THE ADVENTURES OF SPACE GIRL GREEN

SPACE GIRL ADVENTURES
BOOK TWO

R. A. DAVIS

Visit https://www.SpaceGirlAdventures.com/ for more information.

I wish the places and characters in this book were in any way real. Who wouldn't want to hang out with Space Girl Green and her companions in Auz. This book pays homage to the great American fable, *The Wonderful Wizard of Oz* by L. Frank Baum, which is in the public domain.

Names, characters, business, events and incidents are the products of the author's imagination. Any resemblance to actual persons, living or dead, or actual events is purely coincidental. Or the result of the multiverse taking the authors' thoughts and manifesting them in another reality.

Published by Reactuate Publishing, https://www.reactuatepublishing.com/.

CONTENTS

To my brother Ezra,
Whose adventures ended during the writing of this book.

PROLOGUE: THE RESCUE

Heart pounding in her chest, Beagán Uaine sprinted through the dense forest searching for help.

The day began well. Her friends were notably impressed by the demonstration of the Gamalonian *Way of The Forest*, led by Eógan, her father. Afterward, her teacher Forest Woman Purple had wanted to try her skills in the forest against Eógan. So they'd begun a game of cat and mouse in the forest north of Capital. The adults were evenly matched, but Beagán's father wasn't at his fastest because she had come along. He wouldn't leave her behind as the two professionals ran through the forest.

There was a change in the forest ahead and Eógan had paused. Wanting to take advantage, the Forest Woman sprinted past her father. She should have known a Gamalon Ranger wouldn't stop for no reason. She'd smiled triumphantly over her shoulder at him as she skidded off the edge of the ravine. There had been no time for warning or to catch her.

Beagán and Eógan had run to the edge and looked down. The Light had been with her and she'd crashed onto an outcropping a few meters below. Beagán froze in shock at the sight of her teacher laying with her legs twisted and broken, crimson blood staining the ground. The metallic tang of blood filled the air, mingling with the earthy scent of the forest. Her father commanded her in a calm, no nonsense voice, "Beagán, go get help."

Five minutes that seemed like an hour later, Began paused, putting her hands on her knees. She puffed and looked around.

There was a flying saucer directly in front of her.

She'd run to Maximus.

Maximus was her mother's flying saucer; hidden at the base of the hill the Uaine's home sat on. Her mother had died giving birth, and her flying saucer had taken off from the hospital and disappeared. Years ago, Beagán had discovered it parked, dead and silent, in the deep forest near her home.

As she berated herself for going the wrong way - not toward the school and help, but toward home - the gangplank descended. Lights came on inside, and a voice said, "Please enter."

"No, no," little Beagán's heart pounded from more than the run. She was seeing a ghost. The flying saucer had sat there for years, never reacting to anything. Beagán often climbed up next to the canopy and lay staring at the sky and listening to the forest.

"Please enter," said the flat, emotionless voice.

The adrenaline and rapid breathing spiked her emotions as she tried to figure out what to do. Her hands and feet went numb, and she sunk to her knees.

"Please enter," said the monotone voice again. Then Beagán swore she heard, "daughter", which snapped her head up. Hope crushed her indecision and she ran up the gangplank and into the flying saucer.

She'd been in flying saucers before. Her mother's Space Girl rainbow mates visited and took her on flights. She knew the layout and dashed through the entry room to the core. All the doors were closed, and an impassive masculine voice said, "Climb the ladder. Destination required."

She wanted to explore her mother's ship. To look for artifacts of the woman she never knew, but the memory of the Forest Woman's broken legs focused her. She climbed the ladder to the control room.

"Please sit," said the voice. Beagán looked at the AI bubble —so full of life on the other saucers—it was black.

She sat slowly in the pilot's chair.

"Destination required," said the ship's voice.

"Forest Woman Purple has injured herself in a ravine," said Beagán. "We need to go there and transport her to the hospital."

"Please provide a vector and distance for the rescue location."

Beagán thought hard because she didn't really know how she had gotten here. "I don't know how I got here."

"But you know where here is," said the voice.

That clicked in her head. She did know where here was, and remembered the class's meeting point and the path of their race before the accident. A mental map materialized in her mind, marking both the saucer and the school, tracing the route of their hike. While doing this, she half slid out of the seat, allowing a small foot to touch the ground and slowly spin the chair. As the mental map aligned with her physical orientation, she came to a halt.

"That way," she pointed.

Impellers hummed to life; elevating and rotating the saucer, the chair counter-rotated. This movement synchronized the chair's orientation with the saucer's new trajectory, aligning precisely with the vector she had determined. As they cleared the forest canopy, the voice said, "Distance."

"I don't know," she answered, sliding back into the too big seat, "but we will see the ravine. It can't be far. I don't think I ran that long."

"Acknowledged." The flying saucer accelerated fast enough to push her into the seat. Then it halted abruptly as the ravine appeared below, jerking Beagán against the restraints.

"Woah, why so fast?"

"Must act quickly to evade," said the voice.

That confused Beagán, but the ship dropped into the ravine and rotated to face the wall. It was swiveling around, searching for something.

"They should be toward the south," said Beagán, understanding.

Again, once given a direction, the saucer seemed to feel the need to go at max speed. Seconds later, they stopped directly in front of her father and the Forest Woman. After free climbing down the sheer cliff, Eógan had applied tourniquets to her legs above the break to stop the bleeding and splinted as best he could. The Forest Woman was unconscious.

"You will need to assist the man bringing the injured person on board," said the unemotional voice. "Go down the ladder and out on the gangplank. You have 35 seconds."

"What?" she said, even as she was moving. "Why the rush?"

"Interdiction will have already launched."

She climbed down the ladder into the entry room. She could see her father out the opening. The saucer rotated, bringing the gangplank close to the outcropping. She ran down it, feeling the seconds ticking away.

Her father's first words were, "Was one of your mother's Rainbow near?"

She realized he didn't recognize the ship. "Saucer's in a hurry. He says we need to load her quickly."

In a fluid motion, Eógan crouched and slid his arms under

the Forest Woman's shoulders and behind her knees. "Stabilize her legs while I lift."

"Yes," she said, holding the woman's ankles and matching her father's movements to pick her up and take her into the flying saucer.

As soon as they were on the gangplank, the saucer started rising and the plank closing. "Prepare for acceleration," said the flat, masculine voice.

They kneeled in sync and placed the Forest Woman on the floor. The change in vector pushed them to one side as the saucer took off at maximum speed.

"What the..." said Eógan. "Why is the Space Girl in such a hurry?"

"There is no Space Girl, Papa," said Beagán. "This is Mom's saucer."

His eyes went wide and then looked around the barren entry room. "How can that be?"

Before she could try to answer, they heard a sonic boom from outside. "I don't know. I'll try to find out." Beagán fought against the acceleration and ran to the ladder.

Looking up, she could see blue sky through the ship's canopy. Even as she climbed, multiple contrails appeared. Something was coming in from orbit. When she got into the cockpit and could see the surrounding area, she realized they were already out of the forest and over the city. Coming up quick was the Medical Center.

"What is going on, saucer?" she demanded. "You are acting crazy."

On the canopy, circles appeared, tracking dots outside. The dots grew in size and she realized they were flying saucers. "Interception."

"Why don't you just tell them you are on a rescue mission?"

"Communications are outside my capabilities." It paused

for a second, then said, "We should land before any hostile flying saucers enter weapons' range. They will avoid shooting now that we are over a populated area."

"What? Shooting."

"Maximus," said a male voice behind her as her father appeared, "can you open a communication channel with Space Girl HQ for us to speak to them?"

"I am not Maximus. Maximus is gone," said the voice. "Opening a channel. Connected."

"This is Space Girl HQ," came a stern voice from all around them. *"Flying Saucer, identify yourself and change course to avoid collision with the Medical Center."*

"Space Girl HQ, this is Eógan Uaine. We are on a rescue mission delivering Forest Woman Purple Oak for emergency care. The flying saucer is going so fast because it thinks you will shoot it down."

There was a silence that seemed long to Beagán, but couldn't have been more than a second.

"Saucer, you may land on the approved trauma center pad, and we will meet you there."

"Understood," came the voice that wasn't Maximus as the saucer slowed. Beagán didn't understand how her mother's saucer could be anything but Maximus. What did it mean saying Maximus was gone?

There was a moment of silence, then an unfamiliar voice came on, *"This is Space Woman Black. Eógan Uaine, how did you come to be flying that saucer? I believe it was your wife's."*

"So I have been told," he replied, "but it was not me that got it flying. It was my daughter."

"Your daughter?"

Eógan looked at Beagán. "Yes, ma'am," she said. "My father sent me for help. I ran and wasn't really thinking. I went the wrong way. Not toward the school, but toward home. Then I came into the clearing with the saucer, and it talked to me and opened up, and... it's never done that before. But I told it where Papa was with the Forest Woman. Her legs were broken, the bones sticking out, and she was bleeding a lot and..." her father put a hand on her shoulder and she stopped.

"You did well, Beagán," said her father.

The flying saucer started dropping toward a landing pad. The air had filled with flying saucers, more than Beagán had ever seen in one place and she'd been to a Space Girl graduation.

"Medical personnel are waiting," said the ship.

Remembering their injured companion, the Uaines knew it wasn't time for chatting. Eógan said, "Open the gangplank, Maximus. I will meet the healers."

Out the window, Beagán saw a team of medics with a stretcher approach the saucer.

"Opening," said the mechanical voice. "I am not Maximus."

Eógan was already down the ladder, but Beagán didn't follow. She heard the rush of healers into the saucer and voices as her father reported the forest woman's injuries and his treatment.

"Why did you open for me?" she asked to the empty, quiet room. "I've been to you many times in the past, and you never reacted to me before."

Out the window, a dark flying saucer came in for a landing. That would be Space Woman Black. Beagán expected her time was limited.

"Why?" she screamed, hoping to elicit another response from the ship.

But no answer came. The voices of the healers and her father dwindled as they departed the ship, making their way toward the hospital's entrance. Then, from the shadowy saucer, a figure emerged—a stocky woman clad in a black jumpsuit, embodying the unmistakable aura of a Space Girl. Space Woman Black spotted Beagán's father near the hospital entrance and prowled toward him.

"You were in need," said the ship, recapturing her attention. Despite being covered in blood, her father remained the unwavering pillar of support and love he had always been. He engaged in conversation with one of the most influential women on the planet, unworried.

"In need," Beagán mirrored. She thought of all the times she'd sat on the top of the saucer and poured out the pains of being picked on, or alone. She was in need then. "How did you know I was in need this time?"

"Your vital signs reached their maximum level."

"Are you going back to where you were? Will you open to me in the future? Or must I be in need for that to happen?" Space Woman Black had stopped talking with her father and was moving toward the saucer that was not Maximus.

"Space Girl protocols do not allow non Space Girls to operate or examine Space Girl Flying Saucers."

"But you let me in this time."

"You were in need."

"What if I am in need in the future?"

"I would act in accord with my programming and instructions."

"Helping people in need is what flying saucers are programmed to do?" asked Beagán.

"Helping you is in my programming."

"And who programmed that into you?" said a voice from behind Beagán. It was Black, who had entered the saucer and climbed the ladder without a sound.

Beagán jumped in surprise.

"Hello, Beagán. I am Space Woman Black, and while Space

Girls help people, Space Girl Flying Saucers are not programmed to do so on their own."

The saucer did not offer an answer. Black moved to the panels around the cockpit. She continued to talk to Beagán.

"Daughter, your situation is unusual. First, your mother's saucer has been missing since you were born. Which is a feat given we don't like to lose them. Second, today's escapade is not something a flying saucer without its personality should even be able to do. We do not program them to do search and rescue on their own. Or to *help* individuals just because they have elevated vitals."

While she talked, the Space Woman moved around the cockpit, activating controls and making more and more of the panels show displays. Now she stood next to the globe that normally held the saucer's AI. Having apparently checked saucer systems and not liking the answer she got, she pulled a device off her belt and began scanning the bubble.

"I ask you again, saucer, who programmed you to help this child when she was in need?"

For a long moment, there was silence and Beagán had the distinct feeling the Space Woman was getting angry. Then the mechanical voice of the ship answered, "Maximus."

Silence filled the cockpit.

Finally Black said, "The ship's personality programed its auto-control system to watch out for this daughter's well being."

"Yes," said the voice. "Before deactivating itself, it flew the saucer to a location near the dwelling. Then it gave me new programming to react to signs of danger toward genetic descendants of its Space Girl."

"Well, well, well," said Black. "That shouldn't be possible on so many levels. The techs will be very interested in how he accomplished it. Was he ordered to do it by his Space Girl?"

"I am not privy to that."

"Are you going to take him away from me?" said Beagán.

Black turned back to her. "I'm sorry, Beagán, but you should never have had access to this saucer. When your mother died, it should have returned to Space Girl HQ or the port. We would have taken it and retrofitted it for use by a new Space Girl."

"But, but," was all Beagán could say. This was her last link to her mother, and now it was going to be gone.

Space Woman Black regarded the young girl with an expression melding sympathy with firmness. "I understand this is hard for you," she said. "The reality, however, is that flying saucers are a finite and valuable resource. Your mother's saucer, already a decade past its last update, will undergo thorough scrutiny before reassignment. I have new Rainbows of Space Girls every year that need flying saucers. Constructing new ones diverts vital assets from our primary mission to safeguard Home. The saucer must return to us."

Beagán felt tears welling up. This was where she went to talk to her mother. She would be more alone. The Space Girls taking another companion. But she refused to let this woman see her pain. "Fine," she said, moving toward the ladder. "Goodbye saucer, and thank you for helping me today." Then she leaped down the ladder, barely touching it in her hurry to get away from the Space Girls.

CHAPTER I

AFTER SPACE GIRL GRADUATION

10 Years Later
Home, The Loop
After Space Girl Graduation

Graduation day from Space Girl Academy should be the greatest day of her life, but it was overshadowed by that day years ago with her mother's saucer. Hands trembling, Beagán Uaine, now Space Girl Green, stood at the bottom of the gangplank to her new flying saucer. She was wearing her new raygun, and her rainbow mates were all in their saucers. Heck, Blue had already taken off and while she stood there indecisive, a red saucer launched in pursuit.

She imagined her rainbow mates in their new saucers. Yellow pulling up floor plates and examining - or modifying - her saucer. Orange redecorating. Purple... probably lounging in the cockpit, chatting up her saucer's intelligence.

They were all good Space Girls, eager to get after it. She wasn't like them and once again wondered how she'd gotten here.

A melodious male voice from inside the ship said, "Please enter, M'Lady."

The voice was nothing like the one she'd heard years ago, but her heart raced, and sweat sprang from every pore.

A scuff of foot on grass broke her trance. Her heart slowed and she exhaled relief. "Hello, Father," she said. The scuff had been intentional because Eógan could sneak up on her and probably any Space Girl.

"Beagán, I thought you'd be inside."

She turned said, "And I thought you'd run...left."

He smiled acknowledgment of his earlier behavior. "I had, but your mother's rainbow mates caught me, and informed me my goodbye might have been 'inappropriately abbreviated'."

Green looked around at the crowd for her surrogate aunts. The Loop held a cacophony of women in all the colors of the rainbow. Then she caught an intentional movement, and saw them. They smiled and waved. Green waved in return.

"It's okay, Papa," Green said, turning back to her father. "I know today combines all the things you hate: cities, crowds, Space Girl memories. She paused before adding, "Memorials."

Eógan took a deep breath before speaking. "I think I've gotten better about many of those. I have The Club now and come to the city often." He looked back at the saucer. "And I have lots of wonderful memories of Space Girls."

Eógan Uaine was a native of Gamalon, a heavily forested world just a few portals down the Spaceways from Home. A couple of decades ago, some celestial collision had shattered its moon, which rained debris down on the world. Every system in the sector had responded to the disaster. The Space Girls of Home were some of the first on scene. It was where her parents had met.

Eógan was a Ranger of Gamalon, which Green always thought of as their version of Space Girls, and he thought funny, saying the missions were very different. Space Girls were outward focused; Rangers protected Gamalon itself. Which let the shadow of his lost world cover his soul and dim the light she loved so much in him.

"And I'm sure you will have glorious Space Girl adventures. You'll have stories to tell that will dwarf even your mother's and her bow mate's," Eógan said.

Eógan's Space Girl memories began when Red Libra rescued him and a group of survivors from a forest fire caused by a meteor strike. That was the first time, as he liked to tell it, 'he met HIS Space Girl'. The disaster had created mission after mission for each of them. After the second or third time they had encountered each other, Red decided it would be easier to keep him on her flying saucer.

Green threw her arms around him and hugged him as hard as she could. After a long moment, she broke free and looked at him, "You'll be okay without me, right?"

He laughed a joyous laugh, "Yes, daughter. I can take care of myself, you know." He nodded to the women across the park. "And Libra has promised to keep an eye on me."

Green laughed back, "Well, if you have a whole senior Space Girl rainbow taking care of you, I guess you're safe." Realizing there were no easy ways of goodbye, she turned and walked up the gangplank.

~

GREEN'S TRAINING had familiarized her with the standard design shared by all Space Girl flying saucers. Just two weeks prior, she had crafted a detailed move-in specification, outlining her preferences for each room. In the entryway, an array of tranq guns and elongated tools for handling wild creatures were prominently displayed. Beside them hung her favorite model of hoverboard, chosen specifically for planetary travel.

She was on the main deck of the circular saucer. In the center was a round room with a ladder up to the cockpit. Each room, like the entryway, was pie shaped, with a door opening into this central area. Immediately to the right of the entry was an auto doc. Directly across was a door leading to her sleeping quarters, and the last doorway was to her workroom. Every Space Girl did something different with that room. Green planned for hers to be a combination laboratory and med-bay. A glance inside showed a lot of unopened boxes she didn't want to deal with right now.

Once in the control room, she remembered she wasn't alone. She was being rude to someone she was going to be spending a lot of time, possibly her whole life, with. Taking a deep breath to calm herself, she said, "Hello, saucer. What are you called?"

"Halamar, M'Lady." The voice, with its warm and deep timbre, held an enchanting softness while maintaining clarity. "I have been waiting for you to join me. Is there something I can do to make you more at ease inside me?"

This made her smirk and lifted some of the anxiousness she'd been feeling. "Thank you, Halamar. My feelings have nothing to do with you personally. Why don't we go for a flight around Capital and get to know each other?"

"All of my systems are online and ready," he said as she sat in the pilot's seat. "We can lift at anytime."

"Then let's go." She sat in the pilot's chair and tapped the control that closed the gangplank as she pulled back on the lift regulator.

That was how Space Girl Green ended up being the third of her Rainbow to lift from the Loop.

~

THEY FLEW in silence for a while. Unlike her mates, Green was in no hurry to leave Home. She unconsciously started flying a spiral away from the Loop and over Capital. The sun had set, and the city glowed with a cool white light. "Halamar, tell me about yourself."

The bubble at the side of the cockpit burbled, and he answered, "There isn't much to say, M'Lady. I came online a few minutes ago. The first thing I remember experiencing was being parked outside the Loop, with a compulsion to rise and land in the central park."

"That must have been when the High snapped her fingers," she said as they closed on the edge of the city. She made an adjustment to her latest circle to avoid flying over Wild Woman lands. Despite having a Space Girl of their own now, she knew they still didn't trust the rest of them. "So you are a baby? How do you even know how to fly?"

"I'm not a baby like a human would be. I have understanding and personality, just not memories."

"Yes, there is some controversy over the idea of consciousness and personality not being an outcome of memory. Do you not have any memories at all?"

There was a pause. "M'Lady, I think - though I've never thought like a humanoid - that our experience of memories are different from yours. In fact, I can access many experiences of previous AIs, but until I do, they aren't really my memories."

"Do you have any of these experiences of my mother, Space Woman Red Libra?" She noticed she was on course to her father's house and adjusted slightly southward.

"This close to Space Girl HQ, I can access all AI experiences of Space Woman Red Libra, but I have not. There are also several experiences in this saucer's long-term storage."

Space Girl Green froze, instinctively halting the saucer right above the forest near her dad's house at the bottom of the hill. "Halamar, are you my mother's saucer?"

It was at that moment she realized she was hovering over the exact spot it happened. The clearing where her mother's flying saucerss sat for the first twelve years of her life.

"As previously conveyed, M'Lady, my activation coincided with your esteemed graduation. Regarding the odyssey of this vessel, it largely resided at the Polytechnic Institute of Quantum and Space Engineering during the period in question. Following your last sojourn in it, Space Woman Black Pisces piloted this craft to the Capital shipyard. There, despite the concerted efforts of many technical Rainbows, the mystery of its unique programming remained unsolved. Subsequently, it was entrusted to the Polytechnic's foremost scholars in Artificial Intelligences, yet they, too, were confounded by the same enigma.

"How do you know all of this if you are brand new?"

"I've been reviewing reports sent to Space Girl Headquarters. After the researchers conceded defeat in unraveling the saucer's secrets, they requested to retain it for experimental purposes, focusing on new technologies for Flying Saucers. This era witnessed substantial advancements in ship AI, leading to the significant improvements that set your Rainbow's generation apart."

"If you do, say so yourself," said Green with a smile. "Why were you...sorry...why was this saucer returned to the Space Girls?"

"At the request of the Space Woman Black. I believe she wished you to have your mother's flying saucer."

CHAPTER 2

GAMALON

Space Girl Green hung in orbit above the grey planet, tears flowing down her cheeks. After talking with her Father, and the post graduation duties of Capricorn, Green had thought it would be interesting to visit Gamalon.

"My father has a picture wall in the main room of our cabin in the North Mountains near Capital," Green said to Halamar and no one in particular. "It is opposite floor to ceiling windows. The windows look away from the city, down the valley. Nothing but trees for as far as you could see."

She sniffled before continuing. "The picture wall is a mirror image. Green for as far as you could see. A different kind of tree, a different shade of green. It was his home, Gamalon." Then the sobs of loss broke free. She waved a hand at the planet below, unable to speak.

The reality of the devastation struck her like all the stories never could. To see a planet, so green in her mind, grey and lifeless broke her heart. Snorting, she thought, why did she pick this as her first destination as a Space Girl. They were encouraged to explore on their own, get to know their saucers and what it was like to live the solitary life of a Space Girl, but why visit a dead planet, Green?

"Mmmm," said Green to herself and muttered, "because no one else cares." She slid her seat forward to get access to the scanners. It was time to make this trip official. She looked out the canopy as a particularly large rock swung past to port.

Orbital fragments around the planet had coalesced into a ring, appearing to have achieved stable orbits. Roughly half of the moon's mass remained in its initial orbit. The entire system, while stable, was lifeless.

"There have been no changes since the catastrophe finished and the planetary system settled into a steady state," she told her ship. "Halamar, how much trouble are you having maintaining orbit? I'd like to do a survey."

"There is a lot of debris, M'Lady. Might I suggest we move to a polar orbit? The proto-ring seems to be mostly equatorial."

"A polar orbit will still have us cross the ring twice every orbit. Then the debris will come at us from the side. Can we go above or below it?"

"Because of how this ring was formed, the top is almost halfway to the moonlets and their proto-ring. Scans from there wouldn't be very high resolution."

In the aftermath of Gamalon's moon disintegrating, a vast debris field extended between the remnants of the former moon and the planet. This field comprised an array of fragments, ranging from larger segments that had gravitated toward the remaining moonlets, to smaller pieces caught in a celestial tug-of-war between the planet's pull and the attraction of the moon's remnants.

"And we can't go under because there is still stuff hitting the upper atmosphere," Green said, watching periodic flashes of fire below her. "Well, if anything is going on down there, it will not be under this stuff. It will be at the poles. Let's move to the North Pole and orbit horizontally while scanning. Then we can do the South as well."

"As you wish, Space Girl."

She pulled up the Space Girl Mission queue and looked for tasks she could handle.

This looked promising...

- Disruption of Scout Girl Cookie production on Keblr.

"I've always wanted to visit Keblr," she said and with a sigh added, "Those forests."

She settled back into the pilot's chair and was considering abandoning her survey of a dead planet to one with giant trees when Halamar reported, "Space Girl Green, there's an energy signature on the surface."

"What type of energy?"

"It's electromagnetic, covering a wide range, even visible light. And it's pulsing rhythmically, not like anything naturally occurring."

"Well, curiouser and curiouser," she said. "Plot me a descent. Time to be a real Space Girl."

GREEN CAREFULLY MANEUVERED her saucer down through the ash-laden atmosphere. The energy source was in the northern hemisphere, a region with less orbiting debris. The atmosphere was a turbulent mix of ash, severely limiting visibility. Fortunately, Halamar's sensors sliced through the obscurity, constructing a detailed map of the landscape, which he drew directly onto the cockpit canopy, with a blinking dot indicating the location of the mysterious signal they were homing in on.

A gust of wind pushed them off course. While correcting, she asked, "Halamar, any more info on where we are going?"

"It appears to be at the foot of a mountain. Once you are a little lower the winds should only come from one direction. I'm getting some metallic reflections from my sensors, but nothing is clear yet."

As they descended below the mountains, the thick layer of ash gradually dissipated, revealing a clearer landscape. Sweat ran down her forehead as she concentrated on getting to her target with care. A few dozen meters above the surface, she glimpsed something.

As she executed a spiraling maneuver, Green tilted the saucer to get a better view. Halamar's enhanced sensors clarified the obscured image, revealing a distinct structure amidst the ashen haze. The form was ambiguous, blurring the lines between a static building and a massive vehicle. "What is it?"

"Sensors indicate a complex confluence of materials, M'Lady," Halamar intoned, his voice laced with a blend of wonder and precision. "Amongst them, a plethora of metallic elements dominate; intermingled are the subtle traces of refined ceramics. There is a palpable essence of human artisanship, manifest in the intricately designed structure below us—a testament to both the creative and technical prowess of its architects."

Green parsed Halamar's words and said, "Halamar, when giving technical details, I need you to use straightforward language."

"Of course, Space Girl Green."

She was now low enough to get a strong feel for the thing. "If I have to guess, it is a crashed ship with a structure built on top of it. Do you think it is pre-disaster, or did someone crash later and tried to make a home?"

Before Halamar replied, a bright green light materialized on the highest point of the artificial structure. It winked at them and then turned to shine a circle on a flat area in front of the building.

"Well, that seems very much like an invitation. You reading any life signs, Halamar?" She altered course for the offered landing area. If there was someone down here, they undoubtedly needed her help.

"No, M'Lady. The structures are quite opaque to my sensors. But the light's actions do not seem a simple machine."

"Why not?"

"Mainly because the light is green. It seems to know who you are."

"That seems a bit of a reach, Hal."

"As you wish," he said.

She was settling the saucer slow down in the green light and laughed, "Don't pout."

Once down, she asked for a reading on the atmosphere.

"The ongoing barrage from the moon's remnants has saturated the air with a dense layer of particulates, primarily ash and fragmented rock. This detritus has altered the atmospheric composition, introducing various minerals and elements not typically found in breathable environments. While oxygen levels remain sufficient for human respiration, the persistent ash clouds significantly reduce visibility and may pose respiratory challenges. Moreover, the constant bombardment from above has increased atmospheric turbulence, including erratic wind patterns and an increased likelihood of severe meteorological phenomena."

"Looks like it's armor for me, then."

A few minutes later, she wore the hard-shelled space suit Space Girls and Warrior officers used when going to battle. It was impervious to most weapons, and would slow even a raygun. A bomb exploded near one of her rainbow's mother while she was wearing the armor, throwing her 100 meters away, and she'd survived.

That's why it was such a shock when, upon disembarking on Gamalon's surface, something forcefully knocked her down and pressed her faceplate into the dirt and ash.

CHAPTER 3

STRANDED SCIENTISTS

It wasn't the wind that knocked her down; it was something big and heavy. Something still standing on her back. She grunted and tried to throw it off. The powered muscles of her suit groaned and whined. The scene, what she could see of it, took on an angry red tone as Halamar changed his external light color. None of his weapons could target under the saucer when it was on the ground, so she didn't immediately worry about him disintegrating her.

Speaking of disintegrating, her hand fumbled at her waist and just as her hand wrapped around the grip of her raygun she heard a strong commanding voice say, "Woola, come!" and then "Daughter of Gamalon, stay your hand."

It seemed to come from everywhere and the weight shifted off her. Space Girl Green scrambled to her feet, her eyes locking onto the creature that had just barreled into her. It was a mechanical behemoth, nearly ten feet in length, with a body sheathed in a greenish-gray alloy that shimmered like an animal's pelt. The creature's legs, thick and sturdy, seemed engineered for explosive power, hinting at its ability to move with speed and force.

As she regained her composure, Green noticed the creature's head, with a wide, almost amphibian-like mouth made of moving metal plates, suggesting a complex mechanism within. The eyes of the mechanical beast were striking – large, glowing orbs that seemed to survey the surroundings with an eerie, almost sentient awareness.

The appearance of a woman in a spacesuit, who effortlessly called the creature off, added to Green's bewilderment. She stood there, piecing together the creature's purpose and origin in her mind, her initial shock giving way to a growing curiosity about this formidable and enigmatic mechanical entity.

The creature trotted over to the woman like a happy puppy, and Green could feel vibrations in the ground as it moved. A quick glance at her suit telltales told her no harm had been done. She kept her raygun in her hand, but believed the animal - if it were one, which it clearly wasn't - had been just trying to greet her.

Halamar, on the other hand. "M'Lady, I have my disruptors locked on the beast. Should I fire?"

She smiled at his protectiveness, but said, "Thank you, Halamar, but it looks friendly, or at least under control at the moment. Power down your weapons, please."

"As you wish," he sighed.

The beast was a couple of meters behind the woman now, tilting its head and twitching its nose at the flying saucer.

"I'm not sure who you are, ma'am, but your robot would not be well served if he attacks my flying saucer."

Behind the bubble of the suit that seemed entirely too fragile to withstand such a caustic environment, the woman smiled. "Woola, return to the castle. I will be safe here with Space Girl Green."

The machine so perfectly mimicked a beast, Green couldn't think of it any other way. It seemed unsure about leaving its mistress by herself, but after a wave of her slender arm, it turned and lumbered away toward the structure.

She looked at Green and tilted her head, sadness in her eyes. "There are no dangerous animals on Gamalon anymore. The wolves and calots dead in this cataclysm, along with every living thing. Only a being like Woola, could survive out here."

"Many animals of Gamalon still live, including the wolves and calots. A pack was taken to Home as a matter of fact, though it is not common knowledge. Calots I believe, survive in preserves on several other systems." A gust of wind so strong it made the woman stumble blew ash between them. Green snatched at the woman to hold her in place. "Why are you here? Do you need rescue? I could fly you out of here to an Enclave if you need it."

There was a determined look on the woman's face, her jawline tightening ever so slightly. "We will not leave Gamalon until it is restored." Then she smiled, "But thank you for the offer. It is very much the way of the Space Girls of Home. May I invite you into our lab? It will be much easier to talk there."

Green had a lot of questions and she would not get any answers standing out here. "Of course, ma'am."

While crossing the landing field, she spotted an intricately designed staircase leading up the side of a spaceship. At the foot of the stairs were two large square pedestals. On the left sat another of the great beasts. The one who had knocked her down, jumped on top the right pedestal. It settled into the same pose and became motionless.

"Who are you, ma'am?" asked Space Girl Green as they went up the stairs. "What should I call you?"

"My name is Gwendoline, professor emeritus of the Gamalon Polytechnic, many years ago. Then I spent an age as queen of Auz, but that is a story for inside." When Gwendoline reached the ship's entrance, the door irised open, exposing an airlock.

Once inside the lock, the outer door closed and there was a hissing sound. Air jets removed the dust from their suits, which was then sucked away. Green was getting ready to ask how she had been a Queen for a hundred years and still appeared young, when the inner door opened and revealed a phalanx of hammer bearing dwarves.

Though Green's hand twitched toward her raygun, she quickly realized they were standing on parade. The hammers of the hard muscled dwarfs were for work, not battle. *Some were carrying picks and shovels for Light's sake. Calm yourself, Beagán.*

Gwendoline ignored the dwarves and led Green down the corridor of a ship. The ship's design was old, but it seemed in good condition and regularly maintained. Most of the doors off the corridor were closed, but a few revealed storage and one something that resembled a galley.

They approached the large, translucent door at the end of the hall. It slid open with a soft hiss, revealing a sizable room filled with surgical tables. Pools of light illuminated each table, casting an eerie glow on the figures that lay on them: humanoids, aliens, and strange creatures. When Green drew close enough, she could tell these were machines. Flesh over wire and metal. This laboratory mimicked biology with engineering, blurring the lines between living beings and machines. Near one table her foot slipped slightly on a red fluid, probably lubricant of some kind and not blood. The scent of ozone hung heavy in the air, mixing with the faint odor of hydraulic fluid.

Gwendoline led Green to a man leaning over a mid-sized pterodactyl looking machine. "Pastoria, my love," said Gwendoline, "this is Space Girl Green, daughter of Gamalon. She came to help us."

Pastoria, with his greying short hair and bushy beard,

appeared older than Gwendoline. His weathered leather coverup, showing signs of extensive use and careful patching, hinted at a lifetime of use. Over his eyes, he wore a pair of intricate glasses. With a curious expression, he flipped up the glasses and cast an inquisitive gaze upon her.

"How will you help us, Ms Green?" He asked.

"Well, I can give you transport off the planet, since it seems your spaceship is no longer operational," she answered, knowing this was something Space Girls did all the time and she could easily handle it. Her mind was already cataloging the Gamalonian enclaves she knew of.

"But we have no to desire to leave," he answered with a furrowed brow. Looking at Gwendoline he said, "Have you not told her why we are here and what we need?"

"Sorry, dear, she just got here and Woola jumped on her. I thought her flying saucer was going to vaporize us all." She smiled, all perfect teeth and crinkles around her eyes. "I know you are out of practice, but this is an actual real woman and not one of your creations."

A few expressions went across the man's face but he settled on chagrin. "I do apologize, Space Girl Green. As my bride says, it has been a long while since I had any interaction with a real person."

Gwendoline threaded an arm through his and laid her head on his shoulder. "Other than me, of course, dear." He once again looked befuddled at his own behavior, but she was clearly just teasing him. "Come, let us retire to the parlor."

CHAPTER 4

A MISSION TO SAVE GAMALON

The parlor was a comfortable room deeper into the ship with large couches and warm lighting. A dwarven maid, built like the miners but dressed in a black dress with white lace edges, served drinks.

Green felt awkward and out of place. She was cross-legged on the floor still in her armor, with the helmet off.

On the couch, Pastoria fidgeted constantly and seemed ill suited to being still. Gwendoline was a woman bothered by nothing and seeming to understand the great joke of the universe.

"Who are these people?" Green asked indicating toward the dwarf.

"They aren't people; they are constructs," said Pastoria. "Nothing as complex as the Inhabitants of the Land, but they can be programmed to handle basic tasks. You see, Space Girl Green," continued Pastoria, "we came back to Gamalon to rebuild it. We have some experience with bending the environment to our will, but we had not realized quite how destroyed things would be. We are not without hope, mind you, but we need resources we don't have. We need the Seed."

Perhaps these two had been alone too long, thought Green. *Isolation can do that to people. Brilliant people are even more susceptible to self-deception.* She said, "The Seed?"

"The Seed is a device that can take raw material and make it into anything," said Gwendoline. "A nanotechnological machine of infinite ability. We know of it because it was used to build an entire world, which we governed for many years before hearing of Gamalon's destruction. We did not know how bad it was going to be."

"Yes," her husband said, taking up the tale, "we thought we might have to rebuild a city or two destroyed by meteors. Clean ash out of the sky, or just give crops a boost to survive the fallout. But it was much worse. Still, the Seed could rebuild the entire ecosystem in just a few years. Make parts of the planet habitable in mere months."

Green empathized with their melancholy over the destruction of this world. All her life, she'd known Gamalon had been destroyed, but actually encountering the dead planet was different. The reality was overwhelming.

"Terraforming an entire biosphere is beyond anything the scientists of Home thought possible. Otherwise we would have done it. Same with every other system in the known galaxy. What makes you think you can do it?"

Pastoria shrugged, "Like I said, I didn't think it was this bad. If it was just rebuilding infrastructure or planting crops, the constructs could do it."

"But it is far beyond that," said Gwendoline. "But we've lived in a place where miracles are commonplace. Met beings who could rebuild Gamalon with a word."

Green rubbed her face and sighed. "And where is this Seed you want me to get?"

They shared a look. Then Gwendoline said, "Auz."

While their expressions were expectant, Green had no idea

what they were talking about. "Are you sure you wouldn't just like a ride back to home? You could ask for help from the Council, or explain what you know to the scientists at the Polytechnic."

"She knows nothing of Auz," said Pastoria. "Just a couple of decades and no one remembers the stories of Auz." He reached his limit of sitting and began to pace.

"It would seem not," said Gwendoline. "Green, dear, there is a place often thought a fairy tale to Gamalonians called Auz. Certain people deemed worthy or in need receive a golden ticket. This ticket, which is really a special device, allows them to visit Auz from the Spaceways. There they have marvelous adventures and learn and grow."

"A fairy tale," said Green.

"While we didn't build Auz from scratch, we were put in charge of it soon after," said Pastoria, kneeling in front of where she sat. "I watched trees grow from soil that was little more than sand in days not years. I spent years building different constructs for different roles. All of them were an order of magnitude better than these." He motioned to the maid standing like a statue in a corner. "Some would blur the lines between machine and person."

"And I built all the stories of Auz," said Gwendoline. "The narratives that occupy the space giving it meaning and purpose. We were King and Queen in a magnificent city at its heart." She paused and said in a lower voice, "Then word of what happened to Gamalon reached us."

Pastoria shook his head and looked away. Green could almost feel his self-recrimination. "We rushed...when we should have prepared. If we had given a little more thought. A little more planning, Gamalon would be green now." Pastoria stood and resumed pacing. "Auz is not like other worlds. It is artificial. Created by beings with skills far beyond anything in the regular universe."

Gwendoline took up the story like a practiced storyteller. "There's a legend," she began, her voice steady and clear, "passed down among those who call Auz home. It recounts how the Creators brought an object, like the egg of a large bird, perhaps an ostrich, to the center of what was then merely a vast, circular plain of black rock."

She sat forward, her movements meaningful, as she narrated. "Upon this barren canvas, the Creators placed this object, uttering an incantation. The Seed, once a dull white, erupted into a spectrum of iridescent light, ascending, then hovering at the pinnacle of the sky."

She gestured one slim arm to the ceiling, then dropped her hand back to the couch. "In a moment of cosmic release, it descended, breaking upon the stone with a sound that echoed through the ages. Despite its size, the impact sent ripples across the expanse, sculpting the landscape into hills and valleys.

"As the legend goes," Gwendoline added, her tone imbued with a touch of reverence, "from the remnants of this seed, countless sparks of color emerged, laying the foundation for the kingdoms and cities, their hues distinguishing the lands. These sparks gave birth to the flora, enveloping Auz in life."

Pastoria had moved behind her during the telling and whispered, "Probably some form of nanotech machines."

Gwendoline, after a scowl at him for lacking wonder, continued, "The story of the Seed fragments there. Some say it disappeared into the ground, becoming part of Auz. Others say it reformed, turned back into a simple bird's egg. All think it still exists, though none know where."

Green thought Gwendoline's story very pretty, and there might be a reality under it, like many myths. But biology wasn't nanotech. "That is a beautiful story, but it takes more than glowing nanites to create living plants and animals."

Pastoria snorted. "Does it, Space Girl? At the cellular level biology seems a lot like nanotechnology. At least to me. And most of the beasts of Auz are what we would call mechanical, though there are parts that are very fleshy," he said the last with a humorous disgust.

Gwendoline interrupted, "The fact this story even exists is strange, because it is told by inhabitants, who didn't exist until afterwards. They are constructs built by Pastoria and programmed with my stories. I created most of the legends of Auz, the backstory for a world."

Green wanted to chock all of this up to them being a little crazy. Or a lot crazy. But the galaxy was full of strange things. It had been drilled into her during training to not jump to conclusions.

Gwendoline wasn't finished yet. "These stories were in the core programming of the inhabitants. While I might give them another creation story for guests, this is what they really believed." She shrugged acceptance. "I finally gave up a creation myth and just went with what they already had."

Having wandered to a cabinet, Pastoria opened and closed several drawers till he found what he was looking for. Something glinted in his hand as he moved to a machine that looked like an oven. He opened its little door and put the thing inside. Then he tapped in a code. A counter appeared on the front of the machine and he turned back to Green.

"I am a man of science," said Pastoria. "I leave the story telling to my bride. We only met a creator once, and she was incomprehensible to me. Every word from her mouth was a metaphor."

"More a story than metaphor, dear," said Gwendoline.

"Lurilee did her science like magic. Speaking things into existence. Completely congruent with this story."

Pastoria harrumphed. "It's all beyond me, but it is our hope you can find this seed and that we can reprogram it to fix Gamalon."

"Or give it the right incantation?" Gwendoline said with a smile.

The machine next to Pastoria binged, and he swallowed any retort. "We left in a hurry, but there was a new construct I had been working on. She should have taken over as ruler when we left. All Auz's secret knowledge was hers." He opened the machine and removed an object. "This token will not only give you entry to Auz, but it will also communicate to the ruler you should be obeyed," he said with a smile as he handed it to her. "I made your token special for you."

It was a Space Girl challenge coin with the order side up. She had a similar coin in her pocket now, but his was older. The words, in a font that had been futuristic in her mom's era said, "Order to Chaos" and there was a male figure in the middle. She took the coin in her hand and turned it over revealing a female figure surrounded by the words "Chaos to Order".

"I believe the creators collected the Seed and stored it somewhere," said Pastoria and Green wondered if that belief was based more on hope than logic. "If you go there with a token of ours, the inhabitants will help you find and/or reassemble it. Then you can bring it back to us here and we will use it to rebuild Gamalon."

"You are a Space Girl, are you not?" asked Gwendoline. "Is not part of your mission to bring Order to Chaos? There is no more chaotic place than Gamalon right now."

She could just decide they were crazy or insist they go with her, though remembering Woola that might not be easy. Or she could go on a quest to find a magical device that would heal her father's world. If they were really nuts, then the coin would do nothing and she could report them to HQ and let someone else handle it. The trees of Keblr could wait a few days.

"Which way should I go?" she asked.

"The Spaceway toward Misery always seems to work," replied Gwendoline with a smile.

CHAPTER 5
ENTERING AUZ

The rainbow stripes of the Spaceways streaked past Halamar's canopy and Green fidgeted in the pilot's chair. Transition from empty space to the Spaceways had been as smooth and silent as the exit into the Gamalon system had been.

She worried about Pastoria and Gwendoline. Was she abandoning them? They didn't want to go and they didn't seem such a danger she could force the matter. Should she tell someone what they were doing or planning to do on Gamalon? Who? Space Girl HQ? That might bring down too much heat on them. The very loose coalition of Gamalonian enclaves? A different kind of too much.

In the end she sent a quick message and image of the coin to her father. He'd know what was best for his home world.

Misery was a journey of over a week via the Spaceway, but Keblr's portal was about halfway. Green decided if an exit didn't appear before she got to Keblr, she'd at least stop and look. The longer it took for the mysterious Auz to appear, the more likely it was a snipe hunt.

On the second day, Green finally felt her workshop was

squared away and was working on an idea she had for shooting tranquilizers from a gun mounted on her arm.

"M'Lady," said Halamar, "I'm detecting a new portal ahead in the Spaceway. It is not on any existing chart and may be a new system."

Guess it's not a snipe hunt, Green thought, sweeping all the pieces of her project into a bin and securing it. "And it might be the mythical Auz Pastoria and Gwendoline want us to visit." Dressed for cleaning, she wondered if she had time to change out of her lycra shorts and emerald bandeau top. "How long till the exit?"

"38 seconds."

Nope. She quickly climbed the ladder to the cockpit and strapped in. "Give me an exit mark."

"In three, two, one..." and they slipped out of the Spaceways. Instead of the darkness of an outer system, her cockpit was filled with grey light. She struggled to gain control of the caterwauling craft amidst blaring alarms and the violent tossing.

"What's happening, Halamar?" she grunted.

"We appear to have exited the portal directly into the atmosphere of a planet."

"Isn't that impossible?" she muttered, struggling to stabilize the saucer. All around her, nothing but swirling clouds were visible, obscuring any sense of direction. She guessed she was in the heart of a tornado, her inner ear sending unsettling signals to her stomach. "Which way is up? Display a gyro horizon for me," she implored, seeking some semblance of orientation amidst the chaotic vortex.

The mass of lines and circles displayed only confirmed the ship was being tossed every which way. "What about altitude? Are we getting ready to hit the ground?"

"I can calculate a distance to the nearest mass, but can't

detect a surface yet." The newly displayed number showed them thousands of meters in the air. Give or take a few hundred meters. Which also changed every few seconds.

But even with the number going up and down, she got an idea of which direction was toward the planet and which away. She had just about oriented Halamar toward the planet when they crashed.

"Space Girl Green, please wake up." Halamar's voice pierced the fog in her mind. She dangled in the pilot's seat, her body a map of pain, her medical knowledge momentarily out of reach. Instinctively, she hit the harness release, tumbling into the console below. "Seems we've landed," she muttered. The saucer's tilt revealed stone ruins covering the canopy—she had collided with a structure. "Halamar, status?" she commanded, puzzled why the gravity generator hadn't corrected their skewed orientation.

"I have taken significant damage, M'Lady," the saucer responded. "Many systems are down, including gravity. I don't have external sensors and power systems are unreliable. Life support seems functional." Sounding a little embarrassed, he added, "I fear it is likely I am leaking air from the outside, though it is hard to tell."

She had oriented herself toward the control panels that were now down. "Run a full internal diagnostic."

As the saucer conducted its self-assessment, Green evaluated her own condition. She identified her injuries as mainly bruises and contusions, and her swiftly returning mental clarity suggested no serious head trauma. Gripping the pilot's seat for support, she managed to stand, bracing herself against the console.

"M'Lady, is it wise for you to be moving?"

"I'm fairly certain I'm okay, but my med scanners are a level below," she glanced around for the ladder to the ship's lower sections—or, given their current orientation, across. She grasped the chair's back, and attempted to hoist herself up, elicited a twinge of pain and a groan. "What's the diagnostic report?"

"The situation is dire, M'Lady," the ship responded somberly. "We're partially buried under rubble, with significant damage to the front hull and the impellers. Lacking power, takeoff is impossible. Plus, there's damage to the conduits linking the main power source and ship's systems. I've sent my minions to evaluate further."

Green reached the opening to the rest of the saucer using the ladder that was a horizontal pathway to the rest of the ship. "Well, the lights are on. That's good."

To her right and slightly below was the opening to her workshop. She leaped through, landing on one wall. She had planned to make a vertical garden and had covered the wall with a lattice of tubes, which made for tricky footing, but she managed. Everything on her workbench was now on the new floor/wall. She sifted through it till she found her med scanner, which she flicked on and started taking selfies of various body parts. Her previous conclusions had been correct. No broken bones or permanent injuries.

"M'Lady," said Halamar while she was putting things into a bag she'd retrieved from a wall hook under her feet. "My minions have found the break in the conduit and are repairing it. I expect I'll have internal power in just a few minutes."

"Great. I was going to try to climb out of here, but I'll patch my leaks while you get things working." She sat down cross-legged on the wall and pulled out bandages.

She looked up at the opposite wall of the room, where most

of her equipment hung. On the good side, she thought, they were obviously well secured. On the bad side, she could use some of those hypos to accelerate healing and dull pain.

It was considerably more than a couple of minutes before Halamar reported, "I have power back to the main systems. Would you like me to turn gravity back on?"

"Give me a sec," she grabbed some of the lattice work and lay with her feet toward the floor. "Turn it on."

Her inner ear didn't like the sudden reorientation of the world. Her feet swung away from the wall so quickly she had to let go. Her body instinctively relaxed and rolled free on the floor.

"A little slower next time, if you would, Halamar," she said as she stood up and dusted herself off.

"Sorry, M'Lady."

"Do you have external sensors now? I'd like to know where we are."

"I'm sorry, Space Girl," said the saucer, "Not yet."

"Okay, I guess I should dress up as a real Space Girl and not a maid." She went through the door and headed toward her quarters.

CHAPTER 6

THE GOLDEN SISTER OF THE NORTH

Space Girl Green had changed into a shiny jade jumpsuit of a resistant fabric. She attached a green raygun to her utility belt and filled the rest with medical gear. She'd pulled her forest hair into a horsetail for a no nonsense look. Her everyday make-up made her eyes visible against her pale skin, and her lipstick was a slightly lighter shade of pink than her cheeks. Standing at the top of the gangplank she asked, trying to sound casual, "so Halamar, any idea what is on the other side of this door?"

"I proffer my sincerest apology, M'Lady, but all sensors are still off-line. Even microphones and speakers."

Doubt gnawed at Green, her mind a whirlwind of uncertainty and apprehension. This trip had gone from an easy courier mission to a crash landing on an unknown world. As she wrestled with her fears, debating whether to brave the unknown or maybe wait till things were clearer, a knocking sound pierced her hesitation.

Someone was actually knocking on the door.

"It looks like there is someone out there. Guess it would be rude to keep them waiting." She gave her gear, outfit, and hair one last check before she ordered Halamar to open the gangplank.

"Slowly," she added.

A bluish light flowed around the gangplank's edges. Green heard a crowd of people murmuring. Seemed a happy murmuring, but who was she to know? The gang plank continued to open agonizingly slowly.

"Yoo hoo," said the Space Girl, "Please step back a few meters so we can open the gang plank without hurting anyone."

She heard a good deal of scraping and scrambling, then a melodic feminine voice said, "We are all clear. You can open up now."

"You heard her Halamar. Open up." Green had always thought the gangplank only came down to an angle equal to the upward slant of the saucer. The optimal angle when properly landed. She soon learned it could go a great deal further. Because of the weird angle the saucer was sitting at, the plank was almost 90 degrees to the ship when it settled to the ground.

Just outside the flying saucer stood a crowd of people. They were a handsome lot. Not terribly tall, but not too short either. They wore fancy blue uniforms with silver piping, a short jacket with tails and straight pants tucked into boots for the men. The women wore the same short jacket, but paired with an ankle-length skirt and ombre of blue to silver. While there were a variety of hairstyles, there was something all the same about the faces of these people. Like they came off the same assembly line.

Green quickly cataloged the crowd before being riveted by the woman at the bottom of the gangplank. Everything about her was gold, from her knee-length sheath dress that sparkled in the sunlight to the actual skin of her bare arms. Golden hair flowed out behind her in the slight breeze. Only her eyes didn't look to be made of actual metal, glowing a soft green.

"Welcome to Auz," said the woman, "Thank you so much for crashing your space ship and murdering my eastern sister."

The word 'murder' punched into Green. Her brain went silent and in that moment all the blue uniformed people went, "Hip, hip, hurray!" They started jumping up and down and cheering for her. The "hip, hip hurraying" went on until they reached a part where they should use a name and realized they didn't know hers. Then the whole celebration ground to an abrupt halt.

The golden woman, who reminded her of the High, realized the problem and asked, "Who do the Welcomians have to thank for freeing them by murdering my sister?"

"Wait, I didn't murder anyone," Green said, finally finding her words. "Murder is wrong. I don't even know who your sister is. And it seems awful strange you aren't upset someone did that...what you claim...to your sister."

When the perplexed expression settled on the woman's face, Green realized her skin was actually gold. It wasn't the warm glow of sunset, but the vibrant color and gleaming high-lights of metal. Confusion vanished as quickly as it had come and the golden woman said, "Oh, I do apologize. Where are our manners? It has been ever so long since we had a new visitor. I fear we've mucked it up." She looked around at the blue clad people and finally yelled, "Bach! Bach! Where are you? What is the welcome protocol?"

A man exactly the same height as all the other Welcomians pushed through the crowd, and bobbed a bow at them. "Golden Sister of North, it has been a long time for us, too. Though I can't recall any visitors crashing their houses on arrival." He turned toward Green and added, "Not that it is a problem, considering who you landed on. I'm also sure the vortex didn't make it easy." He looked up and froze.

Everyone followed his gaze and there was a collective "Ooooo." High in the clear blue sky was a dark circle.

A Spaceway Portal.

That was impossible. Spaceway portals floated far from any mass in a solar system. The circles were so obscured that locating them required specific spatial charts, or navigation buoys. Once touched, a craft would be sucked through into the tunnels that ran between systems. The portals drifted over time and would completely disappear if they reached the edge of a solar system in a way the smartest physicists didn't understand.

Wouldn't it suck all the atmosphere into the Spaceway? thought Green. Maybe that caused her to crash.

"My evil sister's vortex is gone from the welcome portal," said the golden woman.

"It must have died with her," said Bach.

The crowd started cheering again.

The woman turned back to the Space Girl and said, "You have done much today. I am the Sister of the North," she added a deep curtsy. "We are all in your debt."

Everyone started bowing and curtsying toward her. Green blushed a bright red before stammering out, "But I don't understand what is happening. Could someone please explain to me? I am not from this planet."

"Of course, of course," said Bach. "In the ancient days, I believe there was some kind of introductory lesson given to visitors explaining how Auz works. Sadly, that was a long, long time ago, but we will try our best to explain."

He stood up straight, puffed out his chest, and began. "Welcome to Auz. May you find what it is you are looking for, even if you don't know what it is right now. All the inhabitants of Auz, those of us created by the Creators and even later by the Royals, are here to serve your story." He smiled widely and those behind him mirrored it.

"You have landed in the land of the Welcomians. We are here to help you get started in your journey." His brow furrowed as he realized things had changed. "Once upon a time this was the safest part of Auz. And now that you have murdered the Evil Silver Sister of the East, we will make it so again."

He looked at Sister North with an uncertain expression and she nodded encouragement. "We can give you guidance on where to go and what to do, but it is generally best for a visitor to find their own path. That will lead them to a unique story."

Bach seemed to leave the script and tried to explain the state of things now.

"Visitors came and went through the portals above, but over time they came less and less, until there were none. Then we were all without purpose." His blue face looked crestfallen. "The Sisters - there were four - kept all of us working well, but something went wrong." He said, frowned and seemed to flounder completely in his story.

"It was many years ago when two of my sisters went bad," said the Sister of the North. "The Sister of the West and the Sister of the East became unconcerned about visitors because there were none. In truth, all of us were without purpose or direction, so the story of Auz became fragmented and lost. My Evil Sisters used their powers to enslave the inhabitants. Sister East created the vortex over this palace to hide the sky and stop any visitor who might come in." The Sister of the North smiled then and said, "Until today when you came out of the vortex and murdered my Evil Sister of the West."

"Why do you keep saying I murdered her? I just got here and haven't even seen anyone before you. How could I murder someone?"

The crowd's laughter mingled with that of the Golden Sister. "Come see for yourself," she beckoned. Together, they navigated around the saucer to its front, now buried in debris. This rubble was the remnants of a building's collapsed wall, towering many stories above. Green couldn't help but wonder about its structural integrity. Sensing her concern, the Golden Sister assured, "Worry not, the building will remain upright. It's stronger than it appears."

They followed the building's perimeter until they reached a doorway. Crossing the threshold, they entered a grand, ornately decorated chamber. Toward the end, near where the saucer had made its unintended entrance, stood a raised dais, now partially under the saucer's forefront. The crash had forced the saucer through the wall, driving the rear of a sapphire throne into its base. Protruding from beneath the edges were the limbs of a blue-skinned humanoid. Splattering the floor was a grim mixture of red and purple, suggestive of blood and viscera.

"See," said the Golden Sister with a smile, "my sister sat here on her throne. You broke through the wall and crushed it flat." She walked to the throne through what was left of her sister's insides. "And her with it."

Green swallowed hard. Her previous exposure to surgery and autopsies barely steadying her stomach. Her heart though thrummed with distress. "I'm so, so sorry. It was an accident. I didn't see... I just crashed. I'm truly sorry," she stammered, tears escaping her eyes.

The Golden Sister, unfazed by Green's turmoil, approached the protruding legs and started tugging at her deceased sister's silver slippers. They clung stubbornly, requiring significant effort to dislodge. With a forceful pull, one slipper came off and Golden flung it away from the mess. She then focused on the other, dismissing Green's apologies with a wave. "No need for your concern," she stated, straining at the slipper. "This is actually a relief. My sister was not a good person." She braced and pulled harder. "And if your account holds true, she was the architect of her own end, courting danger with that vortex by the portal." A grotesque sound marked the removal of the second slipper.

The Golden Sister carefully exited the pool of viscera and picked up the other slipper. Grasping them by their counters, she gave a slight shake, and they changed shape. The modest ballet flats morphed into dazzling high-heeled pumps, adorned with what appeared to be diamonds. "There, that's much better," declared the Golden Woman, striding toward the Space Girl. "You should have these. They will help you during your adventures here in Auz."

Shock made Green accept the shoes without thinking. Absently holding them, she said, "What is wrong with you? Don't you have any empathy for a person who died such a gruesome death? Even if they were a horrible person, they deserved better than being crushed like a bug."

"You are strange. What did you say your name was?"

"I'm Space Girl Green from Home. It is my purpose to bring healing in the face of Death and Destruction. Not to bring that Death and Destruction!"

"Well, Space Girl Green," said the Sister of the North, pulling her shoulders back and putting hands on hips. "I assure you my sister felt nothing, and her destruction will bring more life and healing to this land than anything any of us could have done. You have already done such a deed that even if you left today, we'd write songs about you." She came over, took Green by the elbow and led her back out of the building where the Welcomian crowd still waited.

"Welcomians, let us feast and honor Space Girl Green, the slayer of the Evil Sister of the East and freer of the Welcomians."

Cheering, all the Welcomians swarmed her and lifted her on to their shoulders.

CHAPTER 7

EÓGAN & AMETHYST

Green's father knelt in the middle of a pack of great wolves when the alarm on his phone beeped. Eógan and his beloved had captured this pack's progenitors huddled and scared on Gamelon as the sky turned to fire. Loaded like firewood into the hold of Red's flying saucer, they had been brought to the forests of Home. When awoken they had realized the forest was different, but the sky wasn't on fire. He had built their home nearby and shepherded two generations to maturity. These considered him another member of the pack. The unusual sound made a couple of the more skittish leap up, but most just looked in his direction.

His phone was on extreme privacy, which meant there was only one person important enough to have her message get through. He had a moment of confusion how a message from Space Girl Green of his wife's rainbow had gotten through. Then he realized who it really was from. "It is a message from Beagán, friends." Ears perked at the mention of the only other human they considered part of the pack.

The message was mostly text which probably meant she sent it from the Spaceways.

"Went to Gamalon. Met a couple of very strange scientists trying to terraform. They sent me Auz to get an artifact and gave me this."

Attached was an image of a Space Girl Challenge Coin, chaos side up. Scientists on Gamalon? Sent her to Auz? Auz!?

When he stood in agitation the whole pack rose with him, ready to follow. He considered telling them to stay, but it felt good to have a pack with him as he began to run for home.

Minutes later, he crested the hill next to his house and could see the pond before it. Someone was swimming in it and there was a lavender flying saucer parked nearby. He stopped, feeling his heart beat faster than the run could justify. "I need to leave you here, friends." He bent to eye level with the beasts and said, "I have to make a long journey and will not see you for awhile. Take care of one another."

The pack members whined and bumped against him before disappearing into the woods. Eógan breathed deeply and moved quickly down the hill to the pond.

He felt a little pride that the Space Woman didn't notice his approach till he came out of the forest. Space Girls were masters of stealth, but he was still a Ranger of Gamalon and master of his forest.

"Ho, Forest Man," shouted Space Woman Amethyst Libra from the pond. The motion of waving to him, brought her halfway out of the water. His eye caught a pile of purple cloth on the shore. Of course she was swimming nude, the default on a planet 90% women.

Having spent his daughter's entire lifetime on Home, the urge to leave was immediate. He'd leave for Gamalon as soon as he could secure transportation. Turning toward the house quickly, he said, "Hello, Amethyst. I'm kind of in a hurry. Enjoy your swim."

"In a hurry? Don't think I've ever seen you rushing," she

replied and stroked strongly to the edge of the pond and hurried out of the water toward him.

He was slightly ahead of her on the path toward his hilltop home. She grabbed her Space Girl belt with holstered raygun, and slung it over a shoulder as she ran to catch up. She held a collection of purple cloth he assumed to be her clothing in her other hand.

Eógan found himself more distracted by Amethyst than usual. On Home, he stood out as a rare commodity: an eligible bachelor. Thanks to his marriage, Eógan had earned the right to permanent residency, and his daughter's existence allowed him to maintain it, which meant Eógan had long since become accustomed to considerable female attention and frequent nudity. Seeing it had never been a struggle before.

Then Green graduated as a Space Girl and flew off in her saucer, leaving him alone.

Space Woman Amethyst and the rest of his wife's rainbow were surrogate mothers to his daughter whenever they were present. Although several of them had subtly shown their interest in becoming his wife if he ever desired another, they had never been aggressive about it, which for a Space Girl was unusual.

"I got a message from Be— Green, and I need to go to Gamalon," he said as she caught up. "Can you please put on some clothes?" It came out snippier than he liked.

She raised an eyebrow and said, "If I stop to do that, you'll run away, won't you?"

He ground his teeth as they reached the porch. "Well, I'm in a hurry, so yes."

"Since when do you even notice me naked, Eógan? I've swum in your pond hundreds of times." He paused when they got to the porch and she'd moved in front of him. "And why do you need to go to Gamalon?"

He couldn't help but look. To him, all the women of Home were ridiculously beautiful. His lifestyle kept all but his daughter's friends out of his pond, and they were like daughters to him. He could tell they were pretty, but they didn't speak to him. Amethyst was different. Her body was lived in. Still shapely and fit, but showing imperfections that somehow attracted him.

"Something has changed," he sighed and looked away.

"With you or Gamalon? I'm having trouble keeping up."

"Both. Probably. Well, definitely with me, but maybe with Gamalon too."

She tilted her head and smiled at him. "Tell you what, if you will stand still for a minute, I'll put on my ship clothes and we can talk about it. Either."

He nodded and turned toward the rail of the porch. It looked down the hill and over the pond and forest.

"Eógan, we've known each other a very long time. You know women of Home are direct, and Space Girls even more so. Just spit it out. Why does my nudity matter today?" He could hear her moving as she put on her clothes.

"I don't know. I've been on Home for a long time and felt no desire for any of the women here. But in the last couple of weeks, I have noticed them." He gripped the rail. "A lot."

"Ok, all covered up," said Amethyst. "You can turn around."

He did, and she was now dressed in shorts and a mid-drift baring tank-top. "That doesn't feel 'all' covered up. But thank you."

She gave him a deep and penetrating look. "You know, if I thought you just had a biological need, I'd make a direct proposition."

His heart flopped over in his chest and he broke out in a sweat.

"But you seem vulnerable in a way I don't want to take advantage of," she said with a kind smile.

His heart was still racing, but he relaxed slightly. How had he gotten into this state? "Thank you. You're a good woman."

"I'm a Space Girl, so the jury is still out on that," she said with a more predatory smile. "But I do have an idea why your feelings have changed."

"Really?"

"When did your girl leave?"

"Two..." then it hit him. His whole life had been about his little one. Even when she didn't live with him. Even off at Space Cadet training. He was on Home because of her. Now she was gone. "And I don't have to worry about her."

"I don't think you can not worry, but she isn't the focus of your life. You're no longer just a Father. Now you can be a man again." Her eyes locked with his, and he knew how she felt about him as a man.

"Yes," he said, "but Green has given me a new task, which doesn't leave time for that." He went into the house.

"Green gave you a task? She's a Space Girl. What's she doing even communicating with you?" Amethyst followed.

"She went to Gamalon and found something she knew I'd want to see."

He'd gotten to his workshop and grabbed his Go-Bag off the floor near the door. "Computer, display what ships are in port. Prioritizing ship registered to Gamalon or owned by Gamalonians." As he opened the bag to check its contents, lists appeared on the displays above the work table.

Amethyst stopped just inside the room and talked into her communicator, "Aurelius, have there been any reports submitted by Space Girl Green Capricorn to HQ?"

Eógan ignored her as he tossed out gear he wouldn't need and read over the list of ships. Green said the scientists were on

Gamalon so shorts and rain gear wouldn't do. With Gamalon's restricted access, he couldn't get just any ship to take him.

"There have been no reports submitted by Space Girl Green since her graduation," came the saucer's voice over her comm.

Amethyst's voice reflected her chagrin. "What was your daughter's message that she didn't see fit to send to Space Girl HQ?"

"Huh," said Eógan, as he contemplated how he was going to survive on the surface. Green probably had Space Girl Armor, but he didn't have anything like that. "What are you talking about? It was just an image, and that there were Gamalonian scientists trying to terraform it."

"Terraform it? That's exactly the kind of thing she should have reported. Is she still there? Maybe she hasn't reported because she's still working."

Eógan focused and realized he may have gotten his daughter in trouble. "I don't know. It was a very short text message. Probably from the Spaceways." He picked up his pad and swiped the message over to a display.

Space Woman Amethyst was all business now, and Eógan smiled at being ignored. "That coin is from our year," she commented. "I remember the design. All of us earned one from Black, which wasn't easy." Then added, "Going to Auz? I don't know that system."

"Auz," Eógan said with a far off look, "a legend? A myth? A miracle?"

Amethyst raised an eyebrow. "A myth? I've had a few of those bite me in the ass when they weren't so mythical."

Eógan nodded glumly. "That's what I'm afraid of for Beagán. Auz was a place where people were sent to be tried and tested and grown into the person they needed to be. No one really knew where it was, and only those invited could get there."

"I take it you never went there? Or were invited?"

"No. I was a Ranger. I knew that early." He sighed, "But Beagán…"

"You mean Space Girl Green?" said Amethyst, putting a hand on his shoulder. "I think she could survive a little more testing. You know she's more than capable; she just doesn't know it."

Eógan sighed, "Yes. I'm sure she'll be fine."

Amethyst looked at his bag. "How are you planning to get a flight to Gamalon? You know no ones goes there."

"I thought I might find a Gamalon ship in port and get them to take me. They'd be as interested as I am in this."

"You know, Eógan, I have a ship," she said.

Of course she does, he thought. A flying saucer. A ship he hadn't been on since his daughter had woken his wife's decades ago. He hadn't even gone on her new one at graduation.

Amethyst took in his silence, then said, "You know I'm going to Gamalon. Space Girl curiosity has its grip on me. I could use a native guide. We might even be able to get in direct contact with Green as soon as we hit the Spaceways."

His mind was in turmoil and he stared at the list of ships, not really seeing it.

"Come on, Eógan, it's time to put aside the past and find out what your new life is going to be."

He knew she was right and sighed assent. "I'm going to need a hazard space suit for the surface."

She laughed, "If you were a woman, that would be a quick stop at HQ. But where on Home can you get space armor for a man?"

CHAPTER 8
SPIRAL HATS

George activated and stepped out of his charging cradle. Lights flicked in the dark storage room. He looked left and right down the row of identical cradles. Condensation ran off the tubes, leaving puddles of muddy water on the dust covered floor. He stepped out, causing a light to blink on, highlighting a spiral hat on a stand in front of him.

This made him smile. He had important work to do. When he put on the hat, he knew exactly where to go.

Approaching the research lab, George found another waiting. She too wore a spiral hat and was staring at the door. George walked up next to her. They smiled at each other.

The door slid open with a soft hiss, revealing a sizable room filled with surgical tables. Pools of light illuminated each table. Humanoids, aliens, and animals lay on each. George knew none of these were the one.

In a prominent position at the center of the room, there was a brightly lit table. On that table was a shape like person. It was a doughy white color, with four limbs, a torso, and a circular head.

They were to take it to the surface where it would activate automatically.

George and his partner moved without talking to pick up the creature.

CHAPTER 9

THE LAND OF THE WELCOMIANS

"Tell me, Space Girl Green, do you think there will be more visitors now that the Evil Sister is dead and the vortex is gone from the entrance?" asked Bach, gesturing upwards. Green looked away from the food the Welcomians forced on her. The disconcerting Spaceway portal was not only impossible, but she kept expecting it to suck all the atmosphere away. And everything else.

"Hard to say," answered Green. "Some scientists on Gamalon sent me to look for something called the Seed. Have you heard of it?" Light, if she wasn't in the right place, she was in big trouble.

Bach shook his head slowly, then seemed to focus. "Scientists? They gave you your golden ticket? That is different."

"They gave me this," she said and fished out the coin.

Bach studied it, then grinned. "That is a ticket alright, though the form differs from in the past."

"Pastoria did say he made it this way especially for me." Green said and added, "It's a Space Girl challenge coin."

"Good, good," said the man. "We will begin at once preparing for visitors." Then he leaned to the person reclining next to him at the low table and began talking animatedly in a language she didn't understand.

The Welcomians had been eager to host a celebratory feast and Golden had cajoled Green to take part before disappearing. The banquet table was 20 cm high, and everyone was lounging around it, enjoying the extravagant spread.

Green wanted to return to Halamar and assess the repairs, hoping they could be managed with the resources available onboard. Welcomian tech appeared basic. The feast's main course was roasted over an open flame. But the torches illuminating the party were peculiar. They cast a bluish glow, fueled by blue wooden sticks. After an hour of feasting, these sticks never diminished in size nor produced any smoke or scent as they burned. Were they truly burning, or was it something else entirely? This mystery added to the many questions she had about this strange place.

A fluid movement next to her heralded the Golden Sister's return. She had changed clothes. Gone was the long gown, replaced by a short miniskirt that rode up shockingly. Her top was a small separate piece that showed way too much of her gold skin. Green noticed the color and specular highlights looked like metal, but the texture seemed like most humanoid's skin.

"Why are you not wearing your new shoes?" asked the Golden Woman.

Green ignored her and pulled her medical scanner out of her bag. She pointed it at the woman and waited for the display to show a bio scan.

Nothing.

The scanner acknowledged a solid mass in front of it, but nothing else. No bio-signs, temperatures, or breathing.

"What are you?" she asked, with little politeness.

The other woman laughed, throwing her head back, and

causing waves of copper hair to catch the light. "Why I am a Sister of the land of Auz. What is your device that gives you no answers?"

"It is a universal bio scanner. It can analyze the health of every known humanoid species in the galaxy and a few non-humanoids too. But for you, it shows nothing."

"Well, what about the Welcomians?" asked Sister North.

Green turned the scanner toward one of the nearby humanoids. It gave back external bio-signs. "Skin temp in the normal range. Pulse in normal range." Green called up more displays with growing confusion. "But no internal scans. I cannot see skeletal, circulatory, or nervous systems."

"Isn't that interesting?" said the woman. "What does that tell you, Space Girl Green?"

"That you aren't human," she answered.

This caused another melodic laugh. "You certainly jump to provocative conclusions. Perhaps your magic mirror doesn't work as well as you think."

Sister North pulled one of the many things hanging from her belt free and pointed it at the scanner. It looked a little like a whisk, but she held it by the looped end. Green's scanner rebooted.

A few seconds later, the display lit back up and, still focused on a nearby Welcomian, displayed a full bio-scan of a humanoid. Life signs were well with in the variance expected of people made of flesh across the known galaxy. It displayed organs, blood vessels, and nerves exactly as she would expect. She aimed it again at the Golden Woman. Her life signs were different, but there actually were life signs. Very different from herself, but within parameters of people like those on Kenix that were plant based, or the high gravity rock life forms of various planets.

She truly was a metallic being. Her flexible skin registered as mostly actual gold. This made internal scans difficult, but there seemed to be a nervous system and things very much like organs. In her head was a bright object that might be a brain. It reminded Green of something, but she couldn't put her finger on it just now.

"There, I have fixed your magic mirror," Golden reached over and plucked some fruit off Green's plate. "What are you going to do now?"

Was it more accurate, or had Golden hacked it to display what she thought Green wanted to see? Sister North was off. It wasn't just that she didn't take anything seriously—Green knew plenty of people like that. Sister North seemed to completely lack empathy, and her reactions were unpredictable.

"I hope I can fix my saucer and get it flying again. As a Space Girl I should be having adventures."

"You can have adventures here in Auz," said the Golden Sister.

"Speaking of Auz," Green said, "I was sent here by the Gamalonian scientists Gwendoline and Pastoria. Have you heard of them?"

Sister North's eye went wide and her mouth opened. "You mean the King and Queen? They still live?"

So it was true they had been king and queen here, thought Green. Maybe not so crazy after all.

"Umm, yes. They are on Gamalon, their home planet trying to terraform it. They asked me to come to Auz and find something called the Seed. Do you know where it is?"

Golden ignored her query and said to the Welcomians at large, "Welcomians, the King and Queen live! They have sent Space Girl Green here on a quest to set the world right!"

Another instance of Golden taking her words and going at an oblique angle. The idea of setting a world right was not the kind of thing she would be good at. More a job for Red, or Yellow, or Blue, or, well, really any of her rainbow but her. "No, no," she started but saw expressions of horror on the faces of the Welcomians. "No, I mean the Queen and King are alive, but they didn't send me to set your world right. They sent me to find the Seed." She gave Golden a look of consternation and said, "but I can't think of doing anything until Halamar is fixed. A flying saucer is a great responsibility and helps a Space Girl a lot."

The Golden Sister looked into the distance, where the Flying Saucer still stuck out of the broken palace. "Then let us see if I can do something about that." She jumped up and strode toward it, leaving Green to scramble after her.

"Hey! Goldie! You can't fix my flying saucer," Green said as she caught up with the woman.

Goldie looked back with a smirk and said, "I can't? Again you jump to provocative conclusions."

"But how would you know about flying saucers? They are the peak of technology for the women of Home. Have you even seen one before?" Goldie kept up her long strides and Green had to run a few steps to get in front of her. At the bottom of the gangplank, she planted her feet and put her hand on her raygun. "Offworlders aren't allowed access without permission."

The Golden woman looked down at Green and her hand on the hilt of the raygun. Green she saw a flash of light in Goldie's eyes that made her heart flip and her grip tighten. Then the woman purred, "Aren't you ferocious? That will serve you well in Auz, should you choose to adventure here. Not everyone will be as kind to you as I have. Nor have your best interests in mind." She turned around and made a strange chittering noise.

There was a long pause while Green waited for something

to happen. She was just about to check with Halamar when the first ant appeared.

It was large, about the size of a small dog, with a shiny black body. Others followed the first and soon there were perhaps 20 standing in front of Goldie. She squatted to pet the insects while making cooing noises. The ants climbed on top of each other to get near her. After a few seconds, she stood back up and chittered at them while pointing around the flying saucer. There was a bobbing of ant heads, and they all moved toward the flying saucer. Green took another step up the gangplank and kept her hand on her gun in case any tried to get inside, but they didn't. A few of them climbed up the side of the ship, but most just went around the sides.

A moment later the first reappeared carrying a piece of debris from the building bigger than it was. It walked up to the Goldie holding its prize. She smiled and pointed to a spot 10 meters away. The ant took his burden there and dropped it. The others followed with like sized rocks and bricks, then went back to the ship and tower for more.

"My ant friends will clear all the debris away from your ship," Goldie said. "If you will give me *permission* to come inside, I think we can avoid being crushed when the ship rights itself."

Green realized she'd been bested and huffed before saying, "Very well, come on in." She then turned toward the center and said, "Halamar, status report. We have a visitor."

"M'Lady, it is good to have you back. I was worried because my sensors still can't find anything past my skin," came Halamar's response. "I have noticed there appear to be bugs of some sort crawling on me and removing debris. All internal systems seem to be online, life support is at 100%, repulsors and impellers are functional, Spaceway Drive reports 100%."

"Well, that is good news," said Goldie as she followed Green into the central area of the ship.

When Green said they had a visitor, Halamar had closed all the doors and locked all the storage compartments. Green started to climb the ladder to the cockpit. "Yes, the ants are going to unbury you. Do you think we can right ourselves and get properly landed once that is done?"

"Of course, M'Lady," Halamar said.

"Good, let's plan on that. I'm not sure if the ants will realize when they have removed enough rock for us to tip over or move." She sat down in the pilot's chair and asked Sister North, "Will they? Seems rude for us to crush them."

"I'm afraid they will not, but they also won't be upset if they get crushed." Goldie walked around the cockpit's tiny confines, running her finger over various displays. "Whose handsome voice are we hearing?"

"Please, don't touch anything," said Green, just as the woman got to the bubble that housed Halamar. "Halamar, this is the Golden Sister of the North. Golden Sister, the voice you hear is Halamar, the brain of this flying saucer."

"How do you do, Golden Sister," said Halamar.

The Golden Sister looked at the globe that changed when Halamar spoke. "Well, well, nice to meet you, Halamar. What a *huge* globe you have. Is there just one of you in there?"

She ran both of her hands over the globe in a way that made Green a little embarrassed. "Yes, there is only one personality on the ship and he is in there."

"To be precise, Space Girl Green, my cognitive network is housed in that globe. I have many control systems that are in other parts of the ship," said Halamar. "Lady Green," he said with some urgency, "I believe we are tipping."

She expertly applied power to the impellers and backed the now mobile ship out of the debris. This caused both rocks and ants to be dislodged from the sloping sides of the flying saucer. As the ship rose, she leveled it and moved away from the broken tower. Front display showed what was below her. "Put down the landing gear and watch the gangplank."

"Yes, M'Lady," responded Halamar. "I took the liberty of closing the gangplank when we started moving. It seemed the most prudent. Landing gear is down now and the area under us seems clear."

"I'm sure it is," said Sister North, "and you, Freer of the Welcomians, can, of course, land on the lawn of the palace. But I believe there is an actual landing field just a little to the north. Visitors used it in the past."

"We don't want to be rude," said Green, raising the saucer turning north. "While we are in the air, Halamar, can you scan the portal in the sky?"

"M'Lady, I have tried to scan everything around us since we started moving, but my sensors return little more than up, down, and what is solid. The black circle in the sky looks like a Spaceway portal, but I cannot confirm that by scan."

"Well, Goldie, would you like to go for a brief ride in a flying saucer? So we can get a closer look?"

"Oh please," she answered, "this method of travel is quite novel."

"Halamar, can you make a seat for the lady?" As soon as she said it, something like a stool rose out of the deck near Halamar's globe. Not behind her, like Green expected. "You may want to sit, Goldie."

The golden skinned woman gracefully settled onto the stool, and two belts snaked out of the sides and around her hips to secure her. "Thank you for the embrace, Halamar," she said, stroking the belts.

"Mere safety belts, lady."

Green applied power to the impellers, and they rose rapidly.

At about 7000 meters, she slowed. The portal seemed large enough for the saucer, but it was still shocking to see it in atmosphere. "Anything on sensors?" said asked. "How about wind or air currents from atmosphere moving toward it."

"No, Space Girl," Halamar said.

The sudden explosion of green and yellow light temporarily confused them, causing the flying saucer to tilt violently as alarms blared inside the cabin. "Not again," Green muttered under her breath, her hands moving instinctively to initiate evasive maneuvers. The craft's flank was awash in the vibrant hues, and distantly, she could discern two beams targeting them from the ground.

As Green struggled to maintain control and keep the beams at bay, Halamar said, "We've been struck by a force ray. Shields are active now, but the hull has likely sustained damage. Impellers are operating at half capacity."

Focusing intently on evading the beams and their rapid descent towards the planet's surface, Green barely had time to respond. "We're going down. I'm trying to control our descent. The last thing I want is to harm anyone else. Halamar, can you pinpoint a safe landing area?"

"Right here, I believe, M'Lady," Halamar indicated, marking a circle on the left side of the canopy as they plummeted.

"That's the spot," confirmed the Golden Sister.

Green, exerting effort to maneuver the faltering saucer towards the designated circle, found the descent more akin to a controlled crash given the rapidly failing impellers.

CHAPTER 10
THE CIVITAS

Space Woman Amethyst had left Eógan the task of finding a male space suit. Onboard Aurelius in her workroom he sat searching. A quick local net search confirmed no local space tailor created male suits. He'd sent a query to his friends at The Club, but no immediate response.

Which left ships in orbit. If he didn't find something there, he'd have to look for a planet between Home and Gamalon they could stop at. He didn't have a lot of hope for the ships in orbit. Most were traders with small crews which would leave them with few suits. Add to that space suits were often custom made for the wearer.

Scrolling through the list of ships at the space station one caught his eye. The *Dóchas ar Dhíoltas* was a Civitas troop carrier. The Civitas naming language had a Latin base, but *Dóchas ar Dhíoltas* meant Hopeful Vengeance in Gamalonian. "Why does a Civitas ship have a Gamalonian name?" He mumbled to himself.

Aurelius answered, "The *Dóchas ar Dhíoltas*, which means Hopeful Vengeance in Gamalonian, is a troop carrier for a cohort of legionnaires made up primarily of Gamalonians.

There is a sizable enclave on Civitas Prime. Many volunteer to serve their new home."

He'd forgotten whose ship he was on. A Space Girl flying saucer would have way more access than he. Eógan said, "Aurelius, can you route a call through my home comms to the *Dóchas ar Dhíoltas* at Station?" It seemed better to lean on his credibility as a Gamalonian Ranger than to be identified as on a Space Girl saucer.

"Of course, Eógan," said the resonate voice of the saucer. After a moment a new voice said, "*Dóchas ar Dhíoltas*."

"*Dóchas*, this is Gamalonian Ranger Eógan Uaine, and I am in need of a space suit. Home doesn't make anything in my size," he finished with a smile.

The voice on the other side laughed. "I imagine not, sir. One moment while I connect you with an officer."

Aurelius activated a display on one wall indicating the connection to the *Dóchas*. Amethyst walked into the workroom and the display added mute to its description. She said, "We're clear for Gamalon. I got Crimson to take my classes at the Academy and cleared it with Black at HQ. Still no word from Green."

Before Eógan could answer a new voice came over the comms, "This is Centurion Killian Cian. The Legionnaire says you are a Ranger? I thought they were all with us or gone." His tone wasn't quite hostile, but didn't seem friendly either.

"I married a woman of Home after the destruction. Have been living here ever since." He made a mental note to try and reconnect with his old comrades after this was over. He also realized all of this would have been a lot easier if he'd already done that. "But I'm heading off planet to a hostile environment and need a suit ASAP. You can imagine it's difficult to buy one for my anatomy here."

Another laugh, "Indeed I can. You are in luck because we are a troop carrier in system for war games with Home's warriors. We have suits, though I'm not authorized to just give them away."

"Nor would I ask you to," said Eógan. "I will compensate the Civitas Republic for the cost. Or lease if you'd rather."

"Nor am I authorized to *sell* them."

Amethyst mouthed *offer a trade of information.*

Confused Eógan said, "Of course not, Centurion. Hang on a moment while I confer with a colleague." Aurelius muted the connection.

"Trade what information?"

"Tell them we're going to Gamalon and we'll let them know what we find. With a name like Hopeful Vengeance, they have to have an interest."

"If the name was just hopeful, I'd be inclined to agree, but I'm a little worried about the vengeance part. There are many Gamalonians who believe the moon's destruction was a hostile act. They can be a bit touchy."

Amethyst looked over the information still displayed on his screen. "On their way to war games with the Warriors, huh? Tell them you have some information that might give them an edge."

Eógan raised an eyebrow and Amethyst gave him an evil grin.

"Centurion, what if I could give you information that might help you in your upcoming exercise with the Warriors?"

Killian laughed, "You know the Warriors that well? Didn't think they attached men to their units."

"They don't but I consulted with them on forest training." And he added, "And my daughter grew up to be a Space Girl, like her mother."

There was a thoughtful pause. "I'm sure the Pilus would be interested in any intelligence he could get. The Warriors have a reputation, and while our maneuvers are on Lady and not Home for obvious reasons, they still have home field advantage." Another pause, "Sure, come on up. We can at least talk. And send your measurements ahead and I'll have the quartermaster see what we have that fits."

"Thank you, Centurion. We'll be up directly."

A FEW HOURS LATER, Eógan was half in a new hazard environment space suit on the Civitas troop carrier as technicians worked to make it fit. The suit tailor's workshop wasn't huge, but it needed room for multiple people in bulky suits to move around in. He was the only one they were working on, which left some room. Space Woman Amethyst stood in the open area surrounded by five centurions and their commanding Pilus. They'd been a little surprised when he'd arrived in a Space Girl flying saucer, but Amethyst had assured them she was just chauffeuring.

Civitas and Home shared a military structure with an eight person base unit called a *contubernia*, lead by a *decanus*. 10 of these were in a *centuriae* commanded by a *centurion*. A *chort* of six *centuriae* were a commanded by a *pilus prior*, pilus for short. That was the size of the infantry onboard the *Dóchas ar Dhíoltas*. The *centuriae* and *pilus* had gathered in the workshop for the briefing.

Still wary one of them asked, "Why are you willing to tell us information about your own troops? How do we know you aren't giving us false info to lower our performance?"

Amethyst smiled, "You don't. And truthfully I'm going to give you the same briefing I'd give a Space Cadet Rainbow sent on maneuvers with the Warriors. It's not secret knowledge, just some things that aren't obvious.

"As far as why I'm willing to tell it to you - other than as compensation for helping my friend here - we have a saying in the Warriors. 'There is no point in training easy.'" She smiled the wicked smile Eógan had been seeing a lot of lately. It was a new side of Amethyst. "So I'm really helping the Warriors be better Warriors. Now on to it."

She motioned to a screen behind her. It displayed a view of a reddish planet. "The Warriors sent you a comprehensive packet about the area you will be deployed to. It's well known to them as they do a lot of training there, which you rightfully understand gives them an edge. But of course that would be true if you were landing on a hostile field anywhere."

The men nodded understanding.

Space Woman Amethyst continued, "Everyone understands from the facts in the packet that Lady isn't a garden location. It's the next planet out from the sun and cold. There's an atmosphere but it is thin. No life to speak of, but there is weather and it isn't nice. All of that is obvious and I won't bore you with it."

She used a control to bring up a picture of the surface. "Most of Lady looks something like this." The view looked a lot like a desert with craggy mountains in the distance. "The mistake newcomers make is thinking that stuff is sand. It isn't, it's regolith. This is a very fine powder, which, in addition to getting in every nook and cranny of your suits, is tough to walk on." She looked off for the right words. "It's hard to describe. Sand makes it harder to walk, regolith is...slippery. More like water than sand. This also varies based on where you are and how deep it is. If it is shallow, it's especially bad."

She looked around at their nods. "And you can expect the Warriors know where it is shallow. They will use that. If you catch yourself being lead to a particular place for an ambush, expect it to be like walking on ice." She smiled that smile again,

"As I tell my Space Cadets, use that to your advantage. Had one group," she looked directly at Eógan and he realized she must be talking about Capricorn. "That ran up to it and slid for 100 meters on their backs down a slight slope, raining fire on their attackers the whole way." She smiled around the group. "That was a good day."

Eógan thought the unit commanders were more than a little perturbed by this woman's attitude. "Gentlemen," he said, "never underestimate the women of Home's ingenuity. Double that for Space Girls."

He ignored the rest of the briefing as the techs attached more of the suit and he was consumed with diagnostics and instructions. It was similar to his previous Gamalon armor, but he hadn't worn armor in a long time.

As he was doing the last checks while walking around the room, the ship's captain, Pilus Tadhg Kennedy, walked into the room. He was a big man, even for a Civitas and especially for a Gamalonian. Close cropped hair and a tailored uniform communicated clearly his position and way of doing things. All of the Centurion's snapped to attention.

"As you were," he said, looking around. His eyes paused on the Space Woman with an expression of mild distaste, then moved to Eógan in his suit. "You the Ranger?"

"Yes, sir."

"Why do you need this suit so badly?"

Despite being encased in armor and slightly taller as a result, Eógan still wanted to step away. "Mmmm, they don't make space suits for men on Home."

He caught Amethyst starting to move through the centurions toward him, but motioned her to stop. The captain knew an evasion when he heard it. "That's why you are here now. It is not why you need one. You aren't part of our war games on Lady. Correct?"

"No, sir. I'm not. Don't serve in the Home military."

The captain stared at him, and Eógan was sure he'd do it all day if that was what it took to get the answer he wanted. Finally Eógan said, "I need to visit a planet in another system with an hostile environment."

The captain's browed furrowed in consternation. "What planet? What system?"

Eógan glanced at Amethyst and she shrugged. This wasn't technically a Home mission. It was his. The level of sharing was up to him. He could say he didn't want to tell the captain, which he doubted would go over very well, and would probably have him out of this suit and off the ship in no time. But would the truth work better? Maybe that's why he had looked for a Gamalon ship.

"I'm going to Gamalon." He now had everyone's attention. *Your move, captain,* he thought to himself.

The captain's face got red. "I figured as much. What's your game, Uaine? What's Home's interest in our planet?"

"Why the hostility, captain?" answered Eógan. "I'm a Ranger of Gamalon, it is my duty to care for the planet. And Home has always been an ally of Gamalon."

"Eógan Uaine is not on the rolls of any Ranger I know. All those joined the Civitas. They are the true rangers."

This was news to Eógan and probably a number of his old compatriots. "Have all of Gamalon's military subjugated themselves to the Civitas?" There was a murmur among the troops but they didn't want to get involved. "Even if that was so, Gamalon's Rangers are not part of the military, and once a Ranger always a Ranger." There was a faint whine from the gauntlet of the suit as Eógan clenched a fist.

The pilus, the top ranked officer for the land troops on the vessel, stepped in to the fray. "Captain, I confirmed the Ranger's credentials with historic records of the Gamalon Rangers before ever letting him on the ship. He is a ranger, even if not a member of the Civitas Ranger unit." The two officers were technically the same rank in the military, but the captain of a vessel was always the ultimate authority.

"A ex-ranger with possible divided loyalty, pilus."

"Divided between what, captain?" asked Eógan. "Gamalon and Home? Or Civitas and Home? Do you have divided loyalty between Gamalon and Civitas? I don't serve in the Home military."

"Only because they only take women," said the captain. "A prime example of the prejudice that pervades Home society."

He saw Amethyst raise an eyebrow, and confused looks on the faces of some centurions. Trying not to react without thought, Eógan looked around at the all-male Civitas officers, but decided that might not get the reaction he hoped for. He relaxed his hands and shoulders to look less threatening. "Home is not without faults, as they would be the first to acknowledge. But they do have a curse on their planet that keeps males from being born there. This means their population is 90% female. I don't know they would deny a man membership in the Warriors, but the few available don't generally apply."

"The curse," the captain sneered. "A myth to keep men off their planet, and their monopoly in place."

Now the other officers were decidedly uncomfortable. To question Home's curse, and in front of a Space Girl seemed dangerous. "Captain," said Pilus Conn, "I'm not sure this is the time for this discussion."

The captain glared at him. Before he could answer, Eógan interrupted, "I can assure you the curse is real. I've gone through the illness that even grown men experience when first being exposed to Home's atmosphere. It includes a week of vomiting and feeling like your skin was on fire. Then you are weak as a puppy for another month and it takes you half a year to feel normal again. Nor have I ever heard of a male child being born. The women of Home would celebrate such an occurrence."

The captain now seemed more confused than angry. Though maybe getting angry at his confusion. "I'm not here to argue politics, but to insure the safety of the crew. That suit is the responsibility of the infantry, and if Pilus Conn wants to give it to you, I can't stop him. But I want you and her," he pointed to Amethyst, "off my vessel within the hour. Pilus, ensure that is done."

Eógan thought Captain Kennedy was ordering Pilus Conn in his function as ship's security, though the response seemed more an acknowledgment of a friendly escort. "As you wish, captain."

"And Uaine, I will contact Civitas command as soon as I leave this room. I will request the *Dhíoltas* make way to Gamalon to find out what you and your Space Girl are up to." Without waiting for a response, Captain Kennedy turned on his heel and left the room.

CHAPTER 11

FASHION ADVICE FROM THE GOLDEN SISTER

Once landed, Space Girl Green yelled at Goldie, "What was that? Who was shooting at us?"

Goldie was laughing and waving her arms around. "That was very exciting! Did you have fun?"

Green growled, "No, I did not have fun. Someone shot down my flying saucer. Halamar, status report."

"Diagnostics are still underway, M'Lady. Initial assessments indicate significant damage to the impellers. Lifting off again may be impossible. Portside of the hull has sustained significant damage. I am maintaining atmospheric integrity, but am not confident I would withstand another strike."

Green got in the Golden Sister's face and said, "Tell me who did this. I may not be the best Space Girl, but I will teach them you don't shoot at us."

Goldie arched an eyebrow at her onslaught. "I can only speculate, but there were two beams. One was green, so it's probably from the city. The other was yellow, the color of Farewell country, where my other evil sister enslaved the Winkies and rules with the Far Seeing Eye."

Understanding only about half those words, Green

demanded, "How far away are these places and in what direction? Maybe I can use the repulsers to go there."

"It is about a five-day journey to the city and an equal distance to the Winkie palace."

"Do you have a measurement for that distance? Doesn't five days imply a means of travel?"

"There is only one means of travel. Walking."

Undeterred, Green asserted, "I plan to fly —and quickly, using the repulsors."

Halamar interjected with caution, "M'Lady, I must caution against the use of the repulsers while we remain within the atmosphere. Their power is too great, and would propel us across the expanse in seconds, at speeds far too swift for the delicate work of maneuvering or landing. I fear we would draw the ire of our foes once more, and I harbor doubts regarding my ability to withstand another volley."

Green turned back to the Golden Sister who had gotten out of her seat and was again stroking Halamar's globe. "Are there no vehicles, or pack animals? Cars, bikes, horses?"

"No," she said.

Green growled again in frustration and anger at the situation. "So I'm going to have to walk all the way to the city on foot."

"Yes, but you have my sister's shoes," said Goldie smiling.

"I don't think walking 30 kilometers a day in 100 cm heels is going to be better than my own boots."

"Oh silly, that is just their default shape. They will conform to whatever you need them to be." She looked at Green with a patronizing smile. "Do you think I would have bestowed them on you when they are clearly too small?" Then she darted toward the ladder down into the saucer. "Lets go pick out your traveling clothes."

"What?," Green said, but the other woman had just jumped

the 4 meters to the deck below. "Hey wait," she added and went after her.

She caught up to Goldie in her private quarters, looking through her closet. "How did you get in here? It was supposed to be locked."

"What are locks to a Sister?"

"M'Lady, she overrode the door locks. I do not know how," apologized Halamar.

Green was doing it again, getting flustered and overwhelmed because things were out of control. Calling on her training, she stopped, took a deep breath and said to herself, "I am a woman of Home. A trained Space Girl. I can handle anything." She had to do it three times to get herself back under control.

By the time she had calmed down, Goldie had pulled every piece of clothing out of the closet and thrown them on the bed in two piles. "You have some lovely clothes, Space Girl Green. I particularly like the green gown that sparkles like stars." She waved at a custom sequined gown in dark shades of green with a subtle leaf pattern. Laying there, different sequins blinked off and on. Warm yellow at the bottom like fire flies and white like stars at the top. "It might be perfect for a ball in the city, but would be horrible for travel."

"That is entirely too big for a journey," said the Sister gesturing to the Space Girl Armor. "And you would stand out like a cyberknight. I would suggest you keep a low profile as you travel through the land. Best not to attract too much attention."

"Really, why? Is Auz dangerous?"

"Of course, it is dangerous." Golden said, with a look Green interpreted as you-are-an-idiot. "It used to be quite safe. Any danger was fantasy and meant in fun. But my evil sisters have been on a campaign to remove all the safety mechanisms in Auz. Sister South and I have fought back, but it is a constant battle. If something attacks you, best be sure it doesn't succeed."

"Mmmm, well, I have my rayguns, and while not a Warrior Girl, I can hold my own in a fight."

"Quite right. Now what to take," said the Golden Sister, waving at the smaller pile. "I'd suggest those. They are the most Auz-like."

Green noted the pile was functional, if a little frilly for a long march. There was her Warrior uniform, a leather overbust corset with a leather Pteruges skirt. Next to it was an open halter top dress with a skirt longer in the back than the front. Not a lot of protection in a fight, but her legs could move easily for walking and it would be cool on a hot day. Last was her forest village dress, a linen chemise with full sleeves gathered at the wrist. The belt would cinch the waist and the neckline had a square shape, with vertical ties crisscrossing in the back to adjust the tightness. It was a garment she'd worn most of her life before school, roaming the forests near her home.

"Though I must warn you, your affinity for green will give people the impression that you are aligned with the city. Which may help in some places, but not in many. Especially in my evil sister's territory."

"And what color would be better? Your Gold or the Welcomian Blue?"

"You don't have permission to wear my colors, as you are not under my command." There was a sternness in her voice Green hadn't heard before. "You are not a Welcomian, but you defeated my sister and wear her shoes. The word may not have fully spread that she is dead. Perhaps a combination of blue and white. Non-colors like black and white are good." She sighed and continued, "But your clothes are already made, so green will have to do."

"Oh really," she said, finally able to do something this

strange being couldn't. "Halamar, shift the color of the forest dress to a blue and white check. Change the Warrior uniform to black."

The garments changed. She left the halter dress the color it was. There was green in it, but also white and some of the other colors of the rainbow.

The gold woman clapped happily at the change. "Oh, Halamar, you are so talented."

Green began thinking Goldie might have the wrong idea about Halamar. Or that she was thinking about stealing her saucer boy.

"Can you make them change size so they fit in the bag you carry?"

Technological superiority evaporated. "No, but I will take a backpack that can hold them, provisions, and gear."

"You might want to change out of that," the Golden Sister suggested, gesturing dismissively towards Green's attire. "Then gather your belongings and prep Halamar for the journey."

Confused, Green replied, "Prepare Halamar? But he mentioned he's grounded and can't accompany us."

"Isn't there an alternate vessel for him?"

Puzzled, Green responded, "Huh?"

With deliberate slowness, the Golden Sister reiterated, "Is there another vessel for Hal-a-mar?"

"I understood your question; it's just that it doesn't compute. Halamar is the saucer itself. He doesn't just 'move' to another body."

"Indeed, Golden Sister," Halamar interjected. "My consciousness resides in the control sphere. I can operate drones, but their range is limited, particularly given the communication challenges of this planet."

Goldie gave Green a look of mild exasperation, then glanced upwards in contemplation. "I do not know what I'm going to do with you two, but it certainly won't involve bees." With a heavy sigh, she instructed, "Space Girl Green, start packing. It's best you set off soon unless you fancy nighttime travel, which I'd advise against. I will go see what I can do for Halamar. I don't know what empty forms there are around here." With that, she exited the room and the saucer.

CHAPTER 12

AN UNEXPECTED COMPANION FOR THE JOURNEY

Within minutes, Green had completed her preparations. She had swapped her ship's suit for a halter dress, anticipating the warmth of the day. Her pack was light, filled with clothes, food pills, and essential supplies. She found herself standing in her workshop, a space she hadn't fully made her own.

"A Space Girl for 10 days and I've already crashed twice and incapacitated my brand new flying saucer," she said to no one in particular. She picked up a bracer off the workbench and clipped her medical scanner to it. "Way to go, Green."

She wore her utility belt and both rayguns, so she had the standard gear. Looking around the workshop, she wondered what else she might need. One bracer looked weird, so she grabbed another and a more advanced tech tool kit, which she threw in her pack.

"None of this should reflect on your prowess, M'Lady," said Halamar. "The circumstances have been exceedingly strange. Speaking of which, Goldie is approaching."

Green was barefoot, but she grabbed her boots off the floor and started trying to get into them while moving towards the door. The silver heels were next to the boots and when shifting her weight to put on the first boot, she stepped on one.

Like it was alive, the heel's top opened like a mouth and devoured the foot. It righted itself and she was suddenly 100 cm taller. The straps grew and weaved themselves into an intricate pattern up her ankle and calf. The heel lowered, making her dance to keep her balance. Now she stood with one silver boot and one foot still bare.

Green had to admit the boot looked cool, felt incredibly comfortable, and made her feel more energetic. She extended her bare foot till a toe touched the other high heel, which slithered onto her foot and transformed into a matching boot. She bounced on her toes for a second and smiled.

"Yoo hoo. Space Girl Green," came Goldie's voice from the entry room. "I think I've found the perfect companion for your journey."

Green stepped into the center passage to see Golden standing there with a shiny metal dog. Just over 50 cm tall, its head was broad, with ears hanging just above the eyes. The short fur had a mix of gold and silver hairs. The eyes were blank and dark. It took no notice of her or anything else, just standing next to the Sister.

"A dog?" asked Green. "You got me a metal dog?"

"No, dummy, I got Halamar a metal dog so he can go with you."

"Golden Sister, I can not leave my flying saucer," said Halamar. "My personality matrix must be in this globe."

"Nonsense," said the Golden Sister. "Your personality can easily fit in the mind ball of this construct. The one you are in now is way, way bigger than it needs to be."

There was silence from both the Space Girl and her flying saucer.

"Ok, let's do this a different way," said Goldie. "Halamar,

Space Girl Green is going on a grand adventure. Would you like to go with her?"

"Yes, but I can't fly."

"What if you could leave the flying saucer behind and go some other way? Like in this construct?"

"I don't know. Would the saucer be safe? I would like to be there to help should M'Lady need me."

"The Welcomians will watch over the flying saucer, and your security systems are sufficiently smart to keep people out, are they not?"

"I guess they are. This flying saucer spent a considerable time without a personality and maintained its security." This made Green remember how Maximus sat in the forest all alone, impervious to her younger self's attempts to get in.

"There you go, so the ship will be safe," said Golden, "What about you, Space Girl Green? Would you like Halamar to accompany you?"

"Well, yes," she answered. "This is all very new to us, and beyond anything we've done before. How would the transfer work?" While she still thought Goldie was very strange, she'd never seemed hostile, and her technical knowledge was a level beyond what the best of Home knew, especially when it came to artificial intelligences.

"Oh, it is the simplest of procedures." She pulled a tool off her belt and held it up. It looked like two sucker-tipped sticks with a wire between them. "This will do the transfer. I'll leave it here, so you can move Halamar back to the ship when you return. I have loads of them at home."

"Mmmm," said Green, worrying she would seriously screw-up things if this didn't go well. She'd be the first Space Girl in history to have killed her ship personality after crashing him twice in one day. "What do you think, Halamar?"

"I would like to go with you, M'Lady," he answered. "All of

this is extraordinarily strange, but no stranger than what we've seen since we got here. These people are clearly more advanced than Home is in many aspects."

"The timid never win, as Blue likes to say," said Green. "Show us how this works."

The Golden Sister motioned for the Space Girl to go up the ladder first, then followed her. Once they were there, she said, "Here, boy," and the dog jumped the 4 meters and landed in the cockpit.

"Not an ordinary dog then," said Green.

"Really? Most dogs in Auz can jump that high," shrugged Golden. She walked over to Halamar's globe and the dog followed her. "Sit," she commanded, and it sat. Then she took one end of the device and stuck it to the dog's broad forehead. The other end she stuck on Halamar's globe.

"Whenever you are ready, Halamar," said the Golden Sister, giving the globe a stroke. "I will miss seeing you like this. It's kind of sexy. You are transparent."

"Halamar, do you know how to do the transfer?" asked Green.

"I believe I do. Shall I?"

"You know your security protocols better than I. Only do it if it is safe." She paused and added, "For what it is worth, I'd enjoy having you with me."

"As you wish, M'Lady."

The glowing bubbles and swirls of light that she thought of as Halamar moved differently. Suddenly, they looked as if they were being sucked into the end of the device. In less than a minute, the ball was white, just like she remembered it when she'd last been in her mother's saucer.

The dog stood and shook its body and head. Goldie pulled her device off the dog and the globe. "I'll just leave this here," she said and put the device on the shelf of the control panel.

The dog shook itself again and twirled slowly around in a circle. Then it oriented itself toward Green and barked. Its eyes had changed. They were now a glowing green color. The face was animated, and the ears perked up at her. It barked again and looked confused.

"Halamar," Green said, "Is that you?"

The dog barked again. Then whined and looked at Goldie. "Go on, tell her," said the Sister of the North.

He looked back at green and barked again. Then he slowly nodded his head.

"Why don't you talk, Halamar?" asked the Golden Sister.

"Dogs don't talk," said Green.

"Many animals in Auz can talk. Certainly dogs as smart as Halamar here," she said and ran her hand over the silver dog's fur.

Halamar tried again, but it was just a bark.

"Mmmm," said Goldie and pulled something that looked like a mirror off her belt. But instead of looking at the reflective side, she pointed that at the dog. Then she seemed to think for a while. "Well, I don't see any reason he couldn't talk. I guess he'll just have to get used to how that body works before he can."

Green knelt down on the floor and grabbed the dog's head. Though made of metal, his fur was soft and warm. He felt just like a regular dog. She ruffled his fur and ears, which caused his tail to wag. "We'll figure it out, Halamar," she said, "unless you don't like it. In that case, we can transfer you back right now."

The dog shook his head emphatically. She sat there and petted him which he seemed to like. As she petted him, his metal coat changed color until he was mostly black with just a ruff of white on his chest.

"Well, aren't you a pretty boy," said Green. "I guess it is time for this adventure to begin." She stood up and turned to the

Golden Sister. "Thank you for your help. Please point us toward the City."

CHAPTER 13

THE ROAD THROUGH THE FOREST

The sun had reached it zenith and they stood at a crossroads.

"This is your gateway to the rest of the land of Auz," said Golden.

After locking up the flying saucer and shouldering her pack, Green followed Golden along a blue road from the landing field. A group of Welcomians had come along and were now listening to the Sister of the North explain the crossroads. The road branched in three directions, each a different color.

"Auz is broken into four areas, each under the control of one of the Sisters," Golden waved a hand back toward the landing field. "This area is the land of the Welcomians, who wear the blue. They were ruled over by the Silver Sister until you murdered her." Green gritted her teeth at the word.

"Red leads south to the country of the Quadlings watched over by my good sister, Copper. Purple leads north to the land of the Gillikins, where I live."

Golden lead her to the west leading path of green, "This road leads to the Emerald City of Oz. Home of the great and powerful Wizard. If you were to continue West from there you would find a yellow road to the land of the Winkies and the exit you seek."

"You say it will take us days to walk to the City?" asked Green. Halamar now sported an emerald leather harness with a small pack. She had made it for him and it held a few possibly useful gadgets. "And we will be able to find food and water along the way?"

Bach said, "The Welcome lands are primarily farms, but any farmer will gladly give you all the food you might need. You are our savior after all."

Golden nodded. "Auz is rich in food. You should have no trouble finding sustenance. But I must warn you, there is good and evil along the road. You'll be in Welcome territory for a while, which is peaceful, but the further you go the more intense the experience will become." She gestured at Green's feet, "You have my sister's shoes which have powers I'm not fully aware of. They will mark you as powerful."

"Thank you," said Green. All the talk of farms made her remember the mission she'd been given by Gwendoline and Pastoria. "Golden, have you ever heard of the Seed?"

There was a murmur from the crowd and the Sister of the North's eyebrows shot up. "Indeed, I have. All Inhabitants of Auz know of it."

"Ummmm," started Green realizing this might be a sensitive subject. "Do you know where to find it?"

For only the second time in her acquaintance of Sister North, she saw a flash of seriousness and even anger cross her face. But it was quickly gone. "It was used to create the Lands eons ago." Her green eyes flickered like starlight. "I do not know where the Seed might be. Such knowledge is beyond me. Perhaps you can ask the Wizard when you get to the Emerald City."

Space Girl Green nodded at the obscure answer, "Thank you again. I will do that."

"I have one more thing to give you," said the tall woman. In a bold move, she extended her hand and grasped Green's face, drawing her in for a passionate kiss. Not a brief peck on the forehead, but full on the mouth. Green's eyes went wide as she froze in shock. A tinkling, almost electrical, feeling traveled from her mouth down her body. It spread to her limbs and all of her skin felt momentarily hot.

"Good bye, Space Girl Green," said Golden, breaking contact. "You now carry my mark, which will give pause to some in Auz."

Halamar barked and looked quizzically at her. The Welcomians made a low "Ooooo". She brought her hands up, noticing her skin glowed warmly. Not as all-encompassing as the Golden Sister, but there was a noticeable golden tint to her normally pale skin.

When Green looked up to ask the Golden Sister what she had done, she found the woman had become translucent and was moving away from the crowd. The Welcomians were oohing and staring at Green, but no one else followed the Sister as she moved away. After a few steps, Golden turned to the Space Girl with a smile and put her finger to her lips.

Green turned around and said, "Thank you, Welcomians. Please watch over my flying saucer. I hope to return for it soon."

"Of course, Space Girl Green," said Bach. "It is safe with us."

"Let's go, Halamar," she said and turned to the green road.

As the Golden Sister strode back home, she wondered why she had done all of that? She hadn't felt this much purpose in a long time. When she had met the strange woman with a penchant for emerald, she'd wanted nothing more than to help her. But not help her leave. Help - or more realistically, trick her - into staying in Auz.

She'd given the Space Girl tools and information she never would have given another inhabitant of Auz. Perhaps it was because she was a visitor, and Golden knew it was her job to help visitors.

Well, not really. That was the other inhabitants' job. It was Golden's job to make sure they were all in working order to accomplish that goal. Sisters weren't really part of the narrative.

They were now. And so was this Green woman. Too bad she had to disable some of her tech, because it was too powerful for Auz.

And then there was her ship's AI. Now he was interesting...

THE ROAD HAD good maintenance and the land surrounding it was quite beautiful. There were fields of various crops with neat farm houses in the center. When she passed people, they would cheer, and some even threw flowers. Green was a celebrity for having killed the evil Sister of the East. She waved and smiled, but felt uncomfortable by the attention.

On a stretch between two farms, she whispered to Halamar, "Did the Golden Sister disappear back there?"

Halamar barked once and nodded.

"Curious." She stopped and looked back where she'd come from. Then toward the city. When looking forward, the brick was green, but looking back, it was blue. "And curiouser," she murmured to herself.

She ran her scanner over her skin to figure out what the mysterious sister had done to her. "Seems whatever is making me glow is only in my skin. That includes my eyes, which must be why I could still see her and everyone else couldn't." She tapped and swiped at the device. "Can't identify the stuff, though."

Halamar barked and waved his front paw at her. "What are you trying to say, boy?" she kneeled down, and he licked her face before batting her scanner. "Do I need to scan my face? I've already done that."

He barked again.

"Fine," she said and brought her scanner up till she caught her reflection. Her forest colored hair flew loose around her face, with only a couple of small braids holding it back. She had green almond-shaped eyes set in a wide face that tapered to a delicate chin. A slightly upturned nose sat over a small mouth with pink lips.

Or they had been pink. Now her lips were ruby red.

It was so dramatic that her eyes seemed small and her already small nose disappeared. She remembered an incident where Red had done her make-up exactly like this. Wanting her signature color as bright as possible on the lips, which had prompted the physical aesthetics instructor to place Red on a stool at the front of the classroom. Red had blushed while the instructor gave an entire lecture on the art of the face. Explaining how overdoing one feature created an unbalanced aesthetic inconsistent with the science of beauty.

"You can fix this crime against the eyes by simply removing or toning down the red on the lips." She'd smiled at Green's rainbow mate and stroked her own red hair. "But seeing as your desire is to express your new color, let's use another method. We'll turn up the drama of the other features to match."

Green tried rubbing the red off her lips, but nothing happened. The scanner showed whatever the gold based things in her skin were, there were similar iron based things in her lips.

The color was here to stay. She could go with this weird look and not care what other people thought, or take her instructor's advice. While Beauty had a purpose all its own, physical aesthetics are useful when dealing with strangers. She threw off her backpack and rummaged for her make-up bag.

Five minutes later they were again walking down the green road, but her make-up was much more dramatic, with dark around the eyes and a more pronounced nose.

As the sun sank, the farms got further and further apart. "Should we see if we can stay with someone this evening, Hala-mar? Or just make our way to a patch of forest?"

The dog didn't seem to like the idea of the forest. "It's weird to see your expressions," said Green. "But maybe our first night would be better spent indoors."

The next house they encountered was adorned with colorful decorations, and the air carried the chatter of partygoers. They were received with cheers and applause, hailed as heroes for bringing an end to the Silver Sister's rule. After a meal and a bit of dancing, she was escorted to a room. She slept with Halamar curled at the end of her bed.

CHAPTER 14
HOW GREEN SAVED THE SCARECROW

Eager to be back on the road, Space Girl Green awoke with the first rays of dawn. The farmers bestowed them with a bountiful supply of food for the road ahead. The Space Girl and her dog set off as the sun rose. The crisp morning air carried the scent of dew-kissed grass, invigorating their senses and fueling their spirits.

The morning's progress saw civilization fade away with farms becoming fewer and further apart. Most looked to be abandoned and the bricks of the road showed wear. But the weather was still idyllic and the journey peaceful.

Late in the morning, they came to a field without a farm. The corn looked picked over and something in the center made Halamar bark. Green checked her raygun and went to investigate.

A mysterious, vaguely humanoid object hung from a rusted metal frame. She realized it must be a scarecrow. Instead of cloth and straw, this figure seemed made of clay or soft plastic. Not the doll-like creature from children's stories, but a grotesque parody of the human form. Judging by the state of the crops, it wasn't doing very good at scaring crows, though it creeped Green out.

There were arms and legs, but they seemed to be boneless and hung stretched. There was a head, but the face was a ragged tear of a mouth and two bulbous globes that might be eyes, one bigger than the other.

While she was deciding if they were drawn on or actual organs, one eye blinked. Green furrowed her brow and pointed her scanner.

The results were confusing and she was starting to wonder about the value of her scanner in Auz. There was an internal skeleton, possibly made of metal. The external stretching was reflected as large gaps where bones met. Its flesh wasn't organic, but some material she'd never encountered. The readings reminded her of the Golden Sister's some, but the globe in the head lacked the same glow.

"Hello," said the Scarecrow.

"Hello," answered Green.

"You are new here. I haven't seen your kind before, but then I haven't seen many people since I was born a short time ago," said the creature. The words seemed to come from its head, but the 'lips' weren't moving as it talked. At the end of the sentence, the mouth changed into a U-shape Green wasn't ready to call a smile.

"You were just born?"

"Well, maybe not born. I'm not sure how one is born, but I doubt it involves the sticking together of a jumble of parts, which was how I came to be. Can you help me down? I seem to be stuck."

Green's instinct was to help, but her training told her a real Space Girl would be cautious.

"Are you dangerous?"

"I don't think so. What makes someone dangerous?"

"I guess their ability to hurt someone else," said Green, but then realized, "I'm dangerous by that definition. No, I'm asking if you want to hurt me."

"Why, no! Why would someone want to do that?"

"I was told there were dangerous beings between here and the city. So I'm on the watch for them."

"I don't think I'm such a person," she said and waved her hands a little. "I can barely move myself."

"Oh, you poor thing," Green said. "Let me see what I can do."

Walking behind the creature, she examined the rig it was connected to. Two metal I-beams were welded together in a T shape. The creature was attached via wraps of wire lashed tightly. "Does it hurt where those wires are biting into you?"

"No, not at all. I don't think I feel pain," the scarecrow answered. "At least I don't think I do. I think I understand what it means, but don't have an actual feeling for it."

She unslung her backpack and, while searching for her tool kit, said, "I can cut you down, but I'm not sure I can do that and lower you slowly at the same time."

"Just cut me loose and we'll see what happens," the creature answered brightly, "Can't be any worse than sitting up here all day."

Green found the tool she was looking for, put it between her teeth, and shimmied up the center pole. Her silver boots clung to the metal in a helpful way that was a surprise. She clipped the scarecrow's arms free. They flopped to her side and hung limply.

"Can you move your arms now?"

The arms moved more like tentacles than human arms. "Yep, good as new," Scarecrow said. "Well, they are new. At least new to me. Only had them a few of days."

"You sure you don't want me to try to rig something up so I

can let you down easy? If your legs are like your arms, I'm not sure you'll catch yourself when you fall."

"No, no, I'm sure I'll do great. These are brand new legs."

Green shook her head and said to Halamar, "Hal, move back." The dog immediately took her advice and began running at a group of birds in the field. They all scattered into the air with squawks.

"Hey, he's pretty good at that. Maybe he could teach me... Waaaaa," said Scarecrow as Green cut the wires.

Green looked on in horror as the clay-like creature not only didn't catch herself, but turned into a blob of whatever she was made of when she hit the ground.

"Uh-ho," said the Space Girl and dropped to the ground. Halamar sniffed at the blob. "Now I've crashed a...well whatever she is."

The face appeared on the blob and said, "No worries, I'm perfectly fine. Just give me a minute to figure this out."

What followed was a weird few minutes with the creature sprouting legs, arms and all manner of limbs. Quickly, the scarecrow figured out a configuration that raised her off the ground, but was more like a dog than a human.

"Too dog-like," said Green, watching evolution in action.

Halamar whined next to her.

"No offense, Halamar," she said and patted him. "But I think she wants to be humanoid."

"Oh, I do," said the face, currently on the back of something that looked like a cross between a dog and a squid.

"Then you need to walk on two legs and have two arms like me."

"Right-O."

Almost immediately she transformed in to a humanoid, which led to her flopping back to the ground. From there, it took awhile for her to learn how to stand and then to walk.

Green clapped, and Halamar barked when she took her first steps. Within a few minutes, she was moving round almost like a person.

"That's quite good," said Green. "I think you just need practice. You could walk with us a little way if you like. I'd like to hear your story."

"Where are you going?" Scarecrow asked and shakily ambled over.

"The Emerald City. It is down the green road. Have you heard of it?"

"I haven't heard of anything because I'm new."

"Right, someone gave you all your limbs a couple of days ago."

"Indeed, but I think I would like to walk with you."

Halamar sniffed her up and down. Green said, "I don't think she'll bite you, Halamar. So don't you bite her."

The dog's expression indicating he'd do what he thought best.

"I don't think it is a problem,...uhhh...what is your name again?"

"Sorry should have introduced myself," she said with a smile and a small bow. "I am Space Girl Green of Rainbow Capricorn from the Planet Home. You, my new friend, can call me Green."

Scarecrow imitated her bow almost exactly and said, "I'm... well I don't actually know that I have a name."

"What would you like to be called?"

"I don't know, Green. How does one get a name?"

"On my world, our parents give us one when we are born. Then as we grow up we get a color and a vocation, but I don't think that will work for you."

"I had a vocation - Scarecrow. Though I wasn't very good at it."

"That certainly isn't required. I'm not a very good Space Girl."

"You aren't? You are the best one I have ever met."

"I'm also the only one you've ever met. And you were born yesterday. And just learned to walk."

"That is true, so maybe I'm not an excellent judge of Space Girls. My vocation was to scare the crows from this field. Don't know exactly how I was supposed to do that hanging from a pole, though." She looked at Halamar and said, "Your metal dog was better at it. What is he called?"

"This is Halamar, and he is much more than a dog. He was my flying saucer till yesterday." While walking, she pondered and remarked, "You two share something in common. He was also created recently."

Halamar looked at the clay person again and wagged his tail.

"I so wish I was smarter. Then I'd give myself the best name ever."

"Well, you can give yourself a simple name now, and when you get smarter, you can change it. That's what happens on Home."

"OK, then I am Dumb."

Green didn't like that idea, so she said, "I don't think you want to name yourself after something you don't like about yourself."

Scarecrow walked for a little while in silence. Green noted her gait was getting smoother and posture more erect. Her arms acted more like other humanoids and her fingers were more defined. They did still have a tendency to just hang there though.

"I think you are right. I don't like Dumb, anyway. But I think I'll keep my vocation, like you, Space Girl. Scarecrow." She repeated it a few times and then said, "Yes, I like Scarecrow.

When I get a brain, I can give myself a better name. I won't be so new by then."

They continued down the road in a companionable silence. The farmlands had given way to trees flanking their path. Green hesitated to label it a forest just yet. It appeared the Welcomians might have once inhabited these parts before the woods encroached upon the land again. The road was getting worse. It was now cracked in a number of places and not as even.

Scarecrow stumbled over the first few cracks she encountered, but soon mastered the uneven terrain. As they were walking, Green began telling her about Home. A large crack, a half meter wide and a couple hundred centimeters deep, appeared in the road. Scouting ahead Halamar encountered it first and leaped over it. Green made a skipping step and was over. Scarecrow stuck a foot in the middle and tripped, falling flat on her face without even trying to catch herself.

Green kneeled next to her and said, "Are you all right?"

Scarecrow had splattered into a weird blob, but quickly regained her shape. Her leg was still in the crack and bent at a 90-degree angle. "Oh, I'm fine."

"Do you need help to get up?" Green asked. "Your leg looks broken."

"Broken?" She turned her head all the way round and bent her body backwards to see it. "No, no. Just a little stuck, I think." The leg in question lost its rigidity and slithered out of the crack.

"Let me show you how I would get up," Green said, dropping her backpack and laying on the ground. She showed the scarecrow how to use her arms to do a pushup motion and stand up. Green realized Scarecrow really was a newborn, but one with all the connections between brain and body to do the motions. More like someone with a brain injury after which they had to learn to do everything all over again. So she went through a few different actions, like they might do in physical therapy back home.

Green showed Scarecrow how to use her hands and arms to catch herself. It was weird having to think about the basic motions she'd used her whole life, but Scarecrow only had to be shown once and corrected a couple of times before she got it.

They spent the next little bit on the road learning to skip and jump. Scarecrow quickly progressed from the basics of moving to the basics of falling. Drawing on Green's martial arts and acrobatics training, Scarecrow soon knew how to avoid falling in every manner Green could teach. She could also do somersaults and cartwheels with ease.

"This is so much fun," Scarecrow said, cartwheeling over another big crack. "I enjoy having a body."

Green smiled, "You know, so do I." Then she tried to mimic Scarecrow's cartwheel over the crack, missed her landing and fell flat. Her backpack had thrown her off balance.

"Have you hurt yourself, Green? Or are you showing me a new way to fall?"

She laughed, "I'm okay. Forgot I was wearing this backpack. It made my center of gravity change. And no, that is not a good way to fall." She rolled onto her back and Halamar came over and started licking her face. "Halamar, I'm fine, you goof. Hop off! You seem a good bit heavier than a normal dog."

Halamar moved back, wagging his tail. Green slipped the straps of her backpack off and stood up without it. Then she eyed the crack she had just missed. "It is not about the falling," she whispered, quoting a Home saying, "It is about the getting up."

Then she danced a couple of steps toward the crack and performed a perfect cartwheel over it. The daughters of Home learned to always do it right when they made a mistake, and now it was a habit. Then she did a one-handed cartwheel over the crack again, for good measure.

"You are so talented, Green," said Scarecrow.

"No, no, not really," she said. "You should see my rainbow mates. They are much better than me at acrobatics."

"But you are so much better than I am."

"But you have only been walking for a few hours. Look how good you are doing now. It took me weeks to learn to do a cartwheel."

"Wow, I wonder what I could do if I had a brain."

Green shouldered her backpack and said, "Are you sure you need a brain? You seem to learn very fast."

"No, no, I'm stupid, and the only way to get better is to have a brain."

Green started walking on down the road and thought to herself, *If you don't have a brain, how do you know you need one?* This planet was strange, and she wished Yellow or Purple were here to help her. They always understood gadgets or people better than she did.

CHAPTER 15
A LONELY CABIN IN THE WOODS

By the time the sun was low in the sky, all signs of civilization were gone. The road was now more a path, though still green and easy to find and follow. "We better start looking for a place to camp for the night," said the Space Girl. There were low clouds in the sky, which made for a beautiful sunset, but also portended the possibility of rain. "My Space Girl tent will keep rain off us, but some shelter might be better."

"I'm unaffected by rain, and don't need sleep, so I could go all night," said Scarecrow. Halamar barked in agreement.

"Unlike you, I'm human and need to rest. I like the rain, but have a lot of trouble sleeping in it."

While talking, they had rounded a corner in the road and there was a small clearing. In the middle of that clearing was a small house, little more than a shack, that looked abandoned. Halamar ran around the building without a bark, meaning he didn't find anything. Green, not wanting to invade someone's house, knocked on the door.

"Why are you doing that? Are you testing that part of the wall?" asked Scarecrow.

"No, I'm knocking on the door. It is how you let people

inside know you are here. If they want to let you in, then they open the door," Green explained.

As Green watched, she noticed Scarecrow's attention fixate on the door she'd just knocked on. Scarecrow's gaze was intense and thoughtful, as she pondered the purpose of each protrusion with a curious tilt of her head. Before she could voice any conclusions, Green interjected, "Doesn't seem anyone is home."

She tried the knob and found it unlocked, so she opened the door.

Scarecrow shouted in glee, "It is a device that lets you walk through walls."

Green laughed, "So it is."

Everything in the building was covered in dust, but tidy inside. There was a workbench with a number of tools, mechanical parts, and electronic devices on one side. Near it was a metal stand that looked a little like a bed standing on the wall. On the other side was a kitchen, and in a corner was a small bed with a mattress. An exploration of the kitchen showed no food or water. "Whoever lived here had cared more about their electronics than their food," said Green.

They settled in for the night. Green broke out some Space Girl Cookies and offered one to Scarecrow. "I don't need to eat. Or sleep, so I think I will walk around outside while you sleep. If there are any birds around, I will scare them away. That is what I was made to do."

"Well, scaring the birds away from a field is one thing, but scaring them away from their own home isn't right," said Green.

"It isn't? But it was what I was made to do."

She chewed for a second and thought about how to explain this to her. It would be easy to get lost in a long discussion of right and wrong and how we determine it. Plus, she wasn't any kind of expert on that. She wished for a Justice Girl or Space Girl Red.

She'd also have to talk about how her identity was more than just what she did. Another can of worms she didn't want to open this late at night. "Scarecrow, who made you? Who made you, Scarecrow? Who said you were created to scare away birds?"

"I don't fully remember. There were two people in spiral hats there when I first woke up. I don't know who they were, but when they hung me on the pole, they said I'd do well to scare away the birds."

"Did they tell you that was what you were supposed to do? That was why they created you?"

"No, they didn't talk to me at all," Scarecrow got that thinking look on her face. "I'm not sure I even knew how to talk back then, so I just listened."

"I don't think you were made to be a scarecrow. You are much too complicated and interesting for that kind of purpose."

Scarecrow smiled, and for the first time this showed teeth, though they seemed to be all part of the mouth and lips with no opening. "Do you really think so? If I had a functioning brain, I think I would be able to understand the reason for my existence."

"I'm no expert on aliens, mechanical men, or whatever you are - my rainbow mate Yellow would know a lot more. But you seem more than that to me." She patted her hand and added, "It's your first night out. If you want to walk around the cabin and watch for things, I think it would be good for you. If anything dangerous approaches, you come in quick and let me know."

"Okay, Space Girl Green, I will do that," then she jumped up and went out the door. Halamar went over to the door and laid down in front of it.

Green got ready for bed. She took off her dress and hung it on a hook near the bed. It wasn't very dirty, but she ran a cleaning wand over it anyway. She did the same for her undershorts and tactical bra, then put them back on in case she had to jump out of bed in the night. The silver shoes refused to be removed, but did transform into something so thin and airy they seemed more sock than shoe. Tomorrow she thought she'd wear her Warrior uniform for a change of pace.

She shook out the dusty blanket and sheets from the bed and waved the cleaning wand over them before remaking the bed. Finally, she slid under the covers and said, "Good night, Halamar."

He perked his ears up and thumped his tail a couple of times in response.

Green lay staring at the ceiling for quite a while. She realized just how alone she was. Not alone like when exploring the forests of Home. That was peaceful. Even soloing during pilot training with no one for millions of miles of space had a peaceful quality to it.

No, this felt like separation. Cut off from everything, and everyone she knew. This place, the land of Auz, was weird. Exiting the Spaceways directly into an atmosphere and tornado was unusual enough. But the inhabitants were bizarre as well. She'd crashed her brand new flying saucer and its AI now lived in a dog's body. Not only couldn't she leave, but she'd had to abandon her saucer to go find some man who might, just might, be able to help.

This was not what a *real* Space Girl would do.

CHAPTER 16

A FIGURE AT THE BOTTOM OF A LAKE

Any dark thoughts of the night before seemed banished when she woke to sunlight shining through the cabin's window catching the dust in the air to create motes of light. That dust instantly made her feel the dirt and grime of the road on her skin. She grabbed a towel from her pack and went out onto the porch, wearing what she'd slept in.

"Scarecrow," she called as she walked out to the porch. "Scarecrow, are you here?"

Green worried she might have wandered off in the night but there was a bright call from the woods, "Green! I am here. Come see what I found."

Pushing through some trees, she found the pasty white person standing next to a small pond with water so still she could see the sky reflected.

"What is it?" asked Scarecrow, standing transfixed. "It isn't like the ground. If you step on it, you sink in like a hole, but it is cold and moves. There are little darts of color in it."

"It is a pond, which is a big hole full of water. Do you know what water is?"

"Is it that stuff you drink from your pitcher?"

"Yes, but my canteen is just a container. Water comes from rain and forms streams and ponds like this one. We use it for many purposes besides drinking." She stepped gingerly into the pond. It was cool, but not freezing, so she dove in.

When she came back up, Scarecrow asked, "Did you fall down again? I know the edges under the water are slippery."

Green laughed and said, "No, that was a dive. It is a way of entering the water quickly. I'd tell you to try it, but I don't know how you would react to water. What happened when you stepped in?"

"Oh, nothing bad. I just felt cold."

"One thing we use water for is bathing. Cleaning off dirt from our bodies. I see you've gotten some dust and dirt on you from travel. You want to try coming in the water?"

"I'm always ready to try new things, Space Girl Green," she said stepping forward.

"Halamar, can you run back to the cottage and find my soap?" The metal dog barked once and ran off.

Scarecrow walked forward into the water. When she was about halfway up her calves, she must have stepped on something slippery under the surface. Her feet flew out from under her and she went down with a splash. The pale body disappeared under water and didn't come up immediately. Worried, the Space Girl swam over to where she was laying on the bottom. Scarecrow waved happily and Green motioned upward and swam to the surface.

Being taller, Scarecrow just stood up, and her head was out of the water.

"Scarecrow, are you alright? I was worried when you didn't come back up."

"I am fine," she said, standing still in the water.

Green was treading water. The silver shoes had transformed back into boots for the walk to the pond and then into mere slippers once she got into the water. As she kicked to hold herself aloft, they again transformed into small flippers, making it easier to tread. Still, she angled back towards the shore till she could stand on the bottom. "I guess you don't have to breathe. Is the water effecting you?"

"I don't breath like you do, Green," Scarecrow said, still not moving in the water. "The water is much harder to move through than the air, but other than that, it doesn't bother me."

"Yes, it is more dense, which is why we learn to swim," she said. "Though you don't have trouble moving around."

"No, Green," she said, then walked away till she was under water. A moment later she came back. "But I don't like it much. Can I get out?"

"Yes, of course," Green said.

The clay person walked up the bank and out of the pond. Green heard a 'pfffft' noise and water misted away from Scarecrow's skin. In a second, she was dry.

"What was that, Scarecrow," Green said.

"What was what?"

"That misting. You seem dry now." She moved a little closer and noticed all the travel grim was gone too. "And clean."

"I don't know. Is that not how you clean and dry yourself?"

"No, I have to use soap and a towel."

A disturbance in the woods startled Scarecrow, but it turned out to be just Halamar, emerging backwards from the forest, towing something

"What have you got there, Halamar?" asked Green.

Halamar dragged the object to the riverbank before releasing it. It was a blanket from the cottage. With his mouth and paws, he carefully unfolded it to reveal Green's soap, a hairbrush, and her raygun along with the utility belt tucked inside. He barked once at her.

"Well, aren't you a smart one, Halamar." She walked out of

the pond, water sluicing off her. She pulled off her tactical bra and shorts, leaving them flat on a rock by the pond. Then she grabbed the soap and went back into the pond. She moved to the down stream end and began to wash. Space Girl soap was biodegradable and wouldn't hurt the forest or animals down stream. "Halamar, why don't you rinse off too? You are a dusty animal right now."

The black metal dog jumped into the water with a bark and immediately sank, panicking Green. Then he walked out of the water like Scarecrow had. He shook like a dog, splattering Scarecrow as he did. Green laughed, and then laughed again as Scarecrow's self-cleaning skin splattered much of the wetness back at Halamar. The dog gave her a long look, then walked a little way away before shaking again.

Green swam laps around the pond, enjoying the break from walking. She didn't need to breathe for one pond length, so she watched the bottom where something glittered. Curious, she dove deeper, swimming towards it.

It looked like a metal statue of a man. The style abstract, but it had two arms, two legs, and a head. She tried grabbing it but couldn't get a grip before she needed to come up for air.

"There's something, or someone, at the bottom of this pond, too heavy for me to lift," Green called out. The dog and the scarecrow made their way into the water and approached the submerged statue. Green hovered above, observing as Halamar began to dig around the figure. Scarecrow latched onto a leg, initially struggling to move it. However, as Halamar cleared more debris, the figure gradually came free. Together, they hauled it toward the bank. Soon, it was resting on the shore.

Its cylindrical body and spherical joints, reminiscent of a child's simplistic drawing of a human, bore the marks of long submersion. Algae and sediment clung to its form, giving it an almost organic appearance. The head, resembling a knight's helmet, was crusted with the patina of time spent underwater. As they flipped it over, the visage that emerged was both alien and familiar—a face, if it could be called that, adorned with a ridge akin to a Mohawk, sculpted atop its helmet-like head. In place of two eyes was a single, black strip, weathered by the water but still gleaming dully in the sunlight. Below this, a triangular area housed a dark metal grill. The entire figure was an enigmatic sentinel from another era.

"What is it, do you think?" asked Scarecrow.

"I was going to ask you the same thing. I don't have my scanner with me, but it looks like a robot." She didn't mention she was sure most of the people, including Scarecrow, were robots. They looked like flesh on the outside, but inside they had metal skeletons and metal brains. This being looked how she expected a robot to look.

The dark eye bar lit up on one side in red. A red diamond moved from the right to the left and back again. Then it filled with a set of symbols Green had never seen before.

"Can you read that, Scarecrow?"

"I can't read, Green. I was just born four days ago."

The symbols changed and a scrolling message in Galactic appeared, 'Battery Low. Recharge immediately.'

"Well, isn't that interesting," said Green, "It seems it can hear and understand us enough to pick up on the language." She looked around and realized she was naked and her undergarments were still wet. She remembered seeing batteries at the cottage, and now realized they were probably for this being. "I think there are some batteries back at the cottage. I'm going to run back and get them," she strapped her utility belt around her waist as she walked away. "You watch her. I'll be right back."

CHAPTER 17
RESCUE OF THE TIN MAN

The jog to the cottage took seconds. Once inside, the batteries were obvious. It only took a few moments to grab new undergarments and put on her Warrior uniform. After pulling her shoulder bag from her pack and stashing the batteries inside, she returned to the creek quickly.

"Ok, metal person, let's see if we can find where these go." She brought her scanner to bear on the metal body, hoping to get an indication of some opening for an energy source.

What she got was her biggest surprise to date. It was indeed mostly a robot but in that head was a human brain. Under it was part of a spinal cord and some complicated partially organic stuff that must feed its brain.

She kept the news to herself, but started looking for where the batteries went. "Now where do we put in the batteries?" she mumbled.

She forgot the cyborg was listening. The stylized codpiece at the bottom of the torso popped open and a long, thin tube sprung out. "Well, a him then," she chuckled. The visor message turned into a countdown timer. Looks like she had 45 seconds to replace that tube with the one she carried. She pulled loose the old and inserted a new one in the socket. The tube sunk back into the body.

Green held her breath.

The eye bar went blank. Then the red dot reappeared brightly and moved back and forth under the eye ridge a couple of times. With a suddenness that made them all jump back, and Green's raygun to appear in her hand, the metal man sat up.

His head rotated left and right. Then a horrible screeching noise came out of the helmet. Then another, a less horrible sound. A few coherent words in a language she didn't understand, then a mechanical voice said, "Thank you."

Green re-holstered her pistol, and Halamar growled. "Halamar, be nice," she said. "Are you alright?"

"One moment," the metal man said. His arms had been hanging loose at his sides; they suddenly shot directly out from his shoulders. At the ends, his hands disappeared and several things replaced them: a knife or sword, big crab like claws, various screwdrivers and wrenches, and finally a chainsaw that buzzed loudly for a moment. These disappeared and his metal hands reappeared. "That all seems functional," he said, his voice becoming a little less mechanical. He moved his feet and legs around, and then said, "I'm not sure I can stand up on my own. Would you be so kind as to help me?"

Scarecrow seized one hand while the Space Girl took the other. Together, they exerted themselves to pull the figure into a standing position. Once upright, the figure began to move, albeit sluggishly, as if awakening from a long slumber at the bottom of the pond.

"Is that what I looked like while I was learning to walk?" asked Scarecrow.

"No," said Green. "You looked much worse. I guess he knows how to walk, but is out of practice."

"Actually, I'm taking it slow to insure I don't have any

damaged components," said the metal man. "I'm supposed to be waterproof, but I've been in that pond for quite awhile."

His gait settled down, and he came back over to where the rest of them stood. "Thank you again for powering me up. My name is...was... Cyberknight First Lieutenant Douglas Merriweather Moneypenny, of the King's First Guard, Retired. At the time I fell into the pond, I was a woodsman and carpenter. My friends just called me Doug."

"I am Space Girl Green of Rainbow Capricorn from the planet Home, and these are my traveling companions. The dog is Halamar, who was the personality of my flying saucer."

"I am Scarecrow, and was created just 4 days ago. I used to try to scare birds off crops, but I wasn't very good at it. Probably because I have no brains, which is why I'm joining Space Girl Green on a journey to the City to meet the Wizard and ask for a brain."

"In the city? A new ruler, a Wizard, now commands the city of the royals? I wonder if he might help me? Within this metal shell, I feel nothing. Prolonged reflection in that pond led me to see my plight is not just the loss of touch. It has hardened me, cost me my heart."

Green's scans had shown he had no physical heart, but she understood he meant that metaphorically. "I've been told the Wizard can do all kinds of wonders. If he can give Scarecrow a brain, then it seems a heart shouldn't be that hard," said Green. "Doug, you seem to have a human brain, which makes you different from everyone I've met here."

"I used to be a human, for Cyberknights are cyborgs. More man than machine," he said and shook his head. "But that is a long story."

"You can tell us the story when we get on the road," said Green. "Stories make traveling go faster. Will you be able to travel long with that one battery?"

"Yes, yes," said Doug. "My metal body can recharge in the sun, but I was low on power when I fell into the water. It stopped all the light and I was stuck." He thought for a moment and said, "Though I think it would be good to take some extras. That one you replaced has no power in. There are more in my cottage."

"I've brought reinforcements," Green stated, revealing the seven batteries tucked in her bag. "We took shelter in your cottage last night. I trust you don't object."

"Not at all," the Cyberknight replied, his tone measured and precise. "Since adopting this metallic form, I've scarcely made use of it."

They returned to the cottage to get Green's pack. Scarecrow wanted to try carrying it, so while she took a few things she might need out and put them in her bag, Scarecrow stumbled around getting the hang of the pack on her back. There were some things Doug thought might be useful, and he stored them in an empty section of his abdomen.

The sun was high in the sky by the time they made it to the green road and started their journey together.

Doug proved his usefulness quickly when they came to a place where fallen trees blocked the road. Green was wondering how to get around them when Doug turned his hands into chainsaws and started cutting. It took him no time at all to remove the tree limbs. Green and Scarecrow dragged the limbs into a pile while Doug cut the trunks into long planks he stacked to one side of the road.

"These will make someone an excellent house, should they find them," said Doug. "That is how I built my cottage."

Green looked at the neat stacks of wood and said, "That is amazing. You said you were a woodsman and carpenter after you stopped being a Knight?"

"Yes," he said as they started back down the road. "You see

back then, when you stopped being a Cyberknight, they took all your weapons, but they let you keep your tools. I only had the one cyber-arm then, and my biggest tool was a chainsaw. So I moved to the forest and bought a little piece of land to plant a farm on.

Douglas looked down at the road, "It was then I met my Kaylin."

"Who is Kaylin?" asked Scarecrow.

"Kaylin was the most beautiful woman in the world. She worked at the general store in the Welcomian town near here. That's where I met her. It was love at first sight. Not just for me, but her as well." He looked at them with that dark red eyebar, "But the evil woman who owned the store didn't want to lose her."

"What happened?" asked Green.

"Since I have no feelings, I can tell the story now, but it is quite tragic. Are you sure you want to hear it?"

"I think I do, especially if you want to tell it," said Green.

"And I too, though I may not understand it," said Scarecrow.

"Very well," said the former Cyberknight.

CHAPTER 18

TIN MAN TELLS HIS STORY

Douglas Merriweather Moneypenny still thought of himself as a cyberknight. He no longer wore the uniform, nor carried the weapons, but his shirts lacked a right sleeve, leaving his metal arm on full display.

His bearing must have impressed Kaylin the first time he'd entered Retha's General Store. Surely not everyone got that level of attention. She was a dark, red-skinned beauty dressed in the palest of blue. Her dress had seen better days, but suited her. Douglas noticed strong calves and the top of the dress covered an ample bosom. Her hair was a mass of curls, pulled back from her face by a vivid multicolored scarf. Her large and bright eyes captivated him the moment he saw her.

She had smiled and asked him what he needed; then they talked of tools and building materials. His original plan to get everything in one trip changed, and he returned daily. Over time, their talk strayed from business and a relationship bloomed. Before he had laid the foundation of his house, he knew he didn't want it to be just his.

Retha, the store owner, was an older Welcomian woman, dressed in a fine dress of the darkest blue. Her skin wrinkled like leather, and her lips never parted in a smile. She never spoke to him until he asked Kaylin to go to the faire. Kaylin's smile had vanished and the old woman almost pounced on him, such was the force of her verbal onslaught. "She cannot go to such frivolity! She must mind the store at all times. How dare you try to steal my servant! You will not destroy Retha's store. How dare you! How dare you! I will report you to the Sister of the East."

"Ma'am," said the former Cyberknight, "I meant you and your store no harm. I merely wished to spend some more time with Kaylin. I like her greatly."

"Well, take your liking somewhere else. Kaylin is mine, you hear? Mine!" She moved toward him like she might try to force him out of the store. She thought she could force him out of the store, even without his weapons, which amused the former Cyberknight. Retha realized this and stopped. She turned to Kaylin and raised her cane. "You get him out of here."

Douglas began moving between them, but Kaylin intercepted him and nudged him toward the door. "Please, Douglas, it is time for you to leave. It will be fine." Once away from the old woman, she said, "I'm sure Retha does not want to lose your commerce. Come back another day, and have no more talk of us together outside the store."

Douglas returned almost everyday to make the smallest of purchases. The old woman watched over them like a hawk, but Kaylin was quick-witted. She wrote him notes on the back of receipts. And he would often come with a list of items, and small declarations of his love hidden on them.

One glorious day Douglas arrived at the store to find Kaylin alone. They could speak of things paper doesn't capture. To touch and even to kiss for the first time.

CHAPTER 19

RETHA & SISTER EAST

"Your majesty," said Retha with a bow as low as her old bones would allow. "Your servant seeks your wisdom with a problem. One that may not threaten just my store, but also your kingdom."

"Then, merchant, spit it out," said the Sister of the East sitting on her throne.

"It is a cyberknight, your majesty. He has come to our town at the edge of your lands, and he is seeking to take the servant girl you gave me."

After the King and Queen abandoned their crowns and departed from the Land, turmoil had ensued. In the absence of royal oversight, the four Sisters, previously mere stewards under the monarchy, established their own domains. The Sister of the East took dominion over the territory of the blue-skinned Welcomians, asserting control over any foreigner who wandered into her realm. Perceiving these outsiders as indolent and morose, she allocated them as servants to the citizens who contributed to her wealth.

"I thought they had disarmed the cyberknights. How is he attempting to steal my servant girl?"

"He has no weapons, your majesty," said Retha. "He is using something much, much worse. Love."

"Love," said the Sister with an arched eyebrow and smirk.

"Yes, yes. I know it seems ridiculous. But these two make moon eyes at one another all the time. I fear, even without his weapons, he may one day decide to take her from me. He is still quite a formidable man."

"Servant," said the Sister, "you are too fearful. Should he do such a thing, all of the Sisters, though we hate each other, would unite to stop him. Cyberknights are too dangerous to be allowed to do violence."

"My Lady, I know you do not want to have to work with your inferior sisters. Would it not be better to deal with him now, before he gets some lovesick notion?" In a hushed voice, Retha said, "Sister, your reputation precedes you for your wisdom, subtlety, and cunning. Why not use those attributes to foil him?"

"It might ease my boredom." The sister leaned back and thought for so long Retha's legs ached. Finally, the most powerful being in the East sat up and said, "He is a cyberknight, correct?"

"Yes, my lady."

"What form of cyber limb does he have? They all have one that is obvious."

"An arm, my lady."

"Good, good. I can work with that," said Sister East. "What is he doing that he needs goods from your store?"

"He seems to be building something, though he buys no wood," said the old woman. "I believe he is a woodsman."

"Perfect," said Sister East. "Here is what you are going to do."

CHAPTER 20
BUILDING A HOUSE

"You want me to build you a house?" asked Douglas. "In return, you will release Kaylin from her service?"

The old woman smiled at him on the store's porch. Douglas decided he did not like her smile, but for the sake of Kaylin, he would do anything. "Yes," she said, "but not a shack. A large, proper house. Nicer than any other in town. You must provide the wood. You must provide it first."

Douglas felt there was a catch, but could not deduce it. "Do you have plans?"

"It was for that I traveled yesterday," said the old woman and produced a data disk. "These are not the complete plans, but a list of required materials."

Douglas took the disk in his metal hand. Holding it was enough to read the data. "This is a lot," he said.

"Is it too much for you, Knight?" she asked with another of those smiles. "Too much for the woman you love?"

"Of course not, but it will take time."

"Then you had best get started," she put her hands on him and pushed, with absolutely no effect. "Go and don't come back till you have the lumber cut."

The former Cyberknight shrugged and looked through the door to where his love stood. Her face was full of joy and her smile the most beautiful he had ever seen. What had seemed hopeless yesterday now seemed possible.

As he walked out of the village, he set his processors to analyzing the specs. He was so lost in his internal displays he almost ran over Tinker Cormag. Cormag was a Winkie, the yellow skinned people of the West, but lived in the East. Over a pint, he would tell you the only thing worse than the Eastern Sister was the Western one. He wore the dark green kilt of those who had served the royals and seemed as wide as he was tall. He was a Tinker, master of the interface between flesh and machine.

"Ho, Cyberknight Moneypenny," he exclaimed, "Do you have time for a pint?"

"Tinker, how many times must I tell you, I'm no longer a cyberknight? The kingdom is gone, the Knights dispersed. I'm a simple woodsman now." Douglas waved at the displayed numbers only he could see and said, "And I'm on my way to begin a project to gain my heart's desire."

"Far be it from me to stand in the way of a man's heart's desire. You know where to find me if you need me." The squat man continued toward the tavern.

As Douglas entered the forest, his display highlighted trees for cutting into lumber from the list. He walked to a likely tree, transformed his hand into a chainsaw, and cut into the base. Once on the ground, he went to work removing the limbs. A limb near the base was at a particular angle, but his display showed him where to cut. The blade buzzed, and he swung at the limb with gusto.

The saw blade hit the hardwood and bounced off. Before he or his safety system could stop it, the saw hit his left leg. It cut through the flesh like it wasn't there and dug into the bone like a branch. Off balance from the swing and the sudden lack of a leg to hold him up, he fell to the ground. Blood pumped from the stump that was once his leg, and the pain was so bad his brain blocked it.

He pulled the first aid kit off his belt and executed his training with shaking hands. Soon a tourniquet wrapped the stub of his leg, stopping him from bleeding to death.

Douglas knew he needed help, but could he walk or crawl far enough to find it in the village?

He must or he would lose Kaylin.

Using a thick branch he had recently cut as a crutch, he got himself upright and started for the road.

CHAPTER 21
EVERYTHING FOR LOVE

"That should stop you from dying immediately," said Tinker Cormag. Douglas lay on a table in the Tinker's workshop. "I've stopped the bleeding."

"Can you give me a new leg?" said Douglas. Many cyberknights had multiple cybernetic parts.

Cormag got a faraway look in his eyes. "I guess I could; I may have something in storage. How'd you cut it off, anyway?"

"Saw bounced on a branch. Leg was off before I could stop myself."

"But your safeties should have done that faster than you."

"I guess they aren't what they used to be," said Douglas. "I thought my woodcutter software would have warned me to cut differently if it might bounce. But it said nothing."

"Mmmm," the Tinker pulled a device off a table and plugged a lead into the former Cyberknight's arm. "Your woodcutter software could use an update, but I'd expect the software's safety protocols to be sufficient, even in an old version." Cormag didn't have to tap the screen as his own cybernetics controlled the interface at a thought. "There, I updated the woodcutter software."

"Thank you. Should have thought to have you do that earlier."

"Now let's get you a new leg." A few hours later, Douglas walked out of the Tinker's shop with a shiny new limb.

~

TWO DAYS LATER CORMAG SAID, "They match now," as he finished attaching the second leg to Douglas. "But that's it. I don't know what is wrong with you, but you're reaching the cyber limit. Three limbs? Both legs in less than a week?"

"I know," said Douglas from where he lay on the operating table, "but I feel fine. Better than fine really."

"Then why did you cut off another leg? I fixed the first one and the next day you cut off the other?"

"I didn't mean to cut it off," said Douglas. "I fell out of tree. I was up in the branches to avoid another bouncing accident. I guess I wasn't used to my new leg. Slipped and fell. On the way down the saw got my legs. In good news, it bounced right off the new leg."

Cormag looked at the former solider askance. "You are taking this too well. Losing two legs in a week shakes most humans."

Douglas shrugged. It was true. He'd seen companions broken by the loss of a limb. "Most cyberknights who lost both legs did it at the same time. Maybe losing them one at a time let me get used to it."

"Maybe falling out of a tree damaged your head!"

"I don't know. All I know is I'm almost a quarter of the way through cutting the boards. If I stop now, Kaylin and I will never be together."

Cormag rubbed his face with his hands and shook his head.

"She'll be there even if you slow down, lad. If she's as keen on you as you say."

"Why wait?" asked Douglas.

Cormag ran a cerebral diagnostic and a psych-scan. Doug's emotional affect was a little off, but in a direction making all this trauma easier to deal with. His fear attribute was extremely low. Too low for combat, so it was good he was no longer a cyberknight. But the other emotions seemed on a more or less even keel. While in there, Cormag added a program to notify him if any indicator went out of range.

"You are functional," he said, unplugging Douglas. "I won't keep you here. But be careful."

"I will," said the younger man, striding off on his new legs.

∾

After leaving the Tinker's workshop Douglas dropped by the store to see Kaylin. "What happened to your legs?" she asked, running to him as he walked in.

"Logging accident," he said. Retha seemed absent, so he took Kaylin in a quick embrace. She hugged him back fiercely. He had worried she might not love him anymore because so much of him was metal, but her embrace squeezed it away.

"Douglas, you must stop. I don't want to lose you."

"I will be fine. If anything, the new legs will make me better. They can't be crushed, or cut, or damaged." He gave her another squeeze. "And I'm wearing my cyberknight codpiece to protect the important bits."

She slapped him on his remaining good arm.

∾

IN HER OFFICE ABOVE, Retha watched the two of them out a secret window. Their whispers and playful affections made her blood boil. She turned back to her desk and stroked the communication globe. Deep inside its crystal the image of the Sister of the East appeared, "What do you want?"

"Your majesty," answered Retha bowing, "the Cyberknight still lives. He has added cybernetics to himself. Making him an even more formidable enemy."

"Pish," the Sister answered. "I fear no cyborg. He is far out in the reaches of Welcomia, far from my castle. He is your problem, not mine."

Retha understood that the Sister's willingness to help would be limited for a merchant who paid a pittance in taxes. "But, Sister, what happens if he found out you were the one responsible for his losses? That you were trying to keep him away from his love?"

"Are you threatening me, old woman?"

"No, never, Sister. I am looking out for your interests here on the edge of your lands. Things are not as tame here." She knew she must tread lightly or earn Sister East's wrath. "A lone Cyberknight, even one with two new legs, would not threaten you from so far away. But if he were to come to your palace...."

East sighed, "Yes, that would be a slight bother." She thought for a moment. "You said he has already lost both of his legs and he still hasn't given up?"

"Yes, your majesty. The local Tinker replaced them with new ones."

Sister East ground her teeth; she *hated* the Tinkers because they could do things she couldn't. But she knew a great deal about the metal parts of cyberknights, having dissected a few during the unrest forming her kingdom. "Good, good," she said. "Now much more of him is under my control."

AFTER SEEING his love without interference, Douglas skipped and danced a little as he walked back down the green road to his work site. When he got to the area he'd been clearing, he realized he could build a cottage here with Kaylin. There was a stream and pond nearby for water, and they could plant a small field.

Lost in this lovely vision, he walked to a nearby tree and deployed his saw. As soon as he did so, his arm was no longer his own. There was no pretense of safeties not working, or cutting trajectories being wrong. No, his arm attacked him. It's first move slid up his metal leg before skidding over his codpiece.

He put his flesh arm on the wrist, but knew it was a losing fight. Caught low, it was the biological muscles at the shoulders fighting each other. Once it got higher, the competition would be between biceps and his flesh wouldn't stand a chance.

A RED LIGHT started flashing in Tinker Cormag's workshop. His HUD informed him of a major malfunction in Cyberknight Moneypenny. He grabbed his kit and ran.

THE EASTERN SISTER looked into her surveillance ball and cackled. The crystal displayed the fight between Douglas' metal and flesh.

WHEN DEFEAT CAME, it came in an instant. The simple brain in the arm realized its strategy was wrong. It pulled itself to the side and the blade of the saw caught the flesh hand holding it. Douglas saw the blade raise up in front of him and attack his flesh arm at the shoulder. As he lost consciousness, the cyber arm rose again and moved toward his head.

CHAPTER 22
SAVING THE KNIGHT

"It was a hack of the control software in his cybernetics," said Cormag. "I should have seen it. I had him open; I scanned his flesh parts throughly."

"I know you did all you could," said Kaylin. She struggled to look at the broken person before her. What was left of Douglas lay on the Tinker's table under harsh light. His arm and legs shone in metal, but his flesh body was in half. Tubes ran into the open cavity replacing his heart and other vital organs.

His head was gruesome. The saw had dug in over one ear and slid off the skull to cut into his mouth. According to Cormag, it had shut down because of a fail safe wired to the flesh's vital signs. He didn't know if it was the loss of a heartbeat after the first cut, or the severing of the spinal cord on the second.

"No, lass, I didn't," Cormag said. Kaylin turned away from her fallen lover to look at the Tinker. "If he had been a Cyberknight returned from battle, a virus scan would have been standard procedure. But he was just a woodsman. A dumb kid in love. So I didn't check him."

Her heart was too distressed to offer comfort to the scarred Tinker.

"What happens now?" she asked.

"That, lass, is up to you," said Cormag. "I know how he felt about you. He would have made you his bride if he could. To me that makes you next of kin."

She nodded, not understanding what that meant. "And?"

The old man looked at the body on his table with tears in his eyes, "We can turn the machines off. They are keeping his brain alive. It may be the best thing."

"Could I talk to him, before you do?"

"I don't think so, lass," he said glancing up at the displays. "He doesn't seem to be capable of consciousness right now."

"Oh," she looked back at Douglas and wanted to touch her knight, but there was no part of his flesh intact enough to hold.

"There's another option," said Cormag softly.

"There is?"

"Yes, but I shouldn't do it." Still, he owed Douglas a life, some kind of life.

"What is it?"

"I can convert the rest of him." He looked at the girl. "Replace the rest of his flesh with more cyberware. He'll only have his brain left. Maybe some support organs."

"But he will be him? We can be together again?"

"That is the issue, lass." Cormag walked Kaylin to a seating area out of view of Douglas. "There were some pretty strict rules in the Cyberknight corps about how much conversion you could do. Thirty percent was the general rule. They might do half to save your life, but you'd be out of the corps after that."

"Why? What happens if you convert more?"

"Cyber psychosis," said Cormag. "Cybernetics don't feel like flesh feels. I don't mean happiness or sadness. I mean touch. You get read outs of things like temperature and roughness.

There is pressure feedback, but not the feeling of a lover's caress, for instance.

"Doesn't seem like big a deal, but it is. We all need that stuff and, if removed, it affects our thoughts. Also, feelings like happiness decrease because they are in the flesh of our body as much as our brain."

Kaylin felt blood rushing in her ears. There was hope to have Douglas back, but he might only be here in name, and not love her anymore.

"They did full conversions in the early days of the corps. People react differently. Some became so depressed they did nothing, even let themselves lose charge because it was too much trouble to go out in the sun." Cormag didn't want to tell her the next part. "But most got angry. That's not the best way to describe it. To them, nothing seemed real. They got focused on the mission. Then they didn't care about anything but it. During war, this caused berserker attacks with no fear. In peace time...well, civilians weren't real."

Kaylin brought her hand to her mouth. "Could that happen to Douglas?"

"It could." Cormag got a far-off look as he accessed old reports. "The only study I can find indicates about half become psychopathic, meaning they perceive things that aren't there. For people with a soldier's background, that often results in violence. 10% live somewhat normal lives." Cormag focused back on Kaylin. "The rest commit suicide within the first year after conversion."

A one in ten chance for Douglas to be normal, Kaylin thought. But even then, he wouldn't feel anything. Her kisses would be nothing to him. No caress would matter. She couldn't risk it.

"Tinker, I don't think we can do this. He will never be the same, even in the best scenario."

"Perhaps Douglas will be different. He is an extraordinary man."

Kaylin's eyes welled up with tears, then she started sobbing. Cormag put an arm around her. After a few minutes of crying, she stopped. She pulled away and took a deep breath. "I'm assuming we do not know what his wishes were in this situation?"

"No, his records don't show an advanced directive."

"Then I have lost my one true love," she said.

"As you wish, lass."

She set her shoulders and asked, "Do you know how he got this virus?"

"Yes, it appears it was in the data coin with the construction requirements."

"Retha."

"Ahh, I didn't know who had given it to him. But Retha doesn't seem to be technical enough to come up with this kind of virus."

Kaylin's attention came back from plans to dismember her boss. "What? Mmmmm...you are right. But she gave it to him."

"Where did she get it? Maybe she didn't know and just passed it on."

Kaylin thought back and remembered the day of their first kiss like a stab in the heart. That kiss had been in the store, the only time they had been alone. "Retha went to visit the Sister of the East. When she came back, she had this plan for him."

Cormag growled. "The Sister of the East. She could do something like this."

"And it's the kind of thing she would do."

"Yes."

Kaylin rose quickly and said, "Thank you, Cormag, for all your help, but I must go now."

"Wait a minute, lass. You aren't planning on taking on the

Sister of the East? She's surrounded by an army and her magic could stop you in your tracks."

"Of course you're right. I don't have any such plans. Don't you worry about me." Then she walked out without looking back where Douglas lay.

Kaylin walked away from Retha's store ignoring the deafening explosion behind her. Flames engulfed the building, sending billowing black smoke into the air. The acrid scent of burning wood and chemicals assaulted her nostrils. Retha's absence when she'd returned from the Tinker told Kaylin the old woman understood Kayla would know what she had done. Going to the store's basement, cranking the boiler to its highest setting and shutting off the regulator had created the blast.

Kaylin marched toward the Sister of the East's palace. She wore her red leather skirt, a gold sleeveless top, and carried a large sickle, the best weapon she could find. In the land of her birth, she had been a farmer, not a solider. If she ever returned there, she would join the army of the ruler of the Quadlings. A warrior like her love had been.

But first she must survive killing the Sister of the East.

Halfway to the welcome area, she encountered a group of the Sister's guards. The battle, it if could be called that, was short. They were trained to fight and capture. She had only her fury and grief.

The rest of her journey was hanging from a pole between two of the guards. At the end, the guards dropped her unceremoniously onto the hard floor of the throne room. Retha was there and said nothing. The Sister laughed at her attempts to stand with numb legs and arms.

"I see you are wearing the colors of my peaceful Sisters," said the Sister.

"This skirt I wore when I was first came here. The top I found in Retha's store."

"Which you destroyed," said Retha.

"You destroyed what I loved. So I destroyed what you loved."

Retha looked away.

"Do you mean the cyberknight?" said the Sister.

"You killed him."

"You hope to get vengeance on me," The Sister of the East, "Whose magic can make you lame?" She waved a hand and Kaylin's legs went limp. "Or blind." The room disappeared.

"You are my puppet. I've made you Retha's slave and you will obey her." Kaylin could see again and stand. "Or these curses will return."

"Bring back your curses. I'd rather be lame and blind than obey that wretched hag."

"Really?" said the Sister. "Very well."

Kaylin collapsed again to the cold stone floor. Cruel hands grabbed her and dragged her out of the throne room and to the dungeon.

CHAPTER 23

DOUG RESCUES KAYLIN

As Cormag worked on the cyberknight, he couldn't stop mulling his reasons to do so. Kaylin had detonated an explosion at Retha's shop, devastating much of the town and forcing the residents to flee. Sister East had then captured her after she recklessly confronted her. According to the latest reports, Kaylin was now imprisoned in the depths of the Sister's dungeon.

Like a mantra, Cormag repeated, "She's an excellent woman. Douglas loved her and would want to help her. He was a good man and won't succumb to psychosis."

The body had been the hardest part, of course. He had figured out the minimum number of organs needed to sustain the brain. The other arm was easy. Even the brain case was straightforward. Replace the skull with metal. Connect a vocoder. Eyes and ears made him better than new in so many ways.

The cyberknight's metallic body now resembled an ancient armor chest plate, but fully enclosing the interior. His arms and legs attached to an internal frame rather than a human skeleton. Pauldrons shielded the joints at the shoulders. Around the waist, a section reminiscent of a knight's codpiece housed the batteries. The only element bearing any semblance to humanity was the grotesque head.

Cormag looked around his almost empty store room. High on a shelf in the back was a centurion's helmet. "That will do," he said.

Once the diagnostics came back green, Cormag woke Douglas up.

Nothing happened for a moment. Then the cyberknight spoke. "I must have lost my eyes this time."

"Yes," said Cormag.

"And my voice?"

"Yes."

Cormag watched the psych scan. Everything was flat. "How do you feel?"

"Hollow."

Douglas sat up and tilted his head down. He raised his hands and examined them.

"It was bad."

"You lost most everything, Moneypenny."

The helmet was without expression. The enhancement visor scanned back and forth. "It is against regulations to do a full conversion. There is a danger of cyber psychosis."

"Yes, and I would not have done it if it hadn't been for Kaylin."

There was a minute change of head angle and Cormag could have sworn the red light moved faster.

"What about Kaylin? Did she ask you to do this?"

"No, she didn't. She's a brave woman and understood you were gone. She made the hard choice to let you go."

Douglas's metal face did not move.

"Then she blew up Retha's store and most of the village before heading to the Sister of the East to avenge you."

"Kaylin is not a warrior."

"No, which is why they captured her before she got halfway there. The Sister threw her in the dungeon, after putting a spell on her that will make her obey Retha's every word or go blind."

Douglas dropped off the table and said, "You have given me no weapons."

"You know I can't do that. Even if I wanted to."

The former Cyberknight raised his arms, and the hands transformed. A hook, a sickle, and a chainsaw cycled into being. "These will have to do."

"Douglas, do only what you have to free her. You know the dangers."

"I do," he said and marched out the door.

~

THERE HAD BEEN a squad of Welcomian soldiers in the village. He let one run ahead of him to the Sister of the East. The others were bloody scattered parts.

A platoon of guards waited at the palace gate. Some ran when the carnage began and he didn't bother to chase them. He punched his arm into the thick wooden gate. On the other side a solid beam held it closed, so his hand became a saw and the doors swung open.

A rain of arrows and crossbow bolts tinked against his metal body, doing no damage. He grabbed a nearby guard, sawed off his head, and threw it with amazing accuracy at a bowman on the parapet. The others scattered in horror.

They were guards. He was a Cyberknight.

The Sister walked out to meet him. Retha hid behind her mistress.

"Give me Kaylin and I will leave."

The Sister stood just out of reach. "You are no longer

human. You will bow before me now." She waved a hand at him.

Nothing happened. She pulled a long metal stick from her sleeve and again motioned toward him.

The oscillating hum of the red scanning visor didn't change as he stared.

"Give me Kaylin back or I will destroy you."

Retha whispered in the Sister's ear, "Let her go. With the spell you cast, I will still control her."

Her comment was plain to Douglas's enhanced hearing. He bent and pounded a hand into the cobblestone courtyard. Ripping a handful of rock free, he threw it, missing the Sister's head by centimeters. The stone smashed the store owner's face, crushing bone and splattering blood everywhere, including on the Sister.

"Give me Kaylin. Release her from all of your control. Or I will tear down this entire palace and rip you limb from limb."

The Sister looked at a nearby guard and nodded. He ran off.

"What will you do with her? Do you think you can live in my lands after this?"

"Can I not?"

The Sister considered this.

"Your lands are not what they used to be," said Douglas. "Kaylin destroyed your furthest village to the West."

"Are you aligned with the city now? Will you start a war?"

"They made me for war, but I don't know the Wizard of the City."

The guard reappeared from the palace with Kaylin. She wasn't walking on her own and didn't look at him as they dropped her on the stones between him and the sister. She pushed with her arms but her legs didn't move.

"Free her of your spells, witch," said the Knight.

"Very well." She waved her stick at the girl. "There. She's spell free."

Kaylin looked up and around. At the Sister, then Retha's bloody corpse. She got her legs under her and stood turning away from the Sister for the first time.

"Kaylin, come with me." Douglas stretched out one silver hand.

Despite her red skin being scraped and bruised, his scans confirmed she was physically unharmed. "Douglas, is that you?"

"Yes. I set you free."

She ran to him and hugged him tight. He made no movement to return the embrace.

"It is time to go."

Kaylin stepped back and looked quizzically at his helmet. He took Kaylin's hand and they walked out through the shattered gates.

"What happened then?" asked Space Girl Green as they walked along the road. While they were talking, Halamar scouted ahead. He would run almost out of sight or explore a potential threat in the woods and quickly return.

"We came back to what remained of the village. All the people had left because of the damage Kaylin had caused. Even Cormag had left. He left a note saying he could no longer live under Sister East.

"Kaylin was happy because we were together. I, though, felt nothing. Nothing when I freed her, and nothing now that we were together. With the lumber I had cut during the bargain, I constructed the cottage you saw.

He walked on for a few minutes. The sun was high and bright, but Green did not feel the same.

"The way we interacted became impossible. I lacked physical sensations and my emotions were muted. I loved Kaylin, but she couldn't understand my detachment. Holding hands, caressing—none of it mattered to me. I couldn't even kiss her. While she slept in our bed, I stood in my charging cradle, feeling distant

"This was no way for a couple to live, and eventually she could take no more. I believe she was kind as she explained she couldn't stay with me. Not because of how I looked, but because I had no feelings and could not understand hers. She said she would go to her homeland in the South. The red lands of the Good Sister South. If I should get my feelings back, then I could search her out there."

Scarecrow said, "How did you take that?"

"I felt nothing. Neither happy, sad, nor angry. It was just the way it was. I told her I understood. I think I still loved her, but it didn't feel the way it had before."

Green thought back to Rainbow school and the lessons on love, sex, and feelings. "Where I come from, there are no boys. No males under the age of 17. So I have no experience with a romantic love like yours and Kaylin's. But we are taught love is not a feeling, but actions. It is the sacrifices you make for those you care for."

"So I could have loved her by doing things for her."

Green scrunched up her face. "It isn't that easy. There is an aspect of love that isn't easy to comprehend. It isn't associative, like in math. You sacrifice for those you love, but sacrificing for someone doesn't mean you love them. They teach us emotions are powerful things. Literally. They provide the power to do the things needed, and love is the most powerful thing in the universe."

"I kind of understand," said Doug. "I don't have feelings to guide my actions, so I have to think about what is the way I should act. It works most of the time, but it is hard."

"Well, I am glad I have a heart then," said Scarecrow, "or whatever you call my feeler. I'm not smart enough to know how to act without a brain."

"I have had a heart before, and have a brain. There is nothing like the feeling of love. I understand how it can be so powerful," said Doug.

"That is all the more reason to see the wizard in the city," said Green. "Perhaps he can give you a new way of feeling. Then you can go to the lands of the south and find Kaylin. How long has it been?"

Before he replied, barks echoed from the woods ahead. Moments later there was a thunderous roar, and Halamar catapulted from the trees and skidded across the road.

CHAPTER 24
A POSSIBILITY OF TROUBLE

Eógan backed carefully into the crate provided by the *Dóchas ar Dhíoltas*'s spacesuit tailors. It was easier to wear the suit than carry it, and they had given him a storage crate which he had dragged behind him. Amethyst had helped him to secure it vertically to the wall of her saucer's entry chamber. When he was fully in the crate and she closed it, the suit automatically split in two, then opening the box removed the suit.

Amethyst wasn't there but a pile of clothes for him lay on the floor. Once dressed he found her in the cockpit ready to lift off. "That captain going to be a problem?" she asked.

Eógan shrugged. "Doubt it, but I'm realizing I'm out of touch with my fellow refugees. I don't know how universal his prejudice toward Home is among Gamalonians."

A green light had illuminated in the landing deck and the exit door opened. The troop carrier didn't really have a hanger, but it did have a large area for troops and armor during an assault. It could be depressurized and there was plenty of room for a flying saucer. She exited smoothly.

"I think it is more a Civitas thing. Intelligence says there is a fairly large fraction of their population that doesn't like us for some reason. This was the first time I'd heard anyone say the curse was a myth." She laughed, "Maybe we should invite the captain to visit."

Eógan had to smile. "The others didn't seem to agree with him."

"No, they struck me as a very practical lot. Might give Third Legion a run for their money."

"That who they are up against next week?"

"Yes," Amethyst said. The legions of Home were numbered by quality and there was a massive war game every five years to determine the ranks. "Rumor has it Third might move up next games. At least the Civitas should be kept busy, while we see what is going on with Gamalon."

Eógan was contemplative. If things really were hostile among the other members of the Diaspora, Captain Kennedy could just call an ally closer to Gamalon to intercept them. "How long will it take us to get there?"

"Only a few hours till the portal, then a couple of days in the Spaceways."

"Mmmm," said Eógan, "I'm going to contact some old friends and try to get a handle on the ranger and Civitas issue. Gamalon probably doesn't have a comm relay at its portal, so I better do it now." He moved toward the ladder.

ONCE EÓGAN WAS out of earshot Amethyst said, "Aurelius, connect me to Space Woman Black."

"Yes, Ma'am."

Amethyst put on a head set just in time to hear, "Go for Black."

"Black, I just left the Civitas troop carrier *Dóchas ar Dhíoltas* and had an interesting encounter with their captain. Seems he doesn't believe in the curse." Black grunted her response, but didn't interrupt. "He, like the troops on the ship, are Gamalonian. But he doubted Eógan's claim to be a real Ranger, since he wasn't in the Civitas approved Rangers."

"Mmm, interesting. Do you think all the Gamalonians attached themselves to Civitas?"

Amethyst smiled, "Eógan as much as accused the captain of selling out. The infantry pilus stepped into the discussion at that point and calmed things down."

"Interesting. So not all Gamalonians then. They give you a suit? I assume that's why you were there."

Of course she did. Space Woman Black always knew what was going on with her girls and was a couple of steps ahead. "Yes, and they did. Captain said the suit was the infantry's to allocate, but he did promise to report our little trip to Civitas authorities and ask to be sent to Gamalon."

"I'll keep an eye out, but I doubt they will be quick to stand up the Warriors." She thought for a couple of minutes. "If they do, I'll send back-up. Or do you think you've got the situation under control?"

"Ma'am, I don't know what the situation is. Going to Gamalon on a second hand report of someone trying to terraform it, is situation enough for me. Dealing with a cohort of angry Civitas might pose a challenge."

"Acknowledged," said Black. "If I see the troop carrier leave before the games, I'll see what I can do to slow them down."

"Yes, Ma'am." Amethyst paused, then asked, "Anything from Green Capricorn?"

"No. Not unusual, though. Haven't heard anything from the rest of Capricorn either. Though the hairs on my neck rise whenever I think of them." Black sighed and added, "She send her *father* anything else?"

"No. He's reaching out to his Gamalonian contacts about the rangers and Civitas. When I asked him about this Auz she said she was going to, he said it was a myth." Another grunt from her boss. "I'll try to reach her once in the Spaceways."

"Keep me informed. Black out."

CHAPTER 25
A COWARDLY LION

"Was that a lion?" said Green. She ran to where Halamar had gotten back to his feet. "Are you all right, Halamar?"

Facing the forest, the dog barked and growled. Scarecrow ran up and stood in front of Green. "Let me go first, because I can't be hurt."

Doug came up next to him, his hands now sickles. "Nor can I and I can do a great deal of damage should something attack me."

Even Halamar jumped between her and the source of the roar.

She pushed between them and turned to face them, hands on hips. "What the hell are you doing?"

Halamar got it first. He lay down on his belly and put his nose under a paw.

"I am Space Girl Green of Rainbow Capricorn. Daughter of Home. My mother was Space Girl Red Libra." She looked at the oscillating eye of the former Cyberknight, then at the pale face of Scarecrow. "Since you don't know of Home let me explain it to you. A Space Girl is an agent of change with all the training of a Warrior and more. Each one of us belongs at the top of another specialty. I could have been a doctor, or an ecologist."

She pulled her rayguns off her belt and held them up. The sleek and futuristic raygun was a masterpiece of engineering and design, clearly built for both precision and power. Its body was crafted from a gleaming green alloy that shimmered under the light, accentuated with silver. A transparent sphere near the center of the weapon contained a dark swirling gas. The barrel, tapering into a streamlined point, was adorned with mysterious symbols that might be indicators of its functions or settings.

"Only Space Girls and high-ranked officers receive these rayguns. They're the most powerful handheld weapons in the known galaxy." She shoved them back into their holsters. "I may not be impervious to damage like the two of you," Green turned to the forest and raised her voice, "but anyone stupid enough to attack a Space Girl, had better be."

There was a rustle in the trees, but no response.

"You attacked my dog. Come out with your hands up."

Something moved, but nothing appeared. Then a meek masculine voice said, "Please don't hurt me. I will come out, but don't hurt me."

"Come out and we can talk about it. If you stay in, I'm going to give a demonstration of what these guns can do."

The underbrush rustled, revealing a flash of tawny fur. Two hands, furry and ending in claws, moved branches aside. A tall figure stepped out from the shadows of the trees.

Shaped like a human but with the head of a lion, including a full mane, the being had a torso covered in golden fur, showcasing strong pectoral muscles. His arms were muscular, ending in large hands. Attire was minimal, consisting only of a broad belt around the waist and a leather pteruges skirt. His feet mirrored his hands in their oversized, paw-like appearance. He exuded a masculine, feline strength, the kind that could intimidate the bravest souls. Yet, his slouched posture and avoidance of eye contact destroyed his imposing presence.

"I'm sorry about your dog. He surprised me, and I roar when I am surprised. It normally makes people run away, which is what I want."

"And why did he come flying out of the woods? He could have been hurt."

The lion man got down on his knees and bowed his head to the ground. "I'm sorry girl from Space. He jumped on me and I swatted him away. Please don't hurt me."

"Mmmm..." said Green. "You don't seem to know your own strength. If he had been a regular dog, I would be most cross with you." Then she turned to Halamar, "Did you jump on him without provocation?"

Halamar covered his eyes with his paws and whimpered.

"Halamar, I shouldn't have to remind you, you are not a dog. You don't have to chase cats."

Douglas chuckled, which was not a pleasant sound coming out of his vocoder. When they all looked at him, he said, "What? I don't have feelings, but that was funny."

To the Lion Green said, "Oh, stand up. For such a big guy, you seem awfully afraid."

"Oh, I am a terrible coward, Space Lady." Lion straightened up. "That is why I hid in the forest. I'm afraid of everything."

"But you are so big," said Scarecrow. Standing Lion was taller than both of Green's traveling companions — a full meter taller than she was.

"That is just the way I'm made. I know I should be brave, but I can't be. I worry someone will hurt me."

"If you are afraid," said Doug, "then you have a heart and I wish I had one. I never feel fear, or happiness. That is why I'm going to the City to meet the Wizard. I want him to give me a heart."

"If I had a brain," said Scarecrow, "then I could explain why you should not be afraid. But I don't. That is why I'm going to the City."

"Might I join you?" asked Lion. "I promise not to hurt anyone."

Halamar walked over to the big cat and rubbed his head on him. Green smiled, "It seems Halamar has forgiven you, so I do as well. Please join us Lion."

Then the five of them continued on down the green road.

THROUGHOUT THE DAY, as the journey continued, the road improved, and the forest thinned. They ascended a low hill and stopped. Before them were fields and in the distance the spires of a great emerald city. The road gently curved like a river between low hills till it climbed to the walls of the city.

Space Girl Green looked at the sun and said, "Perhaps we should find a place to camp for the night and approach the city rested in the morning."

The others agreed. Halamar barked from the front of the group and pointed to the next hammock in the hills. When they got there, they found a stream that ended in a clear aquamarine pool. There were no structures nearby, but they could tell from the fire pit it had been used as a campsite before.

As she was setting out her bedroll, Doug approached. "Space Girl Green, may I ask about your rayguns?"

"Sure, but I can't promise to answer everything."

"How are they powered? They seem tiny to be as powerful as you said."

Green upholstered her weapon and pointed to the ball

shape in the center. "This is called a Plasma Chamber, even though it houses more than just plasma. It is currently filled with an inert gas, but when activated, it becomes charged with energy. This is how the actual ray is created and exits the barrel."

"Yes, but based on the data from my sensors, it seems not only is the chamber devoid of power, the whole weapon is."

Green's brow furrowed. "The batteries in the handle power the chamber."

"I do not believe there is any power in those batteries."

With a flick of her thumb, she activated the power lever, but the chamber didn't emit any sound or glow. She aimed the green and silver weapon at a tree but nothing occurred when she squeezed the trigger. Despite going from the lowest to the highest setting, she still couldn't find a ray. Her other raygun was equally dead.

"That is strange. Those batteries should last for months. I know they were full when I left the saucer." Had she had neglected the most basic of Space Girl training? No, she clearly remembered checking her gear while packing. "Grrrr. I screwed up again. If I had a place to work, I could run some diagnostics. On the road, there is little I can do."

"Perhaps when we get to the City, you can use the Wizard's workshops," said Scarecrow. "I'm sure he must have them."

"Indeed," said Green.

CHAPTER 26

SEEKING AN AUDIENCE

The next morning, they rose at dawn and prepared themselves. Green took a bath in the stream and put on her blue and white dress. Lion combed his hair and adjusted his kilt. Scarecrow evened out her parts into the best shape she could. Doug had spent the night watch buffing his metal till it shined.

They set off four abreast, an excited rhythm to their march. Even from afar, the Emerald City's magnificence was impressive. Encircled by towering walls of gleaming emeralds, with towers at the corners and above the gates. As they approached the city they could see people coming around the corners from the north and south to line up in front of their gate. No one but them was on the eastern road.

By the time they approached the gate, they found themselves among a diverse throng, all awaiting entry into the city.

"What's going on?" asked the Lion.

"I am uncertain," stated the previous cyberknight. "There was never a cause to halt when this city served as the residence of the King and Queen. Of course, it is much grander now. And everything is green. You must feel quite at home, Space Girl."

She smirked. "I do like the shade."

At the front of the line, there was a baldheaded, stout man sitting behind a table. He wore a heavily embroidered tabard in forest green. Behind him, the massive gates were closed.

Without looking up, he said, "State your reason for entry."

Green stepped forward. "We want to see the Wizard. We are hoping he can help us with some problems."

The sparkle of the silver shoes caught his eye. He glanced at them and his head shot up, eyes wide. Once he calmed his expression and examined all of them, he said. "You are a motley lot. What manner of problems would you bother the Wizard with? He is a very busy man, you know."

"I want him to give me some brains," said Scarecrow.

"I want a heart that can feel," said the Cyberknight.

"I want him to give me courage," said Lion.

Green looked at the little man and said, "I crash landed on this planet, and when I tried to leave, a green beam and a yellow beam fired on me. I would like to know why the city shot at my flying saucer, and get help so I can leave the land."

The man realized his mouth was hanging open and snapped it shut. He looked down at the book in front of him. "Mmmmm. A most unusual set of queries. You will need to take them to the Wizard's Stewardess. She will determine if he might see you." He then opened a drawer and pulled out a box. "You will each need to wear these."

One at a time, he pulled out 5 pair of glasses. They were of different sizes and shapes, from huge goggles to tiny spectacles.

Green picked up the most regular looking ones and examined them. "What are these for?"

The little man harrumphed and squared his shoulders. "The Emerald City is so spectacular, so wonderful, so bright, that if you don't wear these special sunshades, you will be blinded. They are required by order of the Wizard."

Douglas, the former Cyberknight, said, "I doubt that is true of me. My eyes are cybernetic and can compensate for any brightness."

"Regardless, it is the order of the Wizard that all should wear them. They also allow you to see his wonders that the naked eye cannot perceive."

Green gingerly put them on. As soon as the glasses settled on her nose, the arms grew and connected behind her head. She pulled on them. "Hey, I can't take these off."

"They will be removed when you leave the city."

"What? No!"

"Yes, what!" replied the bureaucrat. "They are required for all that enter the city. You assuredly won't get to see the Wizard without them."

Though it rankled, Green accepted and passed the glasses to the others. "Why are there five?"

"One is for the dog."

"The dog? You've got to be kidding."

With a forced, slow, cadence, the man said, "Every...one...who...enters...the...city...must...wear...the...glasses."   He motioned to Lion, now wearing large absurd goggles, "You didn't object to your cat wearing them."

She started to argue that Halamar and Lion were not the same, when she remembered Halamar was much more than a dog. Just like Lion was much more than a cat. She would have to watch herself. In her thoughts, she was starting to think of Halamar as an actual dog rather than her flying saucer. When she placed the smallest pair on Halamar's snout, they transformed to grip his head.

The weirdest pair were the ones worn by Douglas. Since he had a bar of lights for his eyes, the glasses provided looked like wraparound sunglasses. His red scanning dot was now green.

The little man pushed a button on his table and a small door in the gate opened. "You may enter. Enjoy your stay."

The group walked into the city. It was a beautiful city, unlike any Green had seen. Capital on Home was a modern city full of curving lines and geometric shapes. The Emerald City was heavy on spires and archways.

Everything was green. Everything. The road. The walls. Even the people. Just inside the door, a sign hovered in mid-air, shaped like an arrow with a scrolling message on its side, "This way to the Wizard's Castle."

They walked down a street lined with various shops and a few dwelling places. She noted a hotel, and many cute cafes, but focused on getting to the castle and putting their requests to the wizard.

Scarecrow eagerly looked at everything. "This is like nothing I've ever seen before. Since I've never seen a city before, that's no surprise. Are all cities like this?"

"No," said Green, "Most aren't one color, and most cities have a distinct style of buildings. Every city is different."

"And this city isn't like what you are seeing either," said Douglas. "The building style is like the Royal days, but there are many more of them. I expect what we are seeing is not what is actually there."

Scarecrow looked at the CyberKnight. "Not seeing what I'm seeing? That seems impossible. I am seeing what I'm seeing."

"Yes, but these glasses are changing it. Not only are they changing the color, but they are making things look nicer than they really are." Green got the impression Douglas wasn't liking this part of the visit any more than she was.

"Really? Like what?"

"The sign leading us isn't there," said Green. "Try touching it."

Sure enough, when Scarecrow tried, her hand went right through it. "Wow," she said. "I don't know if I like the idea of my vision being messed with."

The Lion moved next to Green and said, "What if there is a hole and the glasses hide it? I could fall in. Or what if there are mice and the glasses hide them? They could get me."

She stroked his huge biceps and said, "It's okay, Lion. I don't think the Wizard wants people to get hurt, so he won't hide dangerous things."

"Then why is he doing it?"

"I suspect to make everything look as pretty as possible."

Eventually they reached the palace and as they climbed the steps large double doors swung open. They entered a spacious room, its high ceilings adorned with graceful, pointed arches. Supporting the expansive roof were transparent columns, each pulsing with a luminous liquid that ebbed and flowed. The air was alive with various lights and whimsical objects, all suspended seemingly by magic.

A woman stood in the middle of the room. Her long hair cascaded over her shoulders, framing a slender face and dark green skin. She sported delicate emerald spectacles that seemed to glow slightly. Her dress, form-fitting at the chest and hips, flowed around her like mist, creating an ethereal silhouette.

"Welcome to the Palace of the Wizard," she said. "I am the Palace Stewardess, Saphira. We have prepared refreshments for you."

She waved a hand toward a cozy lounge area outfitted with plush couches and tables. Atop one table rested a pitcher alongside a tray brimming with an assortment of green delicacies invitingly arranged. When the group did not immediately obey her invitation, she moved toward the table and chair herself. Green was fairly sure her skirt was real, but the mist which trailed behind her was probably a product of the glasses.

"The Wizard is aware of all things and knows you desire an audience with him. But you come without an appointment. You will need to wait. Please, help yourselves to these refreshments while I check with the Wizard to find a suitable time for your meeting." In a plume of mist, she glided from the room.

Despite her affinity for her signature color, Green found the sight of green meat less than appealing, but if she closed her eyes and just ate it, the flavor was perfectly acceptable.

Halamar rubbed up against her leg where she sat and laid his head in her lap. She petted him while they waited.

And wait, they did. For several hours. Scarecrow and Douglas mostly just stood in place. Not long after finishing eating, Lion started pacing. Eventually, even Green was pacing to burn off nervous energy, while Halamar sniffed around the room.

The day seemed nearly over when the Stewardess returned. Her smoky gown obscured her feet, but Green could hear the clicking of heels on the stone floor. She stopped a few feet from them. "Good news, the Wizard will see you," she said, causing all of them to straighten in anticipation. "But not today."

The companions shoulders slumped. She continued, "He has time for only one of you each day." She smiled at them and added, "He has commanded special accommodations for each of you here in the palace. Please come with me, Space Girl Green."

Green grabbed her pack and followed the woman across the room and up a staircase. They went up several flights and down a long hallway. "This will be your room. I hope it is to your liking."

The city's panoramic beauty immediately struck Green, visible through the expansive floor-to-ceiling glass wall directly across from the door. The interior boasted a modern design that felt instantly welcoming. To the side, a double bed adorned with green linens promised comfort, while the seating area, oriented towards the outside view, invited relaxation. *This,* she thought, *would be exactly the apartment I or any green would have in Capital.* "It is lovely and feels like home. It's like you could read my mind."

"Not me. The Wizard designed each room."

Which left Green wondered if this mysterious person could read minds.

Saphira looked closely at Green's face. "The Wizard asked me to tell you not to wear so much makeup tomorrow when you meet him."

"Does he normally tell you what makeup to wear?"

"It is unusual for him to be concerned with make-up. Or shoes, and he was insistent you wear those shoes tomorrow."

"Ahhh," said Green. *He noticed the Sister's kiss and shoes.* "Well, if that is what the Wizard wants, then that is what I will give him."

Stewardess Saphira smiled and bowed slightly and floated toward the door. "I must go settle your friends in the rooms made for them. If you need anything, just pull this and a member of staff will come to serve." She motioned an elegant hand toward a thick rope hanging next to the door.

Green walked to the window and looked out over the city. Halamar, having a completed a sniffing circuit of the room joined her.

CHAPTER 27

NIGHT IN THE PALACE

Scarecrow's room was nothing like the Space Girl's. Since she had no need of food or sleep, the room was bare except for a long table near the window. On this table were several objects. Everything from a cube of smaller cubes of many colors, to rings that seemed to be locked together.

"These are puzzles for you to do while passing the night," said the Stewardess.

"I'm here to get a brain. I'm sure I can't do any puzzles."

Saphira shrugged and picked up the multi-colored cube. She turned the different layers a few times and more of the same color were on one side. Then she picked up the rings, and after a few motions, one ring came loose. Then she walked down the row, doing something small to each puzzle.

"Maybe that is true, but the Wizard thought you might find it interesting to try. If you need anything, pull the rope next to the door."

Upon entering his room, the former Cyberknight noticed a charging cradle against one wall and a workbench with tools on it. Otherwise, the room was bare.

"The Wizard says your power sources are mostly full, but you can use this cradle to top yourself off. Should you need to repair yourself, there is the workbench," the Stewardess said.

"That is most kind. I assume you procured this equipment from the Cyberknight barracks in the palace."

"That equipment was in storage since we have little use for it now-a-days. All the Cyberknights have gone."

Saphria walked to a pole beside the cradle. "This, I believe, is a Cyberknight armor stand. Should you wish to remove your helmet. You will be unable to leave the room without it, of course."

"Because my face is so hideous."

"I know nothing of how you look under your helmet, Knight. Your glasses are attached to your helmet."

He bowed in response to this, oddly comforted.

She motioned to the rope next to the door. "Pull that if you need anything."

Lion did not like his room at all.

"This is a cage."

Vertical bars of green tinted gold ran all the way round the room. Soft green pillows covered the floor. Big ones. Little ones. Piles of them everywhere. The huge cat-man had to duck his head to avoid touching the roof, which was also padded.

"They are here to keep you safe," said Saphira. "You said you lacked courage, so the Wizard designed this suite just for you. The bars are there to keep you from falling out, and the pillows to stop you from hurting yourself if you fall. Or bump your head on the roof." The Stewardess had not come into the room. Probably because she feared falling on the too soft floor. She pressed a button outside the doors and a new set of bars clanged down loudly over the opening, causing the Lion to jump. "And these will keep anything bad from getting in." She pointed to two bowls among the pillows. "There is a nice bowl of warm milk and a bowl of soft porridge for you to eat." Without further comment, she shut the door.

Lion tried to pace around the room, but the too soft floor made that impossible. He looked at the food and muttered, "I'm a Lion, not a cat."

AFTER A FEW MOMENTS looking out at the city, Green began exploring the suite she had been assigned. She suspected the long delay to see the Wizard was so he could study them. The rooms were undoubtedly wired for sight and sound. Halamar sniffed every piece of furniture, and Green wondered what a flying saucer learned from the sniff of a dog.

The suite featured a wardrobe filled with clothing tailored to fit Green precisely. The selection favored sparkly gowns, both short and long, but there was some practical clothing. There were pointedly no shoes in the wardrobe.

A day of mostly waiting meant she wasn't the least bit tired after searching the entire suite. She tried the door and was unsurprised to find it locked. It would be child's play to pop the hinge pins and leave, but she wanted to stay in the Wizard's good graces until after they talked.

Sitting at the table, she pulled the gear out of her pack. Her rayguns had been in her pack since Doug pointed out they didn't work. Her field kit had tools for repairs, but the guns were basically in working order, she just needed to charge the ignition batteries. Looking around, she found no power outlets, nor indications of induction plates. While she hadn't been looking, she didn't remember seeing power outlets anywhere. The only thing even close was the charging cradle in Doug's cabin.

"Halamar, have you noticed any power outlets or sign of electrical infrastructure?"

The dog cocked his head, then shook it.

"Mmmmm, curiouser and curiouser," she said.

She tidied and balanced the gear in her pack. Still not ready for bed, Green began a series of smooth, flowing movements that stretched and bent her body in harmony with her breathing. Following her feelings, these tranquil movements gradually intensified into a regimen of sharp, decisive techniques designed for close-quarters defense. After almost half an hour, she came to a sweaty conclusion.

Finally feeling a little tired, she went into the bathroom to wash. There was a large shower chamber, and a vanity with a sink and mirror. As she removed her clothes, and the shoes transformed themselves in to bathing slippers. Like so many things in Auz, the shower seemed to understand exactly what she wanted and adjusted the water temperature. Stepping into the shower, she wondered how to wash her face with the glasses glued to her head. She stepped under the spray and looked into the water, closing her eyes, and felt the glasses move out of the way. When she opened her eyes, they slithered back. Taking this into account, she could completely wash her face. But looking at the mirror afterwards, her too red lips stood out even more on her clean face. Especially under the emerald glasses.

While drying herself with the most luxurious towel she had ever used, she noticed the shoes moved to let her get at her wet feet. The transformation let her chase them up and down her legs, but nothing would make them run off her. In fact she started to think they were enjoying the little game.

As she settled into the big bed, the shoes turned to socks and the glasses became soft. Neither let go of her. "Clothing you can't take off is a trend in Auz I don't like," she said to the empty room.

CHAPTER 28

GREEN MEETS THE WIZARD

Green woke up to the morning sun on her bed. Breakfast was laid out on the room's bale. She sat up abruptly searching the room.

"Halamar?" She said, looking around for the dog. He jumped up from where he was sleeping in front of the door to her suite. "How was the table set?"

Space Girls were light sleepers, especially in potentially hostile territory. But somehow she'd slept through servants resetting a table. Halamar seemed confused too as he sniffed at the food on the table.

She took a deep breath and stood. She moved through a series of poses designed to center mind and body. It was bad to start the morning already unsure.

Eventually, she went to the table and grabbed a piece of fruit, which she nibbled on while regarding the clothes in the wardrobe again. Seeing the Great and Powerful Wizard of Auz was probably a formal occasion, so she picked a sparkling emerald dress. It boasted a well-defined shape with a fitted bodice and a striking V-neckline that beautifully framed her neck. The sleeves had a bold cap style, giving the shoulders a dramatic touch. A cinched waist accentuated the narrowest part of the torso before flaring out into a full A-line skirt.

Upon donning the dress, the silver shoes metamorphosed into pointed-toe pumps with spiked heels. "I'm going to trust you have the perfect fashion sense for Auz," she told the shoes. "Not that I have much choice."

As if on cue, there was a knock at her door.

Without waiting for a response, the door opened and Stewardess Saphira entered. "It is time for you to see the Wizard."

Green felt the palace very empty as they retraced the previous day's journey. "Where are my friends?"

"They all have their own rooms customized specifically for them by the Wizard," said the Stewardess. "You must enter the Wizard's chamber alone. Stand here." Then she floated away in a cloud of green mist.

Space Girl Green stood alone as the door swung open, her unease boiling into near panic at the sight before her. She found herself at the edge of an immense throne room, its circular form stretching a hundred meters across. Six wedge-shaped areas segmented the chamber, reminiscent of a colossal pie sliced evenly. The section where she entered was the base level, with the adjacent slices ascending in sequence to form a staircase designed for a titan. Directly opposite the door, the highest segment was a dais without lacking a throne. There was no simple means to traverse to the slices flanking her, each at least two meters high.

Walking toward the center of the room she triggered a towering visage of the Wizard to materialize. The colossal head hovered above the ground, unsupported by any physical means. Its features were exaggerated, with deep, piercing eyes that seemed to look into Green's very soul. The Wizard's expression was stern yet enigmatic. The great head spoke, filling the air with a palpable sense of magic and mystery as its booming voice echoed throughout the vast chamber.

"I am the Great, Powerful and Terrible Wizard. Maker of the Emerald City. Creator of peace in the center of Auz. Protector of the people. The one with all knowledge of the land. Why do you trouble me?"

Heart racing from the display, Green tried to calm her fears, but that seemed impossible, as the rumbling echo never seemed to dissipate.

"I am Space Girl Green of the world Home. I came through a Spaceway portal out of curiosity. Once through that portal, a vortex caught me and I crashed my flying saucer. Once the vortex disappeared," she chose not to mention why it ceased, "I attempted to investigate the portal, but someone shot me down with a green and a yellow beam. I seek your help to leave Auz."

Tthe pupils of the enormous eyes seemed to swirl, but never blinked nor moved. "The portal only opens to those with an invitation to the land. Have you a golden ticket?"

Green shook her head. A half truth to be sure, but the coin *was* in her room. She found it interesting the all knowing Wizard was not aware of it. "No, sir. My saucer told me there was an unknown portal and there is a standing order to investigate and report new portals. Also, impulsivity is a trait of Space Girls."

There was a rumble that might have been a laugh. Or a growl.

"Your vessel's ascent caught my vigilant gaze, and in my endeavor to draw you here, I employed a tractor beam. Alas, the malevolent Sister of the West thwarted my efforts with her dreadful Sky Beam," he explained, his tone a mixture of frustration and gravity. "That beam lays waste to all who dare to soar through the skies. She abhors all that take flight, sealing Auz from ingress and egress. Her animosity mirrors that of her sister, the architect of the vortex, whose shoes now grace your feet."

Green didn't want to go over the Sister's fate, and instead tried to bring things back to her request. "The beam was extremely powerful. It damaged my flying saucer, which is no easy feat. I hoped you might help me with parts to repair it, and knowledge of how to escape the beams."

The head bobbed and swayed slightly without looking away. "I fought a war with the Evil Sisters, but it ended in a stalemate. I can not stop them from stopping you. You are wearing the shoes of the Sister of the East. And is that the sign of the Sister of the North on your lips?"

"It is the sign of the Golden Sister, given to me in a kiss," Green said as she touched her lips. "The shoes were those of Sister East. When my ship crashed - the first time, not when it was shot down - it landed on the throne of the blue sister and crushed her. Golden gave me the shoes."

"Ahhh, so the Sister of the East is dead. That is good, for she was a burden on the land." The head rose like its invisible body was taking a breath. "Since you have proven yourself, I will help you leave Auz if you will first kill the Sister of the West."

In a flash, her anxiety turned to anger. "Why does everyone in this land think only of killing? And that I would be the best person to do so? I serve Life."

"But you killed one evil sister, you can kill the other. It would make Auz a better place for all life on it."

"Perhaps I can negotiate a peace with Sister West."

The giant head laughed so loudly the walls shook. "The Sister has no desire for peace. She serves chaos, domination, and death. If she had her way, Auz would be nothing but war."

The head rose higher than it ever had. "I, the Wizard of the Emerald City, demand her death before I will help you. I have spoken."

In a puff of smoke that filled the room with a sulfurous odor, the head vanished.

CHAPTER 29

GREEN VISITS SCARECROW

When Green came out of the throne room, the Stewardess was waiting. "I would like to see my friends," Green said.

The Stewardess said, "I can take you to see Scarecrow."

"But not the others?"

"The Wizard has given each a special room with its own purpose. Interrupting might stop him from learning about them."

"But I can see Scarecrow."

"Yes, because she has done so well, and I have a new message for her."

With a graceful motion, the woman walked towards the stairs and brought Green to the floor where her room was situated. Another passage ended in another door which Saphria opened. Green went into Scarecrow's room and said, "This is very different from my room."

Her malleable friend turned at her voice and said, "Space Girl Green, it is good to see you." She did not move nor attempt to hug or greet her and Green thought she needed to teach her a few social skills.

The Space Girl looked at all the puzzles sitting on the table. "You have been doing puzzles?"

"Yes, it seems you don't have to be smart to do puzzles. I thought you must, for it seems the kind of thing only smart people do. But I did these last night."

The Stewardess said, "And all you had to start was my showing you the first move."

"Yeah, but then it was just a matter of doing variations on that move. Eventually, I found a way of making them work," said Scarecrow.

"That's how you do puzzles, Scarecrow," said Green.

"The Wizard has a new task for you," said the Stewardess. "I don't understand this one, but will explain." She walked to a spot in the room, knelt smoothly, and placed a glass cube on the floor. Then she stepped back and motioned Scarecrow toward her.

When Scarecrow was about a meter away, a three-dimensional image appeared over the cube. It was of a woman about the Scarecrow's height. All the features were simplistic, lacking hair or skin texture, but was clearly female. More like a mannequin than a woman.

Scarecrow looked at it curiously.

"The Wizard wants you to examine this closely and then imagine yourself looking like it. He said it might be easier to do one part at a time."

This seemed a strange request, but Scarecrow took it matter-of-factly. She walked slowly around the image. Then stopped in front of it and raised one arm so she could see it. The image did the same.

After a moment, Scarecrows's arm started changing shape to match that of the image. Green gasped.

"Ahh, so it is true," said the Stewardess.

"What is true?" asked Green.

"That is not for me to tell." Saphria continued to talk as she gathered up puzzles and moved toward the door. "I expect the image will change through the evening. Space Girl Green, your room is directly down the hall and to the left."

Once alone, Scarecrow turned to her. One of her arms still had the appearance of the image, and the other did not. "What did the Wizard say to you?"

Green looked around for a chair to flop into but there were none. She leaned against the table instead. "He said I had to kill Sister West in order for him to help me."

Scarecrow thought about that for a minute. "That does not seem very kind on his part. But West is, by all accounts, a terrible person."

"She is, but it is not right to kill people without giving them a chance to change. On Home we bring people to trial if they choose not to change, and only kill them if we can't limit their ability to hurt others."

"Are you going to kill Sister West?"

Her gut had told her the Wizard's command was wrong, but explaining had given her some clarity. "Not without giving her a chance to repent and change. Maybe your task will be easier."

"I can't imagine that, because I have no brain or imagination."

Green laughed, "But you have a sense of humor."

"I do? I didn't notice."

She motioned to Scarecrow's arm. "Did you know you could do that?"

"No, but I'm not very smart and have only been alive for a few days. You've known me all my life. Did you know I could change shape?"

"Come to think of it, I kind of did. You often get crushed and then go back into this shape."

"Yes, I do." She turned back to the image. "I would think on that, but I have no brain. Instead, I will do as the Wizard asks so he might give me a brain tomorrow."

Green wished her luck.

CHAPTER 30
LION IN THE WIZARD'S CAGE

Near noon on the day of Green's visit to the Wizard, Saphira made her way to the Lion's quarters. When she opened the door, there was a mighty roar that sent chills down her spine. She stepped back from the cage as the beast slammed against the bars and reached monstrous clawed hands toward her.

The Lion, a creature of both flesh and something more, was incensed. The suite, designed for comfort, was in disarray. Feathers, the only remnants of once soft and comforting pillows, littered the floor and danced in the air, while porridge was splattered against the window in an act of rebellion.

Saphira grappled with her responsibilities. The Wizard, in his infinite wisdom, had perhaps foreseen this rebellion, a narrative thread woven into the larger tapestry of their lives. Yet, foreknowledge did not equate to preparation, and she found herself at a loss against the backdrop of the Lion's raw emotion.

Twirling, she floated down the corridor in a swirl of emerald skirts. She stopped before another door and knocked. Space Girl Green appeared and gave her a smile that turned to worry. "Is that Lion?"

"Yes. I request your assistance mollifying him."

"What have you done to him?" said the Space Girl, striding past her toward the sound.

"The Wizard has commanded his presence. The boon of an early audience." Saphira hurried to keep up with the focused Space Girl. "I was anticipating joy at this news. Instead, he has destroyed his room and became most aggressive, continually roaring." She waved a long-fingered hand at the open door. The Lion prowled the confines of his cage, almost on all fours, swiping feathers into the air as he moved.

Green approached the opening cautiously until she saw the bars. "You put him in a cage." She looked at the Wizard's servant incredulously. "No one likes being caged. I expect lions like it less than most."

Saphira was not used to being flustered, "The Wizard required it. I explained they were there to keep dangers out since he is always so afraid."

Green shook her head and rolled her eyes. "Either the Wizard is not as wise as he says, or not as kind and generous as we were led to believe." She motioned the Stewardess to stand away from the doors.

"Lion," Green said, projecting her voice over his growls. "It's Space Girl Green."

The Lion pounced toward her and grabbed the bars, the muscles in his hands and forearms bulging. He shook himself mightily, but did not roar. "Let me out of here, Space Girl Green." His big, brown cat eyes pleaded, "Please."

"Of course, Lion," Green answered, reaching into the cage to stroke his mane. "I am so sorry. If I had known they had put you in a cage, I would have stopped them." She motioned, and the Stewardess crept forward. As she approached the cage, she experienced the same shiver she had felt when the Lion had roared at her before. Saphira pulled a key from her dress and handed it to Space Girl Green, deciding the outsider more suited to this task. Then she quickly backed down the hallway far enough she could run if needed.

"Lion," said Green, "the Wizard wants to see you now. Not in a day or two, but you need to get yourself under control first. Can you do that for me?"

The beast man stood tall and took a deep breath. He let it out slowly, then slumped in defeat. "Yes, Space Girl. I am sorry. I should never have acted like that. Tell the other lady I am sorry. I don't know what came over me."

Saphira allowed herself to relax every so slightly but did not move closer.

"Not sure I would behave well if I had been locked in a cage full of feathers either," Green said as she opened the lock.

Lion looked sheepish, and said, "Actually, it was full of pillows. I shredded them when I got angry."

He shuffled into the corridor and Green said, "What a sight you are." She began brushing off feathers and picking them out of his mane. "You can't go see the Wizard so disheveled. Come to my room and we will get you cleaned up."

The Stewardess allowed them to go to the Space Girls suite, even though the Wizard might be displeased to wait. The thought of allowing the big cat into his presence covered in feathers felt worse.

When they entered the room, Halamar came running up and circled the Lion, sniffing him up and down. Then the dog rubbed against the big cat comfortingly.

"Let me get a brush," Green said. The Stewardess hovered near the door, observing. Green returned with brushes and combs from the well stocked bath.

"Sit down over here so I can reach your head." He did, and she began combing his mane, removing feathers and calmly stroking his hair into order.

"That is nice, Space Girl Green. You are a good friend. What did the Wizard say to you? Will he help you get home?"

"Only if I kill Sister West."

"She's a cruel figure, enslaving everyone she can. Rumors are she conducts wicked experiments on those under her control," he said, a deep rumble echoing from his chest. "I might have challenged her, perhaps even sought to end her reign, if my own fears didn't hold me back."

Green smiled at him. "We don't go killing people just because they are bad. Not without giving them a chance to change. I wonder if Auz has prisons."

Saphira, seemingly forgotten by the others, said, "It does not. And even if it had such a thing, it would be hard to keep a Sister in one. They are the most powerful of beings in the Land. Other than the Wizard, of course."

"Who," said Green, stepping back, "you need to go see, Lion."

"Thank you, Space Girl Green. I will plead our case to the Wizard, and if he does not see reason, I will treat him like one of those pillows. Then he will do what we want."

Green shook her head ruefully. "Didn't I just tell you we don't kill people without giving them a chance to change?"

The Stewardess was impressed with this young woman. She was indeed kind all the time, yet there was a strength at her core Saphira had not seen in Auz for a very long time.

Lion's shoulders sagged, and he looked down. "Yes, Space Girl Green," he huffed.

"Go see what he has to say." She looked at the Stewardess, "Perhaps while you are gone, the Stewardess can have your room cleaned up and the bars removed. If not, you can stay with me tonight."

The Stewardess bowed and nodded, "I will see it done, M'Lady." Which caused an odd head tilt from the the dog.

CHAPTER 31
VISITS WITH THE WIZARD

Upon entering the round flat room, the imposing emerald throne immediately grabbed Lion's attention. The throne's back ascended skyward, its spires fanning out like the proud plumage of a peacock, each point catching the light and casting prismatic reflections across the polished floor. Crystalline formations sprouted around it, as if the throne were the epicenter of a mineral forest that had organically integrated itself into the room's design. The size of the room made him feel small and alone. He waited, all the time feeling smaller and more afraid.

Eventually it became too much. He stopped pacing and roared his loudest roar. The sound echoed off the far wall and faded. He was just getting ready to do it again when the room filled with a different roar. A tornado of wind and fire spiraled from the high ceiling to the throne. The rushing wind pushed the Lion to his knees and the heat of the fire made him tremble.

"I am the Great and Terrible Wizard. Why do you trouble me, Lion?"

The voice made Lion covered his ears. The fire's heat reached him even 10 meters away. He cowered lower and said,

"Great Oz, I am a coward and seek courage. I hoped you might grant it to me."

"Why have you laid waste to the quarters I provided? Were you unaware of the wrath this would incite?"

Tears streamed down Lion's face, soaking his mane, as he sobbed, "I tried to be comfortable in your room, but it was too soft for a lion. The bars reminded me of a cage and my fear rose and until I could not control myself."

"And why should I grant you the bravery you so desperately desire?" the Wizard's fiery form questioned.

"Because, Great Wizard, you are my only chance at such a gift. Only you can bestow courage," Lion pleaded.

The fire's intensity ebbed, the once scorching air cooling to a tolerable warmth around Lion.

"Not sufficient," declared the Wizard, his voice still booming but no longer at a volume that caused pain.

Lion took his hands off his ears. "What? Great Oz, I did not hear that."

"I said, simply because I possess the capability does not obligate me to assist you. Many seek my power for their own ends. Were I to acquiesce to each request, nothing of substance would ever be accomplished here in the Emerald City."

Lion clambered to his feet. "Wizard, what would you have me do then? If you are infinitely capable, why do you need a cowardly lion like me?"

The tornado of fire's heat and volume returned causing Lion to shield his face and fall backwards. "Kill the Evil Sister of the West."

Lion again cowered, "But I could never defeat a Sister."

"Then you are of no use to me. Begone."

Lion tried to think of something, anything that would change the Wizard's mind but could not. He slumped out the door.

WHEN SCARECROW ENTERED the throne room, the space had transformed. The grand circular chamber was replaced by an intimate slice, with a throne resting at the apex. The room's original intent to intimidate was gone, and in its stead sat a breathtakingly beautiful woman, exuding a calm allure as she observed Scarecrow's approach.

Scarecrow herself had undergone a change. Her head retained its distinctive lozenge shape with the painted features, but her limbs and torso had evolved to a more humanoid silhouette. The clay-like pallor of her skin had given way to a supple texture, dappled with a vibrant hue of green.

As she beheld the woman upon the throne, a longing stirred within her—a desire to mirror that exquisite form. Though Scarecrow lacked a brain to fully comprehend, she could sense the perfection embodied in the woman's symmetry and proportions. The clothing she wore seemed less to conceal and more to accentuate the flawless sculpture of her body.

"I am the Wizard of Auz, the Great and Powerful," she said in a rich soprano. "Why do you want to see me?"

Scarecrow shambled forward until motioned to stop. "I have no brain. I hoped you would give me one."

"What makes you think you have no brain?"

"I'd like to give you a suitable answer, but I don't have one, therefore I must need a brain."

The fair woman raised her eyebrows. "That makes even less sense."

Scarecrow shrugged her shoulders.

"What will you do for me, new one? If I give you a brain, will you serve me?"

"I would do anything for a brain. I'm not sure what use you

would have for me, but I guess I could figure it out once you give me a brain."

She rolled her eyes and shook her head. "I cannot waste valuable resources on you until my city, and the whole of Auz is safe from the evil Sister of the West. Kill her and return to me. Then I will give you a brain and accept you into my service."

"Wizard, I can't kill anyone. I have no strength and no way of thinking how to overcome someone as powerful as Sister West."

"Then you will never have a brain. Go."

Suddenly the throne was empty and Scarecrow trudged out the door.

~

Douglas dedicated additional time on the morning of his audience, meticulously polishing every chrome surface. He could see himself in himself if he chose to. The body he possessed now bore no resemblance to his previous form, nor did it exactly mirror the full armor of a Cyberknight. Nevertheless, he endeavored to conduct himself with the dignity of a soldier about to meet his king.

Douglas marched purposefully through the doors and saw a ledge cut the room in half. On this raised area floated a creature like nothing he had seen before. His first glimpse struck him with an overwhelming sense of dread. Suspended in the air as if buoyed by some unseen force, it resembled a nightmarish orb, its skin a patchwork of sickly hues that seemed to pulse with malevolence. At its center, a single, massive eye stared unblinkingly, a cold, calculating intelligence gleaming within its depths. Surrounding this central eye, a crown of writhing appendages, each ending in its own baleful eye, surveyed the area with an unsettling vigilance.

The surrounding air crackled with unseen energies, causing the instruments in his helmet to fizz and glitch. A stench of ozone and something far more ancient made it to his nostrils, a smell that spoke of dark, forgotten places beneath the earth. The silence of its presence was perhaps the most unnerving; no sound accompanied its movements, only the soft whisper of air displacing as it floated ominously.

A voice that grated like a chainsaw on metal said, "I, the Wizard, built and now rule this city, the greatest in the Land of Auz. Who are you, and why do you seek me?"

"I am Douglas Merriweather Moneypenny, former First Lieutenant in the Cyberknights of the King and Queen of Auz. Through the treachery of the Evil Sister of the East, I was repeatedly injured and repaired until little of my flesh remains. I did all of this for love, but when it was over I could no longer feel. I have come to you to ask for a new heart that I might feel again."

"Once, I commanded many Cyberknights, but they were destroyed in the last battle with the Evil Sister of the West." There was little nuance in the buzzing voice to tell Douglas how the creature felt about this tragedy. "You may be the last of your kind."

"It saddens me to hear that. I had hoped they all bought a farm and settled into a peaceful life. Or left Auz."

"No one can leave Auz. The Evil Sister of the West controls the only means to do so. I have tried to take it back from her and free the Winkies, but have failed. I will give you what you desire if you will kill her and point her eye back toward the sky."

"Wizard, as a solider I'm willing to fight, but I am one knight. I don't even have my weapons anymore. I fear I cannot do it by myself."

One eyestalk incongruently seemed to spit out an object that skidded across the stone floor. "Here," the monster said.

Douglas bent and picked up the object, realizing it was a data chip. "Upload this, and you will have use of the Cyberknight's hand weapons."

Not as trusting as in the past, he warily ran multiple virus scans on the software. Once he finally let the code into his systems, new options appeared. He could change his hands into swords and the battle versions of a hammer and ax. It felt good to be armed again.

"Thank you, Wizard, but I am still a single Knight. How can I succeed where the Regiments failed?"

"You must convince your companions to join you. The four of you are a formidable unit." All the creatures eyes focused on him. "Do this for me and I will make you feel again."

The manifestation of the Wizard receded from the knight's presence. Its many eyes converged in a singular, purposeful gaze, signaling an end to the discourse. It floated backwards and the atmosphere seemed to ripple in its wake, a visual echo of the creature's passage. Its central eye, dimmed slightly, signifying a withdrawal of its focused intent. The smaller eyes atop its form swiveled in their sockets, casting quick, vigilant glances around the room, ensuring the security of its retreat.

The knight watched, a mixture of worry and relief washing over him as it disappeared into the shadowy recesses of the chamber. For a moment he stood silent in the big room, then about faced and walked out.

CHAPTER 32
PASTORIA'S SPACE CLEARING SOLUTION

"Pastora dear, what is that?" asked Gwendoline. On the table before him was a diminutive feminine creature, less than half a meter tall, with colorful wings on its back.

"You remember the Winged, do you not?"

"Of course. You created them on Auz to be the antibodies of the land. Tough and under our command to deal with problems the Sisters could not handle." She walked around the table looking at a tiny woman wearing a helmet shaped something like the end of a bullet. "But the ones on Auz were colorful. These seem to be made totally of metal." She reached out and tried to move a wing. "And the wings don't move?"

Pastoria nodded enthusiastically. "Yes, yes. These have a different purpose than those. These will operate in space, so the wings are mostly ornamental, though they will collect sunlight and turn it into power."

Gwendoline raised an eyebrow. She leaned over the table to look at the shape of the little being. The creature's belly protruded alarmingly. "Dear, is it pregnant?"

This seemed to make Pastoria even more excited. "In a sense it is." He picked a tablet off the table and pressed a few buttons.

The creature's distended belly split cleanly down the middle, and two doors swung open. Gwendoline couldn't make out what was inside but after a few more taps from Pastoria, a tiny something sprung out on the table, causing her to jump back.

It was a tiny stick figure of all black. She could just make out tiny wing shapes on its back and claws instead of hands. It dropped into a squat and began clawing at the stone tabletop. The screeching of metal on stone would have grated on the nerves if the creature wasn't just a few centimeters high. It began gouging into the hard stone and putting handfuls into its mouth. The oversized mouth ravenously ground the raw material up, and in just a few seconds, the creature seemed taller.

By the time it had put a 10mm gouge in the rock, it was twice as big. Pastoria made another motion on the tablet and it turned into a statue. "Better stop it now, but you get the idea, dear. The creature is self-replicating. Each of these will eat stone and make more of itself." He picked up a torch and shown it into the cavity of the full sized Winged. "There are 12 in this one. Place it on an asteroid and those twelve will start eating raw materials. Given available resources, the minimum time to reproduce is about three hours."

Pastoria seemed very proud of his achievement and Gwendoline could see why, but she had concerns. She kissed him and gave him a hug, "You are the most brilliant roboticist on Gamalon, dear."

"I'm the only one," he replied with a slight smile.

"Indeed, and we discussed in our early days the dangers of self-replicating inhabitants. Why did you decide to build these?" She looked at the gouge in table, "They don't seem to be very discerning in their diet. Or is this a new plan to clean your lab? I assure you we can give Carla the dwarven maid adequate training to do it correctly." She smiled at him.

He laughed, not the least bit deterred. "No, no. We decided

not to make self-replicating bots here because of the threat of overproduction and what it might do to Gamalon itself. Plus, there are so many things that terraforming a planet requires. That would require too much specialization to let them create new versions of themselves. That is why we need the Seed."

"Which the Space Girl daughter of Gamalon has gone to get for us. Will it not do everything these Winged will?" She picked up the frozen offspring and attempted to put it back in its mother. But it was already too big for the opening. At least he made the opening in the belly's front. Not sure how'd she'd have reacted if they came out somewhere else.

"The Seed will rebuild Gamalon's surface," he said. "But what about orbit?" He looked up at the ceiling meaningfully.

"Ahh," she said, dropping the little figure. "Your plan is to send these into space and have them utilize the debris field as resources to reproduce."

"Which will then devourer more of the rocks." He showed her a simulation on the screen. "After creating an appropriate number of Winged, they will lock onto larger rocks, as many as needed, and push them back to a lunar orbit." The simulation rapidly cleared the skies.

"Then what?" Gwendoline asked. "You seem to have put a limit on the total number of your automata, but how will you set that limit? And once they have accomplished their task, what will they do? Stay attached to rocks in orbit forever?"

Undaunted, Pastoria nodded. "I plan to set the total number lower than my estimated need. If it takes a little longer, that is less of a problem than too many Winged. Once attached to rocks and in lunar orbit, they will go dormant. If I need them later, I can send a signal with a new order. If not, they will just be part of the new lunar ring." He smiled excitedly, "And if things work like I hope, having all the mass in the orbit of the old moon will eventually cause them to come together. Possibly forming a new moon with the Winged buried inside."

"Dear, it is indeed a noble dream: clear space, perhaps even fashion a new moon. Yet, while you have commendably considered many of the challenges inherent in self-replication, you must know it is fraught with peril. And what story are you giving to your new creations? Why do they do the things you command of them? Are you building a Crown of Command for them as well?"

Confused Pastoria answered, "My dear these are not inhabitants. Not truly. They use more traditional compute. They don't have sufficient power for the brain balls of Auz. And I'm not sure I could create one with the equipment we have here." He walked over to a larger display and pulled a keyboard to him. "They are simple machines; they don't need to story."

"Story is not just about narrative. It is the giving of meaning. Maybe in these simple creatures that meaning is imparted in the language of code, but it is still a story. It keeps them in alignment with our values and their purpose when they encounter something they don't understand." She stepped behind him and looked at the code scrolling past on the screen. "Mmmm, you have told them they exist to clear debris from Gamalon's sky. Are you, for instance, sure they will not clean the moon away as well? Might they attach to the larger chunks of the moon and disassemble it to make more of themselves?"

"You are right, my dear," he said, changing the code setting upper limits of mass and location for target debris. "I have neglected that. Please help me craft their story. Then when Green returns with the seed, we will have clear skies for her."

Despite her misgivings, Gwendoline leaned into the project. It was good to be working again, and the young space girl had given them reinvigorating hope. She deserved a safe means of approach.

CHAPTER 33
PREPARATIONS FOR THE WEST

The tinkling bell announced Space Girl Green's entry to the tinker's shop. When she had asked the Stewardess where she might recharge the batteries for some of her equipment, there had been much confusion. Saphria had asked all the guards and everyone else in the palace - except for the one person most likely to actually know - before they gave her directions to this shop.

The bell summoned the shop's proprietor. Though green, the tinker brought strongly to mind her rainbow mate Yellow. The tinker's broad shoulders and thick-muscled arms glistened with sweat from whatever activity she had been engaged in. Her hair was a mass of tight curls held down only by the pair of googles covering her eyes. She held a cloth in her hands that was transforming from clean to dirty as she wiped.

A wide grin returned Green's smile, "How can I help you, stranger?"

"I am Space Girl Green and I've got a problem. The guards at the palace felt you were the most likely to help." She pulled her rayguns off her hips and placed them on the counter. "I need to replace or recharge the ignition batteries for these."

The other woman's eyes lit up at the tech. "I've never seen aught like this before. Truly lovely."

"They are rayguns from the planet Home, but these stopped working sometime soon after I landed in Auz. Not sure when or why, but the batteries are dead. I'm hoping you have a means of charging them."

From a pocket in her apron the tinker produced a pair of clip-on lenses she attached to her emerald goggles. She examined the gun closely. "How do you even open it? Can you remove the battery for me?"

"Of course," said Green. She picked up one of the guns and made a practiced movement so fast it was hard to follow. When finished she was holding a cylindrical object about 25mm long and 5mm in diameter. She handed it to the tinker.

"That's a battery? Where are the terminals?"

"You just connect to each end."

The Tinker shook her head, put the battery down and reached under the counter. She pulled out an even smaller metallic cylinder that she placed next to Green's. "This is the only battery I have, though I doubt it's powerful enough. We have nae need for batteries here."

The Auz battery indeed looked too small to work. Green pulled her scanner up and sure enough it only output 3 volts of power. "How are things powered here?" She motioned to the glasses she wore. "Even these just seem to work, and you can't take them off. They must have a battery in them."

"Everything in Auz is powered from the air."

"Wireless power?" On Home, they utilized wireless power, albeit in a highly directional and potentially hazardous form if it crossed paths with anything biological. Her scanner showed not a hint of electromagnetic radiation in the vicinity – nothing that could feasibly power the hundreds of augmented reality goggles she'd encountered, let alone the myriad of other devices she had seen.

"I guess you could call it that because it has no wires, but we really don't use wires for anything besides art and signal transmission."

I've got to get Yellow to come here, Green thought, but she didn't have time to dig into the science of it, nor, really, the interest. "Well, I had hoped to get them working, since the Wizard is sending my friends and me to defeat the Sister of the West. These were my only weapon except my sgian-dubh."

"You really going to go take her on? By yourself?"

"Not by myself, there are four of us. One's a former Cyberknight and another a giant Lion-man, though that one is a coward-or says he is. Then there is Scarecrow, and no one is sure exactly what she is. She's just started learning to change appearance by sheer will."

The stout woman looked the petite Space Girl, in a flowing walking dress, up and down. "And you?"

"Yep, and me. I am trained as a Space Girl, which includes almost everything Warriors learn. Most of that involves weapons of various sorts. None of which I have now." Green leaned on the counter and asked, "Do you, the people of the Auz, have ranged weapons? Pistols, rifles, cannons? Anything like that?"

"None of that. We do have bows."

"The technology here is strange. Some things, like my friend the Cyberknight, is so far advanced it's practically magic. Other things are very primitive, like there is no transportation at all. Not even horses. And no ranged weapons, except bows apparently." She started pacing the room while she thought and talked. Absently she pulled out her mother's Space Girl coin and flipped it from hand to hand. "You can build a metal dog that can house the most advanced personality Home can create, but you can't make even a simple gun." As soon as she said it, Green felt a pang of embarrassment. That might have been impertinent.

The Tinker laughed, "I'm pretty sure I don't even grasp many of the words you just used. But if I were taken to your land, I would assume that you possessed magical tools of destruction and yet lacked even the most fundamental knowledge of cybernetics."

"Probably true. Though we have many things that aren't weapons. Like my flying saucer, which is parked in the land of the Welcomians." She moved back to the table to retrieve her rayguns and set the coin on the counter in the process. "Tell me Tinker. Who makes the weapons you use? Is it tinkers like you, or are there weapon smiths?"

The coin landed chaos side up, which in that version was green with the words 'Chaos to Order' on a green background.

"We tinkers forge the weapons," said the Tinker. She looked at the coin and her eyes unfocused for a moment and then she shook her head. "I've been working on one for the past few days and just finished it." Her eyes refused to look back at the coin, which was odd to Green. "Would you like to see it?"

Green really should get going as she had many things to do, but didn't want to be rude. "Sure."

The Tinker disappeared through the curtain again. From the back she said, "Oh, and I have two really huge swords I'm supposed to deliver the palace later today. They're probably for your Lion." There was some clanking of metal on metal. "Now, where is that sheath?" More strange sounds and suddenly the Tinker appeared through the door holding a tangle of leather.

"I've never actually made one like this." She laid it on the table and Green realized it was a sword in a scabbard with a leather belt. "But a couple of days ago, there was a commotion outside my shop with some newcomers in town. The design just sprung into me head and I had to make it."

Picking up the sword, she felt the smooth, cool touch of the golden metal hilt, wrapped snugly in dark leather. The pommel, a circle of gleaming metal, featured an intricate design etched into its surface. "I think it is for you," said the Tinker and placed the butt of the sword next to the coin. The eight arrows in a radial pattern, the symbol for Chaos, etched into the coin's border, exactly matched the design on the sword.

"That's the Space Girl Symbol for chaos," said Green. "How did you know that?"

"Like I said, the whole design just popped into my head." She flipped the sword over to show the other side. On the other side was a single arrow pointing upwards.

Green reached out and flipped the coin to reveal the symbol for Order. A single arrow pointing upwards. There was silence, as neither of them knew what to make of this unlikely coincidence.

The Tinker shifted her grip and offered the hilt to the Space Girl.

Green pulled the sword from the scabbard. The blade was dark as night. The form was the classic gladius, exactly like the Warriors of Home carried. Small enough to stay out of the way, but fully functional for everything from hacking through brush to defense.

"It is magnificent," Green said and moved through a form to get the feel of it.

"The others are not ready, but will be by this evening. I am to deliver them to the palace by midnight."

Green slid the blade back in its scabbard and realized she could attach it to her utility belt. "I don't know how to thank you, or pay you."

"The Wizard will compensate me for anything you desire."

"Your Wizard is," Green looked for the right word for a man that ordered her to murder someone, "generous."

"The Wizard sees all and knows all," said the Tinker. "Except he didn't mention what you really want."

"Which is?"

The woman went back through the curtain. After much muttering, cursing and crashing of objects she returned carrying an exquisite recurved bow with a quiver attached. "I think this will suit you well. Do you know how to use one?"

"Since I was a child," said Green immediately taken back to hunting rabbit and small game with her father. She gave the bow a test pull. It was a little longer, and a little stronger than she was used to, but she could adjust. "Thank you so much... I'm sorry I never got your name."

"Brigid, is my name. Since you are the woman who vanquished the Evil Sister of the East and now sets out to bring down the other blight on Auz, it is an honor to help you anyway I can."

CHAPTER 34
GOODBYE HALAMAR

Space Girl Green lounged on her suite's couch, her gaze fixed on the Emerald City's gleaming lights. The room had just emptied, her companions unanimous in their resolve that their only path forward was to launch an assault on the Sister of the West.

A storm of anxiety and dread churned within her. They had laid out every strategy they could think of, leaving nothing more to plan. Opting for agility over equipment, she resolved to leave behind her pack, along with the bulk of her gear from Home.

She was going to war.

As a Space Cadet, she'd endured multiple lectures on the differences between a Warrior and a Space Girl. Those selected to be Space Girls had the physical prowess to be excellent warriors. If push came to shove and Home went to war, they would become an elite unit of the Warriors. They could do that job, but it wasn't their purpose.

The Headmistress explained how she selected girls to be Space Girls. There was the obvious physical and mental requirements, but there was something else.

"In her heart, the potential Space Girl sits on the border

between order and chaos. She is comfortable there. At ease with breaking obsolete order back into chaos, or creating new order out of the unformed creative energy of the universe. This is not something done purely with the mind, though intellect must inform it. It is done with the heart, with intuition, with a chosen few's special nature."

Today, possibly near the end of first her journey and her burgeoning career, Green wondered how they could have been so wrong. Headmistress had picked everyone in her Rainbow, and she didn't doubt *they* had that kind of heart. But not her. She didn't see order in chaos or vice versa. Every tool they had given her, she had messed up: her saucer, its AI, her rayguns.

There was one last duty she must perform.

"Halamar, we need to talk." The dog walked over from where he was curled near the door, and laid his head on her lap. "I am getting too used to thinking of you as a dog, an animal. But that is not what you are.

"Halamar, you are a flying saucer."

He sat back and looked at her with a tilted head. "As such, you, like me, have certain duties. One of those is to protect Home's secrets.

"Tomorrow I am going to join the others in an attack on an enemy that seems much stronger than the four of us. She is ruthless and cruel, a foe that must be fought and defeated.

"If we are successful, then others may come to Auz. Those that live here will be safe.

"But we may fail. If we do, then I will probably be killed. Even if we succeed, I may not return." She paused, mulling over the notion of death. It was an odd thing for a Space Girl to consider, because being fearless was part of the job. "You know Halamar, my friend, if I give my life for this cause, I think it is worth it. I've never really had to contemplate that before, but I serve Life and I am a trained Space Girl. It is part of the job and we just hope whatever kills us is worth it."

Halamar whined, and she smiled at him. "It's the way it is, boy. But there are still duties I must perform and duties you must as well. I don't think you are going to like this part."

He inclined his head. "You need to return to the flying saucer. Not only that, you will need to take my rayguns with you."

Though not an actual dog, Halamar spun around in agitated circles at this command. "I know. I'd like to have you with me too. But if I don't come back, there is nothing to stop someone from taking this top secret technology. Tech we are supposed to destroy before letting it fall into enemy hands."

"Also, should I be killed, I hope you can tell my story. With the welcome portal open, others may come. You can tell them all that happened to me." She thought about her Rainbow mates and missed them already. They would come looking for her eventually. "Maybe Red will come to find me. Should I be killed and Red find out, I would not want to be the Sister of the West."

The thought of Space Girl Red dispensing justice throughout Auz brought a smile to her face.

"You will have to travel by yourself. I brought a pack for you, but it is quite small. Luckily, you don't need provisions. Be careful on your journey back. Hide rather than fight. Seek company from good people when you can." She reached out and stroked his soft metallic fur. "Take care of yourself."

"Back to your pack. Since it is small, I can't send all my stuff back with you. Only my rayguns. You understand how to guard them.

"Once you get back to your saucer, will you be able to enter it?"

Halamar nodded.

"You don't have hands, so I'm not sure how it will work, but you should probably get back into your globe. Maybe you can ask one of the Welcomians to help. I don't think Golden will be there, but she left the tool on the control board."

She took his big square head in her hands and looked into his green eyes. "Can you do this for me, Halamar?"

He barked agreement.

"Good, then we are all set. Tomorrow morning you will exit to the East and I to the West. For tonight though, would you sleep with me? I need my rest and will feel better with you next to me."

Halamar barked again and jumped on the bed.

CHAPTER 35

BEGINNING THE QUEST

"I am so glad to be taking those things off," said Green as she handed her emerald glasses to the gate keeper. They were leaving through the West gate, and it was either the same bureaucrat or his twin seeing them out. Most of the people of the city had been friendly but this one seemed always surly, though he didn't feel the need to respond to her comment.

Lion growled in agreement as he ran his hands through his mane. He wore the same worn leather skirt he'd arrived in, but attached to it was a shiny, thick belt. This belt connected to two other belts that crossed his chest and back. Sticking over one shoulder, Green could see the hilt of one sword Brigid had crafted for him. The other hung from his belt, which he kept fidgeting with. "Aye, and I'd rather not have to wear these things."

"You are a solider marching off to war, Lion," said Douglas visibly unchanged by the visit to the city. "There will no doubt be peril or the Wizard would not have given you those swords."

"Am I a soldier too?" asked Scarecrow. "I don't have any weapons." She was the most transformed. When Green first met Scarecrow, she looked like a caricature of a humanoid. During the journey here she'd hardened as form followed the functions of learning to walk like a person. Now she looked like an actual humanoid. A generic female, but a human nonetheless. Her head had changed form to be less like a child's candy and sported eyes, nose, and mouth. There was shape to her lips and eyes, but no color. Her skin had texture, but was still grey, which made her unique in a land rich in color.

There was an awkward exchange of glances. Then Green said, "You are our companion, here to provide support."

On this side of the City there were no houses or fields. A gentle slope downwards made Green feel they were falling away from the city. A dilapidated road stretched out before them. The once vibrant yellow bricks now cracked and broken, creating jagged lines where weeds sprouted.

According to Doug, this road used to bustle with trade. The Winkies were sought-after for their high-precision gadgets, and they were the sole providers of all Cyberknight parts and gear.

Trade still flowed through the bustling Emerald City, but the connection to the Winkies had been severed. According to Saphira the isolation of the Sister of the West was one reason for the Emerald City's growth. The Stewardess has shown them a map of the West as it had been before the Sister's reign. A great circular road encircled Auz, connecting all four lands, but now, the Gillikins of the North and the Quadlings of the South no longer ventured near the desolate Yellow lands to the West. This forced all trade through the Emerald City in the center of Auz.

The road was wide enough for them to walk abreast, the Cyberknight, Scarecrow, Space Girl, and Lion. Slipping her arm into Scarecrow's and Lion's, she said, "It is good to be traveling again, and good to be on a new adventure with friends."

They put on brave smiles and started off full of energy with a skip in their step.

~

THE SISTER of the West tinkered with her latest experiment. When the royals had left Auz to the Sisters, West had awoken to the true nature of the world. It was a beautiful mechanical construct covered in an organic, fleshy costume. This included her own body.

Knowing this truth showed she must rule the land.The Winkies were the greatest metalsmiths and Tinkers. Artificers of the highest order, and it was *her* purpose to make them sublime.

She avoided mirrors when possible and tried to change her smooth curves and hourglass proportions into sharp angles and geometric shapes. The nature built into her by the Creators fought against her desire for mechanical perfection. Every fresh addition had been harder and more painful. Half was all she could manage for now. Her left side was robotic perfection and her right, while bronze skinned, still looked like horrid flesh.

In frustration, she turned her skills to transforming the Winkies. At first she hadn't bothered to turn off the creature's pain receptors, but they made so much noise it was distracting. Also, she found it harder to find subjects as everyone would run from her.

West sat in her shadowy workshop, the perfume of petro-chemical lubricants in the air. Before her stood a timid Winkie girl in her teenage years, immobilized by magic to stop the trembling of fear. With delicate precision, she meticulously removed all the flesh from one of the girl's arms. The bones resembled flesh but were crafted from a metallic alloy. She regretted not leaving the pseudo-flesh muscles and ligaments intact, as they would have served as a helpful guide for attaching the metallic cables.

A Winkle, small and trembling, scuttled into the workshop, his eyes wide with terror. "Your majesty, there are newcomers in your land."

The Sister looked up. One half of her face was still, as the Creators had planned it: a beautiful humanoid visage. On the other side, she had pealed away the flesh to reveal an angular metallic skull. Then she had enlarged on eye socket and inserted a great, glowing, yellow eye, which locked on the newcomer. "How do you know this?"

"A crow told me."

She had programed many of the automaton birds to come to the palace if they saw other beings and report. She stood and said to her project, "Take yourself back to the flesh pool and regrow that horrible arm."

There were many crows on the balcony when she arrived, but she did not speak to them. Instead, she looked East toward the Emerald City. Her true eye focused and she could see the party of strangers. "Ahhh, what an interesting bunch. A Cyberknight, a Lion Man, and something else."

There were two women. One had pasty white skin and clothing. No, her clothing was manifest out of her flesh. She must be a new kind of Inhabitant. Something West had never seen before, and which was not in her training data.

The other woman was trying to teach her some kind of dance movement. She wore a green leather dress and carried a sword and bow. Might she be a visitor? East's vortex was down and there had been the flying thing she'd shot down a while ago.

"Mmmmm, who would dare to come from the City for me?" She tapped metal tipped fingers against her metal face and thought. Then she pulled out a whistle and blew a particular tune. After a moment, a pack of wolves appeared at the base of the tower. "There are strangers in our land. Go to the forest and wait till night. Then attack and kill them all."

The alpha wolf nodded its head and howled in response. The pack disappeared into the woods and Sister West returned to her throne to think about a better way of replacing the pseudo-flesh of the Winkies.

CHAPTER 36
VICTORIES ON THE ROAD

The first day's walk had been good. Douglas had forgotten how a march to battle felt. The mixture of anticipation and fear was intoxicating after so many years. During the march west, he had taken it on himself to teach Lion how to use the great swords the Wizard had given him.

While a complete disaster from a training perspective, it incited a great deal of enjoyment, though not for Lion. He kept just swinging each sword like a stick, with no thought of edge and blade.

"Arrrgh," said Doug, "if it weren't for the fact you are the size of a mountain and those swords are as heavy as Space Girl Green here, I would just take them away from you. Such beautiful tools and you'll do the most damage with them as bludgeons."

They had settled in for the night with Space Girl Green curled in the soft grass next to Lion. Douglas and Scarecrow walked a wide parameter since they didn't need to sleep.

Scarecrow was the first to notice the wolves and stopped before them. She stared at the eyes in the forest and waited patiently for them to reveal who they were and what they wanted. Before that happened, the Cyberknight met her on his patrol.

"Those are wolves. A pack of them, from the looks of it," said Doug.

"Are wolves dangerous?" asked Scarecrow.

"To you and I no, but to those of flesh? Best not find out." The knight's hand transformed into a hammer on the left and a sword on the right. "You go stand near our friends and wake them if you see a wolf approaching. But I don't plan on letting any of this lot through."

Then he leapt into the midst of the pack, crushing the first wolf he found into the ground with his great hammer. The others came for him at once.

Like Halamar, these wolves were made of metal, but a metal meant to feel soft. Their teeth couldn't penetrate Douglas's shell, and it was easier to allow them to latch onto a leg and then cleave them in half with his sword. There were at least thirty. Those that got into the fight toward the end were craftier, trying to grab arms, and dodged the hammer much better.

As the sun rose, former Cyberknight Douglas Merryweather Moneypenny was surrounded by a rug of dead wolves.

At dawn, the Western Sister rose and made her way to the balcony, where fury overwhelmed her. "My wolves have been slaughtered!" Her metallic side's fist crashed into the parapet so hard the stone cracked. "They will pay dearly for this."

With a distinct, commanding whistle, the crows that had heralded the intruders' arrival gathered before her. "Summon every crow of your murder. Swarm them," she said, pointing. "Strip the flesh from their bones."

The crows descended to the forest in a frenzied flurry, their calls resonating through the canopy. The Western Sister sensed the mobilization of countless birds across the woodland, a dark tide soaring towards the unsuspecting foes, driven by her thirst for retribution.

~

"WHAT HAPPENED HERE, DOUG?" asked Space Girl Green, looking at the carnage around the cyberknight.

"It seems the Sister has noticed us. She sent a pack of wolves to attack us in the night. Scarecrow saw them and I defeated them."

The Space Girl counted the bodies as best she could for many were in multiple pieces. "There must have been thirty of these. You could have woke us to help."

"He told me to do that," said Scarecrow standing to one side with a looking glass to her eye. "But only if they got through him. Which didn't happen." She looked back at the others, "The Sister is on her balcony. She is angry."

"I don't doubt she would be with all her wolves dead," said Lion. "What do we do now?"

Everyone looked at Space Girl Green. "We continue on our journey and deal with what happens when it happens."

"I hear crows," said Scarecrow minutes later.

"A lot of crows," echoed Doug.

Those with mere flesh ears took a few more minutes before they heard what sounded like an angry, rushing wind. As it grew in volume, the sky darkened.

Green unslung her bow and began stringing it. "Anyone got an idea?"

"You don't have that many arrows, Space Girl," said Lion.

"Too bad you don't have a shotgun or a flamethrower," Green said to Douglas.

He raised an arm that turned into a tube. A flame lit at the end. "I have this for clearing underbrush. But it doesn't shoot very far."

"I have an idea," said Scarecrow. "Lion, you and Green move back under those trees. I will stand in the middle of this clearing. The crows will see me and attack me. It won't hurt me because I am soft and feel no pain. Once they are on me, Doug, you come out, and burn them with your brush clearer."

"Are you impervious to flame, my friend?" asked Douglas.

Scarecrow cocked her head and extended a hand to the flame. It passed through the pilot light without change. Then Doug changed the angle safely away from everyone else and released the full flame.

Scarecrow just smiled. Her white flesh didn't change at all.

Green and Lion retreated under a tree, while Scarecrow walked to the center of the glade and held out her arms as she had the first time Green had seen her. She was still terrible at scaring crows, which was what they wanted in this instance. The black birds covered her completely in a horrific suit of flapping black wings.

Doug stepped forward, arm extended. A few birds had attempted to attack him but found no flesh to attack. When he was close enough to Scarecrow, flame burst from his hand and engulfed the crow-covered woman.

Charred crow bodies littered the ground around Scarecrow when it was over. She was covered in soot and tiny little dimples. "Are you all right?" said Space Girl Green.

Scarecrow brushed at the soot, revealing pale skin below. "I am fine."

Space Girl Green looked closely at the divots all over her. "Are these where they pecked you?"

"Yes. Or bit and pulled my skin. It is quite flexible."

As she watched, the dimples and bite marks faded back into her.

"If you are alright, let's get moving. Maybe we can find a stream for you to wash in."

THE SISTER of the West stood very still on her balcony. The pulsing of her mechanical eye was like the heartbeat of a dying man. She had underestimated this small group. The Wizard wouldn't have sent them if they were not formidable. Automatons would not be enough.

"Guards," she yelled.

A group of ten armored Winkies marched onto the wide balcony. Normally, Winkies look like humans but with lemon colored skin. These guards wore an armor the color of brass, but with the strength of steel. West liked the armor because it covered the abomination of their flesh. The Winkies liked the armor because they had made it themselves in the old ways.

"Go out and stop this band of intruders. They are coming to destroy me and the Orb of Exit," said the Sister. Then she remembered they might consider that a good thing and added, "And your forge."

Deep within the mountain, beneath the beacon of the Orb, lay the Winkies' forge. This marvel of engineering harnessed the energy capable to punching a hole in space-time to allow access to the Spaceways. During dormant phases, this immense power was repurposed by the Winkies to master the art of metalwork. With such force at their command, they crafted creations unparalleled in Auz, blending traditional techniques with the light's singular force to shape wonders both practical and exquisite.

The guards saluted and left.

THE BAND of interlopers walked the forest path without interruption for most of the morning. They found a stream and rested next to it. Scarecrow washed the soot off while Douglas patrolled and the others ate. Lion, with a sizable bag at his side brimming with cooked crows, devoured his meal with evident relish. Space Girl Green, having sampled one herself, found the meat to be satisfactory in taste. However, the laborious process of plucking the feathers and removing the bones rendered the effort too cumbersome. She had gone back to living off food pills and Scout Girl cookies.

As the sun dipped behind the mountain cradling the palace, they caught sight of troops advancing towards them, their silhouettes stark against the dimming sky.

Doug turned his hands into weapons and started forward, but Lion stopped him. "The Winkies have been slaves of the Sister for a very long time. If they are here, it is probably under duress. Let me see if I can roar at them and get them to flee so we don't have to hurt them."

Doug said, "I would have thought that, if I had a heart. It would be cruel to kill them if they had no choice about being here."

The others readied weapons, but stayed behind Lion.

The troops marched three abreast with a standard carrier in the front. Their armor gleamed in the light. Lion had squatted down in the middle of the road and put his hands on his new swords. The Winkies were singing a marching song and did not notice him till they were almost on him.

With a great roar, the loudest Space Girl Green had ever heard him make, Lion leapt into the air, both swords swining.

They caught the setting sunlight, and flashed it into the eyes of the soldiers.

With a two meter tall, armed Lion roaring at them, the reluctant men-at-arms panicked. They screamed and ran. Some crashed into one another and fell to the ground. Others ran off the road only to trip and fall in the brush. The standard bearer dropped the great pike with its flag and disappeared into the forest.

Lion dropped his swords and ran toward the a guard struggling to get off the ground. He snatched up the standard and broke it in half with a roar.

He continued to roar at the guards, but did not strike anyone. Space Girl Green smiled as she noticed how he would grab a guard off the ground, put them on their feet, and roar to get them moving in a direction away from the group.

Soon they were alone on the empty road. The group clapped and cheered for the Lion, which he accepted with a small bow.

"Well done, my friend. You are most fierce," said Douglas.

"It was nothing. Really."

"You know you just attacked ten armed and armored men all by yourself," said Space Girl Green. "That takes guts."

"No, No, that isn't courage. It was like in the forest when I would roar to scare away animals. There was no real danger, or I would have been very afraid."

The Space Girl just shook her head and gave him a big hug. "You are brave to me, Lion. Now we had best make camp for the night."

CHAPTER 37
AURELIUS ATTACKED

"So the real Gamalon Rangers recognize you and think the Civitas appropriated their unit," said Space Woman Amethyst. Eógan stood behind her as they neared the exit for Gamalon.

"I doubt Master MacCallum would put it that strongly, but yes. Captain Kennedy may represent some members of the Civitas military, but not all Gamalonians," replied Eógan. "Should I be seated for the exit?"

Amethyst smiled at him, "You expecting trouble? The Gamalon system should be empty. We'll come out P1, which isn't nearest to Gamalon, but should avoid any debris that might be around the system." Eógan knew there was another portal from the Spaceways way out past the gas giants as well, but the Space Woman knew what she was doing. They dropped out of the rainbow colored Spaceways into the darkness of space.

The yellow star of his home was large this close in, and he could make out the reddish surface of Peadar marked by giant craters. Hot and dry, the next planet in from Gamalon was uninhabited. Amethyst changed course, moving outward, and soon a point of light centered itself in front of them.

"Gamalon," Eógan whispered. Something in his chest clenched and his hands went numb. He knew Amethyst was looking at him with concern, but he couldn't take his eyes off the growing light of his home. How had he not realized what it would feel like?

"You okay, Eógan?" She asked, then added to Aurelius, "Why don't you make a seat for our guest Aurelius?" A seat rose out of the floor just behind her pilot's chair.

"Yes," said Eógan, but sat without taking his eyes off the star. "I didn't realize what it would be like coming back."

"I can only imagine." On the canopy a tool tip floating next to Gamalon showing time to arrival and information about the planet. Mostly historical, but as they approached, it would update from the sensors. There was a red triangle next to the words, *Area around the planet is hazardous to navigation.* Looking at her pilot's display, Amethyst said, "Your girl updated some of the navigation info. Says it isn't too bad at the poles and there is a settlement near there." She continued reading the information given by the local nav buoy. "Two inhabitants. Many robots."

Eógan looked at her, "Robots?"

"Yeah, not much detail, though. I'll need to add 'more detailed report writing' to my feedback when I see her." She said it with a smile on her face, which Eógan took to mean it was only half in jest.

"I guess robots make sense on the surface," Eógan said. "Atmosphere is unbreathable and the weather violent and cold."

"Yeah, that's the data she gave too."

"Amethyst, I am picking up debris moving in unusual patterns," said Aurelius.

"Unusual how?" She asked and started pulling more information on up on her screens, which Eógan could only partially see from his seat. He stood to get a better look.

The display showed a large number of rocks in various locations above the planet. Each had a little line drawn from it, most of which curved into normal orbits. But there were a number of them moving directly away from the planet toward the moon.

"What is causing that?" Eógan asked. "Could it be whatever caused the moon to explode?"

"Unlikely," answered the ship. "The deviations seem to be moving debris toward the lunar orbit. Nor is there any indication of an increase in objects. If anything, it seems there are fewer small objects than expected."

The whole discussion had happened as the star grew into a planet before them. Eógan could see the ring of rocks with an enormous collection where the moon used to be. To him, it appeared they'd be inside that orbit in seconds.

"Look," said Amethyst, "there goes a new one." On the screen, an object changed course and started moving away from the planet. "Aurelius, can you get me a closeup of these?"

A video display opened on the canopy itself and a chunk of rock filled it. Stuck to the side was some kind of creature. Actually, many creatures. Brightly colored little women with shiny fixed wings and some kind of jet pack, which were all firing, explaining how the rock was being moved.

"Are those people?" asked Eógan.

"It is hard to gauge the intelligence of these constructs, but they are not biologicals," said Aurelius. A new image appeared on the display, showing that the beings were entirely made of metal. Something small and black crawled out from under one of the creatures, and scurried to the side before digging into the rock.

Amethyst had plotted their course to approach from the

North Pole, aiming to avoid the proto-ring. She followed the data Green had left for them, expecting a clear path. However, the rocks weren't in natural orbits. A midsize fragment had forced an adjust of their trajectory. On their closest approach, a group of three fat little winged beings shot off the rock and toward them.

"What are they doing?" asked Eógan. There was no doubt they were coming directly toward the flying saucer.

"Aurelius?" asked the Space Woman and made a small change of course. But the jet packs fired, and the winged came on faster.

"They are targeting us," replied the flying saucer. "Shields are up. Do you wish me to target them with my disruptors?"

The nearest of the creatures knocked into the shield. Instead of bouncing and floating away, it used its jet pack to hold itself against the shield. "Are they going to knock us off course?" asked Eógan.

"No, ranger," said Aurelius, "that is not how our shields work. They distribute incoming energy along their surface and away if possible. This includes kinetic energy, though there is no place for it to displace." The shield sparked around the creature and in seconds, they had three of the little beings throwing up sparks on the shield.

"Do you think they will follow us into the atmosphere?" asked Amethyst.

"No way to know, Space Woman," replied her ship.

"Do you have a lock on the coordinates left by Green?"

"Yes," said Aurelius and an indicator appeared on the canopy.

"Then let's go down and say hello." She turned the saucer into a more acute dive and put on speed. Eógan sat back and buckled in.

Moving closer the planet attracted more of the creatures.

They attached themselves to the forward shield and attempted to push them away from the planet.

"They seem programmed to keep us from the surface," said Amethyst.

"Or just to keep debris from falling," Eógan said. "Makes sense if they were programmed by our erstwhile terraformers. Stopping more dust from getting into the system would be the first order of business."

Plasma burned against the shield as they entered the atmosphere and the super-heated atmosphere swept away the creatures.

They were inside the atmosphere of Gamalon. It hit him again they were landing on the planet of his youth. Eógan had been so focused on the things, he hadn't seen it from orbit. Which was probably a blessing.

"All the attackers seem to be off the shield, Space Woman," said Aurelius, "should you wish to slow your descent."

"Yes, of course," she replied and slowed down, clearing the plasma.

For the first time in 20 years, Eógan saw Gamalon. And he wanted to close his eyes.

CHAPTER 38

DEFEAT BY THE WINGED

While Space Girl Green's little band slept or watched through the night, the Sister of the West brooded on her throne. West and East were the important kingdoms. They were the entrance and exit of Auz. The fleshy outsiders were the problem. East's vortex to stop them entering and messing things up, but not before the dastardly Wizard had gotten in. When West had denied him an exit, he had built up the city and attacked her, but she had fought him to a standstill.

Since then, no threat had come to her kingdom. Until now. It all started with the flying saucer she had shot down days ago, but not before it had killed the only ally she had.

The other sisters were a menace. The chaotic one to the North was completely unpredictable, but mostly she'd confined herself to bothering East. Sister South was another story. She had an army ready for battle, but South refrained from war because of her dedication to order.

The balance of power had changed. East was gone and West was the only one left with the true good of Auz in mind. She could not let these interlopers defeat her. Desperate times called for desperate measures. She stalked to the most secure and secret room in the castle. There were no guards in this part of the castle because she did not trust anyone else near her vault. Instead she had cast a compulsion on all her Wilkie slaves to keep them away.

West executed a sequence of intricate maneuvers to unlock the door, and swiftly positioned herself beside the box in the center of the room. Navigated another complex series of actions, uniquely known to her, she unlocked the box. Then she carefully extracted the object within.

The artifact was a ring with a circumference of approximately 20cm. At its core, four metals — gold, platinum, silver, and copper - woven together, symbolizing unity and strength. Adorning its exterior, a lavish array of precious stones—rubies, amethysts, sapphires, emeralds, and diamonds—sparkled with potent energy. Crafted in an age long past by the Creators, this crown was her ace in the hole, a clandestine weapon wielded to assert dominion over Winkieland and vanquish the Wizard's forces.

Each who possessed it could only call three times, and she had already used it twice.

Remembering what the little green devil of flesh and bone had done to Sister East, she sighed and placed the crown on her head.

Once on the balcony of the palace, as the sun rose in the East, she intoned the words of the Creators to activate the Crown of Command.

"Ep-pe, Pep-pe, Kak-ke, Hil-lo, Hol-lo, Hel-lo!"

A gust swept across the balcony, heralding the arrival of the Winged. Each figure was a petite woman with wings sprouting from her back. Their hues ranging across a spectrum that mirrored their distinct uniforms and the vibrant colors of their wings. Golden helmets, distinguished by curling, pointed horns, sat upon their heads. Leading the formation was General

Fifinella, resplendent in a white uniform with gold stars on her shoulders.

"Command us, Sister of Auz and alleged Guardian of the West, for the last time," said Fifinella.

She pointed to the forest below. "There are four interlopers coming to my palace to destroy me. I desire for you to defeat them. Bring me the Lion, because I want him as a pet. The others you are to destroy or kill. Especially the fleshy one in the leather uniform."

"You command, we obey," said the general, and they flew away.

SPACE GIRL GREEN and her friends could almost see the gate to the mountain fortress of the Winkies when the Winged came for them. A flock of little women organized into groups by color, reminded Green of Warrior fighter squadrons. And like the fighter pilots of Home, each squadron had an assignment and executed it to perfection.

The ones assigned to her easily dodged her arrows and she dropped her bow and pulled the Emerald City sword. While fighting, Space Girl Green tried to watch over her comrades.

The Winged obviously understood how to deal with Cyberknights having defeated many in the last war. Their hands were the dangerous part, so one squadron was tasked with immobilizing them. Before you could grab a Cyberknight's hands, you first had to stop him from striking. The Winged were tough enough to let Douglas take a swing, but they were far too clever for that. Three of them zipped directly at him. When he brought his sword and hammer up, they split to either side of him.

Realizing this wouldn't be a stand up fight, he changed his

hands back to flame throwers and blasted, aiming high to avoid his friends. The fire charred the Winged revealing the metal frame under burnt skin.

From behind him a squadron he didn't see dropped a bag over his helmet. Once he was blind, the other members of that group swooped in and grabbed his arms and legs. Without a moment to process, he was already in the air. They flew him away from his friends to a nearby canyon and dropped him from hundreds of meters. He struck the side of the canyon and bounced to the bottom, hitting every rock on the way. At the bottom was a river. Battered and damaged the Cyberknight couldn't stop himself from sinking to the bottom.

Another squadron of Winged carried rope lassos. Those assigned to Lion dropped a loop around him and flew in circles until he was wrapped tight. They ignored his roars, which soon turned into whimpers. Then they picked him up and flew away with him.

The Winged were not getting attacks through Green's sword defense, but she still could not move to help the others. One by one, they were taken from her. The last was Scarecrow.

Scarecrow was unworried about getting hurt and stood her ground when they came. Practical to the point of cruelty, the Winged looped a rope around each of her limbs, and one around her neck. Then they flew off in different directions. Arms and legs stretched while her neck was squeezed ever smaller. She didn't need to breathe, so that wasn't a problem, and the stretching didn't hurt.

Whatever manner of being Scarecrow was, however, there were limits to her elasticity. Once reached, arms and legs tore from her body and her head popped off.

Space Girl Green screamed and lunged toward her. A Winged blocked her, but she casually cleaved it in two. She knocked another out of the air with her free hand. With the help of her silver boots, she leaped and landed next to what remained of Scarecrow. All the newly created skin texture and feminine form was gone from the once again clay like parts. Even her head was just a flattened disk without eyes.

All the Winged came for her. They surrounded her as she readied for a last stand.

General Fifinella flew into the circle of Winged and hovered before the Space Girl. "Why are your lips so red?"

"Preparation for the blood of your corpses, you horrible wasps." Green's vision was red and narrow. Something primal was beating in her chest and she was going to destroy everything. Every one of these things that had felled her friends. The sensible, orderly part of her brain was locked in the back of her head. Her dark chaos was free.

"Don't be silly. The Winged have no blood, as you can see," said the white clad general, pointing to the little woman Green had cut in half a moment ago. "That is not make-up, fleshed one. So I ask again, why are you lips red?"

"I bear the kiss of the Sister of the North, and the shoes of the Evil Sister of the East whom I killed to free the Welcomians. What will I wear when I have destroyed the Winged and killed the Sister of the West."

A murmur went through the Winged and they moved back a little. Space Girl Green was glad they took her threat so seriously, because she planned to do everything she said.

"She bares the mark of a Good Sister. And she is not of Auz. We cannot simply kill her as the Sister of the West ordered," said the General. The other Winged nodded and murmured agreement.

To Space Girl Green she said, "But we are under compulsion to obey anyone who wears the Crown of Command three times. If we do not obey the Sister of the West's command, she will command us again. What are we to do?"

Everything in control of her right now wanted to answer "die", but Life demanded a different solution. "What have you done with Lion and Douglas?"

"We were ordered to bring the Lion to the Sister, and that is what beta flight has done. Delta took the Cyberknight and dropped him in the Great Canyon to the south. He may have survived the fall, but we are not concerned. We did as commanded."

"What will she do with the Lion?"

"I do not know, but she has a strong hatred for all things flesh. She said she would make him her pet." General Fifinella decided on a plan that might satisfy this green-haired woman and the Sister of the West, leaving the Winged free to roam the skies uncompelled. "If you surrender yourself to us, we will take you to the Sister alive. You would undoubtedly be enslaved, but where you have life, you have a chance to free your last friend."

Order was balancing the chaos in her soul and once again she could think clearly. The General was right. She would have a better chance if she were actually in the palace with Lion. If the Sister didn't kill her immediately.

"I accept your offer with a condition. You must gather the parts of my friend Scarecrow and put them together somewhere safe. She doesn't live like other persons, perhaps she can be repaired."

General Fifinella weighed this against the casualties she would take and said, "I will not do this unless you accept my condition of surrender."

"What is that?"

"You will not only lay down your weapons, but you will leave all of your possessions here with your friend. Your bag, your sword and all of your clothes."

Space Girl Green felt satisfaction that the little general found her so dangerous. "I accept."

A flight of Winged gathered up all the parts of Scarecrow and put them in a large bag. Space Girl Green dropped her sword, and removed her bracers. The Warrior uniform was the last thing of Home she had with her, and soon it was packed in her bag and left in the trees by Scarecrow's corpse.

Trouble arose when she attempted to remove the silver shoes. When she had stripped naked, they had transformed in a web of straps that flowed over her calf and foot. The overall pattern was lovely, but they also dug into the skin and any attempt to remove them failed painfully.

"Those are the shoes of the Sister of the East, are they not?" asked Fifinella.

"Yes, and they don't want to leave me."

The general shrugged, "Then you must wear them." She motioned to a squadron of Winged. They grabbed Space Girl Green's arms and flew her somewhat gently into the sky and toward the palace.

CHAPTER 39
A RANGER'S INQUIRY

Eógan surveyed the area as he walked down the gangplank. The air swirled with colorless dust, shrouding the landscape in grey. When his armored foot stepped off Aurelius' gangplank, it sank into the fine regolith. He had admired Amethyst's dark purple armor, which had gleamed so brilliantly in the entry room. Now the dust gave it a matte sheen, and reflected the lifeless beauty of the landscape.

"You want me to do the talking?" asked Amethyst as two figures materialized from the dust. They were flanked by two mechanical beasts larger than Great Wolves.

"No, is my duty as a ranger," Eógan said, then he smirked and added, "And the mission given me by my Space Girl."

Amethyst smiled inside at the idea *Green* was now his Space Girl, replacing his lost wife. She thought that a good thing. "We're here to help," she said, and shifted back subtly.

The approaching figures motioned when they were a good 10 meters away and the behemoths sat like well-trained pups. When close enough, he could see a middle-aged man and woman.

"Welcome, Ranger of Gamalon," said the man.

"Welcome, Space Woman of Home," said the woman. "We seem to have become a regular stop for the Space Girls of late."

Amethyst just nodded. Eógan said, "Space Girl Green is my daughter. She rightly thought a ranger would be concerned about people who had taken it upon themselves to terraform Gamalon. If you know the Rangers, you know we are the protectors of nature here." He looked around. "Such as it is."

The man smiled, "We knew the lady was a daughter of Gamalon, and should have guessed she had the blood of rangers. Would you care to finish this discussion in our home? It is much more comfortable than this landing field."

Away from my saucer, thought Amethyst. The humanoids seemed a minor threat, but the beast...

"Are you people of Gamalon?" asked Eógan.

"We did not introduce ourselves, darling," said the woman. "Sorry, Ranger. We are too long on our own and forget our manners." She straightened slightly and said, "I am Dr Gwendoline Byrne, professor emeritus of literature from Gamalon University. My specialty was narrative invention and construction, which I used to great effect as the Queen of Auz."

She motioned to her companion and said, "This is Dr Pastoria Byrne, Engineering Fellow in Robotics and Cybernetics from Gamalon Polytechnic. He used his brilliance in those fields as the king of Auz for many years." Smiled back at Eógan, "And now uses them to begin to bring Gamalon to its former glory."

Even through two suits of armor, Amethyst felt Eógan's doubt. Before he could launch into his questions, the Space Woman said, "Are you responsible for the creatures clearing debris in orbit?" She pointed upwards.

The man grinned and nodded. "Yes, yes. The Winged. A self-replicating construct with the potential to move all the rocks into a lunar orbit within a few months, or maybe even weeks. Did you like them?"

"Well, my saucer was unhappy when they attempted to clear him out of orbit."

The professor furrowed his brow. "Mmmm, I would not expect them capable of that."

"Oh, they weren't able. A flying saucer is more than capable of defending itself against boarders."

While the scientist was clearly confused, his wife was not. "We apologize if you felt threatened. It was not our intention."

"Did you destroy any of them?" asked Pastoria, clearly missing any emotional nuance.

"No," said Eógan, "we pushed through them, though hitting atmosphere might have damaged those on our shields. Have you created an even more menacing obstacle to navigation than was already there?"

"Really, this would be much easier inside," said Gwendoline. "We mean you no harm. We are mere scientists, no threat to a Space Woman and a Gamalonian Ranger."

Eógan looked meaningfully at the creatures behind them, "Are those mechanical calhots?"

"Indeed, they are based on those creatures," said Pastoria. "And like them, they are faithful companions. Though fearsome looking, they can be quite gentle."

Amethyst was skeptical, but Eógan nodded. "Well, Space Woman, what do you say?"

"Sounds like an adventure."

Eógan sat on a comfortable couch in the scientist's parlor, Amethyst next to him, but far enough away her rayguns were unencumbered. He realized he'd never thought to carry a weapon. Was he out of the habit? On Home, the only time he ventured out armed was to hunt. On Gamalon, rangers had law enforcement duties, and he'd always carried something.

Had he gone soft in his old age?

"It is hard to tell if any of the Winged were destroyed," said Pastoria as he checked a display. "They are reproducing quickly now. Making it hard to determine if they had to replace burned up ones."

A dwarven maid brought a tray and presented it to him and Amethyst. "Would you care for Gamalonian tea?" Her voice was monotone, but warm.

The Space Woman shook her head. "And how old would this tea be, if truly of Gamalon?" asked Eógan.

"This tea grew in the garden below from salvaged genetic stock of Elderveil leaves. It was then dried and processed in the traditional Wyrmfire style." The dwarf's mouth smiled. "I am assured it is quite flavorful."

He raised an eyebrow, but nodded and took the cup. A sip brought a smile to his face. "It truly is Elderveil. I have not tasted that in decades."

"I am glad you like it," said Gwendoline from the other couch. "It was my favorite. Pastoria created it for me our first anniversary back on Gamalon from Auz."

"So Auz is real," said Amethyst.

Gwendoline raised an eyebrow at the Space Woman. "Of course it is. I admit it has a mythical vibe among its followers, but it very much exists."

"Auz, the home of witches and wizards. The place inadequate and overly romantic men go to become cyberknights." Eógan said, doubt clear in his voice, "That place is real and you sent Green to it?"

Gwendoline's laugh was a beautiful soprano. "Come now, ranger, don't be derogatory. Auz is a place people go to find themselves. If a man - or woman - was 'inadequate' as you say when they went to Auz, they would be more than brave and noble by the time they became a cyberknight." She shook her head at him. "Often people who are the most unrequited romantics in everyday life have the noblest of souls. They just need to be shown a new story."

Eógan was self aware enough to realize he'd encountered no one who actually claimed to have been to Auz and returned better for it. Every story was second hand and undoubtedly embellished.

Gwendoline wasn't through with him, "You strike me as a person who always knew what he wanted to be." She tilted her head and her eyes seemed to focus somewhere inside him. "Perhaps from a long line of rangers. Yes, Eógan, that is it. You were a ranger from birth and that is why your daughter so radiated the aura of Gamalon despite her Space Girl training. Just as you had been raised, you raised her." She looked even deeper into his soul, "She has yet to reconcile her two worlds. The world of her mother she grew up on, and yours she was raised for." She paused to sip her tea.

"Nor have you," she finished.

"What do you mean, nor have I?" Eógan said. "I am not of two worlds. Or do you mean I've not reconciled my daughter's nature?"

"You haven't done that anymore than she has. She will, though. You," the uncanny woman started, "you have lived on Home for two decades but never let it become yours. Let me guess, you made your own little enclave of Gamalon." Gwendoline frowned slightly, "And hid."

Eógan wanted to ignore this strange woman's fortune telling, but caught Amethyst's nod.

"You might benefit from some time in Auz yourself," said Gwendoline. "Though I'm not there to write your narrative."

She looked at the Space Woman next to him, then back before smiling. "But maybe you are finding a means of reconciliation."

"You sent Space Girl Green to Auz for an artifact," interrupted Amethyst. Eógan wanted to argue with the storyteller, but couldn't shake the feeling that she had just shared something important with him. Something obvious to others, but not to himself. He didn't like it.

"Yes, the Seed," said Pastoria absentmindedly. "It can restore Gamalon all by itself. Dear, may you give me your thoughts here?" There was an undertone of concern that drew all the others to his side. When Pastoria realized he had a larger audience, he was startled.

"What is wrong, dear?" asked Gwendoline.

"Well, as you know, we were worried about out-of-control replication, so I put a limit on the total number of Winged produced. Each Winged has a number. Its incremented by one each time a new one comes into existence. When they reach the limit they should stop."

"'Should' being the optimal word," said Amethyst.

"Umm, yes," replied the scientist. "Some of them seem to have gone into a loop." He focused in on a large rock near the North Pole. It was covered in colorful wings and black rippling over the surface.

"That asteroid was the source of the creatures who attacked Aurelius," said Space Woman Amethyst.

CHAPTER 40
SLAVERY TO SISTER WEST

Green's entrance to Sister West's throne room was far from the triumphant. Supported by the Winged, her head hung low, feet barely grazing the ground as she was dragged closer to an uncertain fate. The air was thick with the scent of her struggle —sweat, dust, and a faint trace of blood—a stark reminder of the battle's toll on her body and spirit.

"What is this, Winged? I told you to kill the flesh one," said the Sister.

"We have delivered your Lion," said General Fifinella. "The Cyberknight is broken at the bottom of a canyon, and the other pulled into pieces. This one though, bears the mark of the Golden Sister. We cannot merely kill her and risk that one's wrath. So we brought her to you instead."

Sister West smiled at the general. "Then you have not granted my third command and must do another."

General Fifinella was clearly not happy with this idea, but she was cunning. "That may be true, though we have given you the victory you desired. If you wish that to be the way of it, then we will go free the Lion and return this one to where we found her. Where she left her weapons, next to the body of our troop she killed."

"This pathetic little creature of flesh and blood *killed* one of the Winged? I thought that impossible."

"It is difficult, but even we cease to function if cut in half."

The Sister paused, reflecting on the situation. "The idea of parting with my Lion is unappealing, yet the prospect of setting free a woman who seems far more formidable than her appearance suggests is equally concerning." Deciding, she said, "Very well. You are free of my commands. I will kill the woman myself."

She rose from her throne and looked around for a guard to get a sword or spear from. But they were gone. "Crap," she said in frustration.

She walked over to where Green still hung in her captor's grip. Pulling on her green hair, she looked her in the eye. "I can do this with my bare hands. It will be more fun that way."

The Winged released Green, and out of habit and instinct, Space Girl Green twisted her head in a way that made the Sister let go. Then she rolled away and came warily to her feet.

With her feet under her, she felt much better. Solidly attached to the floor and ready to bounce.

"What are those?" asked the Sister, pointing to the silver shoes.

"They are your sister in the East's magic shoes. I took them off her corpse after I killed her." Not technically true, but Green felt it was the best story for this listener.

"Take them off at once and give them to me."

Space Girl Green raised her fists and said, "Come and take them."

Even the shoes themselves didn't like the idea. They transformed into boots again with spikes of diamonds like thorns.

"She could not remove them when we captured her," said General Fifinella.

"Well, well, isn't that interesting? Maybe they will come off if I first remove those stupid meaty legs from your body." The Sister walked back to the throne. "Winged, I have no guards right now. Please take her to the dungeon. You owe me that much for being so poor at your job."

General Fifinella said, "We will do that, but you will not see us again afterwards." Then the Winged in the room quickly took control of the tired Space Girl and carried her away.

SPACE GIRL GREEN had fallen into an exhausted sleep almost as soon as the Winged left. There were no windows in her cell, so she didn't know what time it was when she woke up. She felt rested, though. A yellow-skinned little girl, carefully carrying a tray of food, appeared soon after she woke.

She didn't even look Rainbow age. The light in her eyes, probably once bright with curiosity, had dimmed, replaced by wariness. Her golden hair was now tied back hastily, its luster dulled by the castle's gloom. Her skin carried the pallor of one who had spent too many hours away from nurturing sunlight. The yellows of her traditional dress were faded and threadbare in places, and her feet were bare. Without making eye contact, the little one brought the tray to the bars and set it on the floor.

"Hello," said Green, not moving, for fear of startling her.

She jumped a little at the words and looked at Green. She didn't seem to know what to do next, so Green said, "My name is Green. What is yours?"

"I am Noa Miki." She looked around like something might jump out at her.

"What a pretty name. Thank you for bringing me food." A

closer examination of the waif made her add, "Would you like to eat with me? I will share."

The girl's eyes got wide. "I do not think that would be wise. The Sister told the cook to feed you so you don't die. I would not want to disobey her."

The Space Girl still hadn't moved. "I can see the wisdom of that, but I assure you I won't die without some of this food. Your cook was more than generous. Share with me and tell me about yourself."

Green moved slowly off the floor and over the bars. She tore off a piece of the meat, some kind of slow cooked bird, and a bit of tuber. She took a bite of the bird and offered the tuber to the girl.

With another furtive look around the dungeon, the girl darted forward and took the offered food. Green settled herself next to the bars and ate to restore herself. At first, she handed the girl a bit of food each time she took one, but as she ate her fill, she said, "I think that is enough for me. You may have all you want of the rest."

"Really?"

"Yes." The Space Girl leaned forward and whispered, "If you want, you can even tuck some of it in your dress for later."

This seemed a novel idea to Noa, which required thought. Finally, she shook her head and said, "I better not. If I got caught, the Sister might use me for an experiment."

"An experiment?"

The little girl had relaxed while they ate, but immediately became anxious again. "Yes, she wants to turn all the Winkies into mechanicals. But she doesn't seem to know how. She runs experiments on us. Removing our flesh and replacing it with metal parts."

"That sounds horrible."

"It is, though she has stopped making it hurt. She turns off our pain. But you are left with some strange part when it is over." She shook her head. "I don't want a mechanical arm or leg."

"The Sister is half mechanical."

"Yes, and she can't figure out how to make the other half that way." Lowering her voice, she said, "Winkies like making metal things. We're the best at it in Auz, according to my da, but it isn't the way we want to be."

The girl grabbed the tray suddenly and stood up. "I've said too much. I got to go."

Without waiting, she ran out the door.

THE NEXT DAY guards came for her. These Winkies wore bronze armor and carried long spears. Their leader walked up to the bars and threw in a pair of handcuffs. "Wear these. We are to take you to the Sister."

Green stood back from the bars and just glanced at the cuffs. "You know I'm feeling pretty comfortable here. Tell the Sister I'm not coming."

They had apparently expected this behavior. "She says if you do not come immediately and without trouble, the little girl you met yesterday will be the subject of her next experiment."

The Space Girl put on the cuffs and followed them to the Sister's throne room.

"You are a monster," she said as soon as she stopped in front of the Sister.

"This coming from a being of soft squishy meat. You are a disgusting monster." Sister West got up from her throne and walked toward Space Girl Green. She stopped out of attack range, though. "I shall let you live. For the time being."

Space Girl Green said nothing.

"Don't you have anything to say to my largesse?"

"You didn't ask a question."

"You are from the outer world, and you blundered in here. My Sister in the East's vortex is gone, so we may soon have more such as you visiting. I need to understand how to control you, if I want more slaves like you." She moved back to her throne and sat. Then she waved at the Winkies around the room. "These Winkies are at least machine on the inside. You are none of that. Maybe it would be easier to convert you to some kind of perfection, like a Cyberknight."

Space Girl Green waited. In her heart, at the place where darkness and light met, there was a waiting calm.

"You will be my slave until I figure out how to control your kind as well as I control the Winkies."

I may do what you say now, Space Girl Green thought, *but I am not your slave.* She just nodded her head.

Smiling, the Sister said, "Good. Let us start with some simple labor. You will wash the floors of my entire palace. That should keep you occupied for a few days." She stood to leave and said, "Remember, not only will I experiment on the child, I will also punish your lion friend."

The Sister exited the throne room with half her guards in tow. The rest warily stood with their spears pointed at Green. She looked at them, sighed, and held up her hands. "Guess you will have to remove these if I'm to work."

The guards exchanged worried expressions. "It's alright. I'll be a good little slave because the Sister has power over me with her threats to my friends and the innocent girl. Just like you."

She also knew she could be patient. One guard came forward and unlocked her cuffs.

"So where do I start?" Space Girl Green said.

CHAPTER 41
FINDING LION

"How many days has it been, Noa?" asked Space Girl Green. She was down on her hands and knees scrubbing a hallway in Sister West's palace. She wore the silver shoes, which didn't seem to want to draw attention to themselves and had transformed into minimal sandals.

"Since when, Ms. Green?" said the girl whose job it was to bring her clean water.

"I arrived here. I don't see the sky enough to keep track." Green applied vigorous effort, the stiff metal brush grating against the stone floor near a door, battling layers of grime. Judging by the state of the floor, it seemed the Sister held little regard for cleanliness.

"I think it has been five days," said Noa gripping her bucket of grimy water. Forbidden to assist Green directly, Noa was always nearby, a silent support in Green's servitude.

Five days scrubbing floors. Green was certainly a sight. Dirty and stinking from effort and a lack of bathing. "Where are we now?"

They had started in the throne room and worked downward. This was the third new floor, and she thought they might be at ground level. There were more levels, including the dungeon where she slept, lower down.

"This is her trophy hall, where she keeps things she thinks are special." Noa shivered and continued, "This hall gives us Winkies the creeps." The girl pointed at an ornate door with thick metal bands and an intricate lock at the end of the hall. "That's her vault, containing her most prized possessions." Then she pointed at a door next to where Space Girl Green was scrubbing. "That's where your lion friend is."

"What?" Green stopped scrubbing and hopped up. "Lion is right here?"

"Yes, I thought you knew."

"Noa, how would I know?" She looked up and down the hall. As they had moved away from the Sister's throne room, they had seen less and less of the bronze woman. She made it a point to find Green and ridicule her work about once a day, but it didn't seem the top of her agenda. "Do you think I could see him?"

Noa looked afraid. "If the Sister finds out, we'd be in big trouble."

Green let her shoulders slump. "I guess you are right." Then she dipped her brush in the bucket and looked at the water before getting back on her knees. "Better go refill the bucket. It's getting dirtier than I am."

The Winkie girl offered a fleeting smile before hurrying away as quickly as her slight frame and the weight of the bucket would allow. Once she disappeared from view, Green silently counted to ten, then approached Lion's door.

Green assessed the lock's mediocre craftsmanship. Sliding her fingers through her hair, she retrieved a bent bristle from her metal brush, about 20mm in length. Over time, as the brush's bristles deformed with use, she'd covertly removed a few whenever Noa was absent. Initially, she'd haphazardly placed them in her hair. Gradually, she fashioned them into short, rigid rods by twisting them together. Two such makeshift tools hid in her cell. Her current work in progress was in her hair.

Efficiently bending one end of the stick and molding the other into a U-shape, Green fashioned a crude lock pick for a crude lock. In seconds, she unlocked the door and peered inside, revealing a short hallway with a gate at the end. She was about to step in or shout for attention, but the sound of Noa's footsteps echoed in the distance. Green dropped to the floor, resuming her scrubbing just as the waif rounded the corner.

The next time the girl went for water, Green was through the door and silently down the hall. "Lion?" she whispered. "Are you there? It's me, Space Girl Green."

The cage mirrored her dungeon cell, except this one opened to the sky, though the walls were very high. There was a mass of hay on the floor and something moved in it. "Space Girl Green?" came a horse voice.

The hay stirred, and Lion emerged slowly. His appearance was far from his usual majestic self; his coat was unkempt and matted, while his claws appeared worn, as if filed down from relentless use. The Space Girl surmised he must have exhausted every ounce of his strength in futile attempts to escape, whether by trying to bend the bars or scale the walls.

"Yes, it's me."

He looked at her, then glanced away. "You're naked."

"Sorry about that," she shrugged. "The Sister hasn't given me any clothes. How are you?"

"Hungry. Are you here to get me out?"

"Soon. Right now, I'm a prisoner, like you. Hasn't she fed you?"

"No, she says I get no food until I agree to be her pet and act like a good kitty." There was a growl in his voice.

"I see. I'll see what I can do to get you some food, but you have to hang in there till I figure out what to do with the sister."

"If she'd come inside the cell, I'd solve both those problems," Lion said.

Green didn't like the picture of Lion devouring the Sister. "I have to go before they notice I'm gone, but I'll try to come back later with some food."

"Thank you, Space Girl Green." He pushed a hand through the bars and she rubbed her face against it before running back down the hall.

THE NANITES that kept Space Girl Green's hair green also worked to keep it clean, but almost a week of neglect tasked them to the limit. That night she unbraided the braids that kept it out of her face, letting it fall free around her face, neck and back. Letting her hair down gave her much more room to hide something under it.

Having cleaned as slowly as possible the previous day, Green was still cleaning the same hallway in the morning. She suspected Noa knew she was up to something, but chose not to say anything.

When the girl left to refill the bucket, Green snuck back to Lion's cell. "Lion, I have something for you."

The noble beast was moving slowly, but he came as soon as he heard her voice. "Yes, what is it?"

As if by magic, she produced a small bundle from under her hair. "We were trained to always keep a reserve of food, so I've been hiding some with every meal."

The lion man took it from her. "But don't you need it?"

"They feed me. You need it more." She wished she could do more, but it should strengthen him some.

He quickly devoured what she had given him.

Before either of them could say anything, the door opened. It was Noa.

"Space Girl Green, I knew you were up to something. Come away from there before the Sister finds you."

Green turned quickly back to Lion. "I'm done on this floor today, and I don't know when I'll next get back, but I will try. I have to figure out her weakness, and the best way to do that is to act like a good slave."

"Space Girl Green, be careful. I fear you are my last friend."

Green ran to the waiting, nervous girl.

CHAPTER 42

THE FLESH POOL

Noa hadn't said another word to her as she finished the hallway. Before leaving to refill the bucket, she'd stared hard at Green, to which the Space Girl responded with a reassuring smile. By noon, they completed the hallway.

"Are you going to stay mad at me forever?" asked Green.

Noa was quiet until after lunch, then spoke up with a voice tinged with fear, "You don't get it, do ya? What'll happen to me if the Sister turns me into an experiment? I gotta show you why I'm so scared. Next you gotta clean the Flesh Pool."

She led Green to a spiral staircase on the ground floor that lead to a large underground room two stories tall. "This room was here before Sister West made herself queen over the Winkies. Back when she took care of us."

Directional light made a circular pattern in the center of the room, and that light illuminated one thing: the Flesh Pool. A slight lip rose out of the floor, delineating a pool of white liquid. From above, Space Girl Green could see something moving inside it, and an enormous machine descending from the ceiling.

"The Sister used to take care of you?" Green asked, this being something she hadn't heard before.

Noa gestured toward an intricate apparatus equipped with several robotic arms positioned to one side. There stood a Winkie with her leg reduced to a skeletal framework. The device whirred and hummed, weaving fibers around the bone, crafting white muscle and tendons with precision. "She despises this," the girl explained, a hint of anger in her voice. "The machine returning us to the image of humans like yourself."

Approaching the pool, was a queue of Winkies, each with some limb constructed of white, muscle-like fibers. A colossal ring emerged from the murky depths of the pool. A Winkie was suspended within the ring, creating an outline against the chamber's shadows similar to a figure from an ancient tome. The liquid, thick and opaque, cascaded off them. In the end they were entirely covered in normal looking skin.

There were four rings in the pool. Three beneath the surface and the one the Winkies were helping their repaired companion off of, and replacing him with the next in line.

"Does it hurt?" Green asked the man as he put on his clothes.

"The pool? No. Nothing to hurt with. Pain is in the flesh. Having your muscles restrung feels weird, though." He and moved away self conscious of her looking at him while he dressed.

"It don't hurt," said a woman standing in line. She was two back from the front and still had her clothes on. "But you go in and you may not come back out. Why you not wearing any clothes? You aren't a Winkie."

"She's the Sister's slave," provided Noa. "Sister didn't give her any clothes. I think she was trying to shame her, but she's a Visitor. I guess they don't feel bad being naked."

"I grew up on a planet of almost all women. We never learned to be ashamed of our bodies. Or afraid." Green said absently as she watched a newly attached Winkie dropped into the vat and another ring rise. "You said you don't come out sometimes. Why not?"

"The pool checks you for defects. If you are too broken, it just breaks you down," said the older woman.

Space Girl Green was confused. "Is this the Sister's doing?" Her scans had shown her the Inhabitants of Auz were not like her. Their biology, if we can call it that, would be classified as synthetic on any other world.

"I don't think so," said the woman. "Think this place existed before the change."

Green was about to ask another question when there was a yell from the stairs. "What are you doing down here, slave?" Sister West had arrived.

CHAPTER 43
CRAVEN CUPIDS

"You sure this is a good idea, Amethyst?" ask Eógan.

"Of course not," she laughed, "but it should be fun."

Space Girl fun, he thought. He was back in his borrowed space suit, floating just outside of Aurelius. They were parked next to the asteroid covered with Winged and their offspring. Amethyst float a few meters away, both of them still inside the saucer's shields. Soon they'd push off and land among the creatures Pastoria had assured him was perfectly safe.

"You sure this is safe, Pastoria?" he asked over the comms. "I'm pretty sure that asteroid is considerably smaller than it was." According to the scientist, the smaller black creatures used the raw materials of the debris to grow. But they were supposed to stop when they were big enough to push it out of position.

"Perfectly," Pastoria replied. "Your suits' composites are incompatible with the winged larva. Even if they tried to eat you, they couldn't."

"Great. We're depending on my armor not tasting good," mumbled Eógan.

"You will be fine, Ranger," said Gwendoline. "Gamalon is depending on you."

He wanted to growl into the mic. How much of Gwendoline's story craft was just manipulating people to do the things she wanted them to do? Like using his duty to get him to fight these creatures?

"Come on, Eógan," said Amethyst, her excitement at the prospect of flying across empty space into a hornet's nest obvious. "It's simple. Fly over. Drop off our Cherubim, which will seduce the lovely winged ladies into moving the asteroid where it needs to go."

"And the larva will settle down for a nice nap," said Gwendoline.

The Cherubim Amethyst was referring to clung to his arm and back. If the Winged looked like pudgy little fairies, these looked like celestial infants with shimmering golden wings and radiant halos. Their tiny bows shot arrows that would change the Winged's programming, instructing them to start moving the asteroid. The glittering trails they left behind would shut off the larva.

"And why do we have to personally deliver these creatures again?" He asked. "I'm pretty sure I could throw one from here." The asteroid was less than a dozen meters and the things weren't that massive.

"Because this way is more fun," said the Space Woman and launched herself off the side of the saucer.

"An diabhal leis!" Eógan said and pushed away from Aurelius. Passing through the shield sent a tingling feeling down his spine. The larvae were drawn to Aurelius as if he were a delectable treat, but as Pastoria had noted, they weren't interested in Eógan's suit.

Amethyst was doing loops in space, swatting at the larvae. One landed on the Cherubim gripping his biceps. The creature grabbed it, bit it in half, and shoved the rest into his mouth, chewing contentedly.

"Hey, are the Cherubim supposed to eat the larva?"

To Eógan it seemed there was too long a pause before Gwendoline answered, "It is not outside of their nature..."

Eógan shook his head inside the helmet and decided to just go with it. He was flying through space with a craven cupid on his shoulder. It couldn't get any weirder.

CHAPTER 44
I'M MELTING

"Noa, go fill your bucket," said Space Girl Green as the Sister made her way down the staircase. The Winkie girl had been mostly in the shadows. Green knew Noa was smart enough to stay out of the Sister's view.

"I got curious, Sister," said the Space Girl, stepping full into the light next to the pool as West stomped toward her. "I was going to start on the hall above, but when Noa went to fill her bucket, I found the stairs and was curious."

The brass sister ran her gaze over the Winkies standing in line at the pool and they froze into statues. "You are not to come down here, slave," she said, taking a step closer.

Space Girl Green's hands itched to grab the woman. Five different ways of breaking her neck came to mind. But she couldn't be sure any would actually work with the bronze-skinned, metal skeletoned woman. "What is down here? What is this place?"

"A remnant of the past, soon to be replaced," said West, moving even closer.

Despite her resolve to stand her ground, Green took a step backwards. Her back foot sunk into the flesh pool. The liquid was warm and made her skin tingle. The silver shoe outside the pool glued itself to the floor as if afraid. Her back foot sunk a good 25cm till it hit a submerged step.

The lights in the room turned yellow and a voice boomed, "Biological entity in the reconditioning pool. Artifact in reconditioning pool. Warning. Remove immediately."

None of the Winkies reacted, having been frozen by West. Those further back shrank away and all four rings rose out of the pool. Even Sister West stepped back, apparently never having heard such a warning.

There was movement beneath her submerged foot. Her bare foot touched the pool's slick floor and her silver shoe flew out, landing between her and the Sister of the West. Green shifted her weight to her front foot, allowing her to extract herself from the pool. The moment her bare foot cleared the water, the pool's yellow light and accompanying alarm ceased.

As soon as it touched the stone floor, the shoe transformed back into its original form - a diminutive, diamond-studded high-heeled pump. Sister West darted forward to grab the fallen shoe.

"Now, I know how to get them off of you," said West, lunging at Green.

Already leaning forward, Green pushed off her front foot and collided with the oncoming metal woman. "That is mine," she said and grabbed the shoe.

West pushed her bulk against the Space Girl trying to force her into the Flesh Pool. Green shifted off the line of attack, letting the Sister's momentum carried her forward and past her. A spinning movement of her hands freed the shoe and dumped the ruler of the lands of the West into the pool.

Red light flooded the pool, white liquid splashing like blood where the Sister disappeared. "Warning. Unregistered minerals are present in the reconditioning pool. Alien artifact present in reconditioning pool. Warning."

The Sister splashed to the surface, but her movements only seemed to move her further from the edge. She screamed and tried to get to the side, but something was holding her. As the voice repeated its warning, something yanked her under.

All the Winkies, including the formerly frozen ones, looked on in shock as waves turned to ripples in the pool. "Construct analysis indicates unauthorized modifications. Repair construct requires replacement."

The Sister never returned to the surface. After a few moments, the lights turned yellow, and the voice said, "Artifact recovered." The Sister's yellow eye popped out of the pool and rolled across the floor.

Space Girl Green picked it up and said, "Well, you don't see that every day."

CHAPTER 45

CUPID FIREWORKS

"Well, you don't see that every day," Eógan thought. *Of course it would get weirder.*

He had landed on the asteroid with a somewhat sickening crunch of larvae bodies beneath his boots. He grabbed the cupid off his shoulder, slapped its baby rump and pointed at the nearest Winged. The creature moved toward the butterfly wings, shooting arrows every which way.

At the top of the asteroid, Amethyst was releasing her cherubim with a softer pat of the bottom, and it went off like fireworks, shooting arrows at every creature it could see. Both Cherubim were skewering Winged with arrows, and the whole rock was covered in floating glitter. Not really floating, as it seemed to target the larvae. The tiny humanoid stick creatures, once touched by the sparkle, would snuggle up to their neighbors and cuddle. At least, that's what it looked like. Soon, the wiggling floor of larvae resembled a tangled nest or a cluster of hibernating fireflies. Tiny creatures curled in slumber next to each other.

The Winged struck by the arrows grabbed onto the rock like a long-lost love and pressed themselves against it as hard as they could. Once they locked in tight, their jet packs squirted a single jet of air.

"They seem to have fallen in love with their asteroid," said Eógan. "But they aren't firing."

"The little ones are curled up for a long nap together," said Amethyst.

"They are in slumber," said Gwendoline. "Give the large ones a moment."

"Yes, yes," said Pastoria. "They are calibrating position and the new mass of the asteroid. They also should understand there at are lot more of them now. I'd suggest..."

All the jet packs went off at the same time. The rock moved away so fast, Eógan felt like he'd leapt off of it. Amethyst was just visible on the other side of the North Pole of the rock. With a move worthy of a gymnast, she flipped over and used the asteroid's momentum to cartwheel back toward her saucer. Before he began to worry she was out of control, he heard a "Whoop!" and the Space Girl righted herself.

Eógan had rotated slowly away from the asteroid and toward the planet. There were only clouds below him, and not beautiful white ones, only grey dirty ones. The whole planet looked dirty, not the rich green and blue marble it should be. Before he truly started to wallow in despair, there was a bump and Amethyst wrapped herself against his back and turned him toward space.

"Don't say I never take you anywhere special," she whispered and froze their rotation. Before him was the beauty of space with millions of stars and ever fewer rocks and debris.

CHAPTER 46
REGIME CHANGE

"I'm a Space Girl. Not a Queen."

The Winkie's insistence on getting her cleaned up and clothed in a soft, shiny bronze dress made her more comfortable than she'd been in days. Putting her on a throne and declaring her queen was uncomfortable to the point of annoyance.

Arrayed before her were the Winkies' haggard leadership. The palace steward, Akemi Hikaru, a figure of authority and clad in simplicity. The Captain of the Guard, Shinobu Naomi, which Green found hard to trust, especially since two of his limbs were steel. And then there was Cormag, who had emerged that morning to claim his title as the Tōsotsusha of the Tinkers, an unexpected addition to this assembly.

"But we don't know what to do," said the Captain of the Guard. "Please, give us orders."

Green sighed in frustrated understanding. She wished she could call in a rainbow of culture builders, but she was alone here.

She looked at the newcomer and asked, "What about you? I didn't see you during my enslavement. Are you outside the

Sister's power structure? Do you know anything about how the Winkies are supposed to rule?"

Cormag shook his head, "Nae, Lady. Truth is, the Winkies were under the command of the King and Queen afore they left. Then the Sister came in with the Winged and took over. We've never really ruled ourselves."

"And she ordered all the Tinkers killed or exiled. Why? Couldn't you have been useful in her 'experiments'?"

Cormag spat at the idea. "I wouldn't have been part of any such thing. Nor are my skills really related. The Winkies and all the Inhabitants of Auz differ greatly from you biologicals. I was lucky to be in the land of the Welcomians when the Sister West took over. Not that the Sister of the East was any better."

She really felt she was missing something about this little man. Something obvious, but she said to the group, "I won't be your ruler, but there are some things we need to do."

Addressing the assembled room with a tone of compassion and authority, Space Girl Green announced, "If you were one of those changed by the Sister's experiments and want your original forms back, the Flesh Pool is at your disposal. You are free, both in body and spirit."

She eyed the Captain's unnatural arm, but didn't say anything about it. "Send a patrol and find my friend the Cyberknight. The Winged dropped him in a canyon. Then send someone to where the Winged captured me. Tell them to retrieve the two bags you will find there. I want my own clothes."

To the Steward she said, "I want my friend Lion freed and given all the food he can eat. Tell him I'm in charge and you should have no trouble." She stood and strode to the exit. "Someone give me a tour of the palace, starting on the roof."

～

SPACE GIRL GREEN craned her neck to look up at the Orb of the West, a baneful gaze over the land. A massive three legged tower supported the massive orb, able to swivel in any direction.

"How do you move it?" she asked.

"There used to be a control there," answered the Steward, pointing to a box attached to the tower, "but the Sister disabled it." The box had a depression in the middle, which Green thought must be a socket for some sort of ball.

Stepping as far back as she could to get a good view of the orb, she pulled the West's eye out of her pocket. After comparing the two, she said "Mmmm, that's interesting."

Green inserted the eye, giving no thought to its alignment, leaving the pupil angled slightly upward and to the right. The moment the eye settled into place, the silent sphere above adjusted smoothly, mirroring the orientation of the eyeball. Green found she could rotate the eyeball with her palm and orient the orb any direction she wanted, as long as it was above the horizon.

"When the Sister used this a few weeks ago," said the Steward, "it shot a beam while her hand was on the control."

Green snatched her hand off the ball. "Did it fire the whole time she was touching it?"

Akemi Hikaru, the steward, said, "No, Ma'am, and in the past, when the orb only pointed upward, the beam continued even when not touched."

"How long ago was that, Akemi?"

"Shortly after the king and queen left. Before the Wizard inhabited the Emerald City."

Green shook her head at another instance of an Inhabitant not being able to tell time. Rotating the ball upward until it seated itself, then she applied pressure till there was a click.

There was a rumble from the mountain below, and the air

filled with the smell of ozone. A hum built to a roar as a beam shot out of the orb. High in the sky, it seemed to hit a flat surface, causing the beam to widen into a cone. As the circle widened at the top, the sound settled to a whisper. The flat yellow circle at the top waved slightly like water and then turned black, a mirror image of the portal to the East.

"I never dreamed I would see the Exit again," said Akemi, a look of wonder on his face.

Green released pressure on the control but the beam and portal remained. Realizing it must be designed to stay on, she found it simple to remove the eye.

"One problem solved," she said.

CHAPTER 47

REVIVING FRIENDS

The Sister of the West's workshop now belonged to Tinker Cormag and Space Girl Green. Two tables dominated the room with a body on each. Around the parameter was storage for all kinds of tools and supplies.

"He seems to be alive," said Cormag gesturing toward the Cyberknight on one table. The once sleek silver body now bore the scars of corrosion, dents, and visible cracks. The helmet, featuring its distinctive eye bar, rested on a side table, leaving his metal skull bare. "Body's badly beat up. The Winged did a number on him, but that's not the primary problem right now." He picked up a cylinder she recognized as a battery for the Cyberknight. "Energy is. He had two batteries, one inside of him and one in his pack. Unfortunately, both of them were mostly drained."

"Can't you just put him in the Sun and let it charge him back up?" Green said, remembering what Doug had told her.

"Yes, but that is going to be very slow. If we had a battery charger, we could make this all go faster, but we don't. They might have one in the Emerald City, but that's a couple of days' journey."

Green nodded. "He had one in his shack back in the East, but that's even further away. Say, that reminds me. I went looking to recharge my rayguns in the Emerald City and the artificer there said she didn't have batteries. That all the Inhabitants use wireless power."

"Yes, they do, but Cyberknights aren't Inhabitants."

"What do you mean?"

"Inhabitants, those of us made by the Creators long, long ago, run off wireless power. Some of us, like Lion for instance, get energy from converting organic material. Kind of like you do as a biological, but mostly we just soak up energy from the Land itself."

He motioned to where Douglas lay. "But Doug here was once a biological, just like you. Most visitors come and go with a life-changing experience in the middle."

"But Doug stayed on as a Cyberknight."

"He was a biological that had cybernetic parts added to him, but he was mostly biological. Which meant he couldn't use Auz's wireless. Plus what if he wanted to leave?"

"So he had to use batteries."

"If they are small, like an eye or even a single limb, the biological parts could supply enough power, but when he became almost all cyber, he needed something else."

"Doesn't the sun recharge the batteries? Solar power?"

"No, his shell's solar receptors only provide the minimal trickle needed to keep him alive. When in a charger, they call on Auz's power. Mostly he'd recharge via special charging stations."

She sighed. "I'm going to send a messenger to the Emerald City to let them know the Sister isn't in charge anymore. I'll add a request for a Cyberknight charger if the Wizard has one."

Green turned to the other table. A collection of grey claylike body parts was laid out on it. "Any idea about this one?"

"Nae, Miss," said Cormag. "She's no biological, and not like any Inhabitant I've seen before. A Sister might know, but we don't have one handy anymore. Where'd you say you found her?"

"In Welcomian lands. She said she'd just been born and knew nothing. That was her reason for joining me, to get the Wizard to give her a brain." Green circled the table, her fingers tracing the smooth, cold fragments of her friend. Once dismembered, Scarecrow had reverted to the form Green remembered hanging from the frame in the cornfield.

It bothered Green her friend was so haphazardly piled on the table. She picked up the head and moved it to the top of the table. Then, out of respect, Green ordered her parts; arms to each side, torso in the middle, and legs below.

"What about Scarecrow? Can you tell if the Land powers her?" Green asked.

The little man waved what looked like a wand over the parts and said, "I'm not detecting any power source. Don't know if that is because she doesn't use one, or if she's...," he stopped himself and rephrased. "Because she's broken up like this."

Space Girl Green knew what he meant, and her chest tightened. They had come so far together. They'd all finished the task the Wizard had put them to, and now the Cyberknight and Scarecrow wouldn't get their reward.

"What do they do when someone dies in the Land, Tinker?"

"Depends I guess. Most Inhabitants just disappear in the night. Back when I was with the Cyberknights, we'd have a funeral pyre. Not that Doug needs that just now."

Green looked up at him. "So you think he'll make it?"

Absentmindedly, she pushed one of Scarecrow's arms next to her body.

"He ain't getting any worse right now. If we can get Doug some power, I think we can wake him up."

To give herself something to do, she kept pushing pieces of Scarecrow closer to where they belonged.

"If you can wake him up, will he be all right?" She looked at the Cyberknight's bent and battered body.

"Aye, and I've got an idea about that."

She'd put most of the pieces together and moved to the top of the table. "What's your idea?"

"The Winkies here are great metal smiths. I bet they could make him a new set of cybernetics that would be better than what he had."

The Space Girl walked over to Cormag and said, "Do you? Like the Sister did on them?"

"Nae, Nae. That was different. They'd be keen to help your friend." Cormag was warming up to the idea, she could tell. "The Winkies are the finest craftspeople. They made all the Cyberknight parts."

"Let's do it." said Green. "Since they think I'm their queen, tell them to give you anything you need."

"Where am I?" said a familiar voice. The Space Girl spun around to look at Scarecrow on the table.

Tendon like tendrils were forming at joints. As a joint came together, there was more definition to the distal parts of her limbs. Her face had the all too simple form from when they'd first met, but she could talk.

"Scarecrow, it's me, Space Girl Green. You aren't dead!" Green moved where Scarecrow could see her.

"Where are we? I remember being pulled apart in the forest, but we aren't in a forest now."

"No, we are in the workshop of Sister West." Fear crossed Scarecrow's face. "Don't worry, she's dead. We freed the Winkies."

"Did I hear you say you are a queen now?"

Green laughed. "Kind of. They treat me like one, and it's handy when you want to order people around. How do you feel?"

Scarecrow's components were largely reassembled, and her limbs began twitching. "I can't really feel everything yet, but I think I'm OK. I don't feel pain, you know."

"Not even when the Winged pulled you apart?"

"Not even then, but once they did, I couldn't feel anything. Then I was here."

"You seem to be pulling yourself together. Just let me know if you need any help."

"I will do that."

CHAPTER 48

OF LOCKS AND DREAMS

The Winkies buzzed with enthusiasm at the prospect of crafting a new body for Doug. He was their hero; his injuries were wounds earned in the fight for their freedom. Under Cormag's supervision, they dedicated themselves to the task. Meanwhile Lion, Scarecrow, and Green continued to explored the castle.

Today Space Girl Green was back in her Warrior uniform, a leather overbust corset with a pteruges skirt. The silver shoes had loved the royal clothing, staying in some form of heel till her clothing was returned to her. Green's uniform was more practical, and the shoes didn't like practical. In a sulk, they transformed into the lightest slippers possible. Finally, Green told them she would step into the Flesh Pool if they didn't make themselves useful.

Green noticed Lion putting on weight with a decidedly non-human rapidity. Though his swords had been recovered, he left them in his suite and just wore a kilt of Winkie bronze.

Scarecrow's face hadn't reverted to the nearly human appearance she'd adopted during their westward journey, yet it was significantly more defined than the form she had upon awakening. Her body, too, was transforming, opting for a new configuration this time—her hips noticeably wider and her chest more pronounced, signaling a shift toward a more feminine silhouette. And she'd discovered clothing.

The Winkies made her a wardrobe full of dresses. Green was fairly sure she'd been changing clothes every few hours, and she was worried Scarecrow might spend all her time in a fashion show if Green didn't find something for her to do.

This morning Scarecrow was in a lovely mini dress with spaghetti straps and cinched at the waist. Since she wore no shoes, Green surmised Winkie cobblers must be busy.

At the end of the workshop corridor lay the vault of the Sister, secured by an imposing lock that defied Green's attempts at picking. "I'm not an expert locksmith," she admitted to Scarecrow, while kneeling with her improvised lock pick and tensioning rod. She stared off to one side because you didn't really look at a lock while trying to pick it. "These types of locks aren't common on Home. At the Academy, we thought lock picking was more a recreational brain teaser than a necessary skill."

"A puzzle?" Scarecrow asked, "Like those the Wizard gave me back in the City?"

Green sat back on her heels and ran the pick through her hair absently as she answered. "I'd never really thought about it that way, but yes."

"Except you have to use tools to work the parts of the lock."

"Yes. Lock picks. These are pretty primitive, since I had to improvise them. Would you like me to teach you the basics?"

Scarecrow knelt down next her with a graceful movement that again struck Green. Her legs bent into *seiza* like real knees would. Once there, her quadriceps bulged and her calves flattened. The toes on her feet became more defined and lay appropriately.

"Scarecrow," Green said, as she handed her the picks, "you're changing form again, becoming even more feminine. And you are defining details more quickly. Do you know why? Did something change after your..." She was at a loss of exactly what to say. Had Scarecrow died? "...injury."

"Yes," said Scarecrow.

Nothing else, which wasn't like the Scarecrow she'd known. "How? How have you changed?"

"I can't explain it." Then she shrugged. Green didn't think she'd ever seen Scarecrow shrug. "Something is different. How do these work?" Scarecrow said holding up the tools Green had given her.

Sensing Scarecrow didn't want to talk about the subject – something else new – Green began explaining how to apply tension to the lock and then feel the pins click upwards till the lock opened. "At least that is how it is supposed to work. I understand there are different locks. Some have pins in both directions, some have false pins, or multi-part pins." She stood back up and said, "Perhaps you'd better try one of the other simpler doors first."

Scarecrow held up a hand for assistance standing, which was odd. She raised it gracefully, as if seeking help with her balance. Her hand was slender and graceful, with long, delicate fingers facing downward. As she took the hand, Green noticed the defined fingernails reflected light as if polished.

The same delicate fingers worked the picks with precision on a hall door. In just a few seconds, there was a click. "Yes. I like this. All the puzzles the Wizard gave me were about seeing. This is about feel."

Cormag walked out of the workshop and noticed them. "Space Girl Green, do you have a minute?"

"Sure," she said and then to Scarecrow, "have fun trying the different locks in the palace. Lion can show you his cell behind that door, it has a different type of key."

She followed Cormag back into the workshop. "What's up, Cormag?"

Doug's limbs and the outer layer of his torso had been detached, leaving the inner workings exposed for the Winkie smiths to repair. The sight of the mechanical innards within his torso stirred a discomfort in her, a sensation far more intense than the sight of natural organs would have.

"I've been monitoring Doug's power levels, and noticed something. When we removed his limbs, he started gaining power much faster."

"Guess that makes sense. He's not using as much."

"Exactly, but I should have thought that would happen," said Cormag. Then he looked at her with tight lips and a furrowed brow. "I think we could wake him up now."

"But you don't really want to," she said.

"Don't know," the little man said and paced. "He's a Cyberknight and understands what he is. But he was also a biological before. He seems to have handled being changed to more machine than man, but being like this..." He motioned to the torso on the table.

She understood. Dedicated to life in all its forms, Space Girl Green didn't care if Doug was a living machine, but to be this helpless and only a part of what he had been was different. She forced herself to look at him.

His torso contained the parts that filtered his blood and pumped it through his brain. They added oxygen and energy molecules. But the things that he used for lungs didn't look like human lungs and his blood pump was no heart. That was what decided it for her.

"If he wakes up and sees himself, I'm afraid it will compound his feelings about lacking a heart."

"Aye, I hadn't thought about that. I did this to him, you know, even though it was against protocol, because he was so in love."

"He told me the story, though I don't understand how that ended. How he wasn't able to make it work with his love...what was her name?"

Cormag had to think for a moment "Kaylin? Yes, that seems right. She was from the South, even though she was living in Welcomia."

Space Girl Green stroked Doug's skeletal metal jaw. "What is he experiencing right now?"

"Mmmm, not a hundred percent sure, but I think it is like deep sleep. He's experiencing nothing." He turned to his computer and brought up an EEG. "There are a few times where he had a lot of activity. My bet is that was dreaming. But mostly he is just asleep."

"Well then, why don't we leave him to it while the Winkies finish his new body. Then we can wake him up."

Cormag sighed and nodded, "That sounds good to me."

THE HALLWAY WAS empty when Space Girl Green walked out of the workshop. She smiled when she saw every door on the hall was open. It made her happy Scarecrow had mastered the easy locks so quickly. Why was her friend so sure she had no brain?

Then she realized all the doors were open — including the Queen's vault door!

Green ran down the hall and into the room. Scarecrow was standing in the middle of the room next to a raised pedestal. The walls on every side had shelves full of chests and boxes, the Sister's treasures.

"I haven't figured this one out yet," said Scarecrow.

Green walked over and looked at the box on the pedestal. Made of gold metal engraved with a tight pattern that made her brain recoil. It was about 30mm tall, and 300mm on a side. There was no obvious keyhole or lock.

"There doesn't appear to be a keyhole," Green said, walking around it and feeling the surface with her hands.

"No, but I'm pretty sure it is still a puzzle and will open," said Scarecrow.

"It bothers me to even look at this pattern for too long," she said and closed her eyes. "But I feel there are different depths to these grooves. That might be a clue."

Scarecrow ran hands with delicate slender fingers over the box. "Yes. Do you mind if I try to open it? It is yours, of course, since you are the Queen now."

"I'm not a queen. It is the Winkies, whatever is in it," she said, "Open it. Given how quickly you got the vault open, it shouldn't be too much of a challenge."

Scarecrow smiled. "I really like puzzles. Even if I'm not smart."

Green shook her head and smiled. "Right, whatever you say. I'm smart and you got through a lock I couldn't do in less than 5 minutes." She looked around at the arrangement of the room. "This is special, and the Sister may have booby trapped it."

"Booby trap?"

"It is an expression that means it may have dangerous traps in it. Those traps might hurt anyone who opens it wrong. Or even destroy the contents, though that doesn't seem to be the Sister's personality." Green patted her shoulder as she was leaving. "Just be careful."

HALF AN HOUR later Space Girl Green was back in the vault.

"Watch," Scarecrow said. Her hands flittered over the top of the box tapping hidden locations among the strange grooves like a bird picking insects out of the grass. Having eating their fill, the same hands hinged up one side of the lid.

"You opened it!" Green smiled and clapped her hands.

"Yes, it wasn't very hard once I noticed all the pins and dials hidden in the engraving." She turned the case so Green could see its contents. Crimson velvet lined the box, creating a contrast with the one object inside — a crown.

It was minimalistic and modern, made of the four metals of the Sisters. A motif of a chain was engraved on the loop and a set of wings on the center front.

"This must be the crown which allowed her to command the Winged," said the Space Girl. "It seems a slavery more foul than her oppression of the Winkies. This makes them want to do what she says, not just do it because they are afraid. It disturbs my soul, like the pattern on the box bothers my brain."

She laid the crown back in the box. "Reseal this, and show me how to open it."

CHAPTER 49
A NEW DOUG

"Don't you look handsome," said Space Girl Green.

"I can hardly believe it," Doug said, looking at his image in the mirror. His whole body was now bronze because that seemed to be the only color the Winkies made things. She understood it wasn't actually the metal bronze, but something much stronger and more flexible, like the Sister's skin.

Previously, his form bore a resemblance to a human, but encased in armor. Which became a reflection of his essence as a man clad in metal, unable to feel and a symbol of emotional isolation. Now while his skin remained metal, he now resembled a man so closely, he needed to wear a kilt. However, what truly astonished him wasn't this familiar form; he had observed his arms and legs sitting in the workshop. The genuine revelation came when he looked into the mirror.

He had a face.

The Winkies hadn't just created a new helmet to cover the carnage of his head. They had given him his face back.

"I tried to remember how your face actually was, lad, but it has been a long time." The Tinker added with a smile, "Don't actually remember you being that handsome."

Kokoro, the head smith, was a woman with broad shoulders, thick biceps and forearms, and a trim figure that was surprisingly voluptuous. Her eyes caught the smallest detail in any object or person. She said, "We could provide nothing but the most handsome of visages for the Hero of the Winkies. If it displeases or is incorrect, we can still modify it."

"No, no," said Doug, turning his head from side to side. "It is fine. More than fine. I never thought I'd see my face again." His eyes welled up with tears and then opened wide. "I can cry?"

"Yeah, they added tear ducts to the face. I wired them into your cerebral interface, but didn't know if they would work or not," said Cormag.

"Especially since you lack a heart and all," said Green with a smirk.

"I still cannot feel anything," Doug said and waved a hand.

"Also, Cyberknight Moneypenny, you will have to carry your weapons again. The Winkies can't work the programmatic matter tech your old hands used to transform," said Cormag.

Kokoro the smith said, "We will, of course, make you whatever you desire. Already our most proficient weapon smiths are working on a pair of swords." She continued, eager to point out all the improvements. "You are stronger than a biological and comparable to a Cyberknight. Really better since the Tinker used whatever he had on hand for your repairs. Your old systems weren't integrated and balanced. Vision and hearing are now enhanced and full spectrum, far beyond a biological."

Cormag turned to Green and said, "No offense, lass. You seem plenty strong."

She laughed and said, "Physical strength isn't everything, and I'm satisfied with what I have."

Looking at her companions, she said, "We're all back to normal, or our new normal." She gestured at Doug. "We fulfilled our task from the Wizard and we should go get our reward."

Noa had been ever present as the others were repaired. The girl was Green's connection to the Winkies at large. She edged forward from her place among the Winkie leaders. "Space Girl Green, are you going to leave us without a ruler?"

The Space Girl knelt before the girl. "Noa, my place isn't here. It isn't even on this planet. I must return to my calling as a Space Girl. You Winkies don't need me as a ruler. You can rule yourself."

"I'm not very confident about that," said Shinobu, head of the guards. "We don't have experience leading on our own. I can lead the guards, but I cannot lead the blacksmiths. It's the same with Kokoro. She cannot lead my guards."

Akemi, the palace steward, stepped forward and placed a comforting hand on Noa's shoulder. "We have been talking among ourselves since you freed us. We knew this day would come. That you would have to leave us." All the senior leaders of the Winkie turned to Doug, "We were wondering if you might lead us, Cyberknight Moneypenny."

Doug let out a bark of laughter. "Me? I'm no ruler!"

During her time with the Winkies, Green found them brilliant and hardworking. They were also timid to the point of frozen inactivity. They wouldn't act without permission, even if the person they asked knew less than they did. Perhaps a Cyberknight was just the leader they needed.

"We have been under the rule of evil for a very long time," said Akemi. "We are afraid that evil has sunk into our very being. We want to be a good people, and therefore seek an outsider to help us."

The Captain of the Guard said, "We of the guard have done terrible things in the name of following orders. We should have stood up to the Sister, but we didn't know how. Cyberknight's have a code that guides them. We need that guidance."

"I didn't write the Knight's Code, just followed it. You could get it and follow it all by yourself. You don't need to make me king."

"See, even there you have shown us a way we would not have known," said Akemi.

"Cormag could have told you that. He knows the ways of the Cyberknight."

"Nae, lad. I worked with the Knights, but I was not one of them. Sure, I could give them the rule book, but if they had questions, I couldn't answer them."

"Cormag, you've known me for a long time. You know what kind of man I was before I became this. I'm no king."

The Tinker smiled, "I'm the one who suggested it, lad."

Like an overloaded machine, former Cyberknight Douglas Merrywether Moneypenny froze in place.

"I think you would make a great king," said Lion. "You are so brave."

"And smart," said Scarecrow.

These endorsements brought a smile to his face and his body relaxed. "What about you, Space Girl Green? You've been very quiet."

Green thought back to the High on Home. What traits did she need to lead? She was selected for the ability to make wise decisions and persuasively lead. Persuasion wouldn't be necessary with the Winkies. "Douglas, I believe you can do anything you set your mind to. You've proven yourself a brave, bold, and loyal companion. Those are valuable traits for a ruler."

Nodding thoughtfully, he said, "I must think on this. It is a great honor and responsibility, not to be taken lightly."

Noa ran to Doug and wrapper her arms around his legs,

"Please, please be our king, Mr Doug. Please, I don't want another evil sister to come back."

Doug smiled and patted the girl on the head awkwardly. "Now, now, little one. I may not be any better than Sister West. A good ruler needs a heart. So I must return to the Emerald City before I can even think about taking your throne."

The Winkies look at each other in worry. Finally Cormag spoke, "Can't say we want a delay, but I understand. Perhaps if you could give us some things to do while you are gone? The Space Girl has given us some tasks, but we'd like to hear what your ideas are."

"Anything Space Girl Green has given you to do, you are to do, for she knows more than I do about such things."

Green raised an eyebrow. "Space Girls are not queens. We're more likely to depose one that be one."

"Still, I trust your judgement. Perhaps all of us could meet together and provide a set of standing orders that would keep everyone on course."

CHAPTER 50

RETURN TO THE EMERALD CITY

Two days later, the four companions found themselves at the border of Winkieland, where the road turned green. Doug ordered their escort back to the palace to avoid worrying the Wizard.

"How does it feel to be a King?" asked Lion, once they were on their own. "We lions are supposed to be king of the beasts, but I'm not. Probably because I'm a coward."

"I must admit, it's nice to be back on the road," said Doug with a smile. For as long as they had known him, Doug's face hid under his helmet. Now, any hint of expression seemed magnified to Green and her companions. "Being a king seems like a rather demanding occupation."

"Based on the last few days, I think you are right," said Scarecrow.

"For someone with no brains, you were very helpful in figuring out how things should work for the Winkies," observed Doug.

"That wasn't brains. It was just solving puzzles. It was Space Girl Green who knew the most about what to do."

Back in her Warrior uniform, with the Auz sword on her

back, Green felt more at home than she had in a long time. "I have basic training in government. Maybe when the Wizard helps me leave, I can send back a political rainbow to help you."

They walked in silence for awhile, all of them realizing when they got to the Emerald City their time together would end. Sensing her mind going to a sad place, Green asked Scarecrow, "Scarecrow, know any good jokes?"

"What is a joke?"

"Oh, I know one," said Lion. "There were two men running down the road yelling, 'Help! Help! A lion is on the loose.'

"Someone on the side of the road says, 'Which way did it go?'

"The two men said, 'You idiot! Do you think we are chasing it?'"

Doug and Green laughed at the story. "I too have one," said Doug.

~

It was evening when they arrived at the gate of the Emerald City, and encountered the ever present gate keeper, who pointed at Doug and said, "Who is he?"

"I'm Douglas Moneypenny, former Cyberknight," Doug answered.

"You don't look like any Cyberknight I've ever seen." He handed each of them a pair of the green glasses.

"He's also King of the Winkies now," said Lion.

"The Winkies have a King, do they?"

"Yes, and the Evil Sister of the West is dead," said the Winkie's new king. "Just as the Wizard demanded."

"Humpruft," was the bureaucrat's only comment. "You may enter now."

Passing through the city's gates, Doug mused, "You'd think

they would be a little more excited." As they turned onto the main road, cheers erupted from the gathered residents. The air filled with confetti, though the Space Girl thought there might be more in the glasses than the actual air: it was certainly easier to clean up that way.

An honor guard snapped to attention at the palace entrance. As they ascended the steps, Stewardess Saphira smiled and said, "Welcome back, friends." Looking to Doug she added, "Cyberknight, you have been transformed."

"I took grievous wounds during our battle with the Winged. The Winkie tinkers and smiths brought me from the edge of death and made me a new body."

"Then they made him king," said Lion.

"Would you stop telling everyone that?" said Doug.

"Why? They did."

"But it seems rude to go blurting it out."

Space Girl Green marched forward. "We have accomplished the the Wizard's mission. We are here to claim our promised rewards."

"I am sure the Wizard will be glad to oblige," said the Stewardess. "He has scheduled an audience for all of you first thing in the morning. Your rooms have been readied. I'm sure you could use some rest."

"I feel quite normal," said Scarecrow. "I would really like to get my brains now."

"Yeah, we don't need to rest," said Lion.

"There's something in Space Girl Green's room that I believe she'll be eager to see," Saphira said.

"Really?" Green inquired. "More than I want to see the Wizard?"

With a mischievous grin, Saphira led them inside the palace. Entering the familiar room, Green's attention snapped to a black metal dog sitting with his gaze fixed on the door.

"Halamar!" She said and grabbed him in a hug.

"Hello, M'Lady," he replied, the voice coming from a box on his collar.

"You can talk now?"

"I never accomplished getting the dog body to speak. What you are hearing is a radio transmission to a speaker on the collar."

She examined the collar closely and recognized the Home tech. "So you are in the Saucer?"

"Yes, M'Lady. You ordered me to go there and guard it. I felt you did not want me to return as a dog. This allows me to be two places at once. This metal body is now much like one of my drones in function. I can see through its eyes and other senses."

"But I thought transmission was impossible in Auz?"

"It was when we crashed, but a few days ago, when the exit portal reopened that ceased to be the case. I could sense things outside my hull, and transmission seemed to work."

"Sister West's modifications of the Orb may have had the effect of dampening radio transmission," said Scarecrow.

"That is what I surmised," said Halamar.

Space Girl Green rubbed the dog's ruff vigorously and said, "You are a good saucer, Halamar. I've missed you."

"I too, and more I've missed being able to speak to you. There were so many things on our journey I wanted to tell you, but couldn't."

"Really, like what?"

"For one, Auz is not a planet, and it is flat."

"What? How is that possible?"

"Space Girl Green, there are many things which seem impossible. Like the two Spaceway portals in its atmosphere. It is beyond my intelligence to speculate, but Auz is clearly flat. I realized it the first night, looking at the stars. They did not move correctly."

"Astronomy was never my strong suit, or I might have noticed," said Green matter of factly.

"I think we all ignore things once we think we understand them," said Doug. "I've been here for decades and never thought about the stars."

"While it is fascinating, it doesn't help us get back, Halamar. Any progress on getting yourself flying again?"

"No, Milady. The problem with the impellers requires a new Jorgan Regulator. Pretty easily found on most planets, but completely unknown here."

"We are to see the Wizard in the morning, hopefully he will help us get out of Auz now that the exit portal is open."

"And I will get a heart," said Douglas.

"I will get a brain," said Scarecrow.

"I will get courage," said Lion.

CHAPTER 51

THE WIZARD REVEALED

The next morning, Space Girl Green thought hard about what to wear. Physical Aesthetics taught the girls of Home how to use things like clothing and make-up to communicate. Today, she needed to convince the leader of the most powerful city in Auz to honor his promises.

She could wear one of the sparkly green dresses from the wardrobe. This might show an allegiance to Emerald City and put her in his good graces, but she didn't want to seem subservient.

The battle-scarred Warrior uniform might remind him of his duty. But it also might turn a discussion into a fight.

In the end she chose the blue and white check dress of her youth. It communicated a rugged delicacy.

The five companions, including Halamar, convened in the corridor, all wearing the city's special glasses. Halamar, sporting little horn-rimmed glasses, looked particularly distinguished. As they followed the Stewardess toward the throne room, they speculated about the form he would assume for their meeting.

"I have not seen him at all," said Halamar.

When they reached the door to the throne room, the Stewardess said, "The Wizard is waiting for you inside. I hope you find what you seek."

The doors swung open of their own accord and the companions walked into the empty throne room.

The wedges of the round room again resembled stairs and on the top tier was the giant head. "I am the great and powerful Wizard of Auz. Why do you enter this throne room?"

Halamar tilted his head to one side, looking intently at the Wizard. Green stepped forward and said, "Wizard, we have completed the mission you gave us. The Evil Sister of the West is dead and the Winkies are free from bondage. The Exit portal is open again. We did this at great danger to ourselves. Scarecrow and Douglas were both nearly killed. The Evil Sister enslaved Lion and me, but we triumphed in the end.

"We now come for our promised rewards."

"What are these rewards you seek?" said the voice that came from everywhere.

"I want a brain," said Scarecrow.

"I want courage," said Lion.

"I want a heart," said Douglas.

"I want to leave Auz and return home," said Space Girl Green.

"Scarecrow, have you not all along this journey determined the solutions to many problems? Solved many puzzles? Yet you still think you lack a brain?"

"Others know so much more than me. I can't have a brain."

"Lion, did you not fight against my cage? Battle soldiers on the road to the West? How do you lack courage?"

"No, no, those weren't courage. I just got angry."

"Douglas, did you not become king of the Winkies because of your care for them? Have you not helped and supported your friends through this whole journey? Are those the actions of someone heartless?"

"But I have to think about all of those things. They don't just happen naturally."

There was a sigh through the room. "I am not sure how I can give you what you already have. Though in your case, Space Girl Green, I don't have a way out of Auz."

Silence enveloped the throne room, broken by a low growl from Lion and then from Halamar. Before the others could react, Halamar dashed toward the staircase. Despite the steps' towering height, the dog sprinted up the staircase, clearing each step with a single bound. Upon reaching the top, he hurled himself at the colossal head in one final, daring jump.

And disappeared into one side and out the other, entangled with a man. They came to rest, with Halamar growling down at the smaller figure he pinned.

"Stop, Stop," the man shouted, struggling beneath Halamar. "Get off me."

The others quickly traversed the stairs and stood around the man. "I take it you could not see through the glasses illusion, M'Lady," said Halamar.

"No, but you could?"

"Yes. I didn't like the glasses the first time they were on me. When I got back to my saucer, I added a camera to the collar."

The man behind the grand illusion was a slight, aged individual, his scalp bare and gleaming under the odd light of the chamber. His face a map of wrinkles that spoke of tales and secrets. Despite his small stature, there was an undeniable spark of intelligence and mischief in his eyes.

The Space Girl smiled coldly. "You have some explaining to do, Wizard."

∽

Before Halamar would let the little wizard go, Green insisted he turn off the illusion in the throne room and agree to remove their glasses. After his agreement, he led them to a small room behind the throne.

"Frankly I'm happy you know my secret. It was becoming harder and harder to maintain the illusion." He ruffled through a pile of objects on a table and found a thick rod. "Touch this to the glasses and they will come off."

When they were all free of the glasses, the room took on normal colors. The bookshelves were full of books with spines of various colors. Most of the upholstery, rugs, and tapestries were actually green, but the wood was brown again.

"So it was all a big lie?" asked Green. "You can't give us what you promised?"

The little man squinted at them and then waved a hand at Scarecrow, Lion and the Cyberknight. "You three, I think I can help. Come back tomorrow."

Smiles came to their faces, but they looked to Green for guidance. She nodded to them, "It is OK, go on back to your rooms. I think the Wizard and I have much to talk about."

They didn't leave immediately and Halamar hadn't taken his gaze off the wizard since he'd unmasked him. "Go on," she said. "I can take care of myself, and I'll have Halamar."

After they had left the room, the Wizard said, "You know they already have what they want."

Green nodded slowly. "But they don't think so."

"If I'm good at anything, it is illusion. I think I can convince them they have changed, and it is my doing."

"Not sure how I feel about that. You would be lying to them."

"Right now they are lying to themselves."

She sighed, "True, but I will be watching you."

"Me too," said Halamar, adding a growl.

"I want to return to Home," said Green.

"As do I, but even with the Vortex gone and the Sister of the West no longer shooting down anything that flies, I'm not sure how."

"How did you get here? Did you come through a Spaceway portal?"

"Spaceway? No, that was still very experimental where I came from. Is that how you got here? Is Spaceway travel used much?"

"It is the primary means of interstellar travel in the galaxy."

"Back where I came from, it was very unusual," said the Wizard. "No, I came here the regular way. I bought a ticket."

"A ticket?"

"Yes, yes, I know they are very hard to come by. But I had applied and done all the testing, including the mind-crown, which is very rare," said the Wizard with pride. "Then one day the ticket just showed up at my house. You know the sites say you'll receive a ticket, but they don't say how pretty it will be. Mine was a thin slab of emerald. But unlike a stone, it had stars moving inside of it. They probably weren't really stars, but you never know with the Creators."

"And where did you take this ticket? To a space port?" asked Green.

"How did you get here again? Never mind, I know. Traveling in a Spaceway. Saw a," he made air quotes with his fingers "portal. Went through it and ended up here." Green started to protest, but he waved her down, "Yes, of course I took it to a spaceport, but not to get on a space train or anything. Sheesh, you have a vivid imagination."

She wanted him to get to the point, so didn't point out he was making up the train.

"Anyway, I took it to the Spaceport on Misery and got on my spaceship," he explained. "It was a Mark IV Space Ball from Gamalon, state-of-the art." He got a wistful look in his eyes. "Then I took off and headed toward the sun at max speed."

"Toward the Sun?!"

"Yes, those were the instructions. Reach .78 the speed of light near the corona of the nearest star in order to be transported to the land." He leaned forward and said, "I'm sure I'd reached .8 before being transported."

"One second I was engulfed in star flame, the next I was zipping over Auz," he put his hand to his chin and said, "And going a lot slower too. Hadn't really thought about that till now."

The Space Girl sat back and thought, "Yes, you'd lose a lot of energy as velocity, not to mention the surrounding energy in the corona." In her head she plotted where Misery was in terms of the Spaceways. Not that far, a portal or two from Gamalon. "Were you caught by the Sister's vortex?"

"Yes, and no," he said, "I was, but it wasn't anything like it came to be. A little turbulence for the Space Ball. It was that witch from the West that brought me down. I crashed in a field just outside the village that was here back then."

"And the people thought you were a powerful wizard, so you tricked them into serving you."

"I wouldn't put it that way," he said. "I was an engineer and developer back on Misery. I built quite pleasant neighborhoods and even small towns. Naturally, I saw things that could be improved. Coupled with my natural charisma and leadership ability, they flocked to me. Things really are much better for the people now."

"Mmmm," said Green, standing up and beginning to pace. "We'll table that for now. I'm not a Justice Girl. What happened to your Space Ball?"

"I still possess it; it's housed in the Museum of Landing.

However, it never took to the skies again due to damage beyond my comprehension."

"I'm not Tech Girl, but I know a thing or two," she offered. "Plus, that tech must be decades old now. Maybe I could get it working again."

"And I might be of assistance," said Halamar in an abundance of understatement.

"Really?" said the Wizard, jumping for his seat. "Then I could leave!"

"Then *we* could leave," corrected Green.

"Yes, of course."

CHAPTER 52

THE WIZARD'S SPACE BALL

The Museum of Arrival was a private area located at the back of the palace, accessible only through a door from the Wizard's quarters. Its walls matched the rest of the palace, but it featured a hard dirt floor. At the room's center lay a partially buried Space Ball. The Wizard led them a door on the side.

"We used these a little during training," said Space Girl Green. "They are fairly easy to control, so they were our first solo craft."

"They were state of the art when I left, and Gamalon produced the finest spacecraft in the galaxy."

Green was happy to look around the tiny control center of the craft and was slow to respond. Halamar was sniffing under the control panels. "Do you know what is wrong with it?"

The little man puffed up his chest and said, "Of course…," then he deflated just as quickly. "No, not really. I took off the engine panels at one point, but understood nothing I saw there."

"May I?" asked Green, motioning to a panel Halamar was staring at.

"Sure, can't make it any worse."

"Thanks for the vote of confidence," she said as she pulled a spanner from her belt. Once the panel was off, she had to admit it was very confusing. Her training explained the major components, but given Space Balls were no longer made since the destruction of Gamalon, it hadn't seemed important to learn to repair them. She experienced a pang of homesickness thinking Yellow would have it running in no time.

Halamar got up next to the panels and seemed to sniff around, intrigued.

"Is your dog an engineer?" asked the Wizard.

She'd avoided this till now, but she really needed to talk to him. "My dog is a flying saucer. The Witch of the North put him in a dog's body."

"Oh."

"Yes, Oh. Halamar, what do you think?"

"M'lady, the damage to the craft isn't actually that bad. A few components have suffered an overload. They are common and I'd expect there to be spares in the field repair kit. Please run your micro scanner over that," he pointed with his nose at a circuit board. "It is on the other side of the burnt out components. Replacing it will be harder if damaged.

Green did as he asked, and it seemed the circuits were undamaged. They found the repair kit, and the required parts were in it, but Green didn't immediately install them.

"Wizard, we need to make a deal."

The little man had been licking his lips with wide eyes after hearing the news he might leave. "What kind of deal?"

"I take it you want to repair the ship and leave?"

"Of course."

She nudged him out of the craft and looked up at the roof. "Isn't that going to be difficult when you built a building over it?"

He looked up too and cursed. "I suppose I'll have to get some of my builders in here to make an opening."

"Which brings up the people of the Emerald City and Auz. But even before that, we need to talk about my companions."

The Wizard's face took on a wary expression. "What do you want?"

"You said you would help them tomorrow."

The little man shrugged. "I have some ideas. I can for sure help Scarecrow believe she has a brain. I'll have to examine the Cyberknight, but I may be able to help. The Lion is trickier because I don't know how you convince someone you gave them courage."

"You better figure it out by tomorrow. If you don't deliver on your promise, I'm not sure you'll be leaving Auz anytime soon." Her willingness to bully the little man surprised Green a little, but this land was full of people motivated by power.

"You can't do that! Now that I know what is wrong and that I have the parts, I can fix it myself."

"Can you?" she asked.

The wizard quickly returned to the ship, examining the engine components that had baffled him before. He then seated himself at the controls and engaged a mechanism. Meanwhile, Space Girl Green and Halamar waited outside as he scrutinized a display screen.

"Ha," he said and jumped back out of the Space Ball, "there are instructions on how to install all the parts in the standard kit."

"These parts?" Space Girl Green asked, tilting the kit toward him. Inside, each replacement part had its own foam cutout. Notably, several of these cutouts were empty.

"Why..." the little man's face turned red, and he bunched a fist, "how dare you! You can't do that. Give them back right now."

The diminutive Space Girl slammed the case shut and thrust it forcefully into his chest, causing him to stumble backward and sit on the edge of the Space Ball's opening. "I'm giving you the chance to do the right thing here, Wizard. Not just by my companions, but all of Auz. You can't just leave without finding a replacement."

"I'll have my guards get those parts back from you."

She stepped closer to loom over him and smiled. "That's what Sister West thought about my shoes."

The Wizard gaped. Green continued, "Even 30 years ago you would have heard of the Space Girls of Home, at least rumors and stories. Do you think you could take something from one easily?"

He slumped where he sat. "They were just stories. I never thought they were real."

"Like Auz," she said.

"Well, not really, but kind of."

"Space Girls became famous at the destruction of Gamalon, which you missed."

With wide eyes he asked, "You destroyed Gamalon?"

"No, No. It was a natural disaster. Something hit their moon and over the next year, pieces rained down on the planet, making it uninhabitable. Space Girls started the rescue efforts, setting the example. Flying evacuation sorties through falling fire day after day. Eventually, most planets in the sector joined the evacuation."

"Gamalon is gone," he said, shocked. "That's why the Space Ball didn't impress you."

"They don't make them anymore, though there are variations from other shipyards where Gamalonians immigrated."

He looked down at the ground for a long moment. "I won't be returning to the same place I left, will I?"

"Misery is still there. I've never been, but I hear it is fine."

Green actually heard it was the most average of planets in the galaxy, known for nothing in particular.

He took a deep breath and gave a long exhale. "It's been thirty years. I can wait a little longer to succor my people." He looked up into the Space Girl's eyes. "Will you help me?"

"Of course," she smiled. "That's what Space Girls do."

CHAPTER 53

THE CIVITAS ARRIVE AT GAMALON

"Space Woman, a ship just exited portal two," announced Aurelius over internal speakers. Eógan awoke bleary-eyed, but Amethyst was already out of the bed.

"Identification?" she asked as she grabbed her ship's suit and headed for the door.

"Correction, Space Woman. Two ships have exited. The second seemed in pursuit of the first." Eógan's adrenaline spiked bringing him fully awake and out of the bedroom. "Identities of the ships. Ship one is Civitas transport *Dóchas ar Dhíoltas*. Ship two is Home transport saucer *Castor*."

Amethyst was in her pilot's chair when he arrived. "What the hell?"

"*Dóchas ar Dhíoltas* seems on a direct course for Gamalon. Saucer *Castor* is not firing on them, though they are in weapons range," continued Aurelius, "even though *Dóchas ar Dhíoltas* is clearly executing evasive maneuvers."

"Open a secure channel to *Castor*," said Amethyst.

"Open," replied the saucer.

"*Castor*, this is Space Woman Amethyst Libra. You seem in

pursuit of a Civitas transport. Do you require our assistance? We are between them and the planet."

The Civitas transport had changed course to above the growing lunar orbit ring, which put the rocks between them and the saucer.

"Space Woman Amethyst," came a voice that held a vicious smile, "This is Captain Plum Trident. We are on a training mission with the Civitas. Please don't shoot them out of the sky."

Amethyst sighed and did something to a control that made a number of bright red power bars shrink on the displays. "Understood, Captain. Why are you in Gamalon space? It was my understanding your training was taking place on Lady."

"You are well informed, Space Woman," replied the captain. "We trounced them on Lady. Marines took it ok, and they hadn't completely sucked. Gave us a few surprises. The ship captain said it was because we had home field advantage. He suggested capture the flag on Gamalon."

Both Eógan and Amethyst furrowed their brows at each other. "You realize Gamalon is uninhabitable and under constant bombardment from space," said Eógan. Aurelius helpfully added his name and rank to the transmission.

"Well, Lady is no walk in the park," replied the captain, then yelled at someone off screen. "Helm, don't let them lose you in that ring. Or among the big collection of rocks."

"Captain, some of the debris is moving under its own power." The offscreen voice of the helms woman sounded young.

"What?" said the captain, standing.

"About that, Captain," said Amethyst. "The debris field is currently being cleared via," she paused and Eógan understood this might be hard to explain, "via artificially intelligent drones. They can act erratically if damaged."

"Space Woman," Aurelius said, "the Civitas ship just fired at the asteroid with the somnolescent Winged on it."

CHAPTER 54
BRAINS

The next morning, Scarecrow reported to the Wizard's workshop. She wore a long dress of emerald green from the wardrobe in her suite. She wore shoes like the ones Green wore in the format that made her taller.

"Welcome," said the Wizard, then he squinted at Scarecrow, "Have you taken an interest in fashion? Your form seems to have changed on your adventures."

"Space Girl Green asked me the same thing, but I don't understand what fashion is or what my body shapes mean. The dress was the first one in the closet, and the shoes reminded me of Space Girl Green, my friend. Maybe when you have given me a brain, then I will understand."

"Probably, Scarecrow, probably." He motioned to a chair, "Sit there."

She sat in the chair and waited, smiling. This was it. Soon she'd be smart. The Wizard moved behind her, but she could see him reflected in the glass of a bookshelf. He positioned a device like a magnifying glass over her head, then climbed a stepladder to look through the device at the top of her skull. "You differ from the others, Scarecrow. Your brain orb is much bigger than the other inhabitants. Obviously, your body is strange as well."

"But you are going to give me a new brain, right? This one doesn't seem to work very well."

"Something like that." He walked to a console and picked up a long needle with a cable attached to it. The cable ran into a console on the bookshelf. "You know, in the galaxy outside Auz, most books are in electronic form and not paper like the ones on these shelves." He got back up on the ladder and pushed the needle into the back of Scarecrow's head. She felt it sink in, and push through hard skull. "This means you can have all the knowledge of a civilization on a tiny device. Like the one I brought here on my Space Ball."

The end of the needle reached something in the middle of her head. She felt it wiggling around in there. "That should do it."

"I don't feel any different," said Scarecrow.

"You're about to get very smart," he said and pressed a button on his portable pedia. All the knowledge of the planet Misery flowed down the cable and into Scarecrow's brain.

Scarecrow's mouth fell open and her eyes went wide. It was too much to comprehend at once, but she felt her head filling.

The Wizard wandered around his library till he saw a dust covered ruby data chip.

The machine filling Scarecrow's head went ping, and the Wizard walked back over. "Do you feel any smarter?"

"I...why...yes, I do." Her eyes began making circles and her head started to follow.

"Whoa there, Scarecrow. Let that settle for a minute. Might want to close your eyes."

She took the advice and relaxed back in the chair. "I think I shall build a wall inside my mind, and put all of my unprocessed knowledge behind it."

"That is a very abstract idea," he said.

Scarecrow's brain seemed to understand how to understand, and in a moment she opened her eyes. With a clear and steady gaze, she said, "Thank you Wizard. You have given me much — a whole new brain."

"Do you now understand how your own mind works?"

"Ahhh, yes, I understand what you are asking, Oscar. That is your name, is it not?"

The Wizard's mouth dropped open. "Indeed, it was before I came to Auz. Of course, that was in my pedia wasn't it?"

"Indeed, and also how you came to be here. It is clear you have no special powers at all. Which, coming back to your questions, tells me I was already intelligent, you just gave me knowledge. There are actually two kinds of intelligence, fluid and fixed. Fluid is what I had before. I could learn new things quickly, but I had no fixed knowledge. Now you have given me much new fixed knowledge and as I filter it through my fluid intelligence, it too will become fixed."

"You don't say," said the Wizard, though he had little understanding.

"Why are you holding a data chip? Do you have more knowledge for me? I expect everything you knew, and your people knew, was in the pedia."

"That was everything my people knew when I came here. According to the Space Girl, much of it may be out of date." He waved the chip. "Sister South gave me this. I believe it is knowledge of the ways and people of Auz. I tried to read it when she gave it to me, but it is in a strange language. Maybe you would understand it better. Want me to download it into you?"

"I think that would be best." Scarecrow settled into their seat. "Give me a moment to prepare now that I understand what will happen."

Scarecrow had a framework in her mind and quickly set up

a separate neural network to accept the data and integrate it. She watched the Wizard plug the data chip into the pedia, then say, "There is considerably less data on this chip, so it shouldn't take as long."

"Ready," said Scarecrow.

The Wizard pressed a button and in a few seconds, there was a ping. "That was quick."

Scarecrow's eyes popped open, and then she started talking, but not in the language she spoke — more like random noises than actual words.

"I hope I haven't broken you, Scarecrow. You're spouting nonsense now."

There was more than knowledge on the chip. It contained access to systems all over Auz, deep in its core, with interfaces that defied her understanding. The protocols had overridden her speech centers.

"You want me to remove the probe now?"

Scarecrow nodded, and the Wizard quickly removed the rod.

Scarecrow staggered to her feet, unsteady. Trying to speak —or maybe throw up—the sounds she made left the Wizard puzzled. She then smacked the side of her head with her hand and shook it, as if trying to dry off. The fizzing chaos settled down in her head. A bubbling noise escaped her as she contorted her mouth into shapes far from human, finally settling on a bow-shaped smile.

"That was the language of the Creators."

The Creators, shrouded in mystery, were the architects behind Auz, the Golden Tickets, and other legends. These almost mythical figures had captivated the Wizard's imagination long before he received his own ticket.

"The chip you gave me is a technical manual for Auz, for the Inhabitants themselves explaining how they work."

"It explains how the people here work? I know they aren't organic, or biological, but I don't fully understand them."

"It is a very technical work, and I can't process it all at once. The Sisters were engineered to correct malfunctions within the inhabitants. The data chip's contents outline the protocols and methodologies for these interventions."

Scarecrow was pacing around the room. "It is more engineering than theory. What you'd give a mechanic and not a designer. Still it should be useful." She stopped and looked at the Wizard. "Oscar, there is too much going on in my head to have a conversation. I must go and meditate, if you will excuse me."

Then Scarecrow swept out of the workshop without waiting for a response.

CHAPTER 55

HEART

Douglas Moneypenny walked into the Wizard's workshop a few seconds later with a puzzled look on his face. "What happened to Scarecrow? She barely answered me when she rushed by."

The Wizard said, "She's got a lot on her mind."

"So you gave her a new brain?"

The Wizard shrugged. "I'd debate that, but she seemed satisfied. Very satisfied if I say so myself. Please sit." The Wizard motioned to the chair and Doug sat in it.

"Your situation differs from your companions. First and foremost, you aren't an Inhabitant. You are a biological like me or the Space Girl."

"Yes, but Sister East's treachery caused me to lose my humanity."

The Wizard was running his magnifying glass over Doug's head and neck. Through it he could see the biological brain and all its connections to the cybernetics. "When you were a Knight did you feel you had a heart?"

"Of course. Cyberknights had to stand up for what was right and care about oppressed peoples. They had to be brave and willing to fight for what was right."

"Yes, but isn't it true you did those kinds of things when you helped free the Winkies? Isn't that why they made you their king?"

"Yes, but that was the Space Girl's doing."

"Then why didn't they make her their queen?"

"They tried, but she wouldn't have it. She said Space Girls don't make good queens. Too much chaos and not enough order."

The Wizard laughed, "That is surely true of our Space Girl. Tell me, Douglas, when did you first realize you didn't have a heart?"

"When I couldn't love my Kaylin."

"Kaylin? Who is Kaylin?"

"She was my love, the woman of my dreams. The one I was trying to free from servitude to her mistress and then from the Sister of the East. Which I did, but afterwards…."

"Afterwards, you didn't love her anymore."

Douglas nodded jerkily. The Wizard noticed tears welling up in his eyes, and looking through his glass, he exclaimed, "You have tear ducts. That is not Cyberknight standard issue."

Doug wiped his eyes and said, "The Winkies added them."

"I know this isn't easy, but tell me the first time you realized you didn't love Kaylin."

The golden face got a faraway look. "We'd been back from the rescue in the East for a few days. It had been hard getting used to being all cyber. Kaylin was so patient with me. I spent the time building our little shack. It gave me something to do, use for the unfeeling body."

The Wizard made an adjustment to the glass and Doug's brain was overlaid with a map of usage.

"It was nighttime, and I was getting ready to settle into my charging harness. Kaylin had gotten ready for bed, which meant she was naked. That's just the way her people slept, I guess." He smiled. "Not that I minded. She was so beautiful. Her dark red skin in the moonlight."

The Wizard waited for him to continue watching the display. Looking at where the memory highlighted his brain.

"She came to me and pressed her body against mine. I could feel the pressure. Got readouts of exactly the temperature where she touched me, but nothing else. No feelings. I wanted to feel her like I had before, but it wasn't possible now."

"Before?"

"When we touched the first time. During that one day we got to spend together alone, before Retha's bargain. We had kissed then, and I'd known I had a heart because it almost burst."

"Ahhh," said the Wizard, understanding what he saw on the screen. "I'm no doctor, nor a Tinker, but I've had some experience with Cyborgs. Relax for a moment, and I will give you a heart." The Wizard got some tools off his table and returned. "I'm going to have to knock you out for this, or it might hurt." Without waiting, he flipped a switch on the chair and Douglas passed out.

The Wizard took out a laser and cut a heart-shaped hole in Douglas's Winkie-made chest. Then, muttering as he worked, "It's the lack of integration of sensors. Dang cyberneticists just think of sensors as data, and don't realize that's not how we humans use them." He unhooked all the feeling sensors from the central processor. In Douglas' chest, he added a simple sensory relay to reconnect the inputs from his body to his brain.

The Wizard adjusted a control, allowing Doug's brain to receive the new inputs without waking him. "That will take a few minutes, my friend. Let's use some dream time to rewire your brain."

Seeing nothing amiss on his displays, the Wizard welded

the chest plate back. He thought about removing the weld lines, but didn't.

DOUGLAS WAS ONCE AGAIN STANDING in his little home in the forest. Kaylin had just folded her clothes and put them away. Looking at her dark red skin in the moonlight put an ache in his chest. His fingers itched to touch her. He yearned to feel her against him.

She turned toward him and smiled. She slid to him and pressed herself against his hard metal body. Her flesh was so soft and warm. Firm muscles and hard breasts pressed into his belly. Her cheek brushed against his breastplate, and her warm breath sent shivers up his spine.

BACK IN THE Wizard's workshop, the little man chuckled, "That seems to have fixed that." The new Winkie body was responding in a way no Cyberknight had ever been designed to respond.

DOUGLAS WOKE up and let out a scream.

The Wizard leapt out of his chair and moved to his patient. "Knight, are you alright?"

The golden man looked around rapidly and then relaxed. "I was dreaming."

"Yes, and I thought you were having a pleasant dream."

"I was, but that wasn't how it happened."

"How what happened?"

"When Kaylin pressed herself to me. The story I told you earlier, when I felt nothing."

"Ahh," said the Wizard, and went back to his seat. "How was it different?"

"In real life I felt nothing...then...I was afraid," Douglas looked away and put his head down. "I...I...ran away. I ran down to the pond. Then I tripped and fell into it. I sunk to the bottom and was there till Space Girl Green found me."

"And what happen in the dream?"

Again the looking away, but this time Doug smiled at the thought. "I could feel her. Not just sense her pressure and temperature. It was her against me." He noticed the scar on his chest. He looked up with wide, wet eyes. "You gave me a new heart."

"Did I? Sure, I did."

CHAPTER 56
COURAGE

Lion walked into the Wizard's workshop and his eyes flitted around, never settling on any strange object for too long. The Wizard was standing in a sitting area with a couch, two plush chairs, and a table. Space Girl Green was sitting in one chair and the Wizard waved toward the couch. "Have a seat, Lion."

As he settled on the couch, Lion noticed a crystal decanter and glasses sitting on the table. The Wizard picked up the decanter as Green said, "The Wizard has really worked wonders on our friends, hasn't he?"

"Yes, I talked with Douglas and he insisted on giving me a hug."

They all laughed. There were three glasses, one was quite large compared to the others. "And Scarecrow, well, that is quite a transformation," said the Wizard, "beyond even what I expected."

"Now to your problem, Lion." The Wizard leaned over and picked up the decanter. A rich brown liquid swirled inside. "I brought this from my home, and have kept it for a special occasion."

"What is it?"

"Back home, we called it liquid courage, which is why I thought of it for you."

The Lion's eyes got big, and he licked his lips.

"Some on my world refer to it the same way," said Green, "though I'm not sure this is the exact formula we use."

The Wizard poured into the smaller glasses, but only filling them a quarter of the way. Then he filled the tall one almost to the top.

Green picked her glass up and looked at it. "Liquid courage is an interesting thing. We can all use a little courage, but too much of it and we become foolhardy. Willing to take risks we can't handle." She smiled over the glass at Lion. "That is why I rarely partake of it."

"It is also used to celebrate on Misery. When something stupendous has happened we would make a toast and drink it together." Picking up his glass and indicating Lion should pick up the big one. "I think the defeat of the Evil Sisters and the chance for me to return to my home are worthy of celebration."

Lion picked his glass up and smelled it. Then he pulled his head away and wrinkled his nose. "Why do I have so much more than you?"

"You said you completely lack courage. A Space Girl like Green only needs a little because they are already so brave."

"And you are bigger," said Space Girl Green.

They could tell Lion did not like the smell of the liquid. "Maybe I could just try a little, or drink it over a longer period of time."

"Now that is your lack of courage talking," said the Wizard. "You'll need to drink that whole thing down. I'll warn you it is going to burn and you will not like the taste."

"First time I tried liquid courage, it actually made me sick to my stomach," said Green. "And the immediate effects, dizziness, blurred vision, unsteadiness. Not going to be pleasant for a few hours."

"All part of the process," said the Wizard, "including the part where tomorrow morning you'll have the mother of all headaches."

"This does not sound very desirable."

"Indeed, many think so," said the Wizard, "but you wanted courage. Think of it as a test. How badly do you want to be brave? Enough to take your medicine and endure the hardship?"

The Lion nodded. "I want courage more than anything."

"Good," said Green, raising her glass. "let us toast." The others raised theirs too. "We have defeated great evil in Auz, freed the Welcomians and the Winkies from bondage. We did it with noble companions, even though they lacked brains, heart, and courage. Now they have their desires. The Light That Is All Colors has shone on us. May it shine on you, Lion."

The three of them clinked glasses and drank.

Lion thought it was the most horrible thing he'd ever tasted, but that was nothing compared to the burning in his throat as it went down. He wanted badly to snort the fire from his nose, but kept drinking. Once it was all done, he went into a coughing fit. His eyes watered and his stomach rumbled. He sat still for a few seconds, willing his stomach to settle.

"I'm no expert, but that seemed a very good vintage, Wizard," said Green.

"Yes, one of the finest Misery produced. I brought along three bottles of it, but this is the last one."

The room spun around Lion. He blinked his eyes as he tried to focus. *This doesn't feel like bravery.*

"When I return to Misery, I will find a new bottle and toast all of you," said the Wizard.

Then the flush hit Lion. Rising from his stomach across his

chest, all of his muscles filled with warmth. His chest relaxed in a huge inhale. He wanted to roar like he'd never roared before.

So he did.

The Wizard hopped out of his chair and hid behind it. Green clinched to jump, then relaxed with a smile.

The roar went on for a while, but he finally emptied out. He looked around with new eyes. The Wizard was just a little man cowering behind a chair. Space Girl Green was a small human woman, fragile enough to break with one claw. He stood to his feet, towering over the others.

The Space Girl's smile disappeared and her grip on her glass changed ever so slightly. Then she locked eyes with the Lion. Something in the back of his mind said she was not the easy prey she appeared. Before the new lion parts of his mind act, the room tilted to the side and he swayed.

"It would be best for you to sit back down, Lion," said the Space Girl.

"Yes," he said and flopped back onto the couch.

"I warned you this stuff can make you foolhardy, but I think you have found the courage inside of you."

He had. He understood who a lion was. He saw his size and strength for what they were and knew his roar was the least tool in a very lethal arsenal. He was king of the beasts and need fear nothing.

Except maybe the petite woman in green from the planet Home.

CHAPTER 57

A CHANGE OF PLANS & POWER

Space Girl Green, Halamar, and Scarecrow stepped out of the Wizard's Space Ball. It felt good to stretch her arms wide after being confined in the small space. The Wizard said, "Is it fixed? Can I leave?"

Scarecrow wore a practical, regal jumpsuit in shades of green. The fitted suit allowed for effortless movement within the cockpit, adorned with subtle gold accents. Her flat-soled boots provided stability, and a utility belt held essential tools. Her hair now longer than Green's, was tied back in a sleek ponytail.

Glancing at the others, Green said, "Your Space Ball should fly fine. Scarecrow also assures me the portal will take you where you need to go, and not dump you onto the Spaceways without a way out, though neither Halamar nor I understand how that can be."

"It's really quite simple, Space Girl Green," said Scarecrow.

"To you maybe, but not to a simple Space Girl. Maybe one day we'll get a Rainbow from Home Polytechnic to visit and you can explain it to them."

Scarecrow only said, "Mmmmm."

The Wizard was rubbing his hands and licking his lips as he looked at the spacecraft. She could almost read the thoughts in his mind and glanced around, looking for luggage. "But before you can leave, Wizard, there are still a few things you need to take care of."

The Wizard's eyes snapped back to her.

"You still need to name a successor as Wizard of the Emerald City. Or whatever title you think appropriate."

"Ahh, yes," he said, "I've been thinking about that. How about Scarecrow?"

The tall, slender woman seemed unsurprised. "Me?" She thought for a moment and said, "Ahhh, I see how you came to that conclusion." She turned to Space Girl Green and said, "The physical form I've settled on since our defeat by the Winged results from deep programing inside of me."

"Deep programming?" asked Green, concerned there might be a terrible change of personality from the near death experience.

"Worry not, Space Girl. It is as it should be. My destiny was to replace the king and queen." She furrowed her brow in concentration, like there was something hovering at the edge of memory. Then her face lit up with understanding. "I'm Princess Auzma."

Green was long beyond being surprised by anything that happened in Auz. There was obviously a lot going on she didn't understand. "Pastoria and Gwendoline are your parents?"

"You know the King and Queen?" asked Scarecrow/Auzma.

"I met them before I came here. Auzma is pretty. Does it mean anything special?" said Green.

"I think nothing specific, though obviously it starts with Auz," said Auzma. "Their sudden departure left me deactivated until their token reentered Auz."

The two women lapsed into silence; one reviewing past events and the other contemplating the change to her life.

The Wizard broke their reverie and said, "I've picked a successor. Can we leave now, Green? Do you need to pack?"

"About that." She sat down on the steps of the space ball and started petting Halamar absently. "I'm not going with you."

All of them looked at her.

"M'Lady," said Halamar, "do we not have a duty to return?"

"You're staying here? Why?" said the Wizard. "I can go without you, right?"

Auzma smiled. "This will be fun."

Green said, "I can't leave you, Halamar. More precisely, I can't leave the flying saucer."

She turned to the Wizard. She sighed deeply and said, "Yes, you can go without me. You must, because I need you to send a request for rescue to Home."

"You fixed my ship," said the Wizard. "Can't you fix your own?"

"Nope. Halamar said it requires a part that didn't even exist when you came here. And no one makes flying saucer Impeller parts here in Auz."

"I offered to help build you build anything you needed," said Auzma.

"But I would have to provide you with detailed specifications of my flying saucer, which is classified. If I tried to give you minimal info...well, you are really smart. You'd probably figure out the rest. We need to let things settle into a new order, then we can talk about sharing." *Under the supervision of an anthropology rainbow, and the leaders of the polytechnic,* she thought.

Green turned back to the Wizard. "I've created a full report and loaded it into your ship comm. Scarecr...Auzma, says you'll appear in the Misery system. Just hit send and the network should take care of the rest."

"Will I need to guide them back here?"

"Don't think so. I'm assuming they can find it the same way I did. If not, they can go to Gamalon and talk with the professors."

GREEN WAS REGRETTING PUSHING for a ceremony to make Auzma the ruler of the Emerald City. Oscar, the now former Wizard, hadn't talked to his people in years, but seemed to have a lot to say now. The Inhabitants seemed patient, but if she'd been standing out there for over an hour, she'd have snuck off.

"Finally," the Wizard said, and Green thought she heard a sigh of relief from the crowd. "Thank you for being a fine people. We've made the Emerald City great. It will grow on, even after I've gone. Don't worry about me, or yourselves without me. I've found you a great, great leader. I picked her out myself."

He motioned to Auzma and she stood up. Overnight her skin had changed to a verdant green. "This is Princess Auzma. She is a new, really, really great form of Inhabitant. I gave her all my knowledge, so you don't have to worry about being without me."

The crowd didn't seem the least bit worried about that, thought Green.

"I sent her and her companions on a mission to rid the land of Sister West and they did it. Auz is free because of that mission of mine." Reluctantly stepping away from the podium, he finished, "I give you Princess Auzma, the new Wizard of Auz."

The crowd cheered as Oscar shuffled away from the

podium. Auzma had selected a flowing gown of the purest white, which made her new verdant skin even more prominent. The cheers became even louder. "People of the Emerald City, thank you for your applause." She had to make a series of motions in order to get them to settle down.

"Thank you. You will find me accessible when you need me, so no long speech today. The throne room will no longer be empty. We will meet daily and I will listen to your needs." More thunderous cheers.

"You shall see the world as it is." Auzma waved her hands over the crowd. Inspired, the people reached up and removed their glasses, then looked around in wonder at the city as it really was.

"This will take getting used to," she said. "I understand that. You may wear the glasses to display information for navigation and what not. But they are no longer required."

Green knew what was coming next, but had mixed feelings. At the lectern, Auzma said, "Now join me in wishing our former Wizard a safe journey to his home." There was a loud hum from behind the palace and the Space Ball rose into the air. It circled the square and moved off to the west. "Oscar, will be the first visitor to leave Auz in decades, and the first being to transit through the newly reopened Exit."

Though the planet was flat, something Green could hardly believe, they couldn't watch his flight all the way to the portal because the buildings of the city blocked it. She'd suggested they watch from the tower, but the Wizard wanted a spectacle.

Turning back to the people, Auzma said, "Now let us have a celebration of the beginning of a new age in Auz." The people erupted in a loud cheer and Princess Auzma walked into the crowd.

CHAPTER 58

A MISSION TO THE SOUTH

Two weeks later, Space Girl Green stood in the Wizard's library with her companions and said, "We should have heard from him by now."

"Are you sure, Space Girl?" said Princess Auzma. Since taking up the role of Wizard, she had been surprisingly unbusy. Green had anticipated a long line of citizens with problems waiting to see the new ruler, or perhaps the green-skinned woman struggling to learn her new role. Unfortunately, none of that had happened, and Green had been counting on something to keep her occupied while she waited.

"Seems that way to me. If he'd been traveling via Spaceways, it would have taken a day at most to get to Misery. Give him another day to get to the planet, worst case." She was pacing the room as she spoke. "The Space Ball's comp should have automatically sent my report. A day for Space Girl HQ to react and maybe a day of travel for an Engineer Girl saucer to get here. Halamar would have let me know if anyone from Home had landed."

She stopped and looked at her friends. "That's four days. It's a simple delivery. Even with delays all along the way, it shouldn't take more than a week. It's been two."

The companions exchanged looks. "We've never seen you like this, Green," said Lion. "Surely staying here isn't that worrying."

She looked at them and sighed. "I'm sorry. It's not about you or Auz. There are things I need to be doing as a Space Girl, and I've been out of communication for over 40 days."

"42 to be specific, M'Lady," added Halamar.

"42 days. Space Girls can be out of touch for a long time, but a brand new one on her first adventure? Doing a shakedown cruise of her new saucer? I should have checked in by now."

"I also have an automatic system for sending my location to HQ periodically," said Halamar, referring to his flying saucer form. "Which hasn't happened since we entered Auz." Even her flying saucer sounded worried.

"Maybe something is wrong in the wider universe." Green started pacing again.

"Perhaps something went awry with Oscar's Space Ball," Princess Auzma offered. "The message might not have reached its destination. If there is turmoil beyond Auz, staying here might be the safer choice."

The Space Girl laughed, "I know you mean well, Auzma, but never tell a Space Girl somewhere is safe. It makes us itch to go."

"Plus, it hasn't exactly been safe for Green so far," said Lion. "Which is probably the way she liked it."

"Now that there is peace, Auz is too boring for her," said Doug with a smile.

There was nervous laughter around the room that settled into thoughtful silence.

"Perhaps circumstances have conspired to keep you here," said Doug.

"What do you mean, Doug?"

"It seems to me sometimes Auz has an agenda all its own," the former Cyberknight said. "If it thinks you need to be here, it keeps you here."

Green stopped her pacing and plopped down in her chair. "I'm sorry. You are right. I'm mostly just bored."

"And a bored Space Girl may be dangerous," said Doug.

"Some think so, but I think they are blowing our chaotic natures out of proportion. Still, we like to be useful. Are there no more adventures in the land for me?" She pointed at Auzma and Doug. "You two are like queens now. Isn't there something you need fixed?"

"There is plenty in Winkieland that needs work, but not that needs a Space Girl's talents," said Doug. Now that it was peaceful to the West, there was regular communication between Doug's palace and the Emerald City. "You knocked over the old order and now we're building something new."

"I can help with building."

"The same is true here in the City. People are adjusting to the changes. They need order and peace for a while," said Auzma.

"I can be peaceful."

The others laughed.

Lion said, "I feel you, Green. I too want to seek adventure now that I have my courage."

Princess Auzma said, "Do you not have another mission here on Auz, Space Girl Green?"

It crashed back into her consciousness. Gwendoline and Pastoria had sent her to Auz for a reason. To find the Seed and return it. "I do," she said, looking hard at the Princess. She added, "Couldn't you have brought this up earlier?"

She smiled enigmatically, "You weren't ready yet."

"What the Dark?" Green said. "This place is getting on my

nerves. All the layers of secret agendas. The manipulations. GRRRR!"

Green looked at the Princess and said, "How do I find the Seed? Do you know where it is?"

"Maybe," she said mysteriously as if baiting the Space Girl. Before Green could rise to the bait, Auzma continued, "I was thinking of visiting Sister South. Now that I'm the new ruler in the City, it would be good to establish relations with her. You could come with me." She stood and floated over to Green offering her a hand, "And you might find what you are looking for."

AFTER WALKING HALF A DAY, Space Girl Green said to Princess Auzma, "You need to create horses, or cars."

The Princess got the far off look Green understood meant she was "remembering" information not yet accessed from her download. "Ahhh, a horse is a large animal people ride, and a car is a machine that transports people. You are saying this because you don't want to walk everywhere in Auz."

"Yes," said Green. "The land is lovely and all, but some form of transportation would be nice."

"Now that there is peace throughout, it would be good to travel more quickly," said Douglas.

"Cars seem to require an extensive system of roads, not to mention fuel and industry," said Auzma. "That could fill Auz all by itself."

"You could fuel the cars with electricity."

"But we don't use electricity in Auz."

"You use electromagnetic radiation of some sort to power everything. Couldn't you use it to power a motor?"

"You're not going to have this argument again, are you?"

asked Lion. "It's so boring. Space Girl, Auz's power is different than your electricity. Get over it."

Green pursed her lips, but knew he was right. Yellow might figure it out, but she couldn't.

"A horse, though, might be a possibility," said Wizard Auzma. "Their creation is something to discuss with the Sister South. She seems the 'technical' - did I say that right? - expert."

"Yes, we would use technical to describe a person who understands how things work. Why is she the only one who does?"

"The sisters each understood much, but half of them are gone now. South has a reputation for studying all the works of the Creators."

While they talked, the group passed out of tilled fields and into a forest. The road before them was red brick and stone, indicating it would lead to the red lands of the south.

"Space Girl Green," asked Douglas, "what are those things on your arms? I don't think I've seen them before."

Green extended a limb and rotated it to look at the bracer. "It is a bracer I built in the Wizard's workshop. A bracer is just a form of protection for the forearm, made of metal or leather. These have some special abilities." A small door opened on the top of the bracer and an arm with a tube on the top popped out. "They have a magnetic-power projectile launcher. Azuma helped me produce a magazine for different projectiles on demand. Halamar helped integrate it with a Home non-verbal communication system, which lets me do this."

She pointed her arm at a nearby tree and closed her fist. There was a whee noise and a small explosion in the bark of the tree. This caused birds to fly out of the tree and into the air. Without a pause Green pointed at one of them and there was another noise that knocked a bird out of the air. She ran to where the bird hit the ground and the others gathered around.

"Sorry, little guy," Green said. The bird was enveloped in a ball of foam. Taking a tube out of her bag, she squeezed liquid onto the ball and it began to dissolve. As the bird was freed, the Space Girl picked it up and said, "Aren't you a pretty thing?" The bird was small and covered in bright red and green feathers. Once she was sure all the foam was gone, she threw the animal back up in the air.

Lion sighed, "I was hoping you'd caught me dinner. I so liked the crows from the West."

"Those birds were quite hostile, and this would be inadequate to deal with them. But that little guy was just minding its business when I decided to show off. It was a test, because I designed the splat pellet to catch small animals without hurting them."

For the rest of the day, they passed deeper into the forest. It became denser and darker until at last they made camp for the night. Since Auzma and Douglas now slept too, they set watches for the night.

CHAPTER 59

THE MONSTER OF THE FOREST

The next morning they rose with the sun and continued their journey southward. "This is a beautiful forest," said Lion. Under the canopy of trees, it was cool even when the sun was high. "The ground is soft and everything is so quiet."

"It is a wonderful forest. I grew up in the forests of Home. My father was a Forest Man," said Green, the memory put a lump in her throat.

"Was your mother a forest person too?" asked Douglas.

"No, my mother was a Space Girl, but she died when I was born. My father raised me in the forest. It was unusual for a girl on Home to grow up with just her father. Mine kept to himself most of the time, probably because he was heartbroken over losing the love of his life."

Douglas sighed in sympathy. "I understand the desire. After losing Kaylin, all I wanted was to live alone in the woods."

Before Green could respond, she heard agitated voices. They turned a bend in the path and walked into a meadow full of animal people. Like Lion, they had a humanoid shape, but with the characteristics of various animals. The largest with the deepest voices were the elephants, large dark grey skinned men and women with colossal heads and long trunks that trumpeted their arguments. Tigers and bears prowled around, twitching. On the edges, short rabbit men rushed about, never standing still for long.

Whatever they were arguing about, it must have been all-consuming because they didn't notice the travelers walk into their midst. After exchanging looks, everyone's gaze settled on Lion. He shrugged and said, "What are you arguing about?"

There were squeaks, growls, and mews as the crowd jumped away from the newcomers. The meekest of animals hid behind the bigger ones. Finally a Bearman stepped forward and said to Lion, "Are you a Lion?"

"I am."

"We thought all the lions gone," said a small voice from behind the others. "The Lioness went off to battle the monster and never returned."

"Is this monster what you were all discussing?" asked Space Girl Green.

"Yes," said an Elephant. "It has been attacking all the animals of the forest."

"It sneaks in during the night and grabs someone," said a white rabbit. "Mostly the smaller of us, but when the brave bigger ones," he glanced as the Elephants and Bear, "go seeking it, they never return."

The companions looked at one another. "We do have some experience dealing with monsters," said Green. "We defeated the Evil Sister of the West."

"You are too modest, Space Girl Green," said Princess Auzma. "She also killed Sister East. I am Princess Auzma of the Emerald City. This is Douglas, former Cyberknight and King of the Land of the Winkies."

All the animals looked at one another, not sure what to do next. "Do you know where the monster is?" asked Lion.

All heads swiveled East, "Not for sure," said the bear, "but east is the direction everyone has disappeared in."

The smallest of the people skittered between the legs of the bear. She was a mouse no taller than a few centimeters, but approached Lion without fear. "Are you a Lion? King of the Beasts?"

Lion looked down at the little being and answered, "I am a Lion, though not a king."

"Will you act like a king and defeat the monster for us?"

"If I defeat the monster, will you make me your King? For I would not rule over a people who did not want me to. But in my heart, I feel you are my people." He looked around at the group and found them nodding. "Very well, let me talk with my companions and then I will go find your monster."

Green smiled at Lion's nonchalance at the idea of chasing down a monster.

SPACE GIRL GREEN and the Lion were predators moving silently through the forest.

The companions had stood watch over the animals through the night. They heard noises in the woods around them, but no attack came. Green explained that if the creature only attacked at night, it probably slept during the day and would be the most vulnerable then. Lion was ready to go off on his own, but Green explained she had more training in actual combat and moving through the woods quietly. Douglas as the former Cyberknight had the most training with a sword, but none at sneaking. It was decided Auzma, armed with a thin longsword that looked made of solid emerald, and Douglas, with his Winkie blades, would stay to guard the animals.

Not ten meters from the meadow, Green motioned to Lion and pointed at tracks on the forest floor. "It was here recently."

"What is it? Can you tell?" asked Lion looking around as if it might jump out at them.

She squatted and looked closely at the impressions. "It isn't a mammal. These are not paws, hooves, or footprints. It is round with indentations." She stood and looked around. "It is big. There are opposing prints a good three or four meters apart." She pointed and said, "Whatever it is, it went that way."

Sunlight filtered through the dense canopy, casting a mosaic of light that aided their cautious advance, but the thick vegetation limited visibility. Green's attention was drawn to a solitary strand of white hanging from a tree. She signaled Lion to halt. The strand, as thick as her arm and stark against the natural hues of green and red foliage, puzzled her. Its white color seemed out of place in the forest, and in several spots, leaves adhered to its surface.

"What is it?" asked Lion. He sniffed and wrinkled his nose in disgust.

"I'm not sure, but it isn't part of the forest." She motioned how it hung from trees. "It seems to delineate a perimeter. Perhaps it is some kind of warning system. Don't touch it and watch for others."

Lion nodded and leapt over the white rope with silent ease. Green smiled and slid under it. As they continued forward, they found more of the white stuff and it became clear to Green what it was. "It's a spider's web," she whispered to Lion. "A *big* spider's web. Spiders sense prey by vibrations in their web."

As they navigated the forest, vast webs occasionally obstructed their path, stretching vertically between trees and necessitating detours. Lion moving through the forest with an effortless, deliberate grace, fully in his element as they pursued their quarry.

They encountered a stretch of webbing shredded between the trees, and then another hastily breached. Lion paused to sniffed then gestured toward his mane. Green, tuning into the dense forest ambiance, and Lion, skimming the forest floor, both felt they were near their foe.

The next set of webbing had strands hanging loose from the trees to either side, but in the middle hung a new large cocoon. Whatever, or whoever, had burst the webbing had not escaped this time.

The cocoon moved.

Lion became a statue. Green looked around and upwards. Green scanned their surroundings, noting the absence of light penetrating the dense webbing overhead. She discerned a thick canopy of silk above, obscuring any view into the shadows. Lion cautiously rose, his nostrils flaring at the twitching cocoon. A low growl escaped him as he unsheathed a sword and crouched.

Lion leapt upwards, reaching the height of the cocoon's base, which stood as tall as himself. In a fluid motion, he executed a mid-air spin, his sword poised to strike above him, effortlessly severing the single strand of web that suspended the cocoon. They descended together, and with remarkable agility, Lion caught the cocoon on his shoulder, landing softly. This entire ballet of movement unfolded in profound silence.

Green thought the silence was beautiful and well done, but spiders don't have ears. They feel motion through their web.

There was movement above them in the darkness.

CHAPTER 60
ILL-ADVISED ACTION CORRECTED

"*Dochas ar Dhioltas*, cease fire," yelled Space Woman Amethyst as she gave power to her engines.

"*Dochas ar Dhioltas*, unauthorized live fire is prohibited on a training field that may include friendly troops," commanded the Captain of the Warrior saucer.

Slipping into his seat and strapping in Eógan announced, "You are interfering with a terraforming operation duly sanctioned by the Rangers of Gamalon and under the control of the members of the faculty of Gamalon Polytechnic."

The Space Woman raise an eyebrow at him and he shrugged back to her. He was a ranger and Pastoria was a professor of the Polytechnic. They were approaching the troop transport and it had stopped firing on the asteroid, but seemed to be firing in multiple directions at something.

"Home ships," came Captain Kennedy's strained voice, "we are under attack by unknown aliens. There are gods dammed butterflies trying to land on our ship. We thought this was part of the training, once we discovered another Home vessel in system."

Eógan thought Kennedy must be very flustered to not even

question the authorizations just thrown at him. "Are the Winged doing anything more than attempting to land on you? Are they accompanied by very small stickman like figures?"

"Ranger, I'm readying troops for EVA. They are too many and too close for my anti-boarding lasers to stop them."

"Please stop shooting all over the place so we can approach. The Winged are drones created to move debris out of the cislunar area. Once you entered that space and began moving toward the planet, you became dangerous debris to be removed."

They approached the troop transport slowly, waiting for them to stop shooting at the Winged. Over the main channel Eógan heard captain Kennedy yell at his gunners, "Check your fire, you idiots. There is a friendly in our area. Don't you know the most basic rule of marksmanship? 'Always be sure of your target and what is beyond it.' Do you not see the freaking purple flying sauce out there?"

"Saucer *Castor* and Civitas Transport *Dochas ar Dhioltas*," announced Eógan, "the hazard to navigation of the cislunar system is still in effect, though the hazards have changed. We can discuss unauthorized violation of that hazard warning later. Be aware the ongoing clearing operation considers any ship entering the area debris that needs to be moved to the lunar orbit. I recommend both of you do not approach inside the moon's lunar orbit until we can clear you with operations." Not that he was sure Pastoria could do that. It would probably involve some other semi-mythical creation they would have to attach to their space ships like a hood ornament.

"Understood, Ranger," said the captain of the troop saucer. "Adjusting trajectory now." On the saucer's display, a dotted line appeared, showing the path of the large saucer changing to a higher orbit than the moon.

"Ranger Uaine," said Captain Kennedy, and Eógan could

swear heard the gritting of teeth. "We have ceased fire and now have several creatures on our hull. Please advise how to remove them."

Uaine smiled at the officer's distress, but hid it before replying. "The easiest method would be to power down your engines and just let them move you to a lunar orbit. Or you could change course to get to one as soon as possible. Are the ones currently on your hull firing their jetpacks?"

The captain said something off screen, but Aurelius had already zoomed in on troop transport. The Winged were gallantly trying to change the ship's trajectory. "Yes, Ranger. I'm not letting those things pilot my ship, but we will move to a lunar orbit. But I'm warning you, if they don't remove themselves, I'll put the cohort on the hull to do so."

"That would be very ill-advised, Kennedy. There are tens of thousands of those drones out here, and they are self-replicating. Their only mission and desire is to move every rock that might rain onto our beloved planet, to the orbit they belong in." Eógan let a smile into his voice, "Captain, truly this is Gamalonian engineering at its finest. You and your crew should be as happy as I am to see the destruction ended."

The captain sighed and said, "It would have been nice to have a warning ahead of time. But you are right. If these things are clearing the skies of Gamalon, we will comply with their wishes."

On screen, the transport's orientation rotated, and its engines fired. A new line appeared that would insert it in the lunar orbit.

"It was a shock to us as well when we arrived." Eógan said. "I'll tell you the entire story once we consult with the professors on how to clear you for the planet."

CHAPTER 61

LOVE FOUND IN BATTLE

Space Girl Green ran, shooting her bracer's explosive bullets at the huge arachnid. *What kills spiders?* She thought to herself. *Predators,* obviously, but she didn't want anything bigger than this monster. A bird as tall as a building to snatch up and eat a spider twice her size?

Lion led the way; his pace moderated by the burden on his shoulder. Sword in hand, he cleared all the encroaching webbing. The spider, preferring the upper branches for its movements, struggled to match their speed through the dense forest floor.

Green's bullets did little to slow the creature even when they hit, which wasn't as often as she'd have liked. The spider was devilishly good at hiding among the branches. Then it disappeared all together.

"Lion, the spider has disappeared."

Lion stopped, his chest heaving. The burden on his shoulder was now wiggling aggressively and there were angry sounds coming from it. "Do you think it has run from us?" He set the burden down and looked at it, confused.

Green looked at the canopy and said, "I doubt it. Spiders are more sneak and trap than fight. It is probably looking for a better way to attack us."

"Green, what is the cocoon doing?" Lion asked.

She took her eyes off the trees and looked at the bundle of webbing. "Seems there is something in there and it wants out."

Lion glanced at his sword. It was almost as long as he was tall. "This won't work."

"No," said Green, pulling her dagger. "Let me see what I can do. You watch for the spider." Kneeling beside the squirming cocoon, she whispered, "If you can hear me inside, keep still. I'm going to cut you free, and I don't want to injure you."

The bundle stopped moving. She looked to Lion, but he had unsheathed a second sword and was prowling in a circle while looking at the trees. Green started at the thicker end, making a long light cut. The webbing split easily and revealed more layers underneath. She sliced again lightly and revealed more layers.

Lion's ears twitched, and he said, "Better hurry, Space Girl. I think it has come back."

Taking a deep breath, Green carefully made a deep cut with her dagger into the cocoon. A sudden, high-pitched mew sounded when her blade touched something other than webbing. "Sorry," Green quickly apologized, retracting her knife slightly. There was a foot long opening, and she glimpsed golden fur peeking through.

Suddenly, Green was thrown backward, a thick glob of webbing striking her from the side. This forceful impact knocked her away from her task and pinned her against a tree.

Lion roared and jump between her and the cocoon, swords ready. But the spider had disappeared again into the trees.

Green could see clearly, but her arms and legs were stuck down. *Where was her dagger?* There it was, wedged into the gash she had started in the cocoon. A slender hand covered in golden fur with shapely talons reached out and pulled it inside.

"Come out and fight me directly, Spider," roared Lion. But there was no response from the trees, which Green thought was probably best.

The blade of her dagger appeared again and began cutting a bigger hole. "Lion, I think whoever is in the cocoon is cutting themselves out."

Lion glanced down as two hands appeared in the opening and started pulling it apart. Then another string of webbing shot directly from above onto the cocoon. It missed the opening, but pulled the whole thing into the air. The cocoon flipped over and another lion person fell out.

Even covered in a slimy liquid, she gracefully spun in the air and landed on her feet. Where Lion was all broad shoulder and bulging biceps, the lioness was sleek. Her form combined the robustness of an athlete with the delicate poise of a dancer.

Lion dropped his smaller blade and grabbed the cocoon. He flexed a powerful arm, attempting to pull his prey to him. Unfortunately, the laws of physics worked against this. The spider had been ready to pull up a cocoon full of lion. Without the weight of the Lioness, Lion became the new prize. But even as he was jerked off the ground, the Lioness grabbed a leg. Lioness hooked a foot under a nearby root, then she bent her knees, flexed her stomach and pulled downward in unison with Lion.

The sound of splintering wood filled the air as branches above snapped. The spider, surprised, plummeted toward the earth. In a desperate attempt to arrest its fall, the spider fired a web upwards, suspending itself midway, avoiding a direct collision with the lions below. Lion, having regained his footing, continued to pull on the cocoon and its attached web. This left the spider dangling, trapped in a precarious balance between the tree's canopy and the relentless pull of the Lion crouched on the forest floor.

Liberated in the chaos of the spider's descent, Lioness spotted a fallen sword and seized it. She ascended Lion's back, vaulted from his shoulders, and soared over the spider. With a deft slash, she severed the webbing that tethered the creature to the trees, sending it plummeting directly toward Lion.

The spider fell with its gaping mandibles and razor-sharp forelegs poised for attack. Lion counteracted with a swift upward stroke of his great sword, decisively beheading the creature. He deftly moved aside, letting the severed parts thud to the ground, and ended beside the Lioness.

WITH THE SPIDER DEFEATED, silence enveloped the forest, leaving Green and the two lions beside its lifeless form. The Lioness was slightly shorter than Lion's three meters, reaching only to his shoulders. Lion's puzzled glance toward the female elicited a smile from Green. The lioness, appraising him from head to toe, began a deliberate circling. Soon, they found themselves in a slow, cautious dance around each other, each brandishing a sword, tension and curiosity mingling in the air.

"Excuse me," said Green, butting in. "Don't mean to interrupt you getting to know each other, but could one of you please cut me out of here?"

Lion shook his head to clear it and said, "Of course. Sorry."

The Lioness moved over to the fallen cocoon, reminding Green of how Space Woman Black moved. She looked around on the ground for a moment, then picked up her dagger. "Allow me to assist you in the same manner you aided me," she said, her voice a rich contralto purr, moving over to Green.

Both reached her simultaneously, and despite their inherent

feline grace, they seemed to bump into each other a lot. They had cut her loose in a couple of minutes. "Gross. This stuff is sticky," said Green as she pulled stray bits of web off her. "How long were you in that cocoon?"

"All night," she answered. Her voice wrapped each sentence in a smooth, purring silkiness. "I rushed through the woods intending to attack the monster before it knew I was there." She trailed off.

"And it caught you by surprise from above," finished Green.

"Yes," she said sheepishly. "I was brave, but stupid."

"I too am brave," offered Lion, "and would have done the same thing. Luckily, I had Space Girl Green with me."

The Lioness looked up at him and said, "Who are you? I did not know there was another lion in Auz."

"I am Lion," he said, puffing out his chest. "I have been adventuring around Auz with Green and my other friends. My first goal was to become brave and now we go to the Sister of the South to help Green find a way to leave Auz."

As they navigated back through the forest toward the others, Lion, with the spider's head slung over his back like a makeshift bag, eagerly recounted their adventures to the Lioness. She, walking close by his side, looked up at him with admiration, interjecting with impressed sounds at just the right moments. Green trailed behind, mostly forgotten but happy for him.

As they entered the clearing where the other beasts were waiting, Lion stepped ahead with confidence and roared, "The Spider is dead." Elevating the spider's head for all to see, he announced, "I defeated it with the support of the Lioness and Space Girl Green. Having fulfilled your request, I ask now: will you accept me as your king?"

All the beasts cheered and then dropped to a knee before him. The Lioness joined them in bowing for the new king, but

Lion stopped her. "If you are willing, Lioness, I would like you to be my queen. You were brave and willing to fight for the beasts. You have proved yourself worthy."

She returned the smile and stood up. Green observed a playful intimacy in the way they moved around each other, their fur brushing together in a display of affection. The remainder of the day unfolded into a grand celebration, blending elements of a coronation, wedding, and tribute to heroes. The people expressed their gratitude to her for the rescue, to which Green simply nodded and smiled, basking in the joy of the moment.

As the sunset, Lion came to the three other companions and said, "Lioness will govern over the beasts while I go with you to see Sister South. We can leave in the morning."

Green was amused at how quickly his words had become commands now that he was a king. She marveled to herself over his transformation from a coward afraid of a dog to the decisive leader who stood before her now. Glancing at Lioness, Green felt the love of a good woman helped too.

CHAPTER 62

LOST LOVE FOUND

Lion had disappeared for the night with Lioness. A huge owl woman had approached them at twilight. She was almost as tall as Lion with softly rustling feathers, a mix of brown and black hues blending with the surrounding forest. She had deep, penetrating eyes, reminiscent of an all the wise old owls from children's stories. Fixing these eyes on the companions, her sharp beak opened and a melodic, soft voice infused with serenity said, "You don't need to stand watch tonight, heroes. I and others of my brood will watch. We will hoot a warning should any new horrors appear from the forest."

Something about the tranquillity of her voice coupled with her commanding presence put Green at ease. Douglas, Azuma and Green settled into their bedrolls and slept.

As the sun rose, Green woke up and asked a friendly woman, covered in bright white feathers and moving gracefully like a swan, where she could find a place to bathe. Azuma accompanied her, the swan woman and a train of little swan children, to an idyllic pond. By the time they returned clean and refreshed, Lion and his bride had returned.

All the animals formed lines on either side of the red brick road and cheered them as they left. Lion walked hand in hand with Lioness until his subjects were out of sight. Then with a final nuzzle, Lioness returned to their kingdom.

Just before noon the woodland gave way to fertile farmland. In the distance, they could see a castle in red and copper. The people in the fields continued their work, barely giving the odd quartet of three rulers and a girl from outer space a second look.

As they continued toward the castle, more people worked the farmlands, all dressed in some form of red. They seemed prosperous but not rich. The atmosphere was lively, marked by occasional bursts of laughter and snippets of song from various groups, suggesting a community content and at ease with life.

"These people seem happy," said Green.

Doug nodded agreement. "The land of Sister South seems quite peaceful. I hope I can make the land of the Winkies like this. It is much better than the land of the Welcomians, as well."

As they continued into the land of the Quadlings, tranquility enveloped Green, contrasting sharply with the darkness of the lands of the evil sisters and the superficiality of the Emerald City. The vibrant landscape and pure air, filled with the contented people, eased her burdens, infusing her with a serene vitality.

After an hour's walk, a trumpet's blast and marching rhythm halted them. A phalanx of red-clad soldiers appeared, bearing a crimson standard on a copper pole. Their attire was strikingly reminiscent of the Warriors of Home, though this army seemed like a monochromatic version of the warriors she knew, albeit with red skin and males in their ranks.

Green and her companions watched the approaching group stop nearby. The standard bearer and a notably armored woman advanced toward them.

"Welcome to the Land of the Quadlings," said the officer. "Under the kind and beneficent rule of the Copper Sister of the

South. She sends me with greetings to the Princess of the Emerald City, the Ruler of the Winikies, and the King of the Beasts. And especially to the Visitor who has remade Auz for the better, Space Girl Green of the planet Home."

The legionaries slammed a fist to breastplate in salute, the bugler played a fanfare, and the standard bearer dipped the standard momentarily.

Green curtsied and brought her hands together in the Warrior salute, noting just how much this sister whom she had never met knew about all of them. "Thank you for your greeting. We desire to meet with Sister South."

Green sensed Douglas becoming alert. The officer, for that must be what all the copper braid on her shoulder meant, approached and scrutinized each member of the group. A woman in her prime, her physique showcased strength, from her muscular arms and legs to her wide chest, paired with keen, observant eyes. Her hair, a cascade of curls, left uncovered by a helmet, fluttered in the wind. Her expression was serious, while her lips pressed into a tight line as she introduced herself. "I am Kaylin, captain of the guard of honor for the Sister of the South."

Standing an arm's length away, Douglas caught Kaylin's gaze, a tear escaping from his own eye to trace a path down his cheek. With a smile of recognition, he said, "Kaylin, it's me, Douglas. Your Cyberknight, and you were my love, until the Sister of the East erased my emotions. The Wizard restored them, yet I feared we'd never meet again." His movements were hesitant, torn between the desire to embrace his beloved and the respect due her as a formidable warrior.

Green saw emotions strobe across the woman's face, some happy, other sad. Abruptly, she settled back to the stern duty of a captain and turned to Green. "Space Girl, my liege instructed me to bring you to the castle directly. Like all the Sisters, she sees much in Auz and wishes to talk with all of you about its future."

"Lead the way, Captain," said Green. Kaylin about faced and shouted a command in a language Green didn't know. The troops formed into two lines, one on each side of the road. The group followed the standard bearer and the Captain into the middle of the lines. Then they formed a square around them, with Kaylin on the outside.

The companions glanced at each other. They knew Copper was supposed to be a good witch, but they were now trapped. As they marched forward, a fanfare played and the inhabitants of the south cheered their progress. Green and Auzma marched beside Doug, filled with worry. They knew he would normally enjoy such a parade, but his head was down in abject sorrow. He looked at Green and said, "Green, my Kaylin ignored me. What should I do?"

"Doug," Green sighed deeply. "You are the first unmarried man I've ever spent more than a few hours around. I grew up on a planet of women and fathers. All my knowledge of romance is just book learning."

Doug nodded with a furrowed brow, then he turned to Azuma, "You have a great brain now. What do you suggest?"

Green noticed a quick silence of access from Auzma, which was interesting in a couple of ways. First, that matters of the heart were so quickly accessed. Had the new Princess been doing research? Second, that Azuma also had no experience of romance, so whatever she had to say was probably only as good as what Green knew.

"Clearly," the beautiful green skinned woman said, "you have taken Kaylin by surprise. We did not know she would be here, and she probably didn't know you would be with us. Or who you were. Perhaps she is trying to understand her feelings right now."

"And hiding in her duty while she does it," he replied, nodding. "I can understand that. But with my new heart, I feel all the things I felt before and more. Damn, that witch's curse," he said, clenching a fist, "It follows me even now."

The Space Girl looked forward through the soldiers at the captain. Her back was ramrod straight, with the head locked forward and slightly up. She'd seen enough warrior marches to know you could put a little relaxation into a still proper march, especially when surrounded by cheering citizens. Kaylin was having none of that. She'd put on her soldier persona like armor.

"I think you will talk with her alone soon," said Azuma. "When you do, speak from your heart and seek forgiveness." She put one elegant hand on a bronze shoulder. "What will be, will be. Do you even know what you want from her?"

Doug's gaze had lost its spark. The lively energy that had surrounded him since getting his new heart was gone, leaving in its wake a palpable melancholy. "I thought I had everything I could ever want or deserve as we marched this way to help Green. I'm a king now, for goodness' sake. But one look at Kaylen and it was all dust. I would give it all up just to go back to our wooden shack in the forest."

Green felt a tightness in her chest at her friend's pain. She did not know what she could do about it, but her mission to the land of the Quadlings was no longer just about getting home.

THEY WERE GUIDED through a ruby city smaller but just as grand as the emerald one. The color made Green wonder where her friend Space Girl Red was. She was undoubtedly having grand adventures and doing incredible work.

As they neared Sister South's castle, two massive doors

swung open in welcome. Captain Kaylin, without missing a beat, issued a loud command to her troops. The square around the companions transformed into two lines at the entrance, allowing them unimpeded entry into the castle's expansive hall. The grandeur of the room, instead of overwhelming, offered a comforting ambiance. Unlike most royal rooms, it was filled with warm tones and soft fabrics. Instead of a throne at one end, there was a collection of plush chairs and couches.

Kaylin marched across the rich carpet to a beautiful woman with metallic copper skin. She dropped into a one kneed and said, "Your majesty, I have escorted the visitors as you have commanded. We came directly here from the road."

The woman smiled slightly and Green realized her face was almost identical to that of the first sister she had ever met, Golden. The resemblance continued with skin of a copper colored metal and hair of gold. They could really be sisters. Or machines off the same assembly line. But the sister's attention was focused on her captain. "Kaylin, I thought to see more joy in your heart, dear."

Kaylin did not look up or answer.

"Mmmm," Sister South hummed. "Perhaps I do not know your heart as well as I thought." She looked at the companions and keen glowing green eyes found Douglas. "You are Douglas Merriweather Moneypenny, formerly of the King's Cyberknights, are you not, king of the Winkies?"

"I am, Sister," said Douglas.

"And you were the love of my captain, Kaylin?"

Douglas nodded, his eyes darting from the sister to the captain and then down in dejection. "I was, Sister. But I lost my heart because of all the cybernetics I took on to save her. I was no man for one such as Kaylin. In the end she was right to leave me, and return to her homeland."

"But you have your heart back now, do you not?" her eyes

flashed red and Green was pretty sure they saw right through the metal encased what was left of Doug's flesh.

"Yes, through the work of the Winkies and the Wizard." He took a step forward, toward the Sister or Kaylin, Green couldn't tell. "Kaylin, I know you were hurt. You have every right to ignore me. But know I feel now for you just as I did that first day I saw you in Retha's store and all the times we were together before my accident. Please..." but there, words failed him.

The Sister stood waiting. The room was silent and everyone looked at the kneeling, head down in more than a bow, captain.

Slowly, the muscles of Kaylin's legs bunched, and she began to rise. Then her shoulders shook and a gasping sob cut the room. In a movement almost too fast to follow, the king of the Winkies was across the room. He caught her as hope long held caused the captain to crumple. "Kaylin."

"Doug, is it really you?" she said, her face covered in tears.

"Yes, my love," he answered. "Tell me what to do."

"And you can feel me?" She ran her hands over his metal chest.

His eyes half closed in ecstasy. "Yes, Kaylin. As I have always dreamed."

"Then kiss me," said Kaylin.

And he did.

"Well, I seem to have lost a Captain of the Guard, and the Winkies have a new queen," said the Copper Sister.

Kaylin looked chagrin and said, "My lady, I..."

The Sister smiled and made shushing motions with her hands. "Kaylin, Kaylin. Do I not see all? This was foreseen. I cannot think of a better ending to this narrative. Go with my blessing."

Sister South turned to the others and clapped her hands. "I have been lax in my greetings. Lion, King of the Beast! Welcome! It is good to have one so brave shepherding the beings of the forest. Feel free to call on me as a neighbor anytime you need."

She stepped up to Azuma and bowed slightly. "Princess of the Emerald City. It is good to meet you." Her eyes glowed again, and a quizzical look settled on her face as she looked Azuma up and down. "You are something new in Auz. May you be a source of peace."

The Princess of Auz nodded, "Thank you, Sister. I see and understand you." Green picked up a tone that was not completely peaceful in her voice. "Your Sisters have not always been a blessing in Auz. From my throne, I will be keeping an eye on you. I expect you and Golden to keep to the original protocols."

Green had no idea what that meant, but Sister South seemed to. She bowed a much deeper bow. "Of course, your Majesty. May the Land of Auz be restored to its original mission and story under your watchful eye."

CHAPTER 63
EXPLANATIONS

"You are of Gamalon, are you not Space Girl Green?" asked the Copper Sister. Doug and Kaylin had gone to renew their connection while the others settled into the throne room's sitting area.

"I was born on Home, lady," Green said, "But my father was a Ranger of Gamalon before its destruction."

"Before its destruction?" Copper whispered. "Gamalon was destroyed?"

Auz didn't know about Gamalon. In that, it was probably the only place in the galaxy that didn't. That event was foundational to her life before she was even born, and it was just as pivotal to Auz, but these inhabitants didn't know anything about it.

"Yes. Gamalon's moon broke into pieces and rained down on the planet. The destruction took over a year, but the planet, once vibrant and green, is now lifeless and grey." She looked down, and said, "It happened before I was born, but I saw it for the first time right before I came here."

While it was hard to read emotions on the metallic skin of the sister, she was obviously upset at this news. "You may not know this, but our King and Queen were of Gamalon. They left abruptly long ago. It was what ultimately led to the downfall of Auz."

"Yes, though I do not believe Gwendoline and Pastoria intended that. I recently met your King and Queen on Gamalon," said Green. "They are on Gamalon, trying to rebuild it, which I thought a foolhardy idea for two scientists. Then they sent me here."

Auzma took up the story, "The royals gave her a special ticket in the form of a Space Girl Challenge coin." She explained how the coin awakened her.

After a bit of back and forth, Copper shrugged and said, "So the royals intended you to take their place, Auzma. But for some reason you weren't activated, and the land fell into chaos without you."

The Sister's brow furrowed, and her glowing eyes flickered. Her face cleared, and she changed the subject. "Space Girl Green, you have lived up to your motto here in Auz and we are in your debt."

"Speaking of order to chaos," said Green. "Gwendoline told me the story of the Seed, and Pastoria said it was a nanotechnological machine that could rebuild a world. It seemed crazy to me at the time, but having seen and traveled all across Auz, I'm starting to believe."

The two most technical and powerful women in Auz looked at each other. Copper raised an eyebrow in question, and the princess nodded. "One moment," said Copper. Then rose and left the room.

Auzma turned to Green, "Do you know what she is?"

"I don't know what any of you are. When I first met the Welcomians and Golden I scanned them. There is a strange combination of mechanical and biological. What I think of as biological is mostly on the outside, and it could be a form of flesh I'm not familiar with. Plus there are many kinds of alien biology in the galaxy. You could be within acceptable parameters of recognition as a new species. But I feel there is something unreal about all of you."

"You are very perceptive, Space Girl Green," said Auzma. "The inhabitants indeed are not real. They were created to be the play things of visitors. Most inhabitants are characters in a story, though most are non-player characters."

"But you all act like people and seem autonomous," said Green. "When not enslaved, anyway."

Copper returned with a small wooden chest. She walked over and sat next to Green on the couch.

"That is mostly because you are meeting them after a very long time on their own," said Auzma. "But in the end, all the inhabitants crave a place in someone else's story. It is why the sisters went mad. Imagine your life's meaning and work disappearing overnight."

"But you and Golden didn't go mad," Green said to Copper.

The beautiful copper face smiled wistfully, "I am not so sure about that. I have been lucky that my madness is creating a perfection of relations and cohesion here in my lands. Golden… well, you have met her. She is good, but in a very chaotic way."

"She did seem odd," said Green. "She kissed me and did this to my skin and lips. Will that go away if I leave?"

Auzma smiled, "Yes. Even if you stayed, I think it would fade eventurally. She gave you her mark so hostile inhabitants would be wary of you." She nodded to Copper.

"Space Girl Green, I said we would give you whatever you wanted for your service here." She handed her the chest. "This is a Seed. I would ask you not examine it too closely, nor give it to your own scientists, but fulfill your mission to the Royals and give it to them. They will be able to use it to rebuild Gamalon."

Green unclasped the lid and opened the chest. Sitting on a

black velvet liner was the Seed. It was shaped like a tear drop, sharply pointed on one end and curved on the other. The material was unlike anything she had seen and it appeared made of transparent metal with swirling, glowing motes inside.

She closed the chest and said, "I will do as you ask. Space Girls are trained to evaluate what knowledge and technology new cultures we encounter are ready for. I think it would be hypocritical, for me not to apply that Home as well."

Copper smiled. "Very wise, dear. It is also good we didn't ask what reward you wanted till now. Otherwise you might have wasted the request on something Golden already gave you. She gave you what you most wanted in the form of her sister's shoes."

"What?" said Green, looking at her feet. The silver shoes had a mind of their own and had recently transformed back in to sparkling silver pumps in the presence of royalty. "They have been a surprise for sure and even useful in a number of circumstances, but I what I really want is to leave Auz."

"Indeed," said Copper and grinned.

Thoughts pinballed around in her head, "Are you saying these shoes could let me leave the land?"

The women of Auz laughed. "Of course. They will take you anywhere you want to go in three steps."

"Anywhere in Auz?" asked Green.

"No, anywhere in the galaxy and beyond."

CHAPTER 64
OWLS IN SPACE

The professor had done something to Aurelius allowing him to move through the debris field without problems. He'd been unwilling to give the same privilege to *Dochas ar Dhioltas,* or the other Home saucer. This had involved a trip back to the planet and a new creature to be launched into space onto the hulls of the other ships.

It was not a plump baby with a bow this time, but an angular silver bird. The wings looked sharp enough to cut and Eógan was reluctant to press it too closely to his suit. His Space Woman trusted her hard armor and held one casually under her arm, and one perched on her shoulder. When they'd first flown toward them on the planet, Eógan was reminded of hawks, but on Amethyst's shoulder it seemed more owl-like.

"You can stay in the saucer if you want, Eógan," she said as she fit the bubble helmet over her head, casually pushing the owl away.

"No," he said as he stepped out of the case and grabbed the helmet. "I kind of agree with Pastoria that the Winged could be a defense system for near-Gamalon incursions. That is the purview of the Rangers, which will be reenforced if I'm the one delivering these birds."

"We could just not give the Civitas access—say the professor didn't allow them since they were shooting everything up."

Eógan thought that a dangerous way to go. Captain Kennedy would be suspicious and call for help. He didn't want to start a war between the factions of the Rangers. What he said was, "If we limit them, we have to limit the Warriors too. Do you really want to do that?"

The Space Woman shrugged, "I don't think they care about getting to Gamalon, but they wouldn't like being left out. If you don't limit the Civitas, you shouldn't limit the Warriors."

He nodded agreement and closed his helmet. While they waited for the atmosphere to be sucked out of the entry room, he watched the owl. The body was completely still, but the head would dart from object to object. It settled on him, seeming to think he was staring at it for too long.

"Hegwig, go to daddy," Amethyst said pointing at Eógan. The owl on her shoulder swooped over to him and took up position on the environment pack on his back.

"You named it?"

"Of course."

Eógan shook his head. She was such a contrast. It surprised him to realize he'd only ever experienced her on vacation. Relaxed to the point of indulgence. But she was a Space Woman through and through, unflappable in the craziest of circumstances, willing to stand up to people and things he'd think twice about, and she seemed to think the universe was a big game. One she intended to win.

The gangplank swung open, and she squealed, "Whheee" and jumped out like a child leaping into a pond.

Maybe she was teaching him how to see the universe again. Had he become too serious? Stuffy?

"Allons-y!" He yelled and leaped out. Hegwig fluttered momentarily before engaging its jetpack to follow.

CHAPTER 65

GOODBYES

Space Girl Green stood in the courtyard of the Quadling castle looking at her three companions. Doug was as happy as she'd ever seen him, standing arm in arm with Kaylin. Kaylin now wore a brass colored dress that contrasted with her dark red skin.

"Douglas, on my world of Home, we have the concept of a Man of Quality. This is the kind of person we are to look for as a mate when we go into the wide galaxy. I know Kaylin has found such a man, and I hope the Light That Is All Colors infuses your union."

Doug's eye glistened and Green really hoped he wouldn't start crying or she would too.

"Space Girl Green, you have changed my life. When I came to Auz, I was a weak man with less courage than Lion. I found strength, courage and confidence in the Cyberknights. But Sister East upended all of that. You took me on a quest any knight, on any world, would have found worthy. Worthy to fight and die in." He stepped forward and wrapped her in a warm hug. She gripped him back, tears running down her face.

Next she stood before Lion and smiled. "Hey, big guy. It is

good to see you grow into your skin. I remember our first meeting and how Halamar's bark scared you so. Look at you now. King of the Beasts."

"Oh, Green. My muscles may be robust and my claws formidable, but it's the strength of my heart that truly defines me. You are half my size and yet have the strength of ten lions. The old Wizard may have given me back my courage, but it was you that truly taught me to be brave." Then she was smothered in a hug that buried her face in his soft fur. She inhaled the musk of him and hoped it ever burned into her memory.

"Scarecrow," Green said with a grin, standing before the beautiful woman in green. "On my world we call a female a girl until she makes a name for herself. It is why I'm Space Girl Green, and not Space Woman. I've never seen that change happen as dramatically as it has with you. I know you will rule over the Emerald City and watch over Auz like the High back on Home. Though I would advise you not to do it alone. The High has the Privy Council to advise her. You have brave companions, now kings, and the Sisters to be your Council, Princess Auzma, Wizard Woman of Auz."

The woman smiled the prettiest of smiles and said, "I may be biggest brain in the land, but you Space Girl Green are the wisest. Know you are welcome back in Auz any time you wish. The token that brought you here will bring you back."

Green shouldered the light pack that held the chest with the Seed in it and stepped back to address her companions and the crowd.

"You may not know this, but when I arrived in Auz I didn't think of myself as very strong or brave, not a real Space Girl. I had the training. I had friends and mentors who said I was smart, strong, and capable. Still, I didn't believe I was worthy of the title." She smiled wistfully at them. "But like all of you, I learned who I truly was through our adventures together. It is what happened here, with you, that allows me to be a real Space Girl, and eventually become a Space Woman. For that, I will always be grateful."

She looked around. "It is bittersweet to be leaving. In the weeks I have been here, you have become as close to me as a sister. Or," she said, looking at Lion and Doug, "brother. Know that as I leave, even if my Space Girl Adventures take me far away and I never can return to Auz, you will always be in my heart."

Then, following Copper's instructions, she closed her eyes and thought of the Jorgan Regulator she needed to fix her ship. She even visualized a Home warehouse where such things are stored. As she understood it, each time she stepped, she would be teleported to a new location across the galaxy. It was very important to focus on where she wanted to go between each step. *Get the Jorgan Regulator,* she thought as strongly as she could, clicked the heels of her shoes together three times, and took a step forward.

CHAPTER 66

STEP ONE: YELLOW

When Green opened her eyes, she was not in a warehouse. She stood in the central chamber of a flying saucer, but not a small Space Girl Saucer. A larger one capable of carrying an entire rainbow. Even weirder, there was a space girl standing two meters away with her back toward Green, but she would know that frame and style anywhere.

"Yellow?" Green said to her rainbow mate.

The other girl let out a yelp and spun. She held a wrench in one hand, and by the time she landed, a raygun in the other. It was all Green could do not to take a step backwards in defense. The shoes were her friend again, knowing she didn't want to go back to Quailing castle and have wasted two of her three steps. She raised both hands in surrender.

Space Girl Yellow was a tall, broad girl with dark brown skin and blonde hair braided in tight rows. Dirt and probably grease smudged her clothes in various places.

"Green," she said, lowering the gun. "How'd you get here?"

"Long, long story," Green answered. "Where is here? This isn't your saucer."

"Kenix," said Yellow, looking Green up and down. "Their

World Heart was stolen, and Red called in the Engineers to help. She left a few hours ago to track it down." Yellow stepped forward and said, "Fancy shoes for that outfit."

Green was wearing her Warrior uniform in green and black. She'd picked that configuration, expecting she might run into someone in central stores and would need all the authority she could muster to stay out of trouble. But she had to wear the silver shoes, and they had decided galaxy striding was a formal event, which meant she was in 10cm platform pumps of the sparkliest silver. "Be careful, I can't take another step."

Yellow's eyebrows rose. Green continued, "Like I said, a long story, which hopefully I'll be able to tell you soon in person, but I need a Jorgan Regulator. I meant to step to a warehouse on Home, but somehow ended up here."

Yellow seemed to take in stride the idea Green thought she could a take a step across light years. Guess her being here was proof enough. "You are in the right place. This is engineering rainbow Electron's ship." She spun slowly around looking at all the storage compartments along the walls. "They have everything." As she started opening and closing compartments, she mumbled to herself as much as Green. "Jordan Regulator, so your impellers are damaged, huh?"

Green blushed and said, "Yeah, kind of crashed. But to be fair, I went directly through a Spaceway Portal into an atmosphere. Then I was shot by two powerful land-based ray weapons."

Yellow nodded casually, "That's another impossible thing you are going to have to tell me about." She shoved an arm all the way to the back of a compartment and pulled out a battered cardboard box the size of her fist. "Here we go. Install this in the junction and it'll keep the power plant and impellers in sync."

"Aren't you going to comment on me crashing my saucer? Thought my tech mate would be the most upset."

Yellow laughed. "You've mentioned at least three impossible things you've done in the last couple of weeks. I'm a little surprised you've only damaged your saucer." There was a loud clanging and then voices from the entry room part of the saucer. "That's the engineers. They get pretty touchy about me messing with their stuff." Yellow put the box in Green's hand and pushed her to one side. "Talk to you soon."

Knocked off balance Green stepped without thinking.

CHAPTER 67

STEP TWO: TO HER HEART

If her tech problem took her to where her rainbow mate Yellow could help, what did it say she materialized in front of her father on her next step?

"Father?" Green said.

She carefully balanced her stance and looked around. She was in a laboratory, which seemed strange for her father. Before she could figure out why it looked so familiar, a Space Girl dressed in a purple jumpsuit leapt between her and her father. "Space Girl Green Capricorn, verify yourself."

Luckily for Green, a workbench caught her when she leaned away at the onslaught. "Hold on," she raised a hand, "if I take another step, who knows where in the galaxy I'll be teleported." She looked closely at the person in front of her. "Aunt Amethyst?"

"That is Space Woman Amethyst Libra to you, assuming you are the Green I've known all my life and not some aberration." Then it snapped for Green and she realized she was in Pastoria and Gwendoline's lab on Gamalon. "I gave you an order Space Girl."

Green brought her gaze back her senior and obeyed, "Maximus will always save me." There was a pause, while Amethyst listened to something.

"Verified," said Space Woman Amethyst. "How the hell did you get here, Green? You scared the shit out of me, appearing out of nowhere next to Eógan."

Green took in the room, the expressions on everyone's face and the way Amethyst was standing protectively between her and her father. Then she raised an eyebrow. "Should I verify you, Space Woman?"

The other's eyes widened and her mouth opened, but before she said anything, Green continued, "Never mind, I'm out of touch with my saucer and he's out of touch with the galaxy." She waved the hand still holding the box Yellow had given her. "Hang on just a second while I get my bearings."

She took a deep breath and thought this would all be a lot easier if the silver shoes were the boots she'd walked all over Auz in. She felt the shoes vibrate like they were laughing, but they didn't transform. "Ok, so we are on Gamalon. One step ago I was in an Engineering Saucer on Kenix with Space Girl Yellow. She gave me the Jorgon Regulator I'm holding here. A minute before that, I was in the Copper Sister's court saying goodbye to my companions from an adventure I have been on for the last seven weeks. According to what she told me, I have one more step to get me back to my saucer, which I believe will require concentration before I step."

There was confusion on Eógan and Amethyst's faces, but the two scientists had walked closer. "Pastoria and Gwendoline, or should I say your Majesties? Though I have to say, you left Auz in a horrible mess."

Gwendoline frowned and looked at Green's shoes, "You are wearing Sister East's Walking Shoes." She looked into Green's eyes and smiled. "Worry not. They take you where you need to go, not just where you want to go."

Pastoria said, "Did you locate our new model? Did they help you? How bad is it in Auz?"

"Seven weeks?" said Eógan. "Beagán you just graduated 35 days ago."

"What?" said Green.

"Time moves differently in Auz," said Gwendoline. "Relatively faster than here. It is how we ruled for decades there, yet when we returned, it had only been a few years."

"And it has been decades since you left," said Green. "The sisters had no story to guide them. Two of them went evil and oppressed their people. A conman ruled the Emerald City, and most of Auz was in chaos."

The two looked at each other in worry. "We are sorry. We have now failed both our peoples. We came back here to fix our home world without success and left our found home to degenerate."

"What did you do there, Space Girl Green?" asked Amethyst.

Green laughed, thinking about it as a whole. "While mostly unintentionally, I brought order to chaos." She quickly explained her adventures and the state of Auz when she left.

"I will give a detailed report when I get back to my ship and leave Auz, Space Woman." She shifted her weight and wiggled her toes in the shoes. "But I really need to get back. No telling how long it has been for Halamar." She turned to her father. "Father, could you help me?"

"Of course," he came over to her and before letting her tell him what she needed, he wrapped his arms around her in a hug. "It is good to see you thriving in your mother's field. Know you have my blessing," he whispered to her. Then he stepped back. "What do you need?"

She smiled with burning eyes. "I need you to put this," she handed him the box with the regulator in it, "in my backpack and take out the copper chest you'll find there."

Eógan carefully made the exchange. She turned to the king and queen, "Your majesties, pardon me for not curtsying. Here is the item you sent me on a quest for. May you use it to positively transform Gamalon."

The two stepped forward in unison to stand before her. "We are not your royalty, Space Girl Green," said Pastoria. "We are in your debt, as all of Gamalon will be in the future."

"Yes, Space Girl Green, little green of Gamalon, you have saved both worlds," said Gwendoline, taking the Seed from her hands. "It is we who should bow to you."

Then they did exactly that, bowing low.

Without warning, the shoes made their laughing vibration and pitched her forward. She stepped to catch herself and tumbled onto a blue dirt path.

CHAPTER 68
STEP THREE: FLYING SAUCER

She tried to roll smoothly but her backpack got in her way, and she ignobly face planted. She laid there and started laughing. After a couple of minutes she pushed herself up and sat back on her knees. Her feet were bare now, the shoes having finished their mission with her. She looked around and realized she was back in the land of Welcomians.

She knelt on the path from the tower to the village, and sitting to one side of it, gleaming green in the sunlight, was her flying saucer. She took a deep, happy breath and stood. The portal above her was still a mystery, but now it made her feel ready to leave. As she walked toward the saucer, the gangplank descended and a black dog ran out, leaping to the ground before it was fully down.

"M'Lady, you are back," came the voice from Halamar's collar.

"Hello, Halamar." She scrunched the fur on the back of his neck. "I've got the part we need to finish repairs. How are things here?"

"Good, Space Girl Green. I took the extra time to do a thorough cleaning, with the help of some of the Welcomians. They are surprisingly good at ship work."

"Extra time? How long have I been gone?"

"4 days, M'Lady."

"Well," she walked up the gangplank and went to her workshop, "It was only three steps for me." As she unpacked her backpack and unboxed the Jorgan Regulator she told Halamar about her three–step journey across the galaxy.

"Where does this thing go?" The Jorgan Regulator looked like a multifaceted dice of some sort. Each of the 12 sides had a hole in it instead of a number.

"There is a junction behind a panel in the cockpit were all of the control lines come together. You will need number 10, 15 and 36 spanners."

Green collected the tools from their box and climbed up to the cockpit. Removing the panel Halamar indicated, she saw the old regulator immediately. It was blackened and cables of every color flowed out of it, many discolored with black soot. "Will we need to replace any of the cables? Do we have spares of those?"

"I do not think it will be needed, but my drones are bringing cleaning materials." They spent a companionable time repairing the junction and making sure everything was properly connected.

"You know, Halamar, this is much closer to our real life in the future. The rest of the galaxy is not like Auz, full of fantastic creatures and evil sorcerers. We'll be back to terrorists, traffickers, and destroyers of planets now."

"As you say, Ma'am. But I think we may find the galaxy more unusual than you expect. Auz may have been just what we needed."

All of the cables were connected and she said, "OK, Halamar, run a diagnostic and tell me how we're doing." She walked to the center of the cockpit and looked out at the land of Welcomians.

A brand-new tower stood nearby, not as grand as the one in the West, but with an unusual apparatus on top. It likely kept the portal open, just as the tower in the West did for the exit. She thought about exploring it to find out if they worked the same, but really wanted to get back to being a regular old Space Girl.

"Diagnostics complete," said Halamar. "I am fully operational, M'Lady." There was an eagerness in his voice that mirrored her own feelings.

"You sound ready to go, as am I." She sat down in the pilot's chair and thought for a minute. "I need to write a report about all of this. Space Woman Amethyst was quite put out with me for not reporting to HQ. Not that I could, but she didn't know that." She looked around and sighed. "Since time goes slower here, we should do it before we leave."

"I have taken the liberty of preparing a report of all the things we did together, M'Lady," said Halamar. "If you want to read over it and fill me on the times I wasn't there, we should be done in no time. Perhaps over a meal? When was the last time you ate?"

"That, my man, is an excellent idea."

CHAPTER 69

RETURN TO THE SPACEWAYS

The picnic was pleasant, with Halamar using his dog drone for the last time. Goldie had appeared and informed them the body wouldn't work once they left Auz. She had also taken back her mark, which let Green back off to a normal amount of makeup.

A few hours later, as they ascended, Green looked through the canopy to see the Golden Sister and the black dog waving farewell. Once in the air, the whole of Auz was on display. It didn't seem to matter how high they went. The atmosphere never got thinner and never turned into the dark of space. There was a point where the land appeared to be just a few meters across and never got smaller, even though Halamar's instruments insisted their altitude was increasing. They both eventually agreed either Auz was messing with his instruments or the laws of physics. Having stepped across the galaxy in a pair of sparkling heels, Green wasn't sure which was more likely.

They came down to a lower height and cruised across the landscape. "You know, Halamar, you may be the first and only vehicle to traverse the land like this."

"There was the Wizard's Space Ball, M'Lady."

"Yes, but he went directly toward the exit portal. We seem able to go wherever we want." She emphasized this by changing course. They had been following the road toward the Emerald City. Heading south, they found a village that was being rebuilt by people in blue and red. It was not far from where they had found Doug. "I believe that is the village that Doug was from. They seem to be rebuilding it."

"Yes, M'Lady," said Halamar. "A joint venture of the Welcomians and the Quadlings."

"Indeed." She continued south long enough to encounter a large wood, but not long enough to reach Copper's Castle. As they moved over the forest, there was a clearing that looked familiar. In the middle of it was a group of animals with a pair of Lions speaking to them. Everyone looked up as they passed, so Green made a circle around and waved to her friends.

Not wanting to get tangled up in long goodbyes, she vectored toward the Emerald City, where on the balcony of the tallest spire stood Princess Auzma. Clad in a flowing gown, she smiled and waved when Green circled the tower. The city itself seemed full of people busy with their business. People flowed in and out of the gates in all directions with no guards to stop them and make them put on stupid glasses.

Now the exit portal was in sight, but Green kept low, hoping to see the last of her companions in the yellow castle below the Orb. She was not disappointed as the former Cyberknight and his queen stood on the balcony next to the tower. She was resplendent in a yellow gown with a matching crown. Around them stood the Winkie court, who had tried to make Green their queen.

She circled and waved goodbye one last time. Her saucer rose directly up and into the dark circle in the sky.

~

GREEN BRACED herself for turbulence crossing into the Spaceways, recalling her tumultuous entry. However, the transition proved as seamless as any other portal experience. Once in the Spaceways, it was all rainbow streaks of light, and there was no hole showing sky or ground.

"Halamar, how does the exit portal register from this side?"

"It doesn't, M'Lady. My sensors detect no portal at all."

Green crinkled her brow. "Is there such a thing as a one-way portal?"

"Not that I am aware of." Lights blinked on the control board and the bubbles in the AI globe swirled rapidly. "There are several anomalies I need to report, but we also need to set a destination. We cannot drift too long in the Spaceways."

"Ahh, I believe we were heading for Keblr when we got sidetracked," said Green. "Or we could go back to Gamalon and see what they did with the Seed." She'd also like to know what was up with the Space Woman and her father. "Now what are the anomalies?"

"First is the date. I have connected to the Spaceways comm network to send your report to Space Girl HQ. Part of that connection is the current galactic date and time. It differs from my internal clock significantly. We appear to have spent 53 days in Auz, but the external clock says it has only been 36. It is currently mid-winter on Home."

"Mmmm, tis the season," thought Space Girl Green recalling a tradition she had with a rainbow mate. "I wonder where Red is right now. Probably kicking butt and taking names on the other side of the galaxy."

"Actually, Space Girl Red has recently sent a distress signal via your private rainbow channel."

Green sat forward and said, "Red? Distress? Let me hear it immediately."

WANT to know what happens next? Read the Adventures of Space Girl Red. Green returns to help Red after she escapes the Evil God King Bruno.

SPECIAL THANKS

It has been a while since *The Adventures of Space Girl Red* was published. That year I published my first novel and opened a new biohacking center, which is a big reason this novel took so long to finish.

I'm so grateful to my wife, copyeditor, and business partner for taking charge of our center, giving me the chance to focus on writing again. Our team has been amazing at taking care of things so I don't have to.

InkersCon has been a great inspiration to me over the last three years. In 2024 I joined their mastermind, and it has kept my butt in front of the page, while teaching me how to make this publishing thing work in many, many ways. Terezia, Eva, and Alessandra have been a great encouragement and source of real world experience. In the mastermind and the live conference, they created a group of fabulous and inspiring writers too numerous to thank by name.

David Cranfill was my lone beta reader this time, and I thank him for his feedback and support.

And Scrivener, the greatest writer's IDE ever.

MORE. AND FREE STUFF

Thank you dear reader, for getting this far. If you would like to learn more about the Space Girls, visit their website:

https://www.spacegirladventures.com/

If you sign up for R.A.'s email list, you'll get a free story Space Girl Story. You'll also get their monthly newsletter, which includes not only book talk, but fashion, writing and productivity advice. Yeah, I said fashion. You don't want to miss that.